PENGUIN CRIME FICTION

FALSE PROFIT

Robert Eversz worked as a brickmason, housepainter, café poet, factory worker, and filmmaker before embarking, much to his own surprise, on a career in business. He has been a consultant to several Fortune 500 companies, and heads his own consulting business on the west side of Los Angeles, where he is at work on another Marston/Cantini novel.

FALSE PROFIT

—

ROBERT EVERSZ

PENGUIN BOOKS

PENGUIN BOOKS
Published by the Penguin Group
Viking Penguin, a division of Penguin Books USA Inc.,
375 Hudson Street, New York, New York 10014, U.S.A.
Penguin Books Ltd, 27 Wrights Lane, London W8 5TZ, England
Penguin Books Australia Ltd, Ringwood, Victoria, Australia
Penguin Books Canada Ltd, 2801 John Street,
Markham, Ontario, Canada L3R 1B4
Penguin Books (N.Z.) Ltd, 182–190 Wairau Road,
Auckland 10, New Zealand

Penguin Books Ltd, Registered Offices:
Harmondsworth, Middlesex, England

First published in the United States of America by
Viking Penguin, a division of Penguin Books USA Inc., 1990
Published in Penguin Books 1991

1 3 5 7 9 10 8 6 4 2

Grateful acknowledgment is made for permission
to reprint an excerpt from "It's Money That I Love," by Randy Newman.
© 1979 Six Pictures Music (BMI).
All rights reserved.

LIBRARY OF CONGRESS CATALOGING IN PUBLICATION DATA
Eversz, Robert.
False profit/Robert Eversz.
p.   cm. — (Penguin crime fiction)
ISBN 0 14 01.2085 8
I. Title.
[PS3555.V39F3   1991]
813'.54—dc20   90–7682

Printed in the United States of America

For Narky and Lois-Gail

It's money that I love
It's money that I love
It's money that I love
     —Randy Newman

Thanks to Richard Esposito,
Dominic Erba, Jeff Isaacs,
Al Hart, Lisa Kaufman,
Claire Paradis, and Aaron Slavin
for the inspiration, counsel, and
assistance provided in the
preparation of this manuscript.

FALSE
PROFIT

1

Jack Burns was acclaimed as a true prophet of the new capitalism, a paper entrepreneur imbued with a Delphian sense of the dollar. The inexplicable mysteries of exponential dollar growth had been revealed to him, and he manipulated diverse investments with the facility of a capitalist Christ multiplying loaves and fishes, or so it was claimed by his select circle of investors. Junk bonds, penny stocks, precious metals, foreign currencies: all manner of investments yielded their secrets to his touch, while breaking the hearts and banks of the most savvy of his competitors.

Jack Burns did not go unrewarded in the temporal plane. The secretary burnishing her nails behind the reception desk was an icon of young and blond Southern California health. His investment business occupied the penthouse suite of the most prestigious bank building in Beverly Hills, and I had heard of a rumored beachfront estate in Malibu. The *Times* had wanted him for their "Movers and Shakers" business column, but he had refused the interview. They ran the piece anyway, and it was picked up nationally by the Associated Press. Jack Burns's name was whispered around the lunch tables of places like Spago, Rex, Citrus, and the Ivy, with a reverence typically reserved for the heads of motion picture studios. In a town where the telephone is mightier than the sword, everybody took his calls, and the message "Jack Burns is on line one" was guaranteed to juice the salivary glands of bankers, and send even the most jaded super-agent, hit producer, or whiz-kid director scurrying to the phone.

Jack Burns was definitely in. His clientele was culled from the Southern California aristocracy of movie stars, rock musicians, and media celebrities. It was not enough merely to have money. Ordinary money was rebuffed at the imposing patinated bronze office door.

Jack Burns comforted the rich and famous with the peace that their money grew not with just any money, but with money equally rich and famous. Prospective investors needed a minimum of fifty thousand dollars and a name that wouldn't embarrass the editors of *Interview* magazine. I had neither.

It didn't bother me that I had been denied my Warholian fifteen minutes of celebrity. It didn't bother me that I didn't have the fifty thousand dollars to invest. What bothered me was his rug. Though it matched the color of his natural hair, it was a woofer. I figured that a guy making his kind of money would be able to buy a wig that didn't sit up on his head and bark like a dog.

Jack Burns was on the phone, waxing ecstatic about an investment opportunity, when I was buzzed into his private office. He was pitching to someone named Warren, who must have been very famous, judging by the number of times Burns said "baby." Burns winked at me with a predatory friendliness and pointed at a chair.

A six-foot aquarium display of a crocodile's habitat stretched along the far wall. It was an unusual decoration, even for Los Angeles, and I ambled across the office to take a look. The aquarium was stocked with ferns, a pond, a miniature tableau of head-hunter dolls decapitating an effigy of the latest Democratic presidential hopeful, and, hidden amid the ferns, a blinking yellow-eyed crocodile. The crocodile reclined on a rock above the waterline. It was about a foot long. Its neck was thin and its legs spindly, and with its wrinkled skin hanging loose, the creature seemed frail and ancient, like a bonsai reptile.

Burns was closing fast on the phone, and I watched his reflection in the polished aquarium glass. He gestured broadly as he spoke, and his standard millionaire-issued diamond rings flashed in the light cutting through the corner window. His skin was a smoothly oiled sepia, no doubt pampered by exotic liniments, such as essence d'argent, and oil of T-bill. He wore a blue wool-and-cashmere-blend Armani sport coat, and a silk shirt open to what half a dozen years ago would have been a gold chain at the neck, but now was merely hair. I couldn't see his shoes beneath the massive black lacquer desk, but imagined them to be the latest in Italian loafers.

I felt vaguely sorry for the crocodile.

"Someone wants to kill me," Jack Burns said, hanging up the phone and glancing down at his Rolex. He said it with great economy of emotion, as though murder was the least of his many pressing problems.

"What makes you think someone wants to kill you?" I asked.

Burns reached into a drawer, and slapped an envelope on the black edge of the desk. I folded back the lip and, holding the envelope by its corner, shook out an eight-by-eleven sheet of paper. The message was written in cut-out newsprint in an unimaginative style, and expressed a threat to kill the recipient at the earliest opportunity.

"It arrived in the mail yesterday," Burns said.

I flipped the envelope, and checked the postmark. It had been mailed from Malibu.

"Have you shown it to the police?"

Burns frowned, and gave his head a vigorous shake.

"The publicity could kill me. The police would want to talk to my clients. The slightest hint of a scandal could have disastrous consequences. If I have an unhappy client, maybe this is his way of working off steam. It was always my impression that these things are mostly hoaxes."

"Most are. It's a risk to assume this one is. The police could check it for fingerprints, maybe run a saliva test."

"Only a fool would leave a fingerprint. My clients are many things, but you won't find a fool among them."

"What makes you think it's a client?"

Burns fingered the wristband on his Rolex, checked the time, then turned his attention to a gold letter opener laying across a bank envelope. He tapped the tip softly on the desk, cleared his throat, and sighed: "I don't think it's a client."

"You twice mentioned it could be a client. Do you have many unhappy clients?"

"Everybody has unhappy clients."

"But not everybody has one threaten to kill him."

Burns stared at me. I stared back. He smiled.

"You don't back off easy, do you?" he remarked, and when I didn't commit an answer, stood and strolled to the aquarium. He reached into his coat pocket, and withdrew a folded sheet of paper. Turning his back to me, he unfolded the paper, read from it, then stuffed it back into his pocket. It was an odd gesture, like that of an old actor using a bit of stage business to conceal that he had forgotten his lines.

"The single-minded appetite of the crocodile has always amazed me," Burns said, and rapped on the aquarium glass with a gold ring. The yellow beast eyes of the crocodile dully blinked. "Like most successful creatures, they are very simple, and very focused. They like to eat. And when they aren't eating, they like to sleep. Very simple.

"Crocodiles will eat almost anything. They know what they need to survive, show no mercy, and never feel remorse. Those are good qualities for an investment counselor, as well."

Burns unscrewed the lid of a black metal canister placed near the aquarium. The crocodile charged with sudden and violent purpose to the perimeter, and tried to scramble up the wall. Its claws scraped futilely against glass. The crocodile dug into the rock and lunged again. Burns prized a lump of raw fish from the canister and dangled it over the open aquarium top, cooing endearments. Jaw gaping, the creature perched, extended on its front claws, waiting like a chick to be fed. Burns dropped the lump of fish down its gullet. The crocodile took it down with a rapid toss of its snout, and clawed against the glass, demanding more.

Burns laughed, and wiped his hands on a handkerchief pulled from his breast pocket. He set the handkerchief carefully next to the canister, and turned toward me a different man. The irritation and doubt were gone. Confidence infused his face with the aggressive vitality of success. His eyes locked a look onto mine so thick with sincerity you could have hung your net worth on it, and in those eyes I saw the pitchman supreme, the man who could sell sand to the Saudis or snow to the Eskimos.

"If you want a safe investment," he preached, "put the money in the bank in a straight passbook account, take your five and half percent, and retire in twenty years to a little house in the suburbs.

"If you want to gamble big, go to Vegas, play the horses, or put your money in the lottery. It's a one-in-a-million shot, but, hey, if you're the one, you can't beat the return."

Burns shook his head sadly, as though pitying the poor fool's penchant for sucker bets.

"Say you don't want either of those options. Say you want to get a better-than-average rate of return, but at a minimum of risk. A minimum of risk, remember, but not totally risk-free. You can't make real money without an element of risk. If you assign a fixed sum for a minimum of six months to one of my investment programs, chances are I'll make you a wealthier man than you are now. Nobody in town has a better track record at my kind of investments. Bull market, bear market, it doesn't matter, because no matter what is going on in the markets, there is always a way to turn a dollar if you've got the touch. Together we can work out an investment program combining fiscal flexibility with maximum return."

Burns's eyes twinkled with a surefire closing joke, and he prodded the air between us with a gold-studded forefinger, as in mock confidence he whispered: "I can make you so much money your accountant will have nightmares trying to figure how to shelter it all come tax time. How much are you in for?"

Burns held the closing smile, and if a man can peer into another's heart and read its contents, Burns did the same with my wallet, to his disappointment. Just as I was trying to figure out how to get an advance on that one-thousand-dollar treasury bond my Aunt Gladys planned to leave me in her will, the pecuniary gleam in his eye faded, and he sighed: "What the hell do I care? You're the type of guy with eyes in the soles of his shoes."

It was a good pitch. I had been held in his sway and did not realize until later that his presentation had been immaculate of detail. He didn't mention how my money would be invested. He merely said that he would make money, and I believed him. Confidence sells. He was surrounded by the trappings of success, acted a success, and had I not seen the death threat against him, he could have sold me my watch for double retail and I would have thought it a steal. "How many of your clients have lost money, Mr. Burns?" I asked.

"None of my clients have lost money, although a few accounts are temporarily running a deficit," he said, and his eyes slid toward me in sly acknowledgment of doublespeak.

"How many are running deficits?" I pressed.

Burns shrugged, dissembling. "A few."

"Assuming 'a few' means less than a hundred, I'd like to start with a list of those clients. People with millions generally let lawyers handle their death threats. Do you represent any small-time investors who have lost big?"

"I haven't made myself very clear. I don't want you or anyone else investigating my clients."

"Then maybe you'd better tell me what you do want," I suggested.

"I want a Scotch on the rocks. You'll find a bottle in the sidebar beneath the aquarium. Would you mind?"

I minded, but didn't say so. The sidebar door swung out on a hinge. A half-high refrigerator had been built into the cabinet. A nearly tapped-out fifth of Glenlivet reposed among a dozen bottles on the top shelf. I filled a tumbler with ice, eyeballed an ounce of Scotch, and swam it over the cubes. When I handed him the drink, he glanced at the chair across from him, and taking his hint, I sat.

"I don't want to get into any discussion about my clients, or the status of their accounts."

There was no room for dissension in his voice. He sipped his Scotch and closed his eyes for a moment, allowing it to soothe him.

"Always judge an investment broker by his long-term performance, and not by the short term. I have a few unhappy clients currently because this bear market has extended longer than I thought it would. Corrective measures are in place, and everything will soon blow over."

"You know who sent you the note, don't you?"

Burns reached swiftly across the desk and punched the intercom button, barking: "Bring me my checkbook," then released the button and reclined in his chair, smiling a secretive smile. "Let's say I have a very good idea. But his identity doesn't matter. All I want from you is a week of protection, without cramping my style."

"Around the clock?"

"Sure, around the clock. But I'm not suggesting we sleep together," he said, laughing.

The intercom squawked back: "Where is it?" cutting into his laugh.

Burns punched the intercom button, irritated, and shouted: "In the left fucking drawer!" He realized the sudden loss of temper was out of character, and grinned sheepishly, explaining: "She's a temp. My regular girl is out on vacation this week."

The temp poked a timid head in the door, and Burns impatiently motioned her in. "Ahh, Miss Moneypenny," he said, with a complicitous wink in my direction.

"But I told you," the temp protested, "my name is—"

"Just a joke, my dear," Burns interrupted, "for those of us who read."

"Havens," she finished, clearly and proudly enunciating both syllables. "And I do read. Just not Ian Fleming."

She presented the check register with a flourish. Burns plucked it from her hands, said: "That's what I get for hiring smartass college girls," and dismissed her with an annoyed flick of his fingers. I told him my rate, and we came to terms. He tore the check out of the book, and held it up, having, for him, a very common thought.

"Tell you what," he said, drilling me with a confident stare. "Why don't you start an investment program with us? I never work accounts this small, but I'd be happy to do you the favor."

I declined.

2

"Let me show you something," Angel Cantini said when I walked into the office later that morning. I dodged her at the entry, but she doubled back and barred the door to my private office with an outstretched arm.

"What kind of something?" I asked, already suspicious.

"A gym something."

"If it's like the last gym something you showed me, I'm not interested," I replied, and ducked her arm.

"This one is different," she protested, clipping my heels as I circled the desk and yanked open the drawer containing my deposit slips. I slid Jack Burns's check out of its envelope, and endorsed the back. Angel peered over my shoulder, and candy-coated her voice, cooing: "Come on. I promise I won't hurt you."

I didn't believe her. Angel is a physically remarkable woman: six feet of classic Italian beauty and American muscle trained in the martial arts. Her body is slim but strong, like a modern Diana, with hands and feet as deadly as the ancient huntress's arrows. Not that Angel seems a murderous woman. She is emotional, and good-natured, if a little zealous in the pursuit of her desires. When I run my hands through her lustrous black curls, trace a finger along the sinuous line of her mouth, and gaze into her smoky green eyes, I am more likely to find passion than murderous intent. But rarely do I forget, despite her beauty and the bliss of her passion, that this body of delights has kicked, punched, and slammed innumerable adversaries into unconsciousness. Angel's body is not for show, though it does that admirably well. It is for beating people into submission, as confirmed by her past titles in women's karate and boxing.

"Do you see this material?" I said, showing her the Oxford button-down sleeve of my custom-tailored shirt.

"Yeah, I see it. So what?"

"Do you see any rips or tears?"

"No."

"Are any of the buttons missing?"

"Come to the point."

"The point is that it's a brand-new shirt, just like the one you turned into confetti the last time you showed me a gym something."

"Okay, I promise I won't hurt your new shirt."

Angel slid my chair away from the desk, spun it around, and politely asking, "Now will you let me show it to you?" pulled me up by my tie to encourage a favorable reply. Hers were not subtle methods.

"Will this require any use of props?" I asked, tremulously.

"Just the letter opener," she said.

"The same letter opener that shredded my shirt during the last gym something?"

My protests were an integral part of the routine, and I allowed her to shove me into the lobby, which, as our business employed an answering machine for a secretary, doubled as Angel's gymnasium. I had traditional notions regarding the physical superiority of the male, and though Angel invariably threw or kicked or punched or bludgeoned me with great success when she showed me her little gym somethings, I believed that I'd figure what she was going to do and beat her to it.

Angel slapped the letter opener into my palm, and commanded: "Wrap your left arm around my stomach, and press the letter opener against my throat with your right hand."

I did as directed, rising to the challenge with all the intelligence of a trout to a lure.

"You feel you have the advantage now, don't you?" she said, relaxed in my grip.

"Theoretically, yes. Practically, no. You are going to do something unpleasant, aren't you?"

"In a normal situation, what would you expect me to do if I wanted to get away?"

"I don't know. Tell me you had syphilis, I suppose."

"Be serious."

I thought for a moment about how I would try escape such a hold, and said I'd expect her to stomp hard on my instep, push the hand with the letter opener away from her throat, and, digging an elbow into my gut, use the leverage to throw me over her shoulder.

"That's a good move," she said, adding: "For a beginner."

"I have a feeling you have something else planned," I sighed, and tightened my grip on her stomach.

"You don't know what I'll do."

"And I don't care, because I've got the knife."

Her body slackened when I said the word "knife," as though she had fainted and gone completely dead. Her weight bent over my left arm, and as she sagged, I shifted my feet for better balance.

The next thing I remembered, I was looking up a stranger's skirt.

I didn't recognize the fabric over my head as a skirt, nor the two smooth ivory pillars as legs. I was aware only of a sense of mystery and awe.

"Is this heaven, or what?" I said.

My head still swam from the fall, and I doubt my tongue got all the way around the words in pushing them out. It sounded like the lecherous moan of a creature indigenous to the back rows of pornographic theaters. The legs scurried away from my head on open-toed black pumps. The toenails were painted scarlet.

I sat up, still in the relative innocence of the semiconscious, curious about the type of face that would match scarlet toenails. The face was unfamiliar. The features did not seem fully formed, as though, despite her twenty-five years, the woman had not yet fully grown into her face. She was beautiful in the way some fashion models are beautiful, semisexed and unformed as a child. Every facial feature appeared independently perfect and appealing in symmetrical relationship to the whole, as though computer-selected and assembled to a photographic ideal. The face disturbed me. It had the characterless perfection of an advertisement for skin-care products.

Her clothes were modeled on the forties femme fatale. A black dress hugged her slim waist, puffed at the bodice, and widened to large padded shoulders, triangling her figure. Her hair, a shade of blond pale as champagne, was wrapped in a turban-style hat the same black as the dress. A pair of dark sunglasses cloaked her eyes. The contrast of her pale features and dark clothes gave her a look not of this time and reality, like a good black-and-white photograph can make a familiar object seem strange by the simple absence of color. Forty years ago, she could have been Veronica Lake, the mysterious and troubled child-woman of *film noir*. I momentarily contemplated dusting off my Humphrey Bogart act.

"I don't believe we've met," I said, pulling on my left earlobe.

"We haven't. And I won't ask what you are doing on the floor."

"Good, because I don't precisely remember."

"I threw you there," Angel volunteered from the corner.

The woman turned her head to the side, lensing Angel from behind her shades. Then she looked down at me with a creasing at the corner of her mouth. It was a smile, disappointed as hell, but a smile.

"She threw you? I thought detectives were supposed to be tough guys."

"I wouldn't know. I'm just the secretary," I said, standing, and pressed the wrinkles from my shirt.

"He is pretty tough—for a guy," Angel said, and introduced us.

"Then this is your agency, Mr. Marston?" she asked, with a slight unbelieving tilt of her chin.

I nodded.

"I wonder if we might speak a moment, in private."

She spoke the last words solemnly, with a gesture of her head toward my office door. People who drop by, unannounced, most often turn out to be crackpots looking for the spirit of their lost poodle. If she was a flake, she was a well-dressed flake. I was curious enough to open the door to my office and usher her in.

She perched on the end of the chair in front of my desk, and carefully folded her hands, gloved in white, over her purse. I pulled a fresh sheet of paper from a drawer, and hunted for a pen. Her head lifted from her gloved hands to different points in the room and back to her hands, as though taking snapshots from behind her sunglasses. Angel shut the door behind us, and took a chair in the corner. The woman looked at Angel, then shifted her shoulders toward me, and said in a voice so small it could have passed for a whisper: "Excuse me, but this is a private matter. Couldn't we speak alone?"

I could have asked Angel to leave the room. Had the woman bothered to take off her sunglasses, or explain why she did not remove them, I might have been less guarded.

"Angel and I are partners. This is as private as it gets," I said.

The woman straightened, and tugging at the fingertips of her left glove, sighed: "I didn't expect to find sexual equality in a business like yours."

"You haven't. Angel is a junior partner. If I give her an important-sounding title and her own parking space, I don't have to pay her as much."

The woman's small pink mouth turned slightly upward, stopping short of an actual smile; against the pale surface of her skin, it looked like the last curl of a wilting rose. Though I couldn't see her eyes, I felt them measure me for some great, to her at least, trust.

"I'm Nina Gamine, and I want you to find my brother." she said.

The metal clasp of her purse snapped as it opened. She slipped a gloved hand into the center of it and withdrew a small photograph, which she discreetly slipped across the desk. I held it between my thumb and forefinger, glanced at the back, which was blank, then turned it again to examine the likeness. When I had finished, I held the photograph out for Angel.

The photograph was that of a young man seated by venetian blinds, his head cocked toward one shoulder, and eyes upraised, as though contemplating the mystery of heaven. He was blond, his skin was pale, and his features were the masculine image of his sister's: a fragile beauty still unformed. At first I sensed a homosexuality in the face, confusing that with the poetic sensuality of his expression. The eyes were blue, and their gaze stretched over the camera in search of something beyond the surface of things. I supposed he was daydreaming. He was beautiful without seeming effeminate, in the way of young men who have not yet been corrupted by the hopelessness of their dreams.

Nina's head remained fixed on the photograph while Angel studied it, then clicked toward me when Angel returned it. I glanced at Angel. She shrugged, then cleared her throat, suggesting: "Why don't you tell us a little about your brother, such as how long he's been gone, and where you think he might be."

Nina straightened, folded her hands over her purse, and turned slightly in her chair, toward Angel. Her voice was clear and sad.

"Francis is my younger brother. Four years younger, to be exact. We're very close, at least we were until he disappeared. Mom and Dad died when I was twelve, in an automobile accident. People in our family die young. Mom had a sister, but she died of cancer. Dad's brother died in Vietnam. Fell out of a helicopter. Broke his neck." Nina Gamine's lips tightened with seeming emotion, and she fixed her head toward the hands clenched on her purse. "Francis and I were wards of the state. Do you know what that means? You're a dog on the street without a name tag. They put you away with other animals like yourself, without anybody. Then they parade you out, because some people want a new pet. You smile, and try to talk, try to be somebody's idea of a good little girl. One day someone comes and tells you that your little brother has found a new home, but not you. You're too old."

It was too heartrending to believe, so I half didn't. I watched her face. It didn't get me much truth. Her mouth smoothed fluidly over a few sentences, only to twist and stutter past the next, as though not capable of totally repressing the emotions that moved her. I couldn't figure her. I worried the pen in my hands, taking it apart in sections.

"First I lost my parents, then they took my only brother. Francis was adopted by a young minister and his wife, in the Bay Area.

Maybe you have to be an orphan to understand what I'm talking about when I say that we were closer than most brothers and sisters. I went from foster home to foster home, never staying in one place longer than a year or two.''

"Weren't you allowed to see each other?" Angel asked, concern showing in the softness of her voice.

"The minister didn't approve of me. He thought I was a bad influence. I've given a lot of thought about why he didn't like me. The minister, I mean. There was nothing wrong with me. I didn't wear thick makeup, or smoke, or take drugs. I did well in school, worked hard, tried to please. I tried so damn hard to be a good little girl, because I thought that if I was just good enough, maybe they'd ask me to live with them. But of course, I could never be good enough. I reminded the minister that Francis was not his son, not his real son.''

I watched Angel while Nina spoke. She was moved. Angel had been born into a large family. Her father hadn't been a great guy, and as a child she'd been knocked around a bit when he'd had too much to drink. Angel had once told me that as a child she blamed herself for her father's drinking, and thought that if she could only be good enough, he wouldn't hit her. But her brothers—six of them—had always come to her aid, and her father, having sired his own downfall, learned it was safer to be a happy drunk than an abusive one. Her family had problems, but always stuck together.

Me, I was an only child.

Nina Gamine noticed my attention was elsewhere, and her narrative paused. I nodded. She continued, her voice gathering determination.

"On Francis's eighteenth birthday, he moved in with me. We lived together for three years, while he was attending college at UCLA. Then he had some problems at school, and when the minister found out, they got into a big argument. Francis flew up to the Bay Area, and the argument got worse. He returned home, picked up his guitar, and said he was going away for a few days. That was a year ago. I haven't seen him since.''

"Why have you waited this long to try to find him?" I asked.

She nodded, the good little girl eager to answer. "He wrote me, twice. Both within the first month after he left. He was traveling in Europe. Said that he needed time to straighten things out, and not to worry if I didn't hear from him for a while. You know how young men are. I thought he needed time to find himself.''

"What were the problems at school?"

She smiled apologetically. I expected a lie to follow, and when she answered: "You know, the usual schoolboy stuff, poor grades, learning to drink, that sort of thing," I thought I had gotten one. I leaned forward and started to flip through the Rolodex. It wasn't the type of work I liked. For two years I had done nothing but corporate cases. I was good at corporate work. I knew how companies operated: manufacturing, marketing, distribution, accounting, and the chains of command in each and how someone could get dirty in each. I was arrogant enough to believe I knew how the executive mind clicked, and at what forks in the mind the drive to get ahead took a shortcut through greed. Missing persons, hell, anybody could do that.

"I don't think we can do anything for you, Miss Gamine."

"But why?" she asked, startled. "It's simple enough, and I'm willing to pay your fee."

Her hands unclenched and rapidly ferreted through her purse, producing a signed cashier's check. I was less than kind.

"We do mostly corporate work, and I never trust anyone who wears sunglasses indoors, unless accompanied by the tapping of a white cane."

It was then that she removed her sunglasses, and I saw her eyes. There was nothing unusual about their color—blue, like her brother's—nor was there any memorable physical detail or defect, but they seemed unforgettably damaged. It was not a problem of vision. The damage was behind the eyes, burning through, as though some tragedy had been indelibly seared into the iris. It was then that I first saw her as beautiful.

"Of course we'll take the case, Miss Gamine," Angel said.

"We will?" I blurted.

"You don't have to put any time into it if you don't want to. It's something I'd like to work on."

I glared at Angel. She glared back.

"Excuse us a moment," I said to Nina Gamine.

Angel followed me into the lobby. I shut the door behind her. Angel crossed her arms, set her mouth, and leveled me with an implacable stare. I knew I was in trouble.

"What are you doing?" I asked, outraged.

"I'm taking the case."

"I think we have an authority problem here. You don't take a case until I tell you to."

"Then go ahead."

"Go ahead and what?"

"Go ahead and tell me to take the case."

"Why should I?"

"Because I want to help her, that's why."

"That's not a good enough reason. We don't handle cases like this, except as a personal favor."

"We only do corporate work. Big deal. Corporate work is fine. It pays the bills. But you know what it doesn't do?"

Angel prodded my chest with her forefinger.

"It doesn't exercise the heart. The work is cold, and it's dry, and if you don't do anything else, it makes all of you cold, and dry. Here's a woman, and maybe she is a bit theatrical, and maybe there is a screw loose under that silly hat she's wearing, but she seems okay to me and you don't have to be Gandhi to want to help her. What she needs isn't that difficult. Just someone to find her brother. If you're too rigid to bend a bit to help, maybe you should ask yourself how cold and dry you already are."

Angel quietly reopened the door to my office and stepped inside.

Conscious of Nina Gamine's eyes, I walked around my desk and sat down. The photograph of her brother stared at me from the corner of the desk.

"We'll need to know a few more details about your brother," I said.

3

Burns drove a silver Rolls-Royce Corniche convertible. He looked great in it. Anybody would look great in it. Traffic north on the Pacific Coast Highway was fierce, but part of the joy of owning such a car, I imagine, never having owned anything like it, is being above the mundane concern of needing to get anywhere in a hurry. In a Rolls, you've already arrived.

I was following in a car that had arrived twenty years ago, and for the past five had been attempting to limp out the back door. The old Mustang's arthritic joints groaned at every road bump, and her skin was sloughing off in patches of bald gray primer, but the motor was strong and she could still outrun most everything on the road.

North of Malibu Beach, Burns swung the nose of the Rolls across the highway and into Point Dume, a gated coastal enclave for the wealthy who have tired of Beverly Hills. A grove of eucalyptus shielded Point Dume from the highway, and lined a drive meandering among stone-walled estates. I cranked down the window, and sucked the mentholated blend of salt air and eucalyptus deep into my lungs. Whitecaps glistened in a dark blue sea, fitfully visible through patches in the tree-line, and the sky was dimming to a blue and rose twilight. A bird called in the branches overhead, piercing the low murmuring of tires on asphalt. My senses filled, and I felt that momentary grace of peace gifted by nature. Then I rounded the corner, and my eyes were struck by an architecture so monstrous that even nature shrank before it.

As the taillights of the Rolls blinked off inside a four-car garage, I gaped at a hulking slab of stone patterned after a medieval castle. The Mad King of Bavaria would have built something like it, had he made his fortune in tract housing. The stone facade was studded with barred stained-glass windows depicting the Knights of the Round Table. A tower flanked the castle, extending it by another story. Above the tower flew a flag, starched to a permanent triangle, like the beak of a rook. A moat circled the front of the castle, its sides sloped in ivy. Wooden lattices were propped against the facade, and ivy tendrils were tied to the crossbars to coax them to scale the walls. A few had succeeded in gaining hold, but most had flopped to the side, repelled by the architecture. The roof was serrated like a parapet, as though intended for archers, who were no doubt needed to discourage the door-to-door salesmen, Jehovah's Witnesses, and homeless vagrants who periodically descend in barbarian hordes upon the coast of Malibu.

"How do you like my little beachfront bungalow?" Burns trumpeted as he strode across the wooden bridge that stretched across the moat.

"I don't," I answered.

"A man's home is his castle, eh?" he joked with blatant pride.

The head of a lion was carved into the oak front door, which was designed as a modern portcullis, shielded by solid iron grating mounted in a vertical groove. Burns pointed to a digital push-button display embedded in the stone beside the grate. "This is what really sold me on the place. Watch," he crowed, and touched a combination on the panel. An electrical motor hummed above the door, and the iron grating slid smoothly up its track. Burns hit the panel again, and the door clicked open. "King Arthur needed two hunchbacks to do that. That's what I love about modern electronics. You can fire the servants."

I followed him into an entry large enough to park a catapult. A knight's suit of armor posed for battle against the wall, its upraised sword preparing to behead a family of philodendrons bunched at its feet. Burns hung his jacket on the upraised sword, and asked if I'd like a drink. When I declined, he jaunted down a hall to get one for himself, telling me to make myself at home, as though home was a concept that could be applied to such a place. I had brought a satchel of window locks and dead bolts, and went to work instead.

I found the alarm system controls in the entry closet. It was a hardwired system relying on perimeter intrusion detection sensors. When activated, the system formed a closed loop, a door or window representing each point on the loop. Any break in the loop activated an alarm in the house, and automatically dialed a private protection service. Twenty minutes later an alarm-company cop would drive by, if things weren't too busy. It's tough to completely ransack a house in twenty minutes, but plenty enough time to kill someone. I went to check the entry points on the ground floor.

The castle was pure facade. I followed the foyer past a winding staircase, and stepped down to a living room with a red-brick-tile floor, adobe washed walls, and plate-glass windows overlooking the Malibu Coast. The interior decorator had been incapable of following the architect's idea through to its absurd conclusion, and so grafted onto it an equally absurd contrasting idea. The furniture was Santa Fe–style pickle-pine: rough hewn, and washed in a greenish white. Navaho rugs were casually thrown at the aesthetically correct places. The walls were hung with art from the interior decorator school of painting, their amorphous swatches of paint blending into the color scheme and offending no one, except perhaps those who like good painting. Two prickly pear cacti in turquoise vases stood in the corner, quietly and discreetly dying of embarrassment.

Burns paced before the plate-glass windows, cradling a cellular telephone against his ear, and pitched a limited partnership between sips at a Scotch and water. It was a helluva deal, he said, his voice warm and conspiratorial, a once-in-a-lifetime opportunity to get in on the ground floor of a hot real-estate development project. His eyebrows shot up in surprise when I blocked his path and ushered him away from the window. He nodded, understanding that a window makes a man an easy target, and huddled with the phone in the corner while I jerked down the Levolor blinds.

The plate-glass windows were sealed shut by the wall. Between the windows a sliding glass door opened onto a wooden deck. The sliding glass door was secured by a simple hook-and-hole lock. My Aunt Gladys could have taken it out in less than thirty seconds. I knelt and screwed a keyed track lock to the base of the door, half listening to Jack Burns make his telephone sales rounds. I about had the lock installed when the door chimes sounded a melody. It took me a moment to recognize the tune as the first few bars of "Camelot." Burns cupped the phone and shot a glance at me.

"It's okay. I'm expecting someone," he whispered while his free hand inscribed a curve signifying the feminine sex.

The mouth of the lion carved into the front door doubled as the peephole. I peeped a shape vaguely corresponding to Burns's air drawing, and opened the door.

"Hi. I'm Mona Demonay," she said, and a warm fragrance of distilled pheromones brushed past me as she stepped inside. Mona was the kind of blonde little seen since the fifties, when certain actresses redefined the art of cosmetics by sculpting idols of feminine artifice with paint, cloth, and spray. The color had been bleached from her hair, then returned to a calculated gold. Her skin was a shade of white two steps into the grave. Her eyebrows were plucked to a narrow arch over blue-shadowed eyes. Nature had not endowed her with a Marilyn-mole, so she had painted one above and to the side of her lip. She wore a black cashmere sweater, bare at the shoulders and cut to the breastbone. The sweater stretched, as if in disbelief, over breasts held in improbable place by a push-up bra.

"I wonder why I haven't seen you before?" she remarked, her eyes traveling my body in frank appraisal.

"Maybe we just don't travel in the same circle," I offered.

"Then maybe we should start tonight," she suggested.

"Sorry. The edges of my circle are a little sharp for your tastes."

"Then you aren't a guest this evening?" she asked, disappointed.

"I'm the bodyguard," I replied.

She brightened with the realization that I was just another paid service. Her hand traced the line of my biceps, and she took another appraising glance at my body. Were I gold coin, she might have bit me.

"You can go ahead and frisk me, if you like. I won't mind," she said, and turned around, modeling her legs and other parts north for inspection.

"If I took the time to frisk you properly, you wouldn't have the energy left for Mr. Burns," I said, and she laughed.

There was little humor in her laugh. It was a recognition, an invitation, and good business. She snapped open a small white clutch purse, and withdrawing a card in two red-tipped fingers, handed it to me. The card listed her name and phone number.

"Give me a call, and I might take you up on that. But I warn you. I'm not a cheap date."

I pocketed the card, and led her into the living room. Burns was hunched over the coffee table, chopping something with a razor blade. It wasn't a carrot. Mona leaned over his back, planting her red lips on his neck.

"Hey, baby. You're just in time for meds," he said, and handed her a small gold straw.

Mona fingered the gold straw and swooped over the coffee table, devouring the fine white powder displayed on the surface. Burns slipped the straw from her fingers and sucked the remainder, with snorts massive enough to vacuum the rug. Mona ran her red-tipped finger over the table, coating the tips with the last of the grains, then brushed the residue along her lips.

"Would you mind?" Burns demanded, rattling the cubes of his empty glass at me. "You'll find a bottle in the den, or the kitchen, or the bedroom. Hell. Bottles are everywhere but here."

"I'm not the houseboy," I said, kneeling to finish the job with the track lock. I fit the key into the lock and gave it a turn. It worked.

A feminine breath buzzed in my ear. I twisted toward the breath, nearly grazing the lips that framed it.

"I apologize for the poor manners of my friend," she whispered, chemical euphoria dilating her eyes and wresting a wry, pleasured smile from her lips.

"Okay," I answered, and stood. The move surprised her, and she crouched, staring down at the carpet, smiling to herself. I think it amused her to be refused. That I liked her for it surprised me.

"What would you like to drink?" I asked.

"A vodka tonic, thanks," she answered, and the look in her eyes when she glanced up gave me an idea I thought it best to not dwell on. I went to mix the drinks. I was amazed that Jack Burns had been able to keep his business afloat. He was a heavy drinker, and the guilelessness with which he publicly consumed cocaine suggested familiar and frequent use. I suspected that substance abuse was affecting his business sense. The old financial tricks weren't working anymore, and his chemical-riddled brain couldn't quite figure why or what to do about it except cut a few more corners. Before I figured it all out, "Camelot" again chimed through the house.

I checked the door. A redhead waited at the other end of the peephole, staring defiantly into the lion's mouth as I looked out. She wore tight blue jeans strapped into white boots, a blue silk blouse, and a black jacket cut at calf level. I could see well enough to judge that the only weapons she wore were the kind issued to all women, though hers were undeniably of a larger caliber. Cradling the drinks in my arm, I swung the door open.

"I'm Dusty," the woman announced, striding into the foyer. She noticed the drink I was holding, and took it. Her head was small, and her face thin, and both were dwarfed by the Rubenesque proportions of her body.

"That's Mona's drink," I said.

"Fuck Mona," she answered.

"No thanks. You fuck Mona."

She smiled, and finished the vodka tonic in two long pulls. "Believe me, I have," she said, and handed me the empty.

There was a drawl in her voice, and she played with it, drawing out the vowels for effect. I guessed Texas, and she said Oklahoma was right. Dusty knew her way to the living room. Dusty knew her way to a lot of places. I followed her in. The living room was empty. Dusty craned her head over one shoulder and cut me with a who-are-you-putting-on look.

"So where are they?" she demanded, and when I suggested that we look in the bedroom, she replied: "But, darlin', that's the last place we'd find them if they were actually doing it."

I was about to ask if she had a better idea when forty decibels of amplified ripping vinyl blasted from the other side of the castle, in what sounded like a phonograph needle digging an extra groove into a record.

"I told you to use the CD player!" Burns's voice boomed down a hall to our left.

"Ahh, they're in the disco," Dusty said.

"The what?"

"The disco," she repeated, and, jerking her head toward the hall, led me down it to a cavernous room illuminated by flashing lights. At the far end of a parquet floor, Mona leaned over a phonograph. Burns squatted on the floor beside her, one arm wrapped around her thigh while he randomly flicked a bank of switches, trying, it seemed, to get the stereo to function properly.

"You haven't done all the drugs already, have you?" Dusty drawled. She accepted a kiss full on the mouth from Mona, and another one from Burns as he struggled to his feet.

"You wouldn't know how to work this thing, would you?" Burns asked, grabbing his Scotch before I offered it to him.

"No," I answered.

"I seemed to have it going last night, but I can't remember how."

Dusty leaned over the stereo, and clicked a switch. Paul Simon pounded from the speakers. I retreated to the den to mix two more vodka tonics. When I returned, the three of them were dancing sloppily around a pedestal blanketed in white powder, passing the gold straw. They took their drinks without comment. I wondered whether Paul Simon would have taken his record back had he known the environment in which it played. Burns draped one arm around each woman, nuzzling each in turn, while the women swayed to the beat and traded secrets with their eyes. Their hands began a practiced dance on his flesh. I fled upstairs.

4

The master bedroom was on the second floor, and opened onto the ocean. The dresser, nightstands, and lamps bore the sleek and futuristic lines of contemporary Italian design. A wet bar ascended from the corner carpet in a black marble monolith, silver spigots gleaming, and a translucent set of martini glasses and shaker were displayed on the surface next to a bottle of Tanqueray. The interior wall of the room projected a few feet forward, enclosing what seemed to be a closet, which momentarily confused me, as a walk-in closet branched off to the side of the bathroom. A red button was positioned to the side of the projection. I pressed it. Hidden machinery whirred, and the door slid smoothly open, revealing a home entertainment center almost identical to the system in the downstairs disco. I knelt and examined the equipment: Accuphase CD player and tuner, Classé amp, Lurné record player, Proton monitor, and NEC laser disk and VHS player. The speakers, which hung suspended from the ceiling, were by Duntach. In my audiophile days, I would have killed for this equipment. The setup cost about one hundred grand. Mere killing wouldn't have been enough.

I scanned the room for photographs, books, paintings, or objects that would reflect upon the nature of the man who slept there. The air in the bedroom seemed lightly oiled, and stuck to my skin. The room was conspicuously bare of private objects testifying to the living of a life. "He who dies with the most toys, wins" seemed to be the guiding principle.

I scouted past a bathroom with twin sinks and gold-plated faucets, and walked into the closet. A row of Italian suits hung neatly over wire racks of cotton dress shirts and wool sweaters. Two dresses, one black and wickedly cut down the back, and the other white and demurely buttoned to a Mandarin collar, hung at the far end of the closet, above several pairs of matching women's pumps. A current playpal, or the vestiges of a former lover? I wondered, and returned to the bedroom to check out the bed. It had gone king one better, to emperor size.

The headboard had twin paneled compartments. Inside the compartment nearest the wall, nestled against the far corner, I fingered a small box, and pulled it into the light. It was a box of 9-millimeter cartridges, originally containing fifty bullets, and now down to thirty-eight. I checked the other compartment for the gun. It was empty. I ran my hand under the pillows, and knelt on the floor to look under the bed. No gun. I hoped Burns wasn't stupid enough to carry it with him, and thought I'd check his briefcase when I next went downstairs.

Across from the bed, sliding glass doors opened onto a small balcony overlooking the sea. I squatted before it and installed another track lock, then stepped out onto the balcony to scope the layout of the back. The more time I spent in Burns's castle, the less I wanted to own anything in it. Money has a pornographic edge that titillates while demeaning the senses. The sound system I initially coveted now seemed part of a greater obscenity.

The castle perched on a cliff that was sliding with slow immutability to the sea. The salt smell of the sea drifted thickly over the edge of the cliff, accompanied by the hissing roar of waves. The moon dangled above the western horizon, casting long lunar shadows over a kidney-shaped swimming pool. The pool began about a dozen yards from the rear of the house, and ended in a jagged edge at the cliff, a victim of winter storms, earthquakes, and unstable soil. The Malibu land rebels against the toil of men, shaking, drowning, and burning it down, but the residents hang on, reveling in life at the edge of the abyss. The waves would pound the foundation of the cliff, and soon take the rest of the pool. Then the yard would tumble down, and the back patio, and in another hundred years or so, the castle would be fragments of granite at the bottom of the sea. Good riddance.

I returned to the stairway and, looking down from the landing, glimpsed in a mirror at the foot of the stairs three figures entwined on the carpet below. Burns had stripped Mona of her black cashmere. Her belly glowed in the gold pool spilled by an overhead track light. Mona's hands were buried beneath the redhead's blouse, and Burns hovered between them, eager for attention. Their three mouths met with a play of tongues, broke away, laughing slyly, then met again, the pink morsels of flesh like a tangle of worms. Dusty felt for the buckle of Burns's belt, and stripped his pants from him with an expert quickness. Burns lay back on one elbow, and availed himself of Mona's dangling breasts like a bacchante suckling grapes. Dusty shifted lower, and coaxed his erection with her mouth. Burns closed his eyes, and the heavy thudding of his breath drifted to my perch on the stairs. He called for a "Roid," and his eyes jerked open as he pointed urgently toward the corner of the room. I had no idea what he meant by the word, but Mona did. She slipped away and returned with an instant-print camera. The room strobed light. The camera clicked and hummed, and the print flickered out like a green tongue. Mona tossed the print on his chest. While Dusty went down on him, Mona snapped a variety of photos. Burns watched them develop with a twisted grin of self-recognition. His eyes flitted from the prints to his flesh, as though uncertain which sight provided the greatest pleasure. When this first variation began to bore him, Burns called for the camera and began directing the action.

I watched all the possible permutations of a camera, two women, and a man, as invisible as an audience to a screen. I was fascinated, yet loathed what I witnessed. My invisibility played a vital part in the pornography. In a hotel room, out of the curiosity and boredom of the business traveler, I had once watched a pornographic movie. I had flipped through the selection of cable channels, and happened on it by chance. I quickly changed the channel, and debated my sense of guilt by downing two quick shots of whiskey before turning back to the movie. I watched it in its entirety, and when the images excited me despite my conscious loathing, I knew then what it was to be a Peeping Tom. Pornography is sanctified voyeurism.

A shuddering gasp lurched from Burns's throat. Mona disentangled herself from the twisting flesh on the carpet, and stood with the camera to her eye. The room flashed incandescent. Burns arched as though lashed by a whip, then collapsed. Dusty heaved against his sodden heap of flesh, and Burns rolled onto his back, spent. The sorry parody of procreation was finished—or so I believed. Mona's eyes drifted from the triad, and fixed, through the mirror, on mine. My sense of distance shattered, as though an actress had looked out from the screen, and called me from the audience by name. A smile developed on her lips, a small revelation of my shared excitement and guilt. She raised the camera, and the flash reflecting against the mirror momentarily blinded me. Mona slid the print from the camera, glanced at it, and saluted me with a cynical smile. I looked away.

The biomechanics of guilt had set my face aflame and my ears to roaring. I took a deep breath. The roar subsided, but my complexion rivaled the color of a sunset sky. I glanced up to see Mona slipping into an oriental print robe.

"Is the Jacuzzi warm, Jack?" she asked.

Burns opened his eyes, surprised to discover both women had backed away from him, and uttered a slurred "What?"

"It's Jacuzzi time," Dusty repeated, tossing a robe onto his chest. I continued down the stairs.

"Jack here says you're a private detective." Mona swung around the sofa, and shook her hair in a studied gesture of abandon. Her eyes aggressively sought mine, confident that I wanted what experience had taught her all men wanted. "Why don't you join us?" she offered. "It would be fun to have a real dick in the tub, for once."

Dusty laughed, her voice trailing to a drawl: "Hot damn, girl, you're faster'n a hawk on a prairie dog."

Burns struggled to his feet, and began: "Ahh, now, girls," but the rest of his sentence was lost to a gunshot. The shot was no more than a distant pop, but a clean round hole was punched out of the plate-glass window over Burns's head, rattling the Levolor blinds. I dove forward, shouldering Mona into the sofa.

"What the hell?" Burns exclaimed, glancing around in bewilderment.

I shouted at him to get down, but he was too far gone for the words to have any effect. I had landed on top of Mona. She looked up at me, and giggled. Given enough drugs, you may find even attempted murder amusing. I rolled off the sofa and hurled myself across the room. My shoulder hit Burns at belly level, and he thudded to the carpet with a surprised grunt. I pinned him, explaining very patiently that someone was shooting at him, and it would be best for him to stay on the floor at present. He nodded, a semblance of reality beginning to penetrate his haze.

My overnight kit contained a .38 revolver for occasions such as this, and I availed myself of it. I switched off the safety before dousing the track lighting and ducking out the side kitchen door.

The moon hung one night short of full above a calm sea, casting long, sharp-edged shadows across the property. I crouched behind the trash cans outside the kitchen door, and listened to the surf pound against the shore, waiting for my eyes to adjust. When the irises had made their adjustments, I crept toward the sound of the surf and peered into the yard. On the edge of the porch stood a small redwood and glass outbuilding. Wisps of steam rose from the open windows, dissipating into the night air. I crossed to it, and glanced through a window. The steam rose from the surface of a hot tub. I remembered Mona had mentioned something about a Jacuzzi, and circled the enclosure. A pine fence, bare wood graying in the elements, marched in vertical stripes to the cliff. A eucalyptus tree spread its branches a few yards inland, where the fence warped to a final twist of splinters at the cliff edge. I considered the angle and location of the room that had been fired upon, and concluded the shooter had used the tree as cover. He wasn't likely to be hanging around waiting for another try, but even a hundred-to-one shot is a bad gamble when your life is the stake. I skirted the back of the house, breaking into a run and using the momentum to vault the fence. I landed cleanly in a field of coastal grasses and rolled onto my stomach. The maneuver had created slightly less noise than a brick falling off a five-story building. No one shot at me. I doubted that the shooter was so awed by my athletic ability that he had forgotten to squeeze the trigger. I doubted that the shooter was there at all. A car door slammed shut in the distance, and it took me a moment to place the location and significance. I leapt to my feet and chugged through the tall grass toward the access road above Burns's castle. When I reached the road, the sight of taillights receding through the trees and a faint stirring of dust in the air were my only reward.

5

"That son of a bitch!" Burns fumed throughout a Scotch-soaked night of insomnia. Mona and Dusty had fled shortly after the shooting, and Burns huddled in a bedroom corner with a blanket and bottle, insisting with a frightened howl that I remain in the room. At three o'clock in the morning, the phrase *That son of a bitch!* became a chant, interspersed with an indignant *Who does that son of a bitch think he's dealing with?* or a self-pitying *Do I need this kind of crap?* and usually ending with an emphatic: *I'll kill the son of a bitch!*

"What son of a bitch, Jack? Who are you talking about?" I intermittently asked.

Drunken cunning slit his eyes, and invariably he would reply: "None of your goddamned business," then finish by calling me shamus, dick, or gumshoe, and cackling at the joke. At four o'clock, I quit asking, and drifted into a couple of hours of fitful sleep.

I woke at six in the morning, when the color of the western horizon shifted from indigo to cerulean blue. Jack Burns curled in a snuffling slumber with the bottle of Scotch under his blanket. I rose quietly and trotted down the steps to the kitchen, where, newspaper in hand, I enjoyed a cup of coffee thick enough to stand on. The sun was visible in the eastern sky about an hour later, and I stood on the back porch, watching the sea birds whirl above the waves. Two brown pelicans skimmed in tandem along the surface of the sea. I was glad to see them. The local pelican population had been decimated during the 1970s. The largest DDT factory in the United States had operated fifty miles south on the coast of Palos Verdes, dumping its waste into the bay. The local fish population had adapted to the new toxic environment, as did most of the people who ate the fish, not counting the few whose lives were somewhat shortened by cancer, but the pelicans proved more fragile. The factory closed down after legislation outlawed DDT, and now, fifteen years later, pelicans have migrated from the north coast, and are again flying along Southern California beaches. The two pelicans spotted breakfast, wheeled high into the sky, and sweeping back their wings, dropped like arrows into the sea. They emerged from the swell and tossed their beaks back, gobbling fish down long necks. I regretted that the privilege of owning this stretch of coast was wasted on a jerk like Jack Burns, and thought it deserved a much more appreciative sort, such as myself. Maybe I could buy it from him when I won the lottery.

I found the slug buried in the wall across the room from the hole in the plate-glass window. The slug was flattened to the shape of a triple-thick nickel. I'm not particularly adept at the arcane art of forensics, and though I know guns, about all I could tell from the slug was that it was ordinary lead, and fired from a small-caliber gun, most likely a pistol.

I pulled a tape measure from my bag. The bullet hole was located six feet and four inches up the wall. I moved over and measured the height of the bullet hole in the window. The tape read six feet. I extended my hand as though it held a gun. The distance from my hand to the floor was five feet three inches. I'm a bit over six feet tall, and estimated a man of average height would hold a pistol five feet above the ground. I figured there had to be a mathematical equation which would estimate the distance of the shooter from the window, and ran the tape measure from the window to the far wall. Thirty feet separated the two.

I sat down with the numbers and a sheet of paper, and drew a graph. The question was quite simple: if a bullet is fired at a height of five feet, passes through the first point at six feet, and the second point thirty feet distant at six feet four inches, how far away from the first point was the gun when fired? I was pleased with myself when I derived the answer of ninety feet, figuring that if a bullet rises one third of a foot in thirty feet, it would rise one foot in ninety feet—the difference between five and six feet. I measured the distance between the eucalyptus tree and the plate-glass window, and discovered it was eighty-six feet. Discounting the possibility that the shooter was a midget or played center in the NBA, I concluded with reasonable certainty that he had hidden behind the tree, and waited for Burns's silhouette in the window to fire. I was proud as hell of my cleverness, but the fact that I knew from where the gun had been fired didn't amount to much. I pocketed the slug and returned to the castle to rouse Burns.

Angel was ready to begin the day watch when I dropped Jack Burns at his office. Her hair was wrapped in a bun, and she wore a crisp gray suit over a silk blouse with ruffled lapels. The skirt was cut a demure two inches above the knees. She carried a steno pad, and wore a giant pair of black eyeglasses, looking like the shy intellectual in any number of James Bond movies before James removes the glasses to discover a smashing beauty. It had been her idea to dress as a secretary for the day watch, and she must have spent the hours since dawn at her mirror, trying to figure out what one looked like. Burns, sunglasses shielding his bloodshot eyes, and suffering the effects of a killer hangover, brushed past her in the lobby with a brusque:

"Sorry, lady. We're not hiring."

I introduced them. Burns looked at me.

"This girl is going to protect me? What is she going to do, blow the guy away with her hair dryer?"

"I can break your neck at the twenty-third vertebrae in less than five seconds. Care to time me?" Angel answered, and smiled very prettily.

Burns backed off and pushed the sunglasses up his forehead with a trembling hand. He had a little trouble focusing, but when the image came together, he whistled.

"This woman works with you?"

I nodded.

"If a woman's body is a temple, she's gotta be the Sistine Chapel."

"I don't care to be talked about as though I'm not in the room when I plainly am," Angel advised, swinging open the door to Burns's private office, "but you don't know me very well yet, and I'll do you the favor of taking your remark as a compliment."

"Wonder Woman, eh?" Burns whispered as we crossed the threshold.

"I'm a piece of cake compared to her," I said, and left them to get better acquainted.

Nina Gamine was waiting in the hall, leaning against my office door and clutching a manila envelope to her chest when I stepped out of the elevator. Her noir-woman attire of the previous day had been switched to a girl-next-door look of summery white linen and silk, as though she had recast herself as Grace Kelly. Nina self-consciously removed her sunglasses when I approached, and offered a timid smile.

"Don't tell me we had an appointment," I said.

She thrust the manila envelope forward and answered with an uncertain question: "You asked me about some records yesterday?"

I unlocked the door, and let her in.

"Sorry to make you wait, but our office hours are a little irregular. You can just push them through the mail slot next time."

"I didn't mind waiting. I kind of hoped I could talk to you for a moment."

I scooped the mail and the morning edition of *The Wall Street Journal* off the floor, and tossed the bundle on the corner of the front desk. Nina Gamine stood in a corner of the reception room, the knuckles on her fingers clenched white around the edges of the envelope. One side of her lower lip was drawn in, worried from the inside by her set of small, perfect teeth.

"Have you had a good day? So far, I mean," she said, and an awkward smile fluttered over her face. She wasn't very good at casual conversation, and I decided to make it a little easier for her, answering: "I haven't had a good day since August 9, 1974."

"Really? What was so important about August 9?"

"Nixon resigned."

"Oh," she said with an earnest nod.

"That was a joke."

She nodded again, and said: "I'm sorry, but I've been told that I don't have much of a sense of humor."

"That's all right. I'll laugh for the both of us."

I settled in behind my desk, and patiently folded my hands, waiting for her to offer the envelope for my inspection. When she didn't, I prompted her with a polite: "The records?"

"Of course," she blurted, and thrust the envelope forward with both hands. I pried it from her fingers, and wondered whether the money she was spending to find her brother might be better spent on therapy. I spilled the contents of the envelope onto the desk, and examined a few postcards her brother had sent from overseas, and a dozen monthly credit card statements. Her brother had financed the first months of his exile on plastic. There were itemized bills from the first few months, including those for airfares and European hotels and restaurants, followed by a series of threatening notes from collection departments.

"Could your brother have other credit cards not billed to your address?"

"No," she said, flatly.

"How about his father."

"His father is dead."

"His adoptive father, then. The minister."

"Everything was changed over when he moved in with me. I saw to it."

"Could he have written to his adoptive father?"

"No. The break was very final."

"I'd like to talk to him."

"I'd rather you leave him out of it."

She looked at her hands. The fingers twisted around one another, the pressure of the grip mottling her fair skin. She noticed me looking at her hands, and tore them apart, hiding them behind her purse.

"His father could tell me about your brother's friends, even if he doesn't know where he is. Maybe Francis has written to one of his old high school pals."

"He didn't have any friends."

"I find that difficult to believe."

"He was an orphan. Orphans don't make friends easily."

"Maybe he had a girlfriend. He ran away with her, or she broke his heart, and he ran away without her."

"He didn't have any girlfriends."

"You mean he didn't tell you about them."

"I mean he didn't have them."

Nina Gamine's timidity concealed a brittle but unyielding stubbornness. Her resolve shielded me from something about her brother that I might need to know, as though she were afraid of my learning it. She would have to break if I were to learn anything of value, and I cast around my mind for something suitably hard, arriving at the query: "Was he gay?"

She looked at me, her lip drooping, her face blank.

"You know. A homosexual. Is that why he left?"

"No. He isn't homosexual, and I pay you to find my brother, not insult him."

"I'm not trying to insult him," I countered, but the phone rang before I could explain that calling someone gay was not an insult, though perhaps to her it was. The phone rang again. I looked at it. Nina Gamine looked at it. I put the interview on hold and answered.

Somebody on the other end asked for Julio in Spanish. I said, *"No en casa,"* and hung up.

"I'm not trying to insult him," I repeated. "I'm just trying to learn something that could give me an idea where he went. That's why I want to talk to other people in his life, such as his father."

"It's his adoptive father, and I'd rather you not contact him."

"We're going in circles. Why don't you want me to talk to your brother's adoptive father?"

"I just don't think it would help."

"Why don't you let me decide that?"

"But I'm telling you he doesn't know anything!"

"How can you be certain that his adoptive father doesn't know where he is?"

"Because he believes Francis is still living here," she cried.

The phone rang again, and she began to weep. I let it ring, waiting for the machine to pick up, but the volume of Nina Gamine's tears increased with each ring, so I answered it, hoping to silence them both. It was another wrong number. I hung up, feeling shitty. I had pushed her until she had broken with her secret, and as far as secrets go, it wasn't very big; just human and a little pitiful. It didn't seem worth the pain. I muttered a few banal platitudes, and after a minute or two, the worst of it was over. Her tears slowed to a sniffle, and the knot in my stomach began to loosen.

I reopened the interview with an immediate but well-intentioned lie: "I'm not trying to badger you, Miss Gamine." She nodded into a handkerchief, and wiped her nose. I wasn't going to get anywhere by backing off, but tried to be as gentle as I could about pressing my point. "You hired me to find your brother. To do that, I need to follow leads. To get leads, I need to talk to people who know him."

She straightened, the perfect blue of her eyes rimmed red, snapped open her clutch purse, and traded her handkerchief for a small slip of paper.

"If I give you his name, do you have to tell him that Francis is missing?"

I shook my head. She pulled a pen from her purse, and scribbled a name and phone number on the slip of paper. She stretched a trembling hand across the desk, and deposited the slip of paper in my palm.

"I'm hoping to leave town soon," she sniffled. "I know I haven't been much help, but I need to find him as quickly as possible."

"Leaving town as in moving?"

She nodded, and stood to leave.

"Where to?" I asked, but the question was clipped by the sharp ring of the telephone, and the second ring obliterated her mumbled response.

"What!" I barked, picking up the phone.

"You don't have to sound so rude," Angel complained as I waved Nina Gamine out the door.

"Maybe I don't have to, but I want to. What's up?"

"We've got problems. Baby wants to back out."

"Where are you?" I asked.

"At a beauty salon."

"Have you lost your mind? This is no time to get your hair done."

"My mind is quite sound, thank you. If you took the time to think, you wouldn't jump to such a stupid conclusion," she observed in an arctic tone.

I was contrite. "May I politely ask what you're doing at a beauty salon?"

"Watching baby get a makeover," she replied.

6

The Masculine Image huddled between clothing boutiques on Rodeo Drive in Beverly Hills, a city on the cutting edge of criminal law, having illegalized parking on the streets, smoking in restaurants, and voting Democratic. The rich can afford to park in pay lots, and smoking is a working-class habit, so the laws didn't stir up much protest, except among the few token Democrats in town, who resisted having their votes outlawed. The city council had once tried to illegalize poor people within the city limits, until some wag had pointed out that the only poor people in Beverly Hills were the servants, who, though forgettable as individuals, were indispensable as a class. The city council had settled on the compromise of requiring entry visas for anyone making less than a hundred grand a year, but I believe there was a constitutional problem with this law that prevented its enaction.

The lettering on the green awning in front of the Masculine Image read SALON DE BEAUTY. Having learned to never trust anything American labeled in French or Old English, I crossed the threshold with some trepidation. The salon was decorated in Early Safari. Wicker furniture, tropical palms, African artifacts, and dead animals pinned to the wall hearkened back to the good old days when men were proud to be imperialists and killed with happy impunity. I glanced up. A leopard skin hung over my head, flattened against the wall above the entrance. I stared at the cat's glass eyes, and wondered what caliber truck had bagged it.

The chief cosmetologist, her eye trained in this sort of thing, spotted me eying the cat, and screeched in alarm: "That scar!" She circled the laced bamboo reception desk, and pinned me against the wall, her fingers deftly probing the two-inch snake above my right eye, which I had received six months before when someone mistook my head for a piñata. The chief cosmetologist was a handsome woman in her late forties, with short-cropped silver hair, black bug eyes, and great skin.

"You really should have come to us earlier," she worried. "It's almost too late, but we'll see what we can do. Regular treatment with our special acacia mint masque can work wonders. It breaks down the calcification of scar tissue in the epidermis, you know."

"Thanks for the tip," I said, backing away, "but I'm here for Jack Burns."

She frowned. That wasn't at all what she wanted to hear. Her eyes went over my face like an art critic scanning the work of a second-rate painter. "We could fit in an appointment while you wait. The skin is absolutely clogged with dead skin cells. Whatever do you use on it, soap?"

Angel sauntered across the waiting room, grinning. I met her under wood-carved grotesques of sullen and horrified masks, which I assumed were replicas of the salon's less-than-satisfied customers.

"Passing on the make-over?" Angel asked.

"I thought I'd get my chest bikini-waxed instead."

"It's all the rage, I hear."

"What's the story on Burns?"

Angel shrugged.

"He just said he wanted to discontinue the service."

"Any explanation?"

"He said he wanted to speak to the top man. I checked below my belt and decided that means you."

"I think the man is a couch-case. What do you think?" I asked.

"I think that when you have a lot of money, you don't worry about what other people think."

Burns reclined on a cart in a private room, covered feet to chin by a green sheet. A large woman slapped an ointment onto his cheeks from her perch on a high chair above his head. When I slipped into the room, the woman was describing the various slaps, pulls, and pokes to his skin as facial aerobics.

"Marston! Pull up a chair," Burns cried. The woman's powerful hands pinned Burns's head to the cart, causing his eyes to roll in their sockets as he traced my path from the door to his feet. "Rhea here was just about to tell me about my eyebrows."

Rhea smiled and nodded, slapping his cheeks. Her pleasantly chubby face was suffused with the cheerful energy of a woman committed to her work. Her voice was improbably high for a woman her size, and fluted from her throat in singsong rhythms. The accent and inventive sense of grammar placed her from somewhere in Eastern Europe: "A man should have powerful eyebrows, yes? Because the eyes they frame, just like a painting. The eyes they must bring out."

"And what about my eyebrows?" Burns asked.

"They are much too light. Light eyebrows drain the power from a man! His eyebrows must command attention!"

"I love it!" Burns chuckled. "Power eyebrows! What about Marston over there?"

Rhea peered at my face. "He has power eyebrows, yes? Very strong. But if he would step over here, I could give them a fast trim. They are strong, but not well groomed."

"Well, Marston? How about it?" Burns winked up at Rhea, then grinned at me. "Marston is much too macho to approve of all this, I'm afraid."

"When he goes older, and like a worn-out old shoe his face looks, then he'll be very sorry, yes?"

A phone rang. Rhea looked around, startled, and observed: "I hear ringing but there is no phone."

Burns motioned to a leather briefcase in the corner. I opened the case, and handed Burns the cellular phone. He sat up, and raised the antenna.

"Yeah, Jack, good to hear from you. What do you think of my proposition?" he asked, with a friendly wink in my direction.

Rhea turned her back and plunged her fingers into a bright metal mixing bowl. Something in the bowl audibly squashed when she flexed her hands. I was afraid to look.

"I don't like what I'm hearing. Maybe you'd better start over," Burns threatened. He listened, and his face, already a bright pink from Rhea's facial aerobics, turned a darker shade of red. He shouted: "You want me to blow the whistle on the whole thing?"

Rhea glanced over her shoulder, cheerful face dismayed. Her hands were covered in green slime.

"You don't think I can?" Burns shrilled. "I can blow this whole deal out of the water in five seconds. All I have to do is hang up the phone. Is that what you want? Five seconds, and the deal is history."

Burns listened. Rhea shrugged, and turned back to the counter. Burns heard something he didn't like.

"That's it. I'm hanging up."

Burns listened again. He nodded. "That's what I wanted to hear." Burns smiled, and began to pour it on.

"Beautiful. We got a deal then? Fantastic."

More smiling and nodding.

"We still friends? Shake hands and forget the whole thing? Beautiful. Ciao, baby."

Burns flipped the switch, cutting transmission. His face turned ugly. "You son of a bitch! How dare you try to fuck with me!" He slammed the antenna back into the receiver, and tossed me the phone. By the time I caught it, his face had changed again, as though the rage was merely a mirage. He was grinning, proud and full of himself.

"I won," he crowed, and lay back down on the cart.

Rhea clucked at him with her tongue, setting a bowl of lime-green paste by his head. "You ruin the whole treatment by this upset. To relax the facial muscles before we apply the mask is the way it must be done."

I was beginning to think that it would not break my heart to lose this job. Rhea coated her hands with the slimy green paste, and spread it smoothly along his cheeks, working down toward the chin. Burns uttered a sigh of contentment. I assumed it was therapeutic.

"I heard that you were thinking of calling off the service," I said.

"That's right. Matters came to a head late this morning. It was all a misunderstanding."

"Mind telling me what it was all about?"

"This feels heavenly, Marston. You really should give it a try."

"It would give the police something to follow. Just in case you're wrong about it being a misunderstanding."

"Don't be so dramatic. I'm as safe as a baby. Rhea here will protect me, won't you, darling?" Burns flirted with his eyes and smiled garishly beneath the green mask.

Rhea clucked at him with her tongue. "Only if you promise to stop speaking. The mask it won't set properly, if you keep your mouth moving."

The green paste coated his face from forehead to chin, and swirled around slits for his mouth, nostrils, and eyes. Rhea examined her work, nodded with satisfaction, and carrying the bowl to a corner sink, filled it with water.

"You've paid a deposit for one week's services. You may recall the deposit was nonrefundable."

"Don't worry about it."

"It won't cost you anything to keep us on through the end of the week."

"Thanks, but I don't think I'll be needing you, much as I've enjoyed your company. To tell you the truth, I find you a bit of a prude, Marston. Constraining. Your girlfriend even more so."

"Partner," I corrected, though I considered her both.

"This morning I pulled a little white pick-me-up out of my drawer, and would you believe she actually advised me to seek help for my 'addiction,' as she so quaintly put it."

"Angel is a little old-fashioned. She still thinks it possible to help people. I may believe you're as flaky as the stuff you put up your nose, but I realize it's none of my business."

"What the fuck do you know?" Burns demanded, rising to one elbow. Rhea briskly shoved him flat with an admonition to remain still, but it did not dissuade his mouth. "You've never had any real money, and never will have. You drive a beat-up piece of crap, and live in a shoe box somewhere in Santa Monica. If you have more than ten grand in the bank, or clear more than fifty grand a year after business expenses, I'll drop dead here and now with a heart attack.''

There wasn't anything to contradict, and I've found it is futile to argue with clients, so I said nothing. I momentarily regretted that Angel wasn't in the room with me, as she becomes emotional in situations such as this, and I would have enjoyed watching her tear into him. Burns laughed.

''I'm still alive, so I guess I'm right. Now, why don't you get out of here before I decide to put a stop order on your check.''

I thought, Why the hell not? and, moving to the sink, lifted the bowl of water and let it fly. Rhea shrieked. Burns bolted upright, sputtering. I pushed him back down with my hand to his chest, and kept him down while I advised in a modulated, polite tone: ''If that check is returned unpaid, I'll consider the client confidentiality clause of our contract dead. The police will certainly be interested to know why someone tried to kill you, and I know a couple of reporters who could milk a story about investment fraud and attempted murder among the rich and famous for a week of headlines.''

I removed my hand from his chest, wiped it clean on the bottom of the green covering sheet, and made one of the more theatrical exits of my life. Dousing Burns was an emotional, irresponsible, and childish thing to do. It was also a hell of a lot of fun.

7

The statement arrived in the mail the following morning. It was in a legal-size envelope, manila brown, with a clear plastic window framing the office address. Santa Monica Bank was stamped on the upper left corner. I ripped it open, not thinking about much of anything, except that it was a sunny day and I was stuck inside doing what bills I could given my limited financial resources. The statement commanded attention as quickly as a death notice. It was a standard form. Two boxes were checked: "Check Returned" on the left, and to the right, "Insufficient Funds." The check number, amount, and sender were typed in. The sender was Jack Burns.

I called his office. His regular secretary had returned from her vacation. She was good at her job. When I asked to speak to Mr. Burns, she said he wasn't in. I asked when he was expected to return. She said she didn't know, and asked what this related to. I told her about the check, and she professed shock and dismay upon hearing that it had bounced. She insisted that something like this had never happened before, which gave me a hint about both her loyalty and credibility. She apologized. She informed me that the firm had employed a new accountant, and that affairs would be straightened out shortly. She promised to look into it immediately. She did everything she could to make me happy, except give me what I wanted, which was Burns or a way to get in touch with him.

I called Burns's castle, and got his machine. I left a message suggesting that bouncing a check was not much better than stopping payment, and to avoid needless publicity, it would be a good idea to quickly clear up the little misunderstanding. A bad check is rarely an innocent mistake. I've received enough of them to know.

Burns didn't get back to me that afternoon. I called his office about closing time. The secretary expertly played the runaround game, claiming not to have heard from him. I stuffed the bank notice in my coat pocket, drove to my apartment, changed into my swimming suit, and went for a two-mile swim as the sun settled into the ocean. The water was cold, and I had to swim hard to stay warm. Anger stiffened my body, and though the sea was calm, I fought it for the first mile. As I tired, the anger and stress flowed away in my wake, and I relaxed. The second mile cleared my mind. The sea sent me a parting gift, a four-footer with a curl as smooth and shapely as the under-curve of a woman's breast, and I rode it in to shore. After a quick shower, I drove up the coast.

The sun was down and the moon out when I parked in the circular drive in front of Burns's castle. The chimes rang "Camelot" when I pressed the button. After the fifth encore, I tired of the tune, and followed a brick path to the garage. The side door was open. My fingers searched the wall, found the switch, and twin overheads cut the garage in sharp lines of light and shadow. The Rolls was parked in the middle stall, flanked by a Porsche 944, and a Mercedes 450 SL. Maybe he took the Schwinn.

The path skirted the garage, and led through an arched side gate into the back, where it joined with the patio at the rear of the house. The wet salt smell of the sea drifted over the cliff, coating my throat when I breathed it in. The sea draws me, and I walked to the edge to look down. The tide was high, and the ground shook when the waves crashed blue to white against the rocks. I glanced around the yard, and ambled to the jagged edge of the pool where it dropped to the rocks. Brackish water cupped a shining full moon in what remained of the deep end. Nature endures. I tracked the arc of the reflection, and admired the original rising in the eastern edge of the night.

My eyes dropped to the castle and scanned it as I approached.

Lights were showing in the living room and master bedroom. The Levelor blinds were not drawn over the plate-glass windows on the ground floor, allowing a clear view of the back rooms. There was no movement inside, and, equally likely a prospect given Jack Burns, nothing passed out on the floor.

I hammered on the sliding glass door. Great rasping squawks chilled my spine, and I whirled in the direction of the sound, unnerved. Nothing within the yard moved. Over the sea-bleached fence, the branches of the eucalyptus swayed. Squawks sounded again, like the shredding of violin strings. A fluttering of wings shook the tree, and a flock of yellow-beaked parrots took sudden flight over my head, singing in joyful cacophony.

The birds receded into silence. A faint gurgling of water skimmed the periphery of my hearing, and I followed the sound to the redwood and glass Jacuzzi enclosure on the edge of the porch. The blinds were lowered, and the glass steamed opaque. I tried the door. It swung open.

Burns drifted face-down in the tub, lit from below by a ghastly green glow. Green bubbles swirled around his body like a swarm of insects. I pulled his face out of the water. The features were badly swollen, though not bruised or marked, and his skin was a bright, boiled red. His eyes were vacant slits half buried by puffing folds of skin. I gently lowered his face into the water, which seemed unnaturally hot, and gripped his arm at the wrist. The pulse was long gone from his body. I fished the temperature gauge, and checked it in the green light of the tub. It peaked at one hundred twenty degrees. Burns's wig floated aimlessly around the tub like a drowned animal.

His death shocked, but did not sadden me. The morning paper had reported the accidental death of a seven-year-old girl in a gang shooting, and I grieved more for her than him. Still, I stood motionless by the tub for a couple of minutes, adjusting to the fact of his death. I was affected because I had known him and was confronted with his corpse. My mind balked at reconciling my image of this very vital though completely fucked-up man with the dead heap of flesh in the tub. The two seemed to have nothing in common.

I've seen enough corpses, but it always surprises me how dead the dead are.

I brightened the lights and scanned the room. His clothes were heaped on a wooden slat bench against the wall. An empty bottle of twenty-year-old Scotch lay on its side within arm's reach of the tub. A tumbler half full of amber fluid was perched on the tub railing. I crouched by the railing and sniffed it. It was what remained of the Scotch, but the only way I would have known whether or not it was poisoned would have been to take a sip and see if I answered my morning wake-up call. The police are good for something, particularly when you have a dead body and don't know what to do with it.

I decided to break into the castle rather than drive to the nearest phone booth. The sliding glass door leading to the living room was locked at the handle, but the track lock I had installed at the base was unlatched. Draping my hand with a handkerchief, I grasped the handle, bumped the glass with my hip, and gave the handle a quick upward jerk. The handle latch unhooked, and I was in.

Nothing seemed out of place in the living room. Glancing around for the cellular phone, I crossed to the foyer, and checked the alarm control panel, not wanting to be surprised by a security guard, who would likely have a gun but not the training to use it. The alarm was off. I tracked down the cellular phone in the master bedroom, and dialed the number of the Malibu sheriff's department. As I called in the report, I wandered through the bathroom and into the walk-in closet. The two dresses and the collection of women's pumps had vanished.

The uniforms were the first to arrive. Plainclothes would follow later, after the fact of the crime had been established. Two men stepped from the squad car, both standard-issue Malibu sheriff deputies: white, over six feet, mustached, and muscular. They gaped at the monstrous structure, elbowed each other, and one of them said, "A man's home is his castle, eh?"

I led them over the moat and through the castle to the Jacuzzi room, then stood aside while they verified that the object floating in the tub was indeed a man, and the man was indeed dead. They asked me if I had touched anything, and when I said that I hadn't, they advised me to continue not touching anything. I accompanied one of them to the car, and listened to him radio in his report.

He was obliged to keep me company until the first backup arrived. We grunted back and forth for a quarter of an hour, in the minimalist way of manly conversation. The arrival of the backup unit rescued him, and he disappeared inside with a third deputy.

The party was in full swing by the time Sheriff Bernie Kohl arrived. Red whirligig lights danced along the huddled carnival of cops, squad cars, and yellow tape barricades, carving red and blue cutouts of the eucalyptus trees surrounding the drive. Kohl ducked under the barricade and conferred a moment with one of the standard-issue deputies, acknowledging me with a brief nod. Kohl was not standard-issue. His salt-and-pepper hair was worn stylishly long, and he had the best tan north of George Hamilton. He was the only cop I'd ever met with a Ph.D. in English literature, and he had lived in Japan for a year, studying Zen Buddhism. The big-city cops in L.A. shrugged him off as an eccentric, but the insular community of Malibu didn't like hard-nosed cops, and had elected him twice running. I liked him.

"A man's home is his castle, eh?" Kohl quipped, ambling over to shake my hand.

"Either that, or his grave."

"You know what they say about accidents in the home. Is the body your client?"

"Ex-client. His check bounced."

"Impolite of him to die before paying up. How much was the check for?"

"Seventy-five hundred," I answered.

"And you dropped by this evening to encourage payment?" Kohl surmised.

I nodded.

"We'll keep this between us, but that gives you what we call in this business a motive."

"You know me better than that. I would have gotten the money first, then killed him."

"Remind me to cross your name off the suspect list," Kohl smiled, and scrutinized the front of the castle. He clapped me on the shoulder, and cheerily advised: "Death waits for no man, and all that, so perhaps you should show me how you came to find the body."

I first led him to the garage, and pointed to where my fingerprints would likely be found. The quarter of a million dollars in horsepower did not impress him.

"Last year's Porsche," he grunted.

Kohl followed me through the side gate, his flashlight skimming the ground behind my feet. I told him that I had been distracted by the sound of water, but did not mention the flock of parrots. He would have thought me drunk, or worse, poetic. He asked me the nature of my business with Burns, and I told him about the death threat, the wild partying, and the attempt on Burns's life two nights previous.

"Where is the bullet hole?" Kohl asked, and I led him to it. His flashlight climbed the window, and fixed on the sharp-edged circle in the glass. He wasn't pleased that I had pried the slug out of the opposing wall, and suggested I return it with an affidavit stating how it had been retrieved. I attempted redemption by detailing my calculations regarding from where the gun had been fired, but he dismissed me with a cursory "We have people much better at that sort of thing than you."

Kohl clicked off his flashlight, and stepped through the sliding glass door into the living room. The bullet hole in the far wall was visible from across the room, but he didn't bother glancing up when I pointed it out. He seemed more interested in the ambience, examining the furniture, and trying out the ocean view. "Two girls, eh?" he said, with a hint of envy in his voice.

"Two girls, cocaine, booze, and wild sex," I elucidated.

An enigmatic smile crossed his face. He said: "How oft when men are at the point of death, have they been merry," and stepped again onto the back porch.

The side door to the Jacuzzi was open. A detective knelt in front of the tub, dusting the glass of Scotch for prints. A photographer shouldered a flash camera, and bitched at him to get out of the way.

There was a lot of the detective to move around. He was about six-four, and weighed three hundred pounds. His suit was crisply pressed, with a three-corner hanky folded out of the breast pocket. The photographer was a small guy with big ears and a reedy voice. Burns still floated face down in the tub.

"Anything?" Kohl asked the detective, ducking into the enclosure.

"Too much. Half of Malibu probably passed through here this week. You wouldn't believe the stuff floating in this water. I've got at least four categories of pubic hair trapped in the filter, and I'm sure lab analysis is gonna turn up every body fluid known to man and woman."

Kohl leaned over the side of the Jacuzzi, and examined the body without touching it.

"Coroner?" he asked.

"On his way," the detective answered.

Kohl borrowed a pair of tongs from the detective's forensics kit, and snared the temperature gauge from the Jacuzzi, remarking upon examination: "Hell should be so hot."

"He looks rather well done, don't you think?" the detective replied.

"Reminds me of the lobster I had for dinner last night," the photographer quipped, and snapped a shot of the body.

Homicide wit. Kohl took a handkerchief from his pocket, and wiped his hands.

"What do you think killed him?" I asked.

"Tub death," he answered.

The detective and photographer laughed.

"We have to wait for the coroner's report, of course, but by the temperature of the water, and the probable consumption of alcohol, I'd guess our friend here died of hyperthermia."

"Hyperwhat?" I said.

"Hyperthermia. A rapid rise in body temperature. If your body heats to over a hundred and seven degrees, you die."

"I take it you've seen this before," I said.

"It's the third leading cause of accidental death in Malibu, behind auto accidents and drug overdoses. Someone ingests too much alcohol and too many drugs, decides to sweat it out in the hot tub, passes out, and boils to death. That's why we call it tub death.''

"The temperature in the tub is over a hundred and ten. I don't care how drunk, it's going to burn when he steps in," I objected.

"The man turns up the heat after he settles in," Kohl explained. "He's accustomed to taking hot tubs, and like anything else, you can build up a tolerance for hot water, so he wants it really hot. The man is drunk, and chances are, he may have taken a sedative or two, such as Valium. The longer he stays in the tub, the hotter the water gets. Hyperthermia is directly related to the amount of time the body is exposed to high heat, and the organ it affects most directly is the brain. It makes the man drowsy and disoriented. In combination with the alcohol and whatever else he's ingested, it's a powerful narcotic.''

The detective paddled Burns's floating wig to the side of the tub and, gripping it with tongs, lifted the dripping scraggly thing from the water.

"Where do you suppose he bought his wig—the local drugstore?" he cracked.

The photographer laughed, and snapped a candid of man, tongs, and wig. The wig hung there, dripping a melody into the water below, then was stuffed into a plastic bag and sealed. Burns was quickly to follow.

8

The loss of seventy-five hundred dollars is not a minor matter to a small business. I was juggling bills on the computer when Angel walked into my office and pulled from the far wall the poster of my favorite painting by Mark Rothko, *Orange and Yellow*, which is the only painting of his that does not in some way remind me of death.

"What the hell are you doing?" I grumbled, watching her spread a map across the wall and stick it in place with pushpins.

"You can see perfectly well what I'm doing," she answered. It was an accordion map of Europe, with arrows, dots, and notations in colored marking pen.

"Are we planning an invasion of the continent, or perhaps just our summer vacation?" I quipped.

"While you've been dragging your depressed butt around the office this week, I've been trying to find Nina Gamine's brother," Angel admonished, and unsheathed a telescoping pointer from the elastic band of her sweatpants. She whipped it to a bright blue line that began at the map's edge in the Atlantic, bisected southern France, and ended at Rome. Rome was circled in green.

"Thirteen months ago, Francis Gamine flew TWA into Rome, where he stayed at the Excelsior Hotel for two weeks. After a night in Milan, his next stop was Bern, Switzerland. There was no record of travel, so I'm assuming that he met someone, or bummed a ride. He traveled around the countryside, staying at small inns, before continuing, by train, to Bonn, in West Germany. He charged everything to American Express, which is how I know all of this. It seems as though he was trying to hold on to his cash, because the credit card statements show at least one charge a day for the first couple of months.''

''Meaning that he knew he was going to stay in Europe for a while and wasn't going to pay the bill.''

Angel nodded. Her pointer touched the Benelux countries. ''In Holland, he purchased a round-trip ferry passage to England, with an open-ended return passage. In London, his American Express card was canceled, and he switched to a Visa card. He used it to pay for cheap hotels. After two months in London, he busted his credit limit.''

''Terminating the paper trail. We lose him in London, with a possible return to the Continent by ferry,'' I concluded.

''That's what I thought. I called the minister, his stepfather, pretending to be an old classmate trying to get in touch with Francis's high school girlfriend.''

''Hoping that he indeed had one.''

''Most men have some kind of a girlfriend in high school. My first boyfriend in high school was gay, although neither of us knew about it then.''

''Francis is gay, then?''

''Not exactly,'' she said, and was momentarily disconcerted, as though aware of a problem but not wanting to mention it. Angel cleared her throat and continued: ''Francis did have a girlfriend, or what passed for one in high school. Nice girl. She told me that Francis had sent her a postcard from Paris about three months ago. He wrote that he had a job playing guitar in a local club.''

''This is great work,'' I said.

Angel beamed, and pulled the map from the wall.

''She did say one thing that was kind of troubling,'' Angel added.

''What?''

I opened a file cabinet. I store almost everything I own in file cabinets. Wading through books, office supplies, and a pair of sneakers, I found the file I wanted and slapped it on the desk.

"She said that she thought that Francis loved his sister."

"What's so troubling about that?" I inquired, opening the file.

"Loved in the physical sense. As in being in love, and making love," she said, haltingly.

"Don't be shocked," I said. "You do remember that Nina Gamine very strongly suggested that they were more than just brother and sister."

"You didn't suspect incest, did you?"

"I didn't think about it. It's really none of our business. But it does give Francis a good reason to flee the country."

"Guilt?" Angel guessed.

"Ranks right up there with hate, love, and greed in motivating human behavior."

"I get the feeling that you enjoy hearing about this," Angel accused.

"Let's just say it confirms my jaded perceptions of human nature," I answered, too comfortably.

"Well, it doesn't confirm mine!" Angel shouted.

It seemed like a non sequitur, one of those emotional outbursts that make little sense out of the context of her own heart. Her face was all hurt and anger as she turned out of my office, and slammed the door of hers. I waited a couple of minutes, and knocked on her door. I could hear her breath coming in short bursts as she counted past the fifty mark. She told me to come in. I opened the door. She was working the ten-pound hand weights, her skin flush with sweat. At the hundred count she dropped the weights and hid her face in a towel. Her expression was matter-of-fact when she pulled the towel away and said: "I'm sorry I pressured you into taking this case. I believed her. I felt for the pain that she was going through. I didn't think it would be . . ."—she struggled for an acceptable word, settling on "dirty."

"Are you disappointed?" I asked.

She shrugged.

"I think that if I'm going to get emotionally involved, I'd better be more tolerant."

I agreed, and said: "I'm glad we took the case."

"I don't get you," she challenged.

"It's the only job we have at the moment. Gotta eat, right?"

Angel smiled, and said: "Right."

I returned to the file on my desk. The phone number I wanted was on a business card clipped to an $8^1/_2$-by-11. On the flip side was the home number. It was just before noon in Los Angeles, nine p.m. Paris. I dialed the home number through the international operator, and talked for fifteen minutes to a French investigator about locating Nina Gamine's brother. I had met the Frenchman, whose name was Henri Grall, at the West Beach Cafe in Venice, when I had overheard him at the bar boasting to two attractive women about being the Philip Marlowe of Paris. I initially thought him just another quick-fuck artist looking for bar love under false pretenses, but after the women left he was equally gregarious with me. We had a couple of drinks together, talked shop, and exchanged numbers.

When I told him that Francis was not a professional musician, but was reportedly playing guitar in a club, Henri said that he had a pretty good idea where he could find him. He asked for a photograph for purposes of identification. I promised to express a copy to him that afternoon, and rang off.

I collected the photograph of Francis Gamine from Angel's desk, told her that I was going to send a copy to an investigator in Paris, and strolled out to my car in the parking lot. A small man in his mid-thirties called out my name and scurried across the lot to intercept me. He wore a Hawaiian-print shirt two sizes too big. It flopped over the belt of blue polyester permanent-pressed slacks. His thinning black hair was slicked away from a face that was all nose and no chin. A two-day growth stubbled what little there was to his jaw, and his eyes looked bruised from lack of sleep. He didn't look like the type of guy I'd want to talk to, and I pretended to not hear him until he called again. I waited by the hood of my car while the small man trotted across the blacktop. A van cranked its engine and pulled out of a stall at the other end of the lot.

"What can I do for you?" I asked.

He held his palms up to show me he meant no harm and said: "I'd like to ask you a few questions about Jack Burns."

The van roared down the line of cars and jerked to a stop in front of my hood. When I glanced back at the small man, he was looking very big with a snub-nosed .38 in hand. The side door of the van ratcheted back. The .38 nestled lightly against my ribs, urging cooperation. A man with enough size on him to gaff Moby Dick reached a meaty hand from the back of the van, grasped my collar, and hauled me aboard. My face was shoved into the carpeted floor. The van ground into gear, and scraped bottom coming out of the lot. A knee wedged into my spine near the shoulders while my hands were pulled back and cinched with rope. I glimpsed a ringless hand as it slipped a blindfold over my eyes. Another hand jerked my head back by the hair and stuffed a greasy rag into my mouth.

"You want me to sit him up?" a voice asked over my head, anxious to please.

The knee came off my spine, and I was grateful.

"I don't want you to sit him up," the small man ordered. "I want you to sit on him."

A mountain settled heavily onto my back, crushing the air from my lungs. I groaned, and the mountain said: "I could really hurt him, you know, Gilbert? I put myself on the scale yesterday."

"What the numbers say?" Gilbert asked.

"Two hundred and eighty-four."

"And how much of that is mouth?"

"Huh?"

The sting of slapped flesh. The mountain whined high in his throat.

"Don't talk. Just sit," Gilbert, the small man, instructed.

The mountain obeyed, and for about half an hour, sound was limited to the road vibrations humming through my skull. The air warmed and lost its humidity. We were traveling east, away from the heavy layer of marine air that stretches a few miles inland from the coast. I tried to figure out who these guys were. Revelations were slow in coming. Murder is mostly metaphorical in the corporate

world, where a stab in the back is more likely to divert the flow of
cash than of blood. These two were definitely not suit-and-tie types,
and hoods don't run much in my circle.

The mountain moved off my back, and I was rolled over and
propped against the van wall. A hand jerked the rag from my mouth.
I squinted against the blindfold, but my eyes didn't even get as far as
vague shapes.

"I thought you should know we've been hired to do you," Gilbert
whispered, mock-conspiratorial.

"Thanks for the news," I said.

"I've got worse news, asshole. We haven't been hired to just pop
you in the back of the head. First, we have to make it hurt."

"Hurt bad," the mountain echoed.

The taste of grease stuffed my mouth again, and I was flipped onto
my back. Hands gripped my shirt and ripped it open. A sharp crack
sparked in the van, and the shock of the noise made me jump.

"A little nervous, are we?" Gilbert said, and laughed.

Massive hands, gloved in something cold and sticky-smooth like
rubber, pinned my shoulders. Metal bit into both sides of my chest
with a sharp sting. Clips of some sort, I thought.

"Now, that didn't hurt so much, did it?" Gilbert soothed, then
laughed. Something clicked behind me, and streaks of pain arced
across my chest, plunged into the skin and rooted through muscle and
tendon. It spread like a red-hot stain over the joints and bones,
invaded the blood cells, and circled the membranes in burning fire.
I was consumed by it, each cell incinerated, the neurons seized and
electrical flow of synapses twisted to an opposite discharge, which
set my body into an uncontrollable dance of muscle, skin, and bone.
When it ended, breath was gasping out of me, and panic raced its
disorienting spin on my brain.

"Life is pain from here on. Got that?"

I nodded. The rag was yanked from my mouth and I greedily
sucked all the air that I could. Gilbert's voice droned in an unctuous
tone, confident in my pain and terror.

"My brother just got back from a trip to Central America. My
brother and I, we're a lot alike. When he was down there he learned

a couple of things from the local security people about how to make people talk. Talk about anything. Sometimes, just for fun, they would get the victims to say the most disgusting things about their own mothers. Can you imagine that? But you don't have to worry. We're not here to have fun.''

The click sounded again, and the jolt of electricity scorched down my spine. I grunted, grinding my teeth, and he cut the juice, giving me just a taste of the pain, a reminder, before shutting it down.

"This was one of my brother's favorites. A simple device, really. Sorry you can't see it. The hobbyist can easily build one at home, using a simple car battery.''

He clicked, and the device surged electrical fire. My body jerked and twisted beyond control. I fought to keep my mouth shut, not wanting to give the bastard anything, but aware with certain dread that another moment of it would yank the screams from my throat. Then, it stopped. Another reminder, another taste.

"We want to know some things. You don't give us the right answer, you hurt. Got that?''

I nodded again.

"Good. What were you doing for Jack Burns?''

"That's privileged client information,'' I said, and waited for the pain.

It came full throttle this time. The rag was stuffed into my mouth, and the mountain pressed my shoulder blades into the carpet. My body raged uncontrolled, and time became something to be survived until the pain stopped. The veins in my head and neck swelled to popping. I tried to breathe, but the air collapsed in my lungs. Nausea rushed to my brain, and I thought, with horror, that I was losing control over the functioning of my body. Soon, a time now measured in seconds, my body would purge itself of all fluids, the ultimate humiliation that would prove I had no dominion over my own being. Then it stopped. A voice, curiously disembodied, drifted into my ear: "Let's try again. What were you doing for Jack Burns?''

"I was his bodyguard,'' I moaned.

"We know that,'' the voice droned.

A little air filtered through my nostrils, and I worked at enlarging that precious passage until I had sufficient oxygen to speak. "He received a death threat. I hired on for a week, maybe longer if it worked out that way. Nothing much happened. He must have cleared up what was worrying him, because the next day, he canceled."

"What about the money?"

"There wasn't any. His check bounced and the son of a bitch died owing me seven grand."

When the click sounded, I tensed, steeling myself to take it without complaint, but the pain reamed through every nerve, twisting up my spine and cresting up the back of my neck, and set my brain aflame in a spume of agony. Consciousness was ravaged, and when the fragments of awareness rejoined, my throat was hoarse. I must have screamed, though I couldn't remember it.

"You need to come up with three million to stay alive," the voice warned.

"Three million?"

"That's right."

I blurted: "You guys are worse than crazy. You're stupid," and was consumed in a quick, merciful explosion that launched my brain out the top of my skull into the nether world, floating, for a few precious moments, on the painless periphery of nothingness.

"He's coming around again," someone said.

I awoke to the smell of burnt flesh, and the thought of death as a sweet sanctuary, like water to a mortal thirst. It gave me certain peace.

"Too much juice, that time," the voice mused. "Blew his mind like a sixty-watt bulb in a one-twenty current."

The road had roughened. I heard gravel slapping against the undercarriage, and tasted dust in the air. The van ground to a stop, and the doors slid open. The carpet slipped out from under me, and I flopped face-first onto hard ground. My mouth tasted of puke and sand.

"You're looking into Death Valley. You're a thimbleful of water on the desert floor. Evaporated," the voice said.

My head was jerked back by the hair, pulling me up to my knees. A revolver was cocked two inches from my ear, so that I couldn't possibly miss the sound.

"Where's the money?"

"I sure as hell don't have it."

My skull smoked with the roar of the pistol. A high-pitched whine cycled around my right ear. The shot had been purposely six inches wide.

"Last chance, asshole."

I waited to die in darkness with the taste of puke and sand in my mouth. A foot shoved my face into the dirt. The van's engine raced the idle. The passenger door slammed, and gravel spat against the undercarriage as the van spun away.

Rolling onto my side, I curled and pressed my knee against the blindfold, forcing it down and away from my eyes. I sat up. I had been dumped on a hill surrounded by desert chaparral, where the dirt road ended in a turnaround. My legs didn't want to balance my weight, and I tumbled twice to my knees before I got the details of standing and moving well enough to get a view of the van as it turned onto the highway below. A deep blue Chevy, license plate unknown.

9

Angel simmered over a red sauce on the kitchen stove. Garlic, rosemary, onions, sausage, red wine, tomatoes and the unmistakable aroma of a hot Italian temper steamed a sweet but dangerous scent through my apartment. Angel buried her head in the refrigerator, emerged with an Amstel light, and cracked it down on the tabletop with a sharp "Your mistake was getting in the van."

I lay on the couch, an ice pack strapped to my chest, and an iced Jameson sliding down my throat. I considered Angel's anger and whether or not I wanted to acknowledge it. I didn't have much energy for confrontation, and lamely offered the excuse: "He had a gun."

"So what?" Angel challenged.

"So I was inclined to do what he said."

"What was he going to do, shoot you in the parking lot?"

"I was more concerned about him shooting me in the back."

"There is very little chance he would have shot you in front of witnesses. And even if he did, someone could have taken you to a hospital."

"If I was still alive," I interrupted, but she rolled right over the remark.

"And a hospital is a hell of a lot better than being dumped into a shallow grave out in the middle of the desert. Do you have any idea how often a van has been used as a rolling slaughterhouse? You run out of options if you let them get you in the back of a van.''

She was right. My body felt like the inside of a trash compactor, and being both in pain and wrong didn't improve my disposition. You may as well be in a hearse as in the belly of a van.

Angel brought the bottle to the couch and refilled my glass. I pulled her down next to me. She slapped my hand away, and perched on the opposite end. I sat up, and sipped at my whiskey. She watched me drink, which I did self-consciously, aware of her eyes. I set down the whiskey, and felt myself hooked by the sadness of her distance from me. My arm lay along the top of the couch. She reached out and grasped my hand with a fierce squeeze.

"You could have been killed," Angel said, and some of the hardness and anger went out of her. She turned her back, but curled her legs and leaned into my side. I wrapped my arm around her, and she accepted it with a soft yielding of her shoulder. She wore faded blue jeans and a light denim jacket over a thin white T-shirt. I slipped my hand under her shirt and ran it along her supple belly. She wrapped her arms around my neck and kissed me. I returned the kiss. Her mouth drew me into her, loosening the pins of consciousness. My mind drifted, riding the sensations of her lips and tongue. We took our time, and the longer we took, the more I felt as though I was floating, charged, through an atmosphere of ineffable pleasure.

Somewhere, bells began to ring.

It was the telephone. Angel picked up the receiver and handed it to me. "Saved by the bell," she said, and padded to the kitchen to attend to the sauce.

A guy I didn't know asked if I was who I was, and when I said yes, announced in a booming Texas twang: "I'd like us to get acquainted. I've got a problem worse than a lit firecracker up a bull's ass, and I hear you're just the guy to give me a hand."

I asked him his name, and he said he couldn't tell me that over the telephone. Okay, I said, and suggested we meet at my office the following day.

"I don't think it's too smart to meet at your office," he objected.

"Then your office," I offered.

"Hell, the last place I wanna meet is my office."

"We could book a hotel room, but I don't know you that well."

He chuckled, countering: "I was thinking I might pick you up at the corner of Santa Monica and Robertson in about half an hour."

"You won't tell me your name, you won't come to my office, and I can't come to yours. You want to meet on a streetcorner. Right?" I repeated.

"Now I know this sounds strange, son, but if you trust me on this, I promise to make it worth your while," the twang soothed.

I laughed, having heard that one before, and hung up.

"Who was that?" Angel called from the kitchen.

"Either a crank, or I'll find out in a few minutes," I said, the last word clipped by the ringing of the phone.

"We lost our connection," the twang smoothly said when I picked up. "All I want to do is talk over a bit of business, in private. If it works out, we can both make some money. Now that's better than a poke in the eye with a sharp stick, ain't it?"

"May I ask who's calling, please?"

"You want a reference?" the twang shouted. "All right, dammit. Harry Selwurst."

Harry Selwurst was a Westside lawyer with a rich client list. I didn't like him. Nobody did.

"I'm listening," I said.

The friendly twang evaporated. The words were hard and sharp. "If I decide I want you to work for me, I don't want anybody to know about it. I don't want to be seen with you, and I don't want my name used. I'll tell you who I am if I see you. But I demand complete confidentiality. I don't know you. You don't know me."

"Are you going to ask me to do something illegal?" I asked.

"I'm not a lawyer. You can break the law crossing the street in the wrong place. What I want is legitimate, but I want it private."

Angel, licking the red sauce from a wooden spoon, drifted closer, eavesdropping.

"Harry Selwurst's name doesn't go very far with me, and sure as hell not far enough to pull me into a blind meeting," I said.

He swore under his breath. I twisted across to pick up my drink, and felt a twinge in my chest. It made me cautious.

"You're a real hard-ass pain in the butt, you know that?"

I didn't answer.

"Jack Burns," he whispered.

"See you in an hour," I said, and hung up.

The corner of Santa Monica and Robertson once was frequented by women whose miniskirts and shorts were as effective as neon in advertising their trade. The city fathers regarded these licentious but unlicensed businesses as an affront to public decency, and ordered them closed, which the police, without taking any special joy in arresting scantily dressed women more likely to give them the clap than a bullet in the head, did. The spirit of capitalism is not easily daunted, however, and the miniskirts gave way to a jeans, T-shirt, and leather-clad crowd of the opposite sex yet identical profession. The serious action picked up closer to Hollywood in an area known by locals as Boys' Town, but every now and then a car would slow and I would peer into the compartment, expecting the twang but finding a face that was anticipating a service I was not willing to provide.

When the twang arrived, there was no mistaking or ignoring him. He was in the back of a Lincoln St. Tropez stretch limousine. It was black and as long as an ocean liner. I was familiar with the limousines owned by the rental services. This wasn't one of them. What gave it away was the set of gold-plated longhorns above the grill. Discreet. The limo stopped in traffic, oblivious to the sounding of smaller horns behind. The rear passenger window slid down. A big bony hand waved at me, accompanied by a Texas twang.

"Howdy and get in," the twang ordered.

I pulled on the door handle, and ducked under the frame into a space slightly smaller than a nightclub. The bony hand motioned me to the jump seat across the aisle, and I took it. The rear seat was plush and deep and looked like it could sleep six. I wanted one for my living room. To my right a wet bar cradled a bottle of bourbon, a bucket of ice, glasses, and a seltzer bottle. I didn't see a television or swimming pool. I was disappointed.

"Glad to meet a man with a skull as hard as mine," the twang drawled.

Even folded in the rear seat, the man looked tall. Six foot six, I guessed, and rail-thin with a round belly. He wore a brown polyester western suit, yellow broad-collar dress shirt, and a silver bolo tie with a turquoise stone the shape of Texas set in the middle. The lettering on his belt buckle spelled *Frank* in gilt rope which split off after the *K* to form a lasso around the name. His cowboy boots were pointy-toed lizardskin things that had never seen a horse or pasture. A broad-brimmed Stetson, dark brown, occupied the seat next to him. On his right hand, which he offered as he said, "Name's Frank Worthy," was another turquoise stone set in silver, like the tie, but modestly smaller, and not shaped like any state, not even Rhode Island. The man looked like he should be selling used cars on late-night television.

"Paul Marston," I said, and took the hand.

Frank Worthy had eyes the same color blue as the stones in his tie and ring. It was a nice touch. He had strong white teeth and a smile that didn't waste any of them. His skin looked like it had seen a lot of sun and worry early on, which had hardened it and furrowed his brow. He was somewhere in his fifties, and age and a steady diet of sixteen-ounce T-bones had fleshed out the angularity of his thin-man features.

"Native Texan, or just like the act?" I asked.

He laughed, and looked at me with genuine merriment. He had the kind of eyes that twinkled when he smiled, and you wanted to let him buy you a drink and shoot the shit and later do anything he asked you to do if the price was close to right.

"I've been Texan long enough and early enough to learn what I need to get by," he explained. "If you're rich, and talk like Texans think you oughta talk and think like they think, if you can play the good ole boy but be a mean sumnabitch underneath it all, well, soon no one remembers if you were born in Texas or not, or cares."

"I guess that makes you Texan enough."

"Guess so," he agreed. "Wanna drink?"

I said no, and he stretched his frame forward to mix one for himself, which put him one up on Burns in my book.

"What are you doing in L.A.?" I asked.

"Live here now. Have for about a year."

"I take it you're not an oilman."

"Hell no. I used to build homes for oilmen."

"And now?"

"Now I build homes out around Diamond Bar, San Berdoo, and a bit of Orange County."

"What's wrong with Texas?"

"It's broke."

"That's a problem, all right."

"I was one of maybe a dozen people to see the oil bust before it happened, and got out with most of my capital intact, thank the good Lord Jesus." He spritzed seltzer over the iced tumbler of bourbon and raised it in my direction. "And that's what this meeting is all about. Keeping that capital intact."

He drank the top off the tumbler, and settled back. I took a wild guess. "How much were you into Jack Burns for?"

His eyes quickened, and I saw a bit of the mean sumnabitch beneath the good ole boy. He sipped at his drink, thinking transparently for a moment about how much I might know about Burns, his clients, and his business. "Hell, you're as sharp as razor wire," he said, breaking into a twinkle.

"I didn't bring up his name. You did."

Worthy nodded, and sipped his drink, taking just enough to keep it active in the style of a good social drinker, but not enough to do it damage. "I had you checked out," he said.

"Did I pass?"

"If you didn't you wouldn't be here," he said, flat and dry, then added with a short grimace: "I'm into Burns for three million."

I resisted the temptation to whistle. Even for a Texas millionaire, that was more than pocket change.

"And with Burns dead, you wonder what's going to happen to it."

"I'm more likely to worry about what's already happened to it," he admitted, edging the twang back into his voice. "On paper, Burns was making money faster'n a hound on a hare, but when I tried to cash my account, I got the runaround. Made me real nervous. Then he hired you. Now he's dead."

"How did you hear he'd hired me?"

"Friends."

"Mine or yours?"

He chuckled, and gave me the twinkle. I knew he was at least ninety percent the material that comes out the back end of bulls, but I couldn't help liking him, even though he never answered the question.

"Hell of a way for a man to go, in his own hot tub like that. I can't believe anyone could be so lacking in sense, but that's Southern California for you. He died true to his lifestyle. I suppose it was an accident."

"That's what the police believe," I said.

"I was shocked to hear that he had died, but hell, I never liked him all that much. I didn't waste any time grieving. I wanted my money back. I asked around town, and heard stories that made me a real worried man. Wild spending, bad investments, sudden credit problems, people getting burned. Financially, Burns was dead in the water."

"Appropriate metaphor," I said.

Frank Worthy's face blanked, then sparked in recognition of the joke. His mouth stretched open, and laughter rasped from his throat.

"If the son of a bitch died owing me three million, at least I get a good joke out of it. Dead in the water. Goddamn." He laughed again.

"That's more than I got," I said.

"He stiff you?"

I nodded.

"Wanna make it back, and then some?"

I nodded again.

"I'm thinking that maybe Burns didn't piss it all away before he died. I think he skimmed a percentage of everything that came in, and sheltered it somewhere. High rollers go bankrupt all the time, but they don't very often go broke. I'll pay your rate, plus expenses, plus a percentage of what you recover. The money won't be found in his name, unless he opened a Swiss account. Maybe he hid it in a hole in the ground. Maybe he set up a dummy company under a false name. If he did, I wanna be there first and loudest when the cash drawer opens.''

"What's the percentage?"

"Five percent," he said, and tried hard to keep a straight face.

"Standard finder's fee begins at twenty percent," I countered.

"But I'm taking care of your salary and up-front costs," he argued.

"Then make it twelve, with a ten-thousand advance against expenses.''

"Fine," he said. He reached into the inside pocket of his polyester brown western suit and produced a cashier's check for ten thousand dollars. "There's one stipulation.''

I waited.

"Burns's company is going to go Chapter Nine. You could find ten million, and I wouldn't see more than ten cents on the dollar if the money is returned to the company. If I have possession of the money, my lawyer tells me there's a way to establish legal ownership. Anything you find comes directly to me, unreported.''

That was a major hitch. Any money located would legally belong to Burns's estate or his company. I should have declined the job, but looking at the check for ten thousand, I said: "We'll worry about that if I find anything.''

Worthy took that as answer enough. He pressed the intercom and instructed the driver to return to Santa Monica and Robertson. I told him I'd catch a cab at the nearest corner and observed: "You don't want to do business over the phone, and I can't drop by to visit. How am I supposed to get in touch with you?"

Worthy reached into the brim of his Stetson and handed me a blank white card, on which was hand-scrawled a telephone number. "Call this number and tell the man who answers you want to talk with me. I'll get in touch."

The limousine slid to the curb and I got out, glancing at Angel's minitruck as it pulled up a block behind.

"If you find any cash and report it to anybody but me, I'll give your percentage to the lawyers," Worthy warned, and with a wave of his hand, the limo glided into traffic.

I watched it go with a definite bad feeling. I didn't like the ethics and I didn't like the secrecy. If I wanted to hire somebody to find something and then kill him once he found it, I wouldn't use the phones or meet in public and I'd make damn sure there was no paper trail linking the two of us. My reservations were quickly glossed by thoughts of three million dollars, and my percentage of it.

"What's twelve percent of three million dollars?" Angel asked, propped on an elbow with a hand cupped under her chin. She was drawing dollar signs on my chest. I summoned myself from the languorous haze where passion had left me idly contemplating the erotic use of walls in the home. We were sprawled in the hallway leading to the bedroom. It had been our intention to reach the bed, but biology had bettered us a good dozen feet short of our target. By using our imaginations, we had made the best of the situation, although we both suffered a case of first-degree wall burn.

"Rent for the next hundred years," I answered.

"In exact figures," she demanded.

"Three hundred and sixty grand."

She traced the numbers out, and her eyes went far away. "What would you do with your share?" she asked, dreamily.

"Pay my bills and get a tune-up."

She pinched a sensitive part of my anatomy. It got my attention.

"I give up. What would I do with it?" I asked.

"We'd take a vacation."

"I understand New Jersey is lovely this time of year."

"In Europe," she specified.

"Why do you want to go some place where the plumbing is bad, the buildings are old, and they don't even speak English?"

"Since when do they speak English in New Jersey?" she countered.

"Good point," I admitted.

"Language isn't a barrier. I speak all the Romance languages. Italian, some French, and a little Spanish."

"What about the fourth Romance language?"

"Which one is that?" she asked.

I showed her. It didn't surprise me that she spoke it fluently.

10

Nina Gamine wore a fashionable black skirt, patterned lace stockings, and a white silk blouse when Angel ushered her into my office, but her sense of style had frayed since I had seen her last, and she wore them badly. The skirt was wrinkled, and her blouse was inadvertently unbuttoned at the navel. Her makeup might have passed in shadow, but when it was struck by the natural light streaming in the window, the effect was glaringly artificial. The eye shadow was too heavy, the lipstick too vibrant a red, and the rouge on her cheeks had not blended with her skin. Her dishabille was so incongruous to her past stylishness that I initially suspected that she had been drinking, until she asked in a nervous but clearly sober voice: "You've heard something, about my brother, that is?" She braved a quick search of my eyes, unable to bear the uncertainty of not knowing what we knew, and hoping to find an answer in my expression. I motioned to a chair in front of my desk, and she glanced back before cupping the hem of her skirt and sitting on the front edge. Her eyes fluttered in constant motion between Angel and me and the wall clock and the door, like a bird trapped in a small room. I put it down to nerves.

Angel sat rigidly at the other end of my desk, her casual jeans and plaid work shirt contrasted by a cold formality in her demeanor. I nodded to her. She opened a manila file on the corner of the desk, folded her hands before her, and tried to banish her private judgments, beginning: "He's in Paris, and like I told you over the phone, he is more or less in good health."

Nina Gamine nodded, a smile twitching at the corner of her mouth as she responded with an eagerness almost pitiful: "I've never been there, but I hear it's beautiful."

"We tracked down a high school friend of your brother's. She reported having received a card from Francis three months ago, postmarked in Paris."

"Who? The friend, I mean."

"Her name is Mary Masterson."

Nina nodded, pursing her lips. "Francis told me about her."

"Sure he did," Angel sighed, and looked to me for help.

"Just the facts," I suggested.

Angel shuffled the papers before her, closed the file, and spoke without notes. "We wired a copy of your brother's photo to a detective agency in Paris. It's a big city, and millions of tourists visit every year, but Parisians have lived with foreigners for centuries, and know who belongs and who doesn't. The agency showed the photograph around the neighborhoods where young Americans usually hang out. They found him playing guitar in the Métro."

"I knew he'd be playing guitar somewhere," she said proudly. "Is the Métro a large club?"

I couldn't resist, and cracked: "One of the biggest, with crowds in the thousands, though they rarely stop for a drink."

Angel's green eyes coldly advised me that it was her client, and her show, and that I could contribute best by remaining silent.

"What kind of club is it?" Nina asked, confused.

"It's not a club. It's a subway," Angel said.

"I don't understand," Nina stammered.

"He plays his guitar in an underground walkway leading to a boarding platform. He lays the guitar case in front of his feet, and sings mostly old songs from the sixties. A steady stream of people passes by, and every now and then someone drops a couple of francs in the guitar case," Angel explained.

Nina cocked her head, and her eyes clouded behind rapidly

blinking eyelids. She sniffled, and reached into her purse for a tissue. She didn't raise the tissue, but clutched it on her lap while her eyes misted. I searched for something soothing to say, and repeated what Henri Grall had told me over the phone: "It's a nice subway. It's big and bright and the cars are punctual. There aren't any graffiti, and they don't let the bums sleep in it unless the weather outside is cold enough to kill them."

So it wasn't soothing. It didn't matter. Nina Gamine didn't hear a word. She pressed her elbows to her sides, locked her knees together, and stared at the tissue in her hands. She was very quiet, and began to rock gently in the chair. I was afraid that she might cry, being a person with a less than firm grasp of her emotions, but a different focus moved behind her eyes, filling the irises with glass until they looked as clear and dead to the physical world as marbles. I had not seen a look quite like it since the last time I had seen Greta Garbo as Camille dying in Robert Taylor's arms. Her face lifted, and her glass eyes rolled back, and I thought I saw suffusing her features the twisted ecstasy of those who have chosen themselves for martyrdom.

"What have I done?" she moaned, the words faint.

"Yes. What have you done?" Angel demanded. There was anger and judgment and no mercy in the voice.

Nina Gamine's head snapped toward Angel with a startled, "What do you mean?"

"I'm just repeating your own words. What have you done?"

"I haven't done anything."

Nina Gamine hurriedly stuffed the tissue back into her purse. She glared at Angel, but soon withered in the controlled fury of Angel's returning stare, uncertain of what we knew, or guessed, or were totally unaware of. To admit having a secret is the first step in telling it, and as Angel had not directly accused her of anything specific Nina said nothing.

"Glad to hear it," Angel continued when Nina Gamine's eyes dropped. "Your brother does not have a legal address, but is sharing a small flat in the Latin Quarter with his reported French girlfriend. Both are using heroin, and may be addicted to the drug, although this hasn't yet been confirmed."

"You're lying," Nina snapped.

"We only report what has been told to us by the French agency," I interjected.

"Then they're lying."

"About what? The girl, or the drugs?" Angel asked.

"Both."

"Can't your brother have a girlfriend?"

"He wouldn't cheapen himself."

"With anyone but you, you mean," Angel charged.

The air went out of Nina Gamine's face. I planted my feet firmly and swiveled the chair to the side, waiting. Terrible secrets can have terrible consequences. I watched her features tighten, and her hands squeeze the life out of her purse. She leaned forward, her body beginning to shake, and her lips curled in a pained grimace as she hissed: "You fucking bitch."

Out of her child-woman face the expletive seemed doubly obscene. It had no visible effect on Angel, who calmly answered: "You don't have to worry about the sex. I hear junkies can't have any. After what you've done to him, it's not surprising that he's found a way to live without it."

I was on my feet and dodging the corner of the desk when Nina Gamine leapt at Angel, shrieking obscenities. She swiped at my face with red claws when I blocked her. I jerked my head back. The swing carried the claws across her body, where they became mere fingernails again. I pinned her hands against her sides, and circled behind, shifting my hip to the side to shield my groin. All her strength went to wildness, and despite her small size I had to brace myself to hold her back.

Angel did not move, further enraging Nina Gamine.

"If it wasn't true, you wouldn't be angry, right?" Angel asserted.

Nina's resistance slowly spent itself, and her body slackened in my arms. She nodded. I let her go.

"It's none of my business, but we found your brother, and now I feel responsible," Angel calmly continued. "I just hope you know exactly what it is you want before you see him again. And I hope that what you want is good for him."

Nina Gamine bent to retrieve her purse. The anger seemed burned out of her, but not the obsession that drove her toward her brother. Romantic obsession is as dangerous as it is irresistible. To desire something so much that life without it is not worth living is to invite self-destruction. A person might do anything to avoid that destruction. Romantic obsession and incest combined seemed outright incendiary. Nina straightened, clutching the purse tightly to her side, and said to Angel: "I know exactly what I want. Thank you for your concern, and thank you for finding Francis." She turned to me, the incredible sadness that had struck me on our first meeting again flawing her eyes, and announced: "I would like to leave now."

I escorted her to the elevator. Waiting for it to reach the fourth floor, I handed her a slip of paper on which was written her brother's Paris address. Nina Gamine folded it carefully in her purse, and when the elevator door opened, she threw her arms around my neck and her kiss was fierce enough to bruise my lips. I was too surprised to either kiss back or push her away. With a whispered thanks, she stepped quickly into the elevator and was whisked away. I couldn't fathom why she had kissed me, but I wasn't her psychiatrist and didn't envy anyone else that task, so I did my best to forget it.

The receipts, postcards, meeting notes, and telephone records that constituted the Nina Gamine file lay spread across her desk as Angel bent over a blank sheet of paper, inscribing her final notes in an elegant script. She would later compile the notes into a final report which would be mailed, with the bill, to Nina Gamine. I stood by the corner of the desk, watching her work and waiting for her to acknowledge my presence, which she did not seem inclined to do.

When the pen clattered onto the desktop and she glanced up in irritation, I said: "You have a soft touch with clients. Kind of like Mike Tyson's right hook."

"I'm not sorry about what I did," she replied, and returned the tip of the pen to the page.

"I thought you might want a little objective criticism."

"Feel free to yell at me, if that's what you want," she offered, and bent her head over the page with the full intent of not listening to my response.

"She was your client. If you're satisfied with the way you handled it, fine."

"Things are right, or they're wrong. She was wrong."

"Okay," I said.

"Maybe it's my Catholic upbringing, but I think it's wrong to seduce your brother and then hound him halfway around the world. The poor kid is so horrified by the experience he's trying to destroy his life with drugs."

"How do you know that he didn't seduce her?"

"Be serious."

"How do you know that they didn't seduce each other?"

"She's the oldest. It was her responsibility."

"How do you know that it wasn't a one-time mistake that she regrets as much as he does?"

"I don't know how I know it. I just know it," Angel cried, exasperated, and threw down the pen.

"You just know it?" I said, angry not about how she had handled Nina Gamine but by her presumption of truth. "Gut feel tells you what to look for and where to look for it. Gut feel doesn't give you the facts, and it sure as hell doesn't convince anybody except yourself. Only when you have the facts do you know anything, and even then you don't know everything, because the human heart is big and dark and you can never see or search it all. You know just enough to get by, to make a decision and live with it knowing it was the best you could do."

"She was wrong," Angel insisted stubbornly.

"Prove it."

"Next time, I will."

Signaling the termination of her part in the conversation, Angel swiveled her back to me, threw open a drawer, and began to rummage its contents with a terse "I have work to do."

I returned to my desk and started to draft an action plan for the Jack Burns investigation. The phone rang. It was Angel, on the extension.

"She was wrong," Angel repeated, and hung up.

11

Just after midnight the doorbell rang and I opened the door to my date for the evening. She brushed her purple lips across my cheek and swept into the living room, casting a pecuniary glance along the modest furnishings.

"So now I know you're not rich." Mona Demonay smirked, tossing her handbag on the couch. The Marilyn outfit had been dispatched for something more contemporary. I couldn't quite identify the look, but it seemed to be a cross between country-and-western and death rock. Black and silver were the operative colors: silver stiletto heels, pleated black slacks, and a western-style shirt with rhinestone buttons and rhinestone-studded collar stays. The shirt was open three buttons down and folded back to display against the crisp black cotton the luminous skin of her breasts. A silver belt in the shape of a snake rode low over her hips, clasping at the fanged head in front. Small silver chainsaws dangled from her ears. Her blond hair was immaculately disheveled, brushed into long spikes fanning out at oblique angles, like the strokes of a modern action painting.

She cocked her hand on her hip and looked at me. Her purple-painted lips turned up at one corner and her eyes flicked up and down my body with an interest both erotic and amused. Her face was bone-white, and she wore too much eye makeup for my taste, but no matter how she dressed, Mona had the kind of looks men fall for like lemmings over a cliff.

"I didn't think you were exactly the Marilyn type. The older guys, you know, teenagers in the fifties, get turned on by it. I was getting tired of her anyway."

"You do it very well."

"This sounds like a cliché I know, but I'm really an actress. Work is a little slow right now."

She continued her uninvited tour, sticking her head into the bedroom and bath before returning to the living room. There wasn't much to see, just the usual bed, couch, television, and stereo. Mona fished a compact from her handbag, and with an appraising look in its mirror, observed: "I suppose money isn't everything, but it does have a little more value than you seem to think. Money helps forgive the faults in a man, particularly when he doesn't offer me a drink though he knows I'd like one."

"Vodka and tonic?"

"Sounds delicious. How did you guess I wanted one?"

I went into the kitchen to mix the drinks. When I returned, Mona was sitting on the floor by the record cabinet, flipping through the stacks. She took the drink and remarked: "You can tell a lot about a person by the kind of music they listen to."

We clicked glasses. I lifted a Clifton Chenier out of the stack and spun it on the turntable. She twisted her head at the first bars of zydeco drumming out of the speakers. It wasn't rock and roll, so she didn't get it right away.

"Is that an accordion?" she asked, incredulous.

I sat on the couch, and she came over to me, beginning to catch the beat. Her hands trailed up to the back of her neck, thrusting her breasts forward as she pushed her hair up. Her hips swayed with the beat, and I was momentarily distracted by the locus of her sex.

"This would be wild music to strip to," she said, laughing.

I set my drink on the table. "Shut up and sit down," I said.

She circled the table and sat next to me, placing her hand on my thigh, meaning it to be a casual but provocative gesture.

"We've got a problem," I said.

She smiled easily. "A good-looking guy like you, I didn't expect it, but I'm good with problems." Her hand traveled another span up my thigh, and she suggested: "Why don't you tell me about it?"

"Jack Burns is dead," I said.

Her hand jumped off my leg.

"How?"

"Boiled to death in his hot tub."

Mona laughed, reproaching me with a you-naughty-boy look. She again set her hand on my thigh, and smiling wryly said: "Good joke."

I removed her hand and told the story. She looked at me and waited for the punch line. When she realized the story didn't have one, Mona slid as far away from me as possible, and worked her drink down to the ice.

"This is too weird," she complained. "If this is your idea of some sex thing, you're too weird, even for me, and believe me, I've seen some weird shit."

I tossed her the *Times* obituaries to read while I mixed her another vodka tonic. I had thought Burns's death would rate the "Metro" section, but accidental deaths don't rate much ink in a town where even mass murderers are old news. Mona was touching up her face with a powder puff when I returned with her drink. Her eyes were red, and their glistening gave evidence of some emotion. Which emotion was a mystery.

"I didn't figure him as a guy you'd cry over," I remarked, handing her the drink.

"He isn't. Or wasn't," she snapped, tossing the compact into her handbag. A stray tear welled out of her eye and escaped down her cheek. She cursed and wiped it away.

"Then why the show of tears?"

"He owed me money. Serves me right to fuck on credit."

She said the line tough and hard, but like ice on a river it concealed a swift-moving current below the surface. I let it slide, and asked: "Did you see him that night?"

She shook her head.

"How about your friend Dusty?"

She shook her head again.

"You work free-lance, or through an escort agency?"

"Free-lance. Just enough to pay the rent, acting workshop fees, and a few luxuries." She flashed the rhinestones on her collar, and asked, like she might have asked if we were going to a movie: "Hey, are we going to fuck tonight, or not?"

"We're not."

"Then I'm getting out of here before the evening turns to a total waste," she announced, and stood.

I pushed her back down onto the couch and dropped a portrait of Grant on her lap. She folded the bill in half and dropped it in her purse.

"There will be another one if we do this right," I said.

"Fire away. I love easy money," she smiled, and settled into the couch, wafting her vodka tonic under her nose before gulping the last of it down.

"How did you meet Jack Burns?"

"He called, and I liked his address."

"When was that?"

"A week ago."

"Sure."

"It's true," she protested.

"You knew him too well."

She gave a come-hither smile, slid next to me on the couch, and leaned forward until her lips were an inch from mine. "It's my business to know men well without wasting any time. If you'd just kiss me instead of being such a priest, you'd know what I mean."

"Why are you trying so hard?" I asked.

"I like challenges."

Her lips lightly brushed the corner of my mouth, retreated, and flicked the other corner. Her eyes glanced at mine, smiling and available, and I felt her breath travel across my cheek to my neck. She was an attractive woman who knew well the erotic arts, and was charged with a sexual energy to which a certain tumescence proved that I was not immune. I took her head in my hands and kissed her.

She drew my tongue into her mouth, and her fingers searched for the clasp of my belt. I felt for her lip between my teeth and bit down hard.

She cried out, jerking back, and covered her mouth with her hand.

"Some challenges are dangerous," I advised.

"You son of a bitch," she blurted, more in revelation than in anger, then asked: "Am I bleeding?"

I pulled her hand away. There was a small trickle of blood inside her lip. I fished an ice cube from my drink, gently pulled the lip down, and pressed the cube against the wound. The bleeding stopped.

"It hurts like hell," she reproached, without seeming genuinely angry. I think it amused her, the surprise of being denied. Mona didn't seem to like me any less for it, but she didn't try to kiss me again, either. She was giving what I wanted. And I returned the favor with money. Commerce. The universal bond we both understood.

"When did you meet Jack Burns?" I repeated.

"I wasn't lying to you. A week ago. I went to see him, we partied, and he told me to come back the next night with a friend. I did. When I met you, it was the third night in a row. The guy acted like he hadn't been laid in a month, or like he'd just decided to do stuff he'd never let himself do before."

"Like what?"

"Fantasy stuff. Two girls. Standard male domination. You saw some of it the other night."

"I get the general idea," I said, and remembering, felt myself blush.

"How did he get your number?"

She shrugged, pressed the cold base of her glass against her lip. "Sometimes I leave my card on the windshield of top-class cars, and he had a few nice ones. He showed us the backseat of his Rolls, if you get my meaning."

She snapped her fingers suddenly, and opening her purse, withdrew a small vial. Cracking the cap, she licked her finger, turned the vial upside down, coating the tip of her finger with a fine white powder, and applied it to her lip with a petulant "You don't believe in having fun, so I won't offer you any." She sealed the vial and dropped it into her purse. "But I know I'd seen him around town."

"Where?"

"Maybe at a party. Maybe he was a producer or something for a film I tried to get on."

"You ask him about it?"

"Yeah, but he said he never went near the movies. I figure he had to be lying, you know, not wanting to admit it because then I'd be asking him for a job or something when all he wanted was to get laid."

I set the matching portrait of Grant on her lap, and thanked her for the help. At the door, she wrapped her arms around my neck.

"If you bite me again, I'll pancake your nuts," she whispered, and kissed me.

I didn't put a lot into it, but that didn't prevent me from enjoying it.

"If you ask, I'll stay. No charge."

There was a human need in her eyes, and it wasn't sex. I smiled back, and said: "I'll have to take a rain check."

She shrugged, and trailing her hand across my chest, swung down the steps.

12

Godfrey's perched on a cliff north of Malibu. The restaurant offered a view of a coastline where property values ran about a buck per grain of sand. The menu was priced accordingly. Sheriff Bernie Kohl had insisted I take him to brunch in exchange for the opportunity to discreetly pump him for information. It was a good deal for both of us. Bernie wouldn't tell me anything that he wouldn't tell a reporter who asked him the right way at the right time. He kept his integrity and got a free meal. I got the public details of his investigation and the bill.

I initially mistook the parking lot for a German auto dealership when I swung across the Pacific Coast Highway and into Godfrey's. The lot parked eighteen Mercedes, twelve BMWs, six Porsches, two Audis, and, hidden behind a tree where it would be least likely to offend, a late-model Chevy sedan. The Chevy was Kohl's. I tossed my keys to the valet, an aspiring actor type with a lion's mane of blond hair and an attitude without the pocketbook or résumé to back it up. He opened the door for Angel and, stepping back to look at the old Mustang, pronounced it almost a classic. He parked it on the back side of the Chevy.

Kohl was on the verge of supplementing his busy social calendar with the drop-dead gorgeous blond hostess when we interrupted him. With his tan and rugged visage jutting out of a burgundy polo shirt, and sporting white shorts and a pair of Reeboks, he looked more like the local tennis pro than like a sheriff. When I introduced him to Angel, he did a cartoon double take, and whispered: "You are a devious son of a bitch."

The hostess waved us forward before I could respond, and led us to our table on the terrace, overlooking the sea. The brunch crowd that owned the million-plus dollars of German engineering in the parking lot was casually dressed in short pants and tennis whites, with a sprinkling of blue jeans, colored polo shirts, and Italian loafers. Still, it was an unmistakably moneyed crowd. I have never been able to understand how the rich can maintain the aura of personal wealth even in casual attire. The brunch crowd wore what most people wear on a sunny Sunday afternoon, but the clothing fitted their trim bodies more precisely, and unlike most people's, their hair stayed in place when the wind blew. Perhaps, I thought, a perfect starched demeanor is the effect of having the help iron your underwear.

Something disturbed their composure that morning, and I had the pleasure of walking behind the source of distraction. Angel wore a simple white linen dress, set off the shoulders and cut sharply down the back. With the sun bronzing the sculpted musculature of her shoulders and back, and the undeniably feminine curve of her breasts taut against the linen, she moved with the power and beauty of a Rodin stepped from the sculptor's pedestal. I could hear the necks of the diners cracking as they craned to watch her stride past.

The hostess seated us and dispensed the menus with a cold formality, having been completely forgotten by Kohl, who accepted his menu without taking his eyes off Angel. As the hostess departed, Kohl huffed: "When you told me your partner was an ex-boxing champion, you neglected to mention her gender or her considerable charms."

Kohl bowed his head in Angel's direction and, his eyes going all liquid, sighed: "Beauty such as yours is genius."

Angel smiled, and thanked him for the compliment.

"Thank Dante. He said it first," Kohl said.

"When I see him, I will," Angel replied, drawing an appreciative chuckle from Kohl.

A waiter dropped by the table and I ordered a bottle of Sonoma Maison Deutz, a crisp and clean sparkling wine from Napa. When it came, we drank a toast to April sunshine, and spent a few minutes in civilized conversation before getting down to business.

"I'm surprised the press hasn't been more interested in the death of Jack Burns," I remarked when the first round nestled toward the stems of our champagne glasses.

"You might see a feature article someday, but not anytime soon," Kohl guessed. "I know Richie Warner at the *Times* has started to snoop around, but he seems interested in Jack Burns's death only as a metaphor of his lifestyle. Certainly not as any criminal act."

"Why not?" Angel inquired.

Kohl savored his champagne, smiled, and began to show off. "My first guess was right. The coroner's report fixed the cause of death as hyperthermia. The blood tests revealed a classic profile: a moderate barbiturate count, and a point-five-percent level of alcohol in the blood. We found a prescription bottle in the bathroom cabinet of the master bedroom. The prescription was in his name. He took a sleeping pill, chased it with several shots of Scotch, settled in for a soak, and fell asleep in the Jacuzzi. The water was very hot—over a hundred and ten. In about an hour, his blood temperature rose to lethal levels. In simple terms, he boiled to death in his hot tub."

"An accident," I said, with some doubt in my voice.

He smiled and, leaning toward Angel, tried for a laugh. "It happens all the time around here. You know what we call it?" He waited a beat, then hit the punch line: "Tub death."

Angel nodded, interested, but serious. Kohl seemed disappointed.

"Some people think that's funny," he reproached.

"Marston told me all about it," Angel admitted.

"Having no wit of his own, he steals mine," Kohl accused, and cracked his menu, deciding that if his jokes were not going to be laughed at, even politely, he would get down to the business end of brunch and order.

Godfrey's specialized in spa food, which was once a euphemism for what was served on the fat farm. There were glowing references in the menu to the healthy California lifestyle, and it listed the nutritional data for each entree, along with the credits of a nutritional consultant. The food was as low in calories, salt, fat, and cholesterol as it was high in price. In the menu, the proprietors referred to spa food as Malibu Manna, knowing that in Southern California people will swallow anything attached to high concept.

"Couldn't someone have lured him into the tub when he was already drunk, and spiked his last drink with a sleeping pill?" Angel suggested when we had made our selections and passed them on to the waiter. "I don't understand why it has to be an accident."

"Because it falls under that category. If a man falls off a ladder, cracks his head, and dies, we don't investigate his wife for murder, even though she could have given him a shove," Kohl explained.

"Why don't you?" Angel demanded.

"Because murder, when it happens, is almost always very simple. Complicated schemes invite chance. Each facet of a plan establishes a new opportunity for something to go wrong. Simple methods work best. A gun, a knife, a blunt object. Nobody would bother with something as Byzantine as boiling a man to death in his own hot tub."

"What about suicide?" I asked.

"I have the same objection. An insurance claims agent came by to discuss the suicide angle, and I'll repeat what I told him. There is no precedent. I can remember three cases like this in Malibu over the past two years, and I've read about a couple of others. All turned out to be accidents."

"What's the policy and who's the beneficiary?" I asked.

Kohl deliberated for a moment and, deciding that it was a matter of public record, opted to tell me. "About half a million, with the standard suicide clause, made out to dear old mom."

"I can see why the insurance company would want to investigate. Have you met Mom?"

"She formally identified the body, as sole surviving relative. You want to talk to her?"

"I don't know why I should. There doesn't seem to be much of anything in this for me," I hedged, not wanting to seem too eager.

"Who the hell are you trying to kid?" Kohl set his glass down and stared across the table with indignation.

I couldn't think of anything to say, so I refilled his champagne glass, and waited with a polite smile which I hoped didn't look too sheepish.

"You knew the guy's reputation as a money-maker. You knew he was having financial problems when he hired you, otherwise he wouldn't have hired you, right?"

I held the smile.

"Then he bounced the check on you, and if by then it didn't register that Burns was hooked into a major fraud operation, you have the intelligence of a four-hoofed animal beginning with the letter A."

I dropped the smile.

"You calling me an armadillo?"

"I think he means ass, dear," Angel corrected.

"Bernie, I'm hurt that you have such a low estimation of me."

Kohl lifted the champagne glass into the sunlight, his large fingers gracefully cupping the base, and examined the pale gold bubbles against the blue sky. He sighed, whether from the pleasure of this sight or from exasperation with me, I couldn't tell.

"You make an ass of yourself, don't blame me for riding you," Kohl pronounced.

"Okay. Maybe I had a suspicion that Burns had a cash-flow problem," I admitted.

"Cash-flow problem, hell. You invited me here not because you're interested in whether Burns was murdered or committed suicide, except perhaps as a side issue relating to what you really want to know, and what you want to know is: What happened to the money?"

"We should tell him, Paul," Angel advised.

She looked at me with a strange gleam in her eyes, which I interpreted to be honesty. I returned the look with a gleam of my own, which could only be interpreted as murderous. I didn't care what Kohl guessed about my business, but I didn't want to advertise it, and Angel should have known that. Different lies raced through my head about my new business with Burns, all implausible.

Angel turned away from me, and confessed: "We were hoping to find an easy way to recover our money. The check that bounced was for over seven grand."

Coming from me, Kohl would never have believed it, but from Angel, he did. Such is the genius of beauty. He ran the statement over in his mind, and stared at Angel for a moment. She didn't waver. Then he laughed.

"What's so funny?" she demanded.

"You're standing at the end of a very long line. Burns died several million dollars in debt."

"If you're going to go, go big," I said.

Angel was indignant. "Here's a guy with offices on Wilshire that have to cost ten grand a month, and the phones are ringing all day. He's got a Rolls Royce, a Porsche, and a Mercedes in his garage. The garage is part of an estate on one of the most expensive beaches in the world. On the beach!"

Kohl watched, fascinated, as Angel's hands, animated by anger, swept back and forth across the table.

"He's got this reputation around town as a hot-shit investor, if you'll pardon the expression. Movie stars and millionaires flock to him. And he dies millions of dollars in debt. I don't get it. How could that happen?"

It was watching her at the table that my appreciation of Angel's expertise deepened. She knew how to ask a question that did not seem to be a question. Kohl had the answer, and was delighted to tell it.

"It was a Ponzi scheme."

Angel frowned and, leaning back in her chair, thought for a moment. "I don't know what that means," she admitted.

"It worked like this," Kohl responded, in the attitude of the expert pleased with himself. "Burns was promising a high rate of return on his fund, which was supposedly a combination of stocks, commodities, and other funds. When you're promising twenty percent on investments, and delivering, people notice. So he wasn't having any problem attracting investors. But what Burns did was a little different from what other investors do, which is take a percentage of the trade. What he did was take the equity and spend it. When somebody gave him money to invest, the cash became blind to everything but the inside of his wallet.''

"He didn't invest it?" Angel exclaimed, shocked.

"Never. You want to know how he paid off come collection time?"

Angel nodded.

"He sold new investors, and used their money to pay off."

"I don't get it," Angel said.

"Okay. Some guy gives you a hundred grand, and you promise to give him a hundred twenty the same time next year. You spend the money, then go to two guys with the same deal. They give you a hundred grand each, that's two hundred grand, and you use that money to pay off the first guy. That leaves you eighty grand clear to live on until you collect four other guys to pay off the second two guys. Every time you need to pay somebody off, you do it with cash coming in from new investors. The first investors, they love you, because you made good money for them, so they give you more money to invest, and recommend you to all their friends.''

"Sounds great while it lasts," Angel admitted.

"That's the problem. It can't last, because you have to keep bringing in the new investors, and sooner or later the scheme collapses.''

"Did he have anything left at all?" I asked, trying to fit my mind around the blind rapaciousness of such a scheme. It has to fail eventually, I thought, so how does one prepare for the end? Suicide, bankruptcy, a change of identity and the same scheme in a new city?

"His bank accounts are as empty as the L.A. River," Kohl answered. "Everything was leased. His house, his cars, even his car phone, all leased. There's no cash, and no equity in anything. He lived in such a way that should he go bankrupt, which was a matter of weeks away when he died, there would be nothing left for his creditors, not even enough for the lawyer fees to file a civil suit. His investors lost their equity, and would have lost even more money trying to sue him to get something back that no longer existed.''

''Sounds pretty slick. I don't know about you, but if somebody did that to me, I'd be mad enough to break his legs. Somebody else might be willing to do even more than that,'' Angel suggested.

''And don't forget that someone did send him a death threat, and put a slug through his window,'' I added.

''Right. The death threat came back from the lab yesterday. Times newsprint on common twenty-weight bond. No prints, no fibers, no hairs. The gunshot could have been fired as a teenage prank. If someone had a gun and was willing to fire it, why would they bother drugging him and setting him in a hot tub? It just doesn't make sense.''

''Maybe someone just wanted to scare him at first, but when he found out that Burns couldn't pay up, decided to kill him in such a way that it would look like an accidental death,'' Angel theorized.

''Too complicated,'' Kohl objected with a vigorous shake. The conversation invigorated him, and he hunched forward, pressing his point. ''I know it looks like somebody killed him. He provided over a dozen people with a motive because he was such an asshole, if you'll excuse my language.'' Burns paused to tip his head at a courtly angle toward Angel, then continued: ''Half of Malibu Colony and the entertainment industry lost money on this guy. We have plenty of motive, and if we worked at it, we might even prove someone had the opportunity. But we still would not be able to demonstrate that a crime was committed, that it was not an accident.''

I contemplated several million dollars in lost investments, and the legal tangle involved in the payback should any of that money ever be found. Others would be interested in tracing what happened to the investors' millions. I needed to know whether Burns was intimately associated with anyone who might be considered equally culpable for fraud, such as a girlfriend or hidden partner, and remarked: ''The LAPD bunco unit must be working double time on Burns, given the amount of money involved.''

''Jack Burns isn't even on their decks. Whatever they had at the time of his death has been swept into the dead-case file.''

"But that's absurd," Angel protested.

"Have you ever tried to prosecute a corpse?" Kohl queried. "You can't have a trial if you don't have someone to try. There is no reason to investigate if you can't have a trial. The whole system of criminal jurisprudence is predicated on having a defendant."

"It becomes a matter for the civil courts. And as there is no money to be recovered, there isn't much reason to file suit," I explained.

Recognition gleamed in Kohl's eyes. He leveled a no-bullshit look at me and held it, watching as he speculated: "Which won't discourage some investors from hiring lawyers to check into the feasibility of a suit, or those lawyers from hiring private investigators, such as yourselves, to track down any money that doesn't show up on the books."

I shrugged, not admitting yes or no, but he knew what I meant by the shrug, and what I meant was yes. Angel read the shrug and, correctly guessing that her earlier story about the check for seven grand was in danger of being compromised, moved the conversation forward by insisting: "I still think Jack Burns was murdered."

Bernie Kohl pursed his lips, and a proud smile seeped from the center to the corners of his mouth. His spine stiffened, and with a dramatic squaring of his shoulders, he quoted in stentorian voice: " 'Foul deeds will rise, though all the earth overwhelms them, to men's eyes.' "

He laughed then, adding: "From Shakespeare's *Hamlet*, which, along with *Macbeth*, is among the greatest murder mysteries ever written."

Kohl raised his glass, having, I guessed from the number of times he quoted him, a soft spot in his heart for the Bard, and we drank to a man almost four centuries dead.

13

Jack Burns's mother lived on a six-figure-income block in the foothills of Sherman Oaks, up the hill from Ventura Boulevard. It was the type of neighborhood where everybody minded his own business unless someone painted a house the wrong color or put a car on blocks in the front yard or played music a little too loud, which would band the remaining neighbors in a suburban lynch party. I parked next to the street number Kohl had scribbled on a napkin at Godfrey's of Malibu. The number belonged to a ranch-style house on an oversize lot, one-story, with a wooden shake roof, and a miniature-house mailbox at the end of a concrete walk. The name on the box was V. Burnside.

A crew of Mexican gardeners swarmed over the front yard with clippers, rakes, brooms, and mowers. Angel took a moment to brush up on her Spanish with a gardener in a Dodger cap, while I walked up a short ramp to the door and rang the bell. Dodger Cap mentioned the name Fernando Valenzuela. Angel said something to Dodger Cap, and he plucked an orange off the tree, calling to a pal wielding a rake and a rubber bucket. His pal crouched, holding the bucket parallel to the ground, and Dodger Cap went into the Fernando windup, complete with eyes rolling back into his head, and fired a strike into the heart of the bucket. Angel laughed, and the Mexican smiled, proud but shy. The door opened behind me and a voice groused before I could turn around: "You shouldn't encourage them. Those are perfectly good oranges."

I turned around and gaped at an empty hallway. My eyes guessed down and dropped awkwardly to a shriveled old woman in a wheelchair. I began to introduce myself, but she cut me off with an abrupt: "I know who you are. Stand aside."

I stepped away from the doorway, and with a brisk turn of the wheels she rolled down the ramp to the edge of the walk. The gardener running the power mower cut the motor. The old woman gripped a wooden cane, which I later learned was used solely as an instrument of intimidation, as her legs were useless and she could no more walk than fly, and rapped it sharply on the concrete.

"If I catch you throwing my oranges again, I'll baseball your head into the next county. Understand?"

The gardener stared blankly at her feet, then glanced back for help. Angel translated. The gardener laughed, his eyes dancing back to his pals, who also laughed, one of them gripping his rake like a bat. The old woman rapped her cane again, and hissed: "INS."

The laughter ceased. The gardener nodded, his eyes a flat black, and after bending to retrieve his shears, began to clip the hedge. The old woman pointed at Angel with her cane and said: "She doesn't look like a wetback. Is she with you?"

I introduced Angel as my partner. Angel didn't offer her hand, and Valerie Burnside didn't look like she would have taken it were it offered.

"Wheel me up the ramp," she commanded, holstering the cane beside her leg.

I gripped the wheelchair from behind and pushed it up the ramp. In the hall, she held her hand up, like a cavalry officer signaling halt, and I stopped. She took control of the chair. Wheeling to the intercom, she pressed the button and shouted: "Mary! Where the hell are you?" then waited impatiently, tapping the handle of her cane with sharp red nails, until an out-of-breath voice answered: "Out back, ma'am."

"You think your job is one long coffee break? Get in here. We have guests."

Valerie Burnside backed away from the intercom and swung into the living room. She rolled the chair into the corner and, holding one wheel still, spun the other to turn the chair toward a gold cloth sofa. She gestured toward the sofa and told us to sit. A pair of blue harlequin glasses dangled from a loop around her neck. She set them carefully on the bridge of her nose and gripped the handle of her cane, setting the tip on the hardwood floor.

"I understand you were hired to protect my son. You didn't do a very good job," she began before we settled.

"He told you about us?"

Her head bobbed forward and back.

"He didn't tell you he fired us," I said.

"We talked once a week, whether we had anything to say or not. If he fired you, he wouldn't call and waste my time with the news unless the week was up."

Valerie Burnside turned her head sharply to the side. I took the direction and saw a young woman uniformed in white bustle into the room. Her legs were short and plump and the white nylons rustled as she moved. A blue badge imprinted with the letters LVN was pinned above her breast. She had a pleasant face, soft and round beneath ginger-colored hair clipped back in a beret. The youthful beginning of smile lines formed at the corners of her mouth. She was trying to smile when she hurried in, but bore instead a harried grimace. Freckles etched a mask pattern under brown, panicked eyes.

I stood when she entered the room. It was a habit ingrained since youth by my grandmother, and I meant nothing special by it. Valerie Burnside did not appreciate the gesture.

"Sit down," she commanded, with a rap on the hardwood floor with her cane. "It's only the hired help."

"I'm your nurse, ma'am," the woman protested.

The old woman's mouth opened, and out trickled a dry cackle. "This is Mary. She is a licensed vocational nurse, which means she's not smart enough to be an RN, or real nurse. What will you have to drink?''

Angel shook her head. I said I'd have a water. Valerie Burnside measured us critically and, finding us not up to standard, rapped her cane to the floor and directed: ''Three lemonades, then.''

Mary bit her lip, and glanced at Angel, and then at me, keeping her eyes on us while her body half-turned to the doorway, trying to simultaneously fulfill the order and wait for clarification. The old woman ended the confusion with a rap of the cane and a sharp bark: ''Get to it, girl.''

Mary completed her turn and disappeared through the doorway. Laying the cane across her lap, Valerie Burnside settled back and forced a smile.

''My regular girl left me four days ago, if you can believe such a thing. She was no prize, but she was a wonder compared to this one.''

''How long had she been with you?'' Angel asked.

The old woman looked at me, and I looked back, waiting for her to respond to the question, which I realized after half a minute of staring back and forth she had no intention of doing. Angel had been crossed off her list. Valerie Burnside was easy to offend and held a grudge. The combination burdened the conversation. I slipped into my mortician's face, the long one with the sympathetic eyes.

''This will be hard for you, I know, but we need to ask you a few questions about your son.''

''You can ask all the questions you want, but I won't answer 'em.''

We stared at each other for another thirty seconds. Her eyes were unyielding jabs of blue, and darted from my face to the handle of her cane. I looked at her hands. The nails had been carefully manicured to ten sharp points, and stained a visceral red. The fingers were long and, though sheathed in withering flesh, gripped her cane's wooden handle as though it were a predator's perch. The tip of the cane rested on the hardwood floor, loosely supporting the weight of her shoulders as she sat erect and imperial in the wheelchair. The paralytic legs shrouded in a blue lap blanket, the thick harlequin glasses and wheelchair, were an illusion of frailty, and crouching behind it was the spirit of a hawk. A crippled hawk is no less fierce. It listens to food, and not reason. I tossed her a scrap.

"You're going to get screwed out of half a million bucks."

She frowned, and the movement dislodged her glasses, requiring a quick centering movement with her forefinger.

"What are you talking about?" she commanded.

"The insurance money."

"I know that, you idiot. What about it?"

I raised the pitch of my voice to the proper tone of incredulity and exclaimed: "You haven't heard?"

Valerie Burnside whitened her knuckles on the handle of her cane, and glared as though she wished to beat me over the shoulders with the other end of it. "If I don't know what you're talking about, I can't tell whether I've heard anything or not, now can I?" she said, the words straining through the hawk set of her jaw.

I shrugged and smiled easily, determined to make her fight for it. "Most insurance policies have a suicide clause."

"So what? Jack didn't commit suicide."

I laughed knowingly. "You don't know much about insurance companies, do you?"

The tip of the cane whipped up and slapped against the arm of her wheelchair. "Come to the point!"

"At the coroner's inquest, your son's death can be ruled one of three ways: accidental death, murder, or suicide. If it's ruled one of the first two, you win, and the insurance company loses. If it's the third . . ."

She cut me off with a slap of the cane. "Nonsense. There was no note, so it can't be suicide."

"Only about half of all suicides leave a note, Mrs. Burnside."

Her jaw dropped a little, then snapped into a frown. She repeated the centering motion with her glasses, and glanced up sharply at the sound of white crepe-soled shoes squeaking on the tongue-and-groove. Mary balanced a sterling silver tray with three crystal goblets brimming with lemonade. She waited uncertainly at the coffee table, looking to Valerie Burnside for further instructions, her feet shifting and squeaking like jittery mice.

"Set them out on the table, and don't forget the coasters," Valerie Burnside commanded.

Mary methodically placed coasters in front of Angel and me, and on the small end table beside Valerie Burnside, and topped each with a goblet. She smiled nervously, and tried to back out of the room.

"The tray. Take the tray, for heaven's sake," the old woman bitched, taking deep breaths to control herself.

Mary lurched to the table, picked up the tray, nearly clipping Angel's lemonade, and hurried from the room. I looked at Angel. Her face seemed set in stone. I moved my eyes toward the doorway through which Mary had passed. She nodded.

"Pardon me, but may I use your rest room?" Angel asked, loud but polite.

"Can't you hold it?" the old woman asked.

Angel stared back in disbelief. "No. I can't."

"The problem with women is they have weak bladders," Valerie Burnside pronounced, and dismissed her with a wave of a hand.

Rising from the couch, Angel moved toward the doorway, saying: "I'll assume it's this way."

The old woman watched, disapproval jutting out her jaw. "If that woman is your partner, it's little wonder my son fired you."

Her paralysis was not a handicap, but a weapon which allowed her to spew bile with impunity. I decided to press a little harder.

"Your son was a crook, Mrs. Burnside."

She looked at me sharply.

"He was running a Ponzi scheme, which means he spent his clients' money instead of investing it as contracted. He used the money collected from new clients to pay the interest on accounts from previous clients, or claimed the investments were a total loss."

"That's an outrageous lie," she accused.

"He died over a million dollars in debt, with millions in yet-to-be-accounted-for investments that have either disappeared or went to support his lifestyle. He was having trouble attracting new clients, and without the infusion of fresh cash, the whole scheme was beginning to collapse. He couldn't meet the payment schedules of his clients, and legal proceedings were being prepared against him for fraud. Someone was threatening his life. With no way out, he killed himself, staging it to look like an accident, so that his poor crippled mother would be able to collect on his insurance policy.''

She fumbled for her cane, trembling with anger, but it slipped from the armrest and clattered to the floor. She glanced down at it, horrified, and going white, shouted: ''You unspeakable piece of garbage. You come into my home and insult my son, my dead son!''

''This is the scenario the insurance company will argue at the coroner's inquest. Personally, I don't believe that is exactly what happened, but right now I have no way to prove it. And neither do you.''

When the old woman realized I had goaded her into losing her temper, she brought her anger slowly under control, lifted a small brass bell from the end table beside her chair, and gave it a vigorous shake. I allowed her a few moments to think things through. Mary, her face brighter than it had been before, no doubt the result of sharing secrets with Angel, entered the room and stood expectantly by the end of the couch.

''My cane,'' Valerie Burnside said, pointing to the floor.

Mary picked up the cane and handed it to her. Stepping back with just a hint of dagger in her pleasant smile, she left with a lilt to her step when dismissed.

Fondling the handle of her cane, Valerie Burnside pursed her lips. A shrewd look composed of distrust and hope for gain moved in her eyes when she looked at me. ''This insurance company. Have you spoken with them?''

''I had lunch with the sheriff handling the case.''

''What's in it for you?'' she asked.

It was a question I had expected, but wasn't certain how I would answer until I had the measure of Valerie Burnside. She wouldn't buy sentiment, so the revenge for a dead client story went out the window. The truth would have given her an advantage I didn't want her to have. Burns could have been laundering money through his mother's account, and until I had a line on the missing money, the fewer people who knew that I was looking for it, the better. I settled for a story that gave me the same monetary interest as the old woman.

"My client recommended your son's services to several of his business associates. If it turns out your son killed himself, or was murdered, the story becomes front-page news because of the fraud angle, and my client will look very bad. If the death was accidental, the fraud case becomes harder to prove, and almost inconsequential, because, after all, he's dead, so why bring it to trial? The whole thing blows over in a few weeks and it's business as usual."

"Who's your client?"

"I can't tell you," I said, and smiled craftily.

"You can tell me how you're being paid, though."

I hesitated, pretending a struggle with my conscience. "I'm getting my rate, expenses, plus a bonus if the coroner rules it an accidental death."

A shrill, dry laugh cracked from her throat, and she smiled as though triumphant. "Ask your questions," she said.

"I need to know who was close to your son."

"I don't think anybody was close to Jack."

"That's bad," I said, and made a show of concern.

"Why is it bad?"

It was bad because the easiest explanation of what had happened to the money, other than that it had been spent, was that it had been laundered through a close friend or associate. I lied: "It's bad because I need someone to testify that Jack was feeling fine, and had never hinted at suicide."

"He never mentioned it to me."

"You have too much financial interest for your testimony to do any good, if you'll pardon my saying so."

"Not at all. I believe in getting the facts out."

"Certainly he had a girlfriend," I pressed.

"None that he brought home to Mother," she said.

Little wonder. "A close friend? Someone he had known for years?"

"Jack's closest friend was the guy he shaved with every morning. He lived by himself, and for himself." She frowned, and examined the tip of her cane, adding, too succinctly: "He was that way since his father died."

"How did his father die?" I asked.

She shook her head. "It's not important."

"Then why not tell me?"

She tapped her cane lightly on the armrest, considering. "It's bound to come out, I guess. He committed suicide," she said.

"You need to tell me more," I said gently.

"Jack's father was convicted of embezzlement in the fifties. I was forced to work in a factory, to support myself and Jack. I ran afoul of a conveyor belt, and lost the use of my legs." She cleared her throat of pain and regret. "When he heard, he hung himself in his cell."

I stood, and thanked her for the hospitality, thinking about parallel lives lived out to the same inevitable conclusion.

14

We drove the canyons from the San Fernando Valley to the Westside, climbed Coldwater Canyon to the crest of the Santa Monica Mountains at Mulholland Drive, and followed the ridge west to Beverly Glen. Los Angeles splayed before us at the crest like a trillion tons of concrete, wood, asphalt and glass lifted twenty thousand feet and dropped. It is a city shaped like an accidental spill: a gridless disarray of high-rises engulfed by no-rises which scatter against the mountains to the east, and fall west into the Pacific Ocean. Still, when the sun is shining and the wind has scoured the sky free of smog, there is beauty at the city fringes of mountains and sea.

Mulholland Drive was winding and sun-dappled and free of traffic. The old Mustang began to feel coltish again, thrilling to the press of the accelerator. Angel hung on to the armrest as we slung around a curve, and she shouted over the roar of the engine: "Every time I begin to feel confident about the moral superiority of women over men, I meet a bitch like Valerie Burnside."

"The exception proves the rule," I answered, powering through the curve.

"It's not her I'm talking about, but me. I wanted to punch her out. So much for moral superiority."

When I had stepped out of Valerie Burnside's front door in

Sherman Oaks, Angel had been surrounded by the crew of Mexican gardeners in what I had at first perceived to be group flirtation, but appeared as I approached to be a serious discussion. Dodger Cap had done most of the talking, clutching garden shears in arms folded across his chest, and the crew had seconded his words with brief nods and bursts of vocal assent. Excitement had animated Angel's glance when I approached the car, and I knew she had learned something important, either from the nurse or from the gardeners.

I downshifted around a Mulholland corner, and asked her about the nurse.

"Mary didn't know much, but what she knew, she was happy to tell," Angel hinted.

"I wonder why?"

"Because they'd arrest her for strangling the old bitch, which is what she really wants to do." Angel gripped the armrest, and braced her feet on the floorboards as the Mustang muscled into passing gear. She watched two slower vehicles slip by on the right, and said: "Mary replaced a woman named Kathy Maddox, who put in over two years as the nurse."

"I like this nurse angle," I interjected. "A nurse would know how to discreetly put someone under with alcohol and barbiturate, and how hot the water would need to be."

"Not to mention knowing about hyperthermia in the first place," Angel added.

In the rearview mirror, I played peek-a-boo with a blue Chrysler. He was doing his best to stay out of sight, but at twice the posted limit on a two-lane highway, he had to either lose me or show his grille. He showed his grille. I swept around a Volkswagen van traveling half my speed, braked into the top of an S-shaped curve, and accelerated out of the bottom, countersteering to bring the rear wheels out of a slide. One of the few traffic lights on the road turned amber ahead, and I was forced to pump the brakes. The wheels locked during the final ten yards of stop. Angel dug the seat belt out of her flesh, gave me a look that could have split concrete, and asked through gritted teeth: "Do you have to drive so damn fast?"

The blue Chrysler was hidden behind the Volkswagen. The van driver was giving me the finger. I deserved it.

"Any reason to believe Kathy Maddox knew Burns other than in a casual way?"

"None."

"Use your imagination. Maybe they were sleeping together on the sly," I suggested.

"Kathy Maddox was not that kind of girl."

The light turned green, and I accelerated through the intersection as rapidly as possible without squealing the tires. The left blinker on the Chrysler was going, and before I lost sight of it around the next curve, it had pulled around the Volkswagen.

"You mean she was a dyke?" I guessed.

"A lesbian. Dikes are what they build in Holland to hold back the sea."

"Dyke, lesbian, same difference," I said.

"You think so? Do you think there is any difference between calling a man gay and queer?"

I dodged the remark, asking: "Do you think she could have faked being straight with Jack Burns?"

"From what I've heard of his sexual tastes, he wouldn't have been interested. Kathy Maddox isn't the sex-bunny type."

Another light flashed to amber ahead. I took a chance and floored the accelerator. The Mustang lurched with a sudden gasp, and we slid through the intersection a half second into the red. The blue Chrysler disappeared behind, stuck at the light. I eased off on the speed, and settled back into my seat, thinking about the money. "Burns seemingly died without money or friends. If he's buried his assets in a dummy account or corporation, it will take months to find it, if there is anything to find, which I am rapidly beginning to doubt."

"What makes you think he died without a friend?" Angel asked.

I was about to answer when I glanced at her and noticed glinting in her eyes the same excitement I had seen earlier during her conversation with the gardening crew. The sun streamed through the windshield as the car pulled out of the canyon, and Angel's face glowed full of pride in a flickering gold light. The beauty of her startled me. My mind raced away from Jack Burns and everything connected to him and whirled around my feelings for this strange and wonderful woman who had come into my life six brief months before. Life seemed utterly changed by her presence. I had been competent before knowing her, and done well enough, but even in my best moments did not feel as complete as I did that moment driving in the sun. The transcendence did not last long, as Angel interrupted it with a laughing: "You're slipping, Paul. If you knew a little Spanish, you could have overheard a few choice bits of gossip."

"What did the gardeners tell you?" I asked, recovering my sense of time and place.

"That Kathy Maddox had a very attractive blond woman friend who dropped by the house every now and then. The two would disappear for an hour during lunch, and one day, when they returned, Jack Burns was at the house. Kathy went in to help Mrs. Burnside, but the blond woman lingered outside, talking to Jack. A couple of days later, the woman dropped by on Kathy's day off. She was with Jack, and the two seemed to have become very good friends. The gardeners reported seeing Jack with the woman several times during the past three months."

"Do we know anything else about this woman?"

"No, but Kathy Maddox would."

Angel flashed a photograph of Kathy Maddox. I held it across the wheel and studied it as I drove. She was a plain-looking woman with brown hair and a square, solid face. Her address, an apartment in the center of West L.A.'s gay and lesbian community, was hand-written on the back. I tossed the photograph to Angel, and almost told her that I loved her.

The drapes to Kathy Maddox's apartment were drawn open to empty rooms. Her apartment, or what had once been her apartment, was on the second floor of an apartment complex built in the early sixties, when the excitement of the space race compelled architects to a futuristic vision of the world. The future, according to this particular architect, consisted of an amoeba-shaped pool and two forlorn palm trees confined in a concrete courtyard, gold sparkles sprinkled liberally through white stucco walls, multicolored track lighting, and the name Galaxy Apartments.

The windows to Kathy Maddox's apartment were veined with sun-bleached dirt. I cleared a circle the size of my head with the palm of my hand and stuck a nose against it. Cardboard boxes and crumpled newspapers littered a ragged carpet the color of wilted spinach. The paint on the walls had faded to off-off-white. Bright squares glared where pictures had once hung. The base to the ceiling light fixture had been unscrewed, the light bulbs removed, and the disc-shaped base left dangling on a thin metal chain. Angel pointed to a black-and-orange For Rent sign in the lower corner of the window.

A thin man in his early thirties stepped out of the apartment next door. He had a blond mustache, immaculately trimmed hair, pressed shorts, and a gay power T-shirt. "It's a nice apartment, once it's painted and the carpets are replaced," he said, shading his eyes against the late-afternoon sun.

"We're more interested in who used to live here," I replied, and giving my name, offered a hand.

We shook.

"Too bad. It would be a relief to get some straight people around here. I long for a little diversity in this haven of perversity."

"If you want to live next to straight people, move to Orange County," I suggested.

He laughed, and said he'd heard they shot Democrats on sight in Orange County, and didn't want to imagine what they would do to a gay Democrat.

"Have any idea where Kathy Maddox moved?" I asked.

He tossed his head to the side and back again. "She left about a week ago. I didn't even hear about it until they started moving her stuff out. Why do you want to see her?"

I let my shoulders rise and fall, as though it were of no great importance. "My mom is getting on in years, and I heard Ms. Maddox provided nursing care."

He seemed to buy that, and said: "I have no idea where she went, but Martha would."

I looked interested. He pointed to a ground-floor apartment on the other side of the courtyard. "She lives over there. They were close friends at one time. She may know more about it."

"How close?" I asked.

"Close."

I thanked him, and waited while he jogged down the steps and out to the streets. Angel took my arm and pulled me close to the wall.

"You know what I think?" she said.

I said that I didn't.

"I think you should wait in the car and let me handle this. I think she might open up more without you around, particularly if she believes I'm gay."

"Do you feel comfortable doing that?" I asked.

"I'm not planning on sleeping with her," she said in a dry tone.

"I should hope not."

"What did I do before I started working with you?" she quizzed.

"You were a prizefighter."

"Just because I like men doesn't mean I don't know a lot of women who don't. How many locker-room seductions do you think I've seen?"

"Give me a hint," I asked. "Are we talking three or four figures?"

"You get the point," she said.

I waited in the car.

A half hour later I tired of listening to talk shows and limited-playlist rock and roll and stepped out to stretch my legs. The Galaxy Apartments were a couple of blocks south of Sunset near Fairfax. I thought I'd walk up to Sunset, and see which motion-picture and singing stars were being ego-stroked with hundred-thousand-dollar billboards on the strip. In entertainment circles, having a studio or record company emblazon your image onto a Sunset Strip billboard was almost as prestigious as having talent. My trek didn't get as far as the next block.

Around the first corner, behind the Mustang and just beyond a clear sight line from its rear window, the blue Chrysler was parked. The driver was in gear and rolling the moment he saw me, cranking the wheel in a U-turn, his tires slamming into and over the curb when the radius of the Chrysler wasn't tight enough to make the turn clean. I got the first number and three letters of his plates, but he was moving fast and I missed the last three numbers. I ran back to the Mustang and caught sight of him again on Sunset. I hoped he would head north, into the hills, where I could catch him, but he knew the limits of his car and mine, and stayed to the city streets, hoping to lose me at the signals. He was very good behind the wheel, and a better tail than I expected. Or lucky. The way he led me through Hollywood, I was betting that he was good. I was good, too, but not as lucky. A motorcycle cop hit his siren behind me, and the chase ended at the corner of Melrose and Highland.

The cop looked like a libertarian's nightmare in helmet, leather, and black jackboots. I rarely tremble before authority, but my hand shook a bit when I handed him my license, remembering my habit of not paying parking tickets until the day before they go to warrant. It is one of the few remaining rebellions from my student days, when I believed parking tickets were symbols of a capitalist police state, and sometimes I make a mistake and the ticket goes to warrant. Then I have to pay triple the amount of the original ticket or risk arrest. It isn't a very effective protest. The cop must not have bothered to check, or maybe my record was clear, because he wrote me a ticket for doing fifty-five in a thirty-mile-per-hour zone and let me go.

When I got back to the Galaxy Apartments, Angel was gone.

15

Angel huddled at the final crest of sand between Santa Monica beach and the sea, a chill offshore breeze whipping her hair as she smoothed sand between her outstretched legs. It was the magic hour, when an atmospheric alchemy transforms daylight blue to twilight gold. She glanced up and watched the waves sweep at low tide across a flat stretch of sand, falter, and fall swirling back into an advancing wave. Two sandpipers chased the wave's receding edge, knifed their long beaks into the sand in search of sand crabs, and dashed to high ground a half-step ahead of the next crash of blue-white water.

"Sorry I missed you," I said, settling into the sand next to Angel. She had written that she would be at the beach watching the sunset, and slipped the note under the door to my apartment.

Angel nodded in brief acknowledgment when I spoke, but didn't turn her head from the sea.

"I had another run-in with the blue Chrysler," I announced.

No nod, or flicker of interest in her eyes. Her hands dropped to the sand. I let my voice wander.

"I thought we had lost him in the hills, but he tailed us to the apartment. I took off after him, and didn't get anything out of it except a speeding ticket."

Nothing. She had sculpted the sand into a scallop shape, and etched parallel lines down the shell with a chewed fingernail. Her hands rested flat, fingers caressing the surface grains of sand. She stared at the sculpture. Her fingers arched and clenched, crushing it. Then she smoothed the sand and began again.

I couldn't tell whether she was mad at me or not. At that moment, I couldn't tell anything about her. She seemed like a stranger, as though a half year of knowing her had disappeared like the images on a roll of film exposed to the sun. The sudden blankness was disturbing. Unnerved, I prattled about chasing the blue Chrysler, being radar-gunned by the motorcycle cop, and returning to the Galaxy Apartments to find her gone. I speculated on the identity of the driver, where he had initially begun to tail us, and what his business might be. I congratulated her on her skills as an interviewer, and how well she had handled Valerie Burnside's new nurse and the gardening crew, but no matter what I said, no matter how quickly or loudly I spoke, or how many words poured from my mouth, it all seemed to disappear the moment I said it, erased by that sudden blankness between us. It defeated me. Like a fool, I babbled on, thinking that my voice could push away the blankness.

"Shut up, Paul," Angel finally said.

The sound of her voice was something, and her three words were more than my thousand. She looked at me, and that too was something arced across the blankness. Then she pushed up from the sand and suggested: "Let's walk for a while."

We skirted the advancing edge of the sea, strolling along sand still wet and hard from the previous high tide. The sandpipers and sea gulls gave us wide berth, their heads bobbing vigilantly as we passed. The reds and golds and lavenders of the twilight sky glistened on the sheen of wet sand.

"I feel like I've been turned inside out," Angel admitted after a few minutes of silence.

"I'll listen, if you want to talk about it. If not, we can just walk," I offered.

"I think I should tell you about my meeting with Martha."

I said that would be fine, and waited. We walked a while longer, and Angel began, hesitantly at first, then speaking with natural animation, running her sentences together in the delightful way she has when thinking and feeling her way around something.

"Kathy Maddox would have to be tough, to care for someone like Valerie Burnside for two years. I figured she might attract someone gentler, more stylish. I was right. Martha looked like she slept standing up. You know what I mean. Not a hair out of place. An hour in front of the mirror perfecting an image maybe no one will see. I think she worries about wrinkling, because she is so pale you can see the blue veins under her skin."

"She let you into her apartment, then," I surmised.

"Of course. I told her I was looking for Kathy. Moved last week, Martha said, and good luck in finding her. When I asked why Kathy disappeared, she asked me if I'd like something to drink, and I said I'd have a beer, a light one if she had it, and she made a joke about keeping our girlish figures. Her apartment was small, but nicely done. It didn't look like she had a lot of money, but most of the things were nice. She had some original artwork on the walls by a woman artist I didn't know, but that doesn't necessarily mean anything, because I don't know many artists. She let me know that the artist was a special friend, and I wasn't at all confused by what she meant by that."

"Was she trying to come on to you?" I asked.

"Why are you so paranoid about women coming on to me?" Angel demanded, and I sensed a deep frustration beneath the anger. I just shrugged, feeling a little defensive. I had thought it an innocent question, but of course it wasn't.

"She was just lonely, okay? Maybe she thought she might have a chance to sleep with me, but mostly she was just lonely. I don't feel good about it, but I used it to get her to tell me things. They had been lovers for about two years. She thought that they were really solid, had almost made the big commitment, and telling me the story, I could tell that she still felt pretty bitter about it. Then Kathy met someone new. What it boiled down to, according to Martha, was that she had been thrown over for a younger woman. And a very pretty younger woman. Thin and blond, like somebody out of the pages of a fashion magazine. Martha called her the Fashion Doll. She said that ten years ago maybe she could have kept up with her, but not now, not at forty, and it was really sad, the way Martha said it. You knew she was really fighting the age thing, and losing badly, which maybe only women can understand.''

I let that judgment filter through my mind, thinking that Angel was probably right. Women develop quicker than men, and society counterbalances this advantage by judging them less attractive at an age when men are still considered in their prime. It's a tough system, but if a man is decent and cares about what's important in a woman, a few lines will only make her more beautiful. The problem, as several woman friends have told me, is that there are damned few decent men. It was strange to hear that a woman would place the same age value on another woman. I broke away from my thoughts, and said: "It sounds as though Martha really got to you."

Angel stooped, picking a stone from the sand. The stone was polished black by sand and water, and glistened in her hand. "I know you're not supposed to get emotionally involved," she admitted, and heaved the stone past the breakers. It felt good to her, and she searched the sand for another stone. Like a small boy, Angel still found the throwing of stones cathartic. "You're supposed to stay detached from the people you talk to in this business, but still, I thought it was really sad." Angel watched the second stone ripple into a wave. "As Martha saw it, the relationship was not that stable. Martha kept thinking that it would end, and Kathy would come back to her. Then just last week, Kathy arrives at the apartment complex with two Great Danes on the end of a leash, and announces that she is moving to Paris. And she's moving there with the Fashion Doll."

The image of two large dogs in a small apartment seemed incongruous, and I asked: "What's this about the Great Danes?"

"Martha said she had never seen them before, but they were supposed to belong to the Fashion Doll, and Kathy was just looking after them for the day. Martha started asking her questions about how Kathy could afford to quit her job and move to Paris, and Kathy lied to her, or so she says."

"Why does Martha believe Kathy was lying?" I asked.

"Kathy said her mother died and left her a lot of money, but Martha knows this is bullshit—her words, not mine—because she knows that Kathy didn't get on well with her mom, and her mom didn't have any money anyway. Maybe they knocked over a bank, I said as a joke, but Martha didn't laugh, and said she had thought the same thing."

The sun had sunk well below the western horizon, and only a dull residue of pink and twilight blue remained. We had passed beneath Santa Monica Pier and neared Venice Beach on our walk, and doubled back toward Santa Monica. I contemplated Angel's recounting of the interview with Martha, and asked: "Do you think Kathy Maddox and her girlfriend could have found access to Jack Burns's bankroll, and killed him for it?"

"You're always telling me not to go just by gut feel, but that's what my gut is telling me. So I guess we should look into it," Angel said and, as we walked, slid her arm through the crook of my elbow.

It was her first gesture of intimacy of the evening, and I allowed myself a moment of contentment before observing: "We're a little short on details. Did Martha tell you this woman's name, or where Kathy Maddox would be staying in Paris?"

I felt Angel's arm tense, and I thought she might pull away, resenting my disappointment at the lack of details. Angel has a healthy resistance to criticism to the point of stubbornness, but when in a highly emotional state, she becomes all nerve ends. I gripped her forearm, and squeezed it to encourage her confidence.

She seemed to relax a bit, and answered: "I know it doesn't leave us much to go on, but Martha swears that Kathy never mentioned her name. Ex-lovers aren't always that truthful or forthcoming. Kathy didn't know where she would be staying in Paris, or so she said, but promised to send Martha a postcard. Martha will call me if she does, but frankly, I don't think there will ever be a postcard. Sorry, but that's the way it is."

"Are you still depressed?" I asked.

Angel didn't answer. We continued on, approaching Santa Monica Pier, now brightly lit against the night sky. Before we reached the pilings—which always gave me an uneasy feeling upon approach, as I had once been forced to shoot a man there—Angel pulled around to face me and, searching my eyes, said: "There is something I'm not telling you."

I waited in the darkness and silence, expecting her to add some troubling detail to the story of Martha and Kathy. She instead confessed: "It's not about Martha. It's something about me, something about myself that I really don't know how to talk about."

I try to remain open to the emotions of others, but her seriousness and my ignorance of what troubled her intensified my disquietude. Perhaps she noticed my resistance, though I tried my best to conceal it, or maybe she just decided that she needed something other than talk.

"Do me a favor?" she asked.

I nodded.

"Hold me?"

I held her. With my arms around her back, and her head against my chest, she clung to me, despair weighting her arms, and need giving them strength. I pressed her closer, awed by her vulnerability.

"We are all a little crazy, aren't we?" she said finally.

I started to say something about that, but she pressed her finger to my lips, and I said nothing.

"Maybe we all have some secret twist in us, some self-destructive twist that keeps us from getting what we want from our lovers."

I quietly held her until she pushed away. She said she needed to be alone for a while, and I watched her slip into the darkness toward Venice Beach until the outline of her body could no longer be discerned against the night-black sea.

16

I'm accustomed to sleeping alone, but when the phone rang just before midnight I was nowhere near sleep and had just poured myself a tumbler of Jameson Irish whiskey to drive from my mind the fear that our relationship might have been what was troubling Angel. I felt as secure in her love as I had with any woman, but being in love is a high-wire act. Trust makes the act work but also sets you up for the fall. I chased the whiskey with a glass of water and answered the phone.

"I want to buy you lunch, strictly business," Mona Demonay offered when I picked up. The low hum of voices and a clattering of dishes filtered through the background.

"Whose business?" I asked.

"Yours, mine and Jack Burns's," she specified. "Can you meet me in, say, half an hour?"

"This is a little late for lunch."

"That depends on your hours, darling. I'm in between shifts, so it's lunch by my clock. I'm at the West Beach Cafe. I presume you can track it down," she said, and hung up.

I saw his headlights flash down the block as I swung the Mustang from the curb and headed toward the beach. This time it was a brown Plymouth, the kind they made in the early seventies before the gas crunch, an ugly monster with eight cylinders and a grille like a gorilla's grin. He was following between two and four car lengths back, but traffic was thin. Sometimes there weren't enough cars to hide behind, and I was watching for him. I made it easy, driving the speed limit on Pacific Avenue and stopping on yellows. Where Venice Boulevard dead-ends into the sea I turned right and pulled into the West Beach Cafe parking lot. The Plymouth cruised past on Pacific, the driver's head swiveling to make my car before turning left. A red-coated valet opened the door and traded a parking stub for my car keys. The Plymouth doubled back and parked across the intersection with a clear view of the café entrance. I went inside.

The West Beach Cafe is a Westside restaurant and bar that goes in and out of style every couple of years and could care less. They hung art on the walls before it became the fashionable thing to do and started serving California cuisine before somebody thought to give it a name. On Friday and Saturday night the place is choked with beautiful babes with big hair and guys who look like they either model for *GQ* magazine or own it. On Sunday nights it is a mixed blue-jean and designer-gown crowd. Some of the neighborhood artists drop by for a drink, and the atmosphere is quiet and amiable. The food is good but the bar is better: a long curve of oak and a list of Scotches that requires a year of dedicated drinking to canvass.

Mona sat alone at the far end of the bar, streaming cigarette smoke over a vodka tonic. A blond Adonis type in a linen jacket, pink shirt, blue jeans, and Topsiders cruised by to check her out, but she waved him off with a quick "No thanks." Her attire wasn't obviously sexual by Southern California standards—a black leather jumpsuit with the silver snake belt and chainsaw earrings I had seen her model the night before—but most of the men were scanning her in the oblique way of those gathering their courage for a pass. She sat at the barstool, one leg hooked over the other. The high heel dangled from her toes, and she held her cigarette aloft with an elegant curve of her arm before slowly molding her lips around the filter tip. She exhaled and cast a playfully bored look about the room, noticing every single man at the bar and whether each was watching her, before spotting me at the entrance and nodding with one short drop of her eyes.

"Can I buy you a drink?" she asked, rising to kiss my cheek when I had crossed to her end of the bar.

One of the twenty-year-old single-malt Scotches would have been fine, but I needed to keep my senses sharp and asked for coffee instead. She said I was boring, but signaled the bartender and ordered it. A phone hung on the wall at the entrance to the rest rooms. I excused myself and used it to call Angel. It was late and Angel didn't seem happy to hear my voice, but it was work and I didn't have time to deal with her displeasure. I told her what I wanted her to do and when I wanted it done. Then I hung up.

The coffee was waiting next to a small object wrapped in tissue paper when I returned. I ignored the object and slid the cup to the other side of Mona to keep an eye on the door while we talked. Mona pushed the object before me again and told me to open it. I did. It was a bronze letter opener with a six-inch blade. The handle was cast in the full-bodied shape of an Egyptian woman. Her raised hands grasped the base of the blade at the top of her head, the line from her elbow to her hands shaping the hilt. Imitation rubies were inlaid at the eyes, and their red gleam evoked an otherworldly expression of seeing beyond the grave. I let it balance in my hand. Mona read the question in my eyes and answered: "So I guessed wrong and it's not your birthday. Now we're even."

I asked her what she meant by that.

"You gave me a hundred dollars last night, and I felt cheap taking it. I was mad at you, and when I get mad at somebody, I always try to take their money. But I was mad at you for the wrong reasons, and the money didn't make me feel any better. Now I feel better."

I could have asked her why she had been angry the night before, but I thought I knew why, and as it seemed to be a point of pride with her, it would only make her angry again to ask. So I just thanked her. She nodded curtly, uncomfortable with the sentimentality of gift-giving, and broached her proposition.

"What would it be worth to you if I could prove that Jack Burns wasn't always the investment hotshot everyone thought he was?"

"Not a hell of a lot," I answered.

Mona rolled her eyes, thinking my response an attempt to bargain, and countered: "I know you've hit a money vein somewhere. Otherwise why would you ask me what I knew about Jack Burns last night?"

"Jack Burns was involved in serious fraud. Multimillion-dollar fraud. From what I've heard, the man died dead broke."

"Don't bullshit me," Mona demanded. "You run a business. You wouldn't come out here to talk about Jack Burns if there wasn't money in it somewhere."

"Maybe I wanted company."

"And maybe I'd believe that if you weren't such a priest last night. If you've changed your mind, let's go out to the car and get down," Mona suggested, and her voice was hard and aggressive, as though challenging me to a fight.

"What is it you want to sell?" I asked, deflecting.

"I told you. Proof that Jack Burns was not what he said he was."

"I already know he was a fraud. It really doesn't make a hell of a lot of difference if you confirm it."

"I don't know this fraud business you're talking about, but I know he was loaded, and I have something I want to sell. So chill out with the dead-broke bullshit, and tell me where I can find a buyer if you're not interested."

She stubbed out her cigarette with a final stubborn blast of smoke. I thought it important to dispel her illusions about Jack Burns, and laid out the Ponzi scheme for her: how it worked and how through the wonders of leasing and investment fraud a man could appear wealthy and die millions in debt. She didn't want to believe me, but the details were compelling, and as the truth wore against her fantasies, her shoulders slumped, and the frequency with which the vodka tonic made the trip from the bar to her lips doubled.

"Shit," was all she said when I had finished, and she propped her elbows on the bar and cupped her head in her hands.

I sipped at my coffee, pretending that it was single-malt Scotch. My taste buds didn't go for it. "What have you got to sell?" I repeated.

Mona straightened and shot me a curious look. "Why are you so interested if the guy died broke?"

Good lies are always at least half-truths. I started with: "My client was one of Jack Burns's investors. He lost a lot of money and he's a little hot about it." Then I improvised: "He wants to know how Jack Burns managed to screw him so completely."

"Jack Burns once screwed people for a living," Mona said, and laughed high and loud. Heads at the bar turned, attracted by the noise. Maybe it was the attention, or the vodka, or just the realization that what she had to sell wasn't worth as much as she had thought, but the edges rounded from her hard-sell stance, and she began to come on with an impish sensual charm. Mona tousled her hair, hit me with a teasing smile, and asked: "Do you remember those pictures I took?"

I nodded, my face beginning to burn with the memory. She dug scarlet nails into her purse and speared a white envelope. "What would it be worth if I could prove that twenty years ago Jack Burns was a porno actor?"

The notion stunned me. I signaled the bartender and ordered a Laphroaig, a dark and smoky single malt from the Isle of Islay. He poured it neat in a large tumbler. I sipped at it, luxuriating in the rich burn sliding down my throat.

"Surprised?" Mona speculated, carefully watching as I sipped at the Scotch.

I shrugged, feigning indifference. The image fit like the torn halves of different portraits. From porno actor to investment con man was a big stretch, but both involved a perverse method of performance, and twenty years is a long time to learn a new act. I realized that I didn't know what Jack Burns had been twenty years ago, and didn't believe anyone else in town was any wiser than I.

"I'll need a little more to take to my client," I said.

"Sure. I give it to you for free, and then you tell me to fuck off. No thanks."

"Not my style. You don't have to give me proof until I ask for it. Just give me something more than an accusation, and if my client sounds interested, I'll ask for the rest."

She studied my face, which is honest enough. We had tested each other enough times by then to rough out the perimeters of our characters, and I guess she trusted me, because she began: "It was the pictures that first set me off. He didn't just ask me to take them. He directed me, like he knew what he was doing. So I figured this was either a regular thing of his, or maybe it fit into his past in some way."

Her scarlet nails tweezered a Polaroid from the white envelope and flipped it onto the table. The shot was microscopically anatomical, and I had difficulty distinguishing the various body parts photographed. It could have been anybody in there. She dipped into the white envelope again, and tossed another faceless shot onto the bar. I could feel her eyes scanning my face for a sexual response as I glanced down at the photographs. The shots were as erotic as plumbing fixtures.

"These are very specific angles. If you've done porno, or maybe if you've watched enough of it, you'd recognize the setups. There are only so many angles you can use to capture the sex act. Jack Burns knew them."

I asked a very stupid question. "How do you know them?"

"Look, I'm an actress, okay? I want to break into films and television, and I'm going to make it. But I have to eat in the meantime, and porn seemed like a good idea, so I acted in a few films. It's not just all fucking and the money is good and you get some on-camera experience. Even Stallone did it, right? Of course I wouldn't do it now, not because of any moral thing, but because you don't really want to become known as a porno actress if you want to do legit stuff, understand?"

Her ambition disturbed me. If you spend any time in this town, you become aware of the human waves assaulting Hollywood with all the intelligence and hope of Australians charging the Turks at Gallipoli. Most don't have any talent but they all have ambition and except for one or two lucky ones the talented fall with the untalented in a heap of dead dreams far short of the gates of Paramount Pictures. Mona was smart and mercenary. I wanted to tell her to quit the high-class hooker act, forget the pursuit of a film career, and find something that wouldn't leave her broken and directionless at thirty. Instead, I just nodded.

"So I know a few people in the biz, and asked around, low-profile so nobody knew what I really wanted. I knew he wouldn't have been in anything recent, and it isn't easy finding porn from the pre–*Deep Throat* days, but I ran across a guy with a collection of old loops, shorts, and features shot in the sixties. I just about went blind looking through it all, but finally, there it was, a flick shot in 1970. It was about the sexual escapades of a television repairman.''

Mona speared another Polaroid and dealt it onto the bar. This one included the closed-eyed and straining face of Jack Burns.

"Jack changed a lot in the twenty years between that film and this," Mona continued, pointing at the Polaroid. "He had his own hair then, and he was about forty pounds lighter. His face was lean, and he sported one of those bushy outlaw mustaches popular at the end of the sixties.''

"How can you be certain it's the same guy?" I asked.

"A man can lose his hair and gain fifty pounds, but two things don't change: his foot size, and his dick.''

"I'll take your word for it," I said, "but I don't think I want to look that close, and my client might want a little confirmation. Do you have any other proof?''

"One of the actresses in the flick went on to be a big star in the seventies. She's pretty much dropped out of the scene, but she still gets a little action now and then. Older woman roles, mom-and-daughter routines. Her stage name is Sash. I'm gonna talk to her tomorrow.''

"What kind of deal do you want me to take to my client?''

Her eyes lasered mine with calculated avarice as she without hesitation quoted the price. "Ten thousand buys you a copy of the film, the Polaroids, a tape of the interview with Sash, and if you want, I don't say a word about this to the newspapers or anybody else.''

"That last bit sounds a little like extortion," I observed.

"I prefer to call it public-relations damage control," Mona answered, and lit a cigarette, waiting for my reaction.

I gave it. "I don't know if I can get anything for you. It won't help my client recover any of his money, and if he wants the film, it would probably be to trash the reputation of a man already dead. But I'll make the offer, and if he's interested, I'll let you know.''

Her eyes laughed behind a veil of smoke and she said: ''You could save me from a life of sin if you make this work. I could take some time off, do a few more auditions, and who knows, I might hit it big and next year invite you skinny-dipping in the pool of my new mansion.''

Mona crushed out her smoke and stood, straightening the pull of the leather jumpsuit across her breast. ''In the meantime, I'm late for my next date.''

She dealt a final Polaroid onto the bar, face up, my face up as I watched that night from my perch on the stairs. She let me take a good look at it, then scooped it with the rest of the photographs into her purse.

''This I'm keeping for sentimental reasons,'' she said, and let linger a more than friendly kiss below my right ear.

I watched the men at the bar watch her leave, and gave her a few minutes to clear the parking lot. I stood, and the bartender hit me with the tab. I paid, noting that Mona still owed me lunch, and walked out to my car. My glance casually passed the Plymouth still parked across the street. I paid the attendant, cranked the engine, and pulled around the block to head north on Pacific. I followed Pacific to Rose Avenue, then cut one street over to Main, one of the principal shopping avenues on the Westside. The shops were all dim but one, a fifties-style café that kept late hours. I turned left across Main, and crossed under an archway to a public lot behind the café. The Plymouth passed up the first entrance to the lot. I stepped from the Mustang and headed for the archway as the Plymouth turned up a side street and entered the lot from the back. I knew then I had him.

The Fifties Cafe was half-crowded with insomniacs and late-night revelers with no place left to go when the bars began to close. Had any other place been open, I'd have chosen it, never having understood the craze for an era when vegetables were canned and political repression in America had reached its peak. The music in the café was too loud, the waitresses chewed gum, and the shell of a 1956 Cadillac was riveted to the ceiling. The café had lots of atmosphere, and all of it annoying. I pulled up a stool at the counter and muscled down a cup of vintage fifties weak but bitter coffee, watching the windows near the door for passing faces. Foot traffic was meager two hours past midnight. I was reasonably certain I spotted the tail midway into my coffee. I didn't see his face. He wore a brown sport coat and swiftly walked on the opposite side of the street, his head swiveling as he passed the café. I gave him a couple of minutes, then tossed down the dregs and dropped a bill on the counter.

I strolled back to the Mustang, debating whether or not I should have asked Angel to bring a handgun, and hoping that I hadn't made the wrong decision when I'd opted to pull this stunt unarmed. I've only carried a gun a couple of times in this business. White-collar types rarely spring an Uzi on you, but I didn't think the guy in the Plymouth was a white-collar type. The problem with carrying a gun is that you might use it, and if you don't, someone will see you have it and shoot you just to be on the safe side.

When I reached the Mustang, I glanced through the windshield and nodded to Angel, who sat slumped in the driver's seat. I went through the motions of opening the driver's door and stepping in, but instead crouched down and slammed the door shut from outside the car.

Angel started the engine and eased out of the parking slot. Profanity streaked through the night from the direction of the Plymouth. The tail had found his tires slashed. Angel cruised in first gear toward the back of the lot, where the Plymouth had parked. I trotted in a low crouch on the other side of the aisle of cars, moving toward the curses. When I caught sight of the Plymouth's fender, I stood. The tail's back was turned. He was watching the Mustang, which pulled behind his Plymouth, trapping him on one side. When he saw the driver, he knew something was up, and quickly whirled to face me. I knew him. He had taken me for a ride a few days ago. Gilbert. The small guy with the tropical shirt and thinning hair who had handled the gun and burned me like a piece of toast.

I had him blocked off from the front. Angel vaulted out of the

Mustang and strode around its rear fender. Gilbert backed against the Plymouth.

"Looks like you've had a little road trouble," I observed, walking slowly toward him. His sharp face was tightly compressed, the lips pulled back over his teeth. He opened the left side of his sport coat to a leather holster and wood-grain gun butt. My feet decided it was time to stop.

"What's this action with the gun, Gilbert? I just want to talk to you, and I don't think you have orders to shoot me."

"I just might change my orders myself," he warned.

"The way I look at it, you were just doing your job the other day. I don't hold any grudges."

He had been afraid, but though there were two of us, he was the only one with a gun, and the fear turned to swagger. "Yeah? Well, I do, asshole. Those were new tires."

"No big deal. Tell us who you're working for, and I'll buy you new ones."

His lopsided grin and flat stare told me he didn't buy the proposition. He crossed his arms, his right hand resting near the gun butt, and leaned back against the Plymouth. The canine look was sharp in his eyes, the fear-sensing stare a dog will give before deciding whether or not to bite.

"How much longer you planning to follow me?" I asked, keeping my voice casual and polite.

"I got nothing to say to you and no time to say it," he said and, in a show of bravado, spat on the ground at my feet.

"Were you driving the blue Chrysler yesterday, or are you working in shifts?"

"You got ears. Use 'em. I'm telling you to fuck off."

I took another couple of steps forward. Gilbert's hand inched up to the gun butt inside his blazer.

"Relax, Gilbert. I told you I don't hold a grudge," I soothed, holding my hands palms up in the universal sign of peace. I was close enough. I let my eyes slide easily toward Angel. His eyes followed mine. I moved in quickly. He thought he'd have time to pull his gun, forgetting to protect his face. My palm clenched to a sharp left hook that jettisoned his head back to the roof of the Plymouth. His knees slumped, and I followed it with a short, chopping right as he went down.

His hand slipped away from the holster when he hit the ground. Angel darted forward and speared the gun while I held him down. Angel opened the Plymouth passenger door. I lifted him by his belt and shirt front and tossed him onto the front seat. He groaned and tried to slap my hand away when I went through his coat pockets, so I hit him again and told him I'd shoot him if he moved. His license gave his name as Gilbert Stern, and listed a San Bernardino address. The license was new, increasing the odds that the address was still good. There was nothing else in his wallet except money. I stepped back and tossed the wallet on the floorboards. One of his feet dangled over the edge of the doorframe. So I lied. I did hold a grudge. I slammed the door on his foot.

17

Angel had her feet propped on the desk and her ear to the phone, going over the details for that night's flight to Paris with the travel agent when I stumbled into the office at a quarter past ten. I waved good morning, and headed for the coffee machine. I had spent an adrenaline-charged two hours pacing my apartment floor after the encounter with Gilbert the night before, and my eyes were slogged from the lack of sleep. I poured myself a cup from Ms. Coffee, chugged it, and poured another. I carried the second cup to my office and turned on the computer. I typed for half an hour, entering names, addresses, descriptions, and observations from the previous day's investigation.

When the coffee had finally fired enough caffeine jolts into my nervous system to allow me to link consecutive thoughts, I summoned the number Frank Worthy had handwritten on a blank card, and gave it a ring. A man answered with a languid "Yeah?" and I told him I wanted to speak with Mr. Worthy. He took down my name and number, and advised me that Mr. Worthy would get in touch when he could. I didn't know when that would be, so used the time to call Ian Waddington on the second line.

Ian was a Young Turk with a national brokerage firm. When I first met him, shortly after he had migrated west from New England, he claimed he had moved to Southern California because there is more money and less intelligence here than anywhere else in the world. He had three primary interests: stocks, bonds, and mutual funds. Anything else to him smacked of frivolity. Ian had serious limitations as a human being but he was a very good broker. Six months previous, he had made a small fortune on information I fed him regarding the murder of a chief executive officer at a Fortune 500 company, so he answered my calls.

"What do you know about Jack Burns?" I asked when his secretary announced he was on the line.

"If you invested any money with that slimeball, you deserved to lose it, so don't come crying to me," Ian asserted, angrily supposing that I had money and hadn't come to him.

"I didn't invest with him."

"Then why are you asking?"

"I was his bodyguard."

There was a pause on the other end of the line. "You did a pretty piss-poor job, didn't you?"

"He fired me," I explained.

"Although I must admit the world is a better place for your incompetence," he mused, ignoring my explanation.

"I take it you didn't think much of him."

"I didn't need to know him to hate him."

"Bad for business?" I guessed.

"Guys like Jack Burns pop up every couple of years, promising unreal rates of return until whatever scam they're working collapses. All it takes is one good fraud scare to jelly-leg the local investment market. The papers have yet to run anything on him, so the mom-and-pops haven't been affected, but my Cadillac accounts are all down ten percent since the story started floating around the big money circles."

"How would you like to do me a favor?"

"Favors are free, and I don't like doing anything for free."

"I need a deep background check. I figured you could get it faster than I can, particularly the financial history."

"Why are you so interested?" Ian asked in a tone of voice openly speculative on what was in it for him.

"My client lost a bundle. He wants to understand what happened."

"Throwing good money after bad?" Ian quizzed, not buying it.

"Something like that. Hold on," I said as the first line began to ring. I cupped the phone against my chest and shouted across the office for Angel to pick up.

"How deep do you want me to check?" Ian asked.

"Twenty years should do it. I'm interested in jobs held, where lived, significant investments, and ownership of any companies or partnerships."

"Give me a couple of days and I'll see what I can do," Ian offered, and rung off.

"Frank Worthy," Angel shouted across the office when I hung up.

I jacked into line one and told Worthy I wanted to meet him at his office.

"Can't do that and you damn well know it," Worthy objected.

"Right. I'll brief you on the phone, then."

"Damn, but your memory is shorter'n the hair on a hog. No substantive contact on the phone. I'll pick you up like I did before, say about six p.m.."

"Things are moving fast and I might be out of town by then. Pick me up in an hour, at the corner of Fourth and Wilshire."

He didn't like it, but when I told him it was either that or I'd talk to him when I got back into town God knows when, he agreed.

I didn't like it either, and decided that I needed to start establishing a record of contact with Frank Worthy.

"Did you finish drafting the Worthy contract?" I asked Angel after softly knocking on her office door.

She reached into a drawer and tossed a manila envelope on her desktop. I pulled out the contract, a standard form stipulating work for hire. Worthy's address had been left blank, but the document at least listed his name and phone number, and with any luck I'd get him to sign it that afternoon.

"We're leaving for Paris on a six o'clock flight. I've found a charming little hotel on the Ile de St. Louis with a room overlooking the Seine," Angel said as I scanned the contract.

"What's wrong with the Holiday Inn?" I asked.

"I thought we'd want something centrally located," Angel calmly replied.

"Are you feeling any better? You seemed a little down last night," I said, sliding the contract back into the envelope.

"I'm going to Paris tonight. I feel great," she answered.

We both knew it was a dodge, but left it at that, and arranged to meet at my apartment at three that afternoon.

Worthy's Lincoln St. Tropez stood out in the surrounding traffic like a bull among a flock of sheep. It was heading south, toward the ocean, and I crossed the street to wait for it. The limousine braked in the middle of the right lane, and I hopped in accompanied by a bleating chorus of horns.

"I hadn't expected anything quite so soon, son. I'm impressed," Worthy said when I had settled into the jump seat across the aisle. He had changed his western-cut brown suit to western-cut blue and his Stetson from brown to white since I had seen him last, but the turquoise stone on the bolo tie was still shaped like Texas, and his belt still spelled his name in gilt rope.

"I've been lucky," I answered, and handed him the manila envelope.

"What's this?" Worthy dug into his side pocket and produced a pair of gold-rimmed spectacles.

"A standard work-for-hire contract."

Worthy frowned when I told him what it was, but pulled the sheaf of papers from the envelope. The spectacles settled low on his nose, he gave the document a careful read. He held each sheet of paper by the edge and twisted his fingertips when he turned a page. I expected him to balk when he reached the signature line, but instead he asked for a pen. I gave him one, and he signed.

"Now, what the hell do you got that's so important I gotta break herd to talk to you?" Worthy grumbled, returning the contract.

I laid out the Ponzi scheme as Sheriff Kohl had explained it, and confirmed that Jack Burns had died legally if fraudulently broke. Worthy listened attentively, interrupting the flow of my narrative with questions about attachable assets and close business associates. That led to the connection between Valerie Burnside and Kathy Maddox, and Kathy's sudden windfall and departure for Paris with a young woman who had been romantically linked with Jack Burns. His attention turned from polite to intense when I mentioned the report that Kathy Maddox had come into an inheritance.

"Sounds like there could be something in that one, doesn't there?" he speculated, palming the Stetson at his side and spearing me with a shrewd glance. "Although I don't quite understand why Mr. Burns would be cavorting with a couple of hookers if this woman you mentioned was doing right by him."

"Maybe they had a falling out," I suggested.

"If I was a woman wanting to steal a man's money, I'd make damn sure I didn't fall out with him until I'd already made the grab."

"Could be she had already run off with the money. Knowing he was broke, Jack Burns decided to enjoy the rich life while it lasted. He called in a couple of hookers, and did all the drugs he could stuff into his system, which indirectly caused his death. Or maybe the woman was angry at being dumped, and came back under the pretext of sleeping with him one last time, and instead killed him with the help of Kathy Maddox."

"It doesn't matter whether she killed him or not. What matters is where's the money," Worthy advised, drawing the bottom line.

"I don't know if she has the money or not, but it warrants a look. Flying to Paris won't be cheap. I wanted to get your approval before I committed."

"Just follow the cash, son, and you'll have my approval wherever you go."

Worthy leaned over his ball-shaped belly, pressed the intercom button, and instructed the chauffeur to return to Wilshire and Fourth. I moved on to other business, asking: "How well did you know Jack Burns?"

"Not well enough, obviously," Worthy answered bitterly.

"How long have you known him?"

"Off and on about six months."

"Would it surprise you if Jack Burns had acted in pornographic movies twenty years ago?"

Worthy blinked and glanced out the window. The limousine had pulled onto the residential avenues north of Wilshire, near my apartment. The avenue was wide and lined with palm trees. Worthy watched the palms flitting by, his mouth stretching from dull hanging shock to wide chagrin. His eyes were far removed from amusement when he turned to me and said: "Yes sir, that would surprise me. That would surprise me one whole hell of a lot. It would surprise me so much I'd have to ask you how the hell you came up with the idea."

"One of the hookers thought she recognized him. She took some candid photographs of Burns getting hot and heavy with the other hooker. She claims she tracked down one of his old films, compared the body parts, arrived at a match, and now she wants to sell the package to you."

"Why the hell would I want to buy a film about Jack Burns's bare ass? The news is pretty damn interesting, but I'm sure as hell not going to watch it."

"She made the offer, and I promised I'd pass it along to you."

"What does she want for it?"

"Ten grand," I said as the limousine pulled to the curb at Wilshire and Fourth.

"Tell her to forget it," Worthy instructed, elbowing open the door. As I stepped onto the asphalt he added: "Just follow the money, son. That's all we're really interested in."

Right. I shut the door and pulled the pen from my pocket as the limousine accelerated into traffic. I wrote the license number on the manila envelope containing the contract. Worthy had signed the contract without reservation, yet in handling the document had been careful to avoid leaving a clear fingerprint. That detail, combined with the secret meetings and payment by cashier's check, led me to suspect that Worthy just might not be his real name.

18

Angel was packed and on my doorstep an hour before we were due to leave for the airport and three hours before our six o'clock flight to Paris. I held the door open while she carted two soft canvas suitcases into the living room. The tops sagged when she set them down. I felt the first of the two. It was half empty. The second was less than that.

"You could pack everything into one of these bags and still have room for a small building," I observed.

"You said to travel light, so I thought I'd compromise. I'm traveling light to Paris, and heavy on the way back."

"Planning a shop?"

"A major shop."

"Are you sure two bags are enough?"

"I thought I'd buy a third while I was there."

She was serious. Angel looked around the apartment for my bags. The apartment is small, and it didn't take her long not to find them.

"Where's your stuff?" she inquired.

"In the closet," I said.

Her eyes doubled in size and her voice hit a frequency usually reserved for sirens and opera singers. "You're not packed?"

"A man isn't really a man unless he can pack for a two-week trip in less than half an hour."

Angel looked at her watch. It was a new digital model that had a stopwatch and listed the time in every part of the known universe. "Prove your *cojones*," she said, and started the stopwatch.

I hung the travel bag by its hook over the open front door, and dropped in my bathroom kit, which I keep under the sink packed and ready to go. In the bedroom, I tossed slacks, a sport coat, jeans, and shirts onto the bed. I grabbed a fistful of socks from a drawer, and clutching bundled underwear against my chest, walked into the living room. A man stood at the door, his fist raised to knock. I was so startled I dropped my shorts.

"Mr. Paul Marston?" he inquired, lowering his fist. His voice was polite, and his posture nonthreatening but ready. I kicked the underwear aside and stuffed the socks into the side pocket next to the bathroom kit. The man watched my hands very carefully. He was a six-footer, about forty and a little out of shape around the middle, but not enough to slow him more than a few ticks. His russet hair was in hasty retreat toward the crown of his head. To compensate, he hung a thick walrus mustache over his upper lip like a shingle of virility. His face was the reddish brown peculiar to pale skin left too long in the sun, and around the weathered cracks of his face, freckles traced a reminder of his youth. His style was heavy on synthetics: vinyl running shoes, white Dacron shirt unbuttoned at the top, brown polyester sport coat, and tan slacks. The sport coat was a size too large, and crossed casually over the front to conceal a large bulge under the left armpit. The man either had a severe anatomical irregularity or was carrying a gun.

I nodded, and slowly pulled my hands out of the bag. He produced from his left coat pocket a slim leather wallet and flipped it open to his identification. His name was Stewart, and he was a detective with the Los Angeles Police Department, Homicide.

"So they finally upgraded Burns to a murder," I assumed, relaxing.

He slipped the ID into his pocket, trading it for a stick of gum, which he slowly unwrapped while scanning the corners of my face.

His glance settled on my eyes. He asked: "What are you talking about?" and popped the gum beneath his mustache.

That stopped me.

"Jack Burns. He died last week. In Malibu," I stammered.

His eyes rolled up and to the side; then he nodded, casually parting his sport coat with a hand placed on one hip, which revealed the butt of a regulation .38 Police Special.

"Going somewhere?" he asked, and cocked his head to watch my answer.

"Paris," I said.

"I hear it's nice this time of year. A little vacation, maybe?"

"Maybe."

Stewart took a quick step back and to the side, looking over my shoulder. I half turned. It was Angel.

"You're losing time," she said, joining me in the doorway. When her eyes hit the bulge in Stewart's coat, she tensed and asked: "What's up?"

I looked at Stewart. He was trying to keep his eyes on Angel and me, and the room behind us. All this while chewing gum. I was impressed.

"Anybody else in the apartment?" he asked.

"A few roaches. The last time I checked, they were unarmed."

He didn't laugh. Neither did Angel. It was a tough audience, and I sensed that it was about to get tougher. The gum in Stewart's mouth was being worked over pretty good. The man was tense.

"Last night. Where were you?" he asked.

"Here," I said.

"All night?"

"No, not all night."

"Where else were you?"

"The West Beach Cafe, Cafe Fifties, and in my car."

"Were you with anybody?"

"Sure, but before I go into details, I'd like to know what kind of a charge I'm looking at."

A row of yellow-stained teeth flashed beneath his mustache, and his head wagged back and forth, as though I had it all wrong. "No charge at all, sir. But I was hoping you might be able to tell me if you've ever seen this woman."

He dipped into his pocket again, and flashed a palm-sized

photograph, in black and white, of a busty blonde leaning against a tree and smiling for the camera.

"Oh shit," I said.

Stewart folded the photograph into his coat pocket and, with a brief lead of his eyes toward Angel, said: "If you want to talk about this in private, it's okay by me," thinking that the woman and I and been engaged in the type of activity I'd prefer to keep secret.

"Her name is Mona, and she's an actress and part-time hooker with a few steady clients. She dropped by my apartment just before midnight Saturday. I saw her again last night at the West Beach Cafe."

Stewart thought it through for a moment, the gum cracking between his teeth while his eyes switched from me to Angel and back again. My forthright explanation threw him, and he had expected some kind of a jealous reaction from Angel. He tried to make the connection more explicit. "Saturday night. I assume it was a professional visit. Whose profession. Yours, or hers?"

"If you're moonlighting for the VD clinic, you don't have to worry about me. I'm clean," I said.

The gum showed pink between his front teeth when he gave me a wise-guy smile. "Glad to hear it. Mind telling me the purpose of Ms. Demonay's visit?" he asked, pulling a small brown notebook from his back pocket.

I told him about Jack Burns, and how I'd met Mona. He asked what we talked about on Saturday and Sunday nights. I gave him about ten percent of it. He made a few notes, nodding and chewing vigorously until I mentioned that I had last seen Mona about two in the morning. Then the gum froze in his mouth and he pointed the tip of the pen toward Angel, asking: "And you were with Mr. Marston until when?"

"Three in the morning, and what is this all about? Because we're going to miss our flight if this takes much longer," Angel demanded in her usual direct manner.

Stewart smiled and shrugged. I had the feeling that Stewart was going to lie. Perhaps not lie. Intentionally mislead. For a forty-year-old homicide cop, innocence is a tough act. "We were just checking up on Ms. Demonay's alibi for that night. Doesn't concern you, though Mr. Marston here may be asked to swear in court that he was with her."

I said that would be fine. He asked when our flight was due to leave as though that was of only casual interest, and thanked me for the cooperation. When he walked away, I didn't think that was the last I'd see of him.

We checked our bags at the curb of the international terminal on schedule. I had moved fast, disturbed by the implication that Mona had involved herself in a murder, and not wanting to get trapped in the spiraling web of a homicide investigation. We crossed the terminal to the airline check-in desk, briefly waiting in line until our turn came and the attendant signaled with a brisk: "Next, please."

When the attendant asked for our tickets, Angel explained that our order had been phoned in that morning. The attendant stood eye-level to my six foot one, and carried the height with a thin elegance. Her skin was paper-white, and she wore her black hair clipped straight across the back in the eighties version of the bob. She asked our names, perching her long fingers on the rim of a small box of alphabetized tickets on the counter. Her fingertips jerked when Angel listed my name, and I thought it was just nerves until I caught the sly upward direction of her glance and saw something like fear in her eyes. She rifled through the box, cleared her throat, and said: "I can't seem to find them."

Angel mentioned the name of the travel agency that had ordered the tickets, and the attendant checked again. "There's no reason to worry," she advised, her face flushing, "but they don't seem to be here. If you'll wait for just one moment, I'll check the office file." The attendant was all smiles and reassuring nods as she backed into the door behind the desk.

We waited.

"What a hassle," Angel remarked, leaning against the counter.

The people waiting behind us selected another line. Time lagged behind the speed of my thoughts as I tried to figure why the delay.

"What do you want to do first thing we get to Paris?" Angel asked, idly passing time.

"Assuming we get to Paris," I said.

Angel squinted in a what-the-hell-are-you-talking-about look, but followed the direction of my eyes and understood when she saw Detective Stewart, flanked by two black-uniformed LAPD officers, moving with brisk, confident strides across the terminal. No guns were drawn, but the two uniformed officers walked with their hands on unstrapped gun butts, and their eyes nervously flicked from the position of my hands to the nearest bystanders, anticipating a hostage situation. Stewart's jaw pumped a wad of gum with each step, and his eyes focused on my belly with the intensity of a middle linebacker plugging the gap on a draw play. The jaw clenched with his final step, and through it he announced, loud and authoritative: "Paul Marston, you're under arrest. Please put your hands on your head, and turn to face the counter."

All activity in the terminal stilled for the absurd drama.

I was stupefied and didn't react immediately. One of the officers bumped my elbow and turned me brusquely around while the second stepped in front of Angel, motioning her to step back. She asked what was going on and was told to keep her hands to her side and her mouth shut. I reluctantly clasped my hands behind my head while the uniform took the usual liberties with my body allowed by law. The attendant slipped out of the back office to watch. Her face was suffused with the pride of her role in bringing a miscreant to justice. I wanted to tell her it was a mistake and that I was really a nice guy, but I didn't think it appropriate and she wouldn't have believed me anyway. The uniform pulled my right hand down from the back of my head, and wrapped the wrist in steel.

"What's the charge?" I asked, glancing over my shoulder at Stewart, who had just read me my rights.

"We're picking you up on a traffic warrant," he said.

The uniform pulled my left hand down and cuffed it to my right.

"You're kidding," I said.

"You didn't pay a parking ticket. It went to warrant this morning," he explained, allowing himself a complacent smile as he grabbed my elbow.

His cleverness and smug satisfaction galled me. I didn't like being arrested, and I'm not above grandstanding if the circumstances call for it.

"Are we living in a police state?" I exclaimed, my voice booming through the suddenly silent terminal. "There are murderers out on the street, and you're arresting me for a parking ticket?"

The outburst prompted hushed murmurs through the terminal. Stewart's face flushed, and he gave me a sharp tug, prodding me toward the exit. "I told you the charge. You know damn well what this is really about. Now shut up," he ordered.

Stewart set a brisk pace, holding my elbow while one of the uniformed officers took a position on my opposite side. Angel darted ahead, maintaining a body-length's distance from the second officer, who ran interference for the two arresting officers.

"What about Paris?" she called, back-pedaling.

"I'll meet you there. Call my lawyer and tell him I've been arrested on a traffic warrant," I instructed.

The officer running interference told her to stay back in a tone of voice that would brook no disagreement, and took a threatening step in her direction. Angel stepped aside. Stewart guided me out of the terminal to the open door of a squad car.

"I'm not going without you," Angel called out from behind, screened by one of the officers.

"Sure you are. Contact Henri Grall and I'll call you the first chance I get," I answered, my last words clipped as Detective Stewart's hand cupped the back of my head and pushed me into the backseat. He slid in beside me and slammed the door while a waiting officer cranked the engine. I craned my neck to look out the back window.

Angel raised her hand. Her eyes were deep with worry, and I held them for a moment before I smiled and mouthed the word "Go." She shook her head, and I mouthed the word again. The squad car popped into drive, and her face receded into memory.

19

The squad car cut inside the airport loop and pulled around a flat yellow building. The view out the window flitted along a row of service garages, then settled onto a sign that read: No Parking—Police Vehicles Only. The police station behind the sign was so small and well hidden among the airport services that I despaired of my lawyer's being able to find it. Stewart escorted me past the front desk to a holding room. He freed my right wrist, and asked me to sit on a long wooden bench. When I sat down, he cuffed me to the bench.

I waited.

Stewart returned an hour later, unlatched the handcuffs, and led me to a cramped room with a table, four chairs, and a two-way mirror on the wall across from the door. Stewart sat in one of the chairs with his back to the two-way mirror, and slapped a manila envelope onto the table. I sat across from him and folded my hands in front of me. He told me I had the right to have a lawyer present, and I replied that I thought I could confess my felonious parking habits without one.

"We can get around to that later," Stewart said. He pulled out a jumbo pack of Wrigley's sugarless, shook out a stick, and offered me one. When I declined, he shrugged and carefully unwrapped a stick, folding it in half before popping it into his mouth. "What I want to talk about first is your relationship to Mona Demonay."

"I don't have much to add to what I told you this afternoon," I replied.

"So my memory isn't so good. Tell me again, and I'll take better notes this time."

When being interviewed by the police, I've always found it a good idea to stick as close to the truth as possible, and to tell the same story the same way every time I'm asked to tell it. If I remember too many details as the interrogation wears on, the interrogator will suspect either that I'm holding back or that my memory improves with questioning. Either suspicion makes for a long night. The interrogator's job is to break my story if he can. My job is to hold fast to my version of events. It becomes a game with stakes that can change a life around.

I had little idea regarding what Stewart wanted from me, so I told the truth in as much detail as client confidentiality allowed. I didn't tell him who my client was, or what he had hired me to investigate, except that it regarded the estate of Jack Burns. I described Mona's relationship to Jack Burns, and how I met her. Her offer to sell me the Polaroids and the pornographic film bordered on client confidentiality, and I decided to omit it. My narrative concluded on the confrontation with Gilbert Stern, although I did not mention that I had either slugged the man or slammed his foot in the car door.

Stewart listened patiently to my story, then asked me to tell it again. On the second go-around, he changed tactics. He aggressively probed for trivial details in an attempt to rattle me. I remained calm. He challenged me on points of fact, such as names, dates, and times. He twice claimed that my recollection of a specific detail had changed since my first telling, when it had in fact been consistent. Angry that I wouldn't go beyond a general description of my conversations with Mona, Stewart pulled the gum from his mouth and pointed the wad at me with a harsh and threatening "So what you're telling me is that after three in the morning, you have no one who can testify to where you were."

"At three in the morning, everyone sleeping alone doesn't have an alibi. Chastity may not be the virtue it once was, but last I heard it wasn't a crime," I countered, beginning to lose my patience.

Stewart wadded the gum into a ball between his forefinger and thumb, and stuck it to the ashtray in the center of the table. His expression was passionless as he dug into the manila envelope and flipped a photograph onto the table. It was a copy of one of the Polaroids Mona had revealed the night before. The photograph was a close-up of Dusty giving head. The only visible presence of her masculine partner was his erection. I felt my face being scrutinized for a reaction as my eyes skipped over the photograph. Stewart tossed a second photographic copy of a Polaroid onto the table next to the first. It was the anatomical shot of the coupling of sex parts, as anonymous and erotic as plumbing.

"Mona offered to sell me these photographs last night," I explained, deciding then to tell him why Mona had been anxious to meet me Sunday night. I didn't get the chance.

Stewart palmed a third photograph and slapped it onto the table. The slap drew my eyes to his hand, which pulled away to reveal the shot Mona had taken of me sitting on the stairs. "It must have made you very angry," he said.

"Not at all," I answered, but he coolly rolled over my sentence with another of his own.

"It made you so angry that when you met with her at four in the morning to make the payoff, you killed her instead. You pulled out a knife."

"Wait a minute," I objected, my mind beginning to reel with the implications of his statement, and the suddenly revealed intent of the interrogation. But Stewart didn't wait.

"You pulled out a knife, and you were so angry, you stabbed her, then you stabbed her again. You were so angry you stabbed her fourteen times," Stewart pressed, his fingers searching the manila envelope as he talked. He pulled out a glossy eight-by-ten color photograph and dangled it in front of my face. Mona lay in an alley, swamped in blood. Her black jumpsuit was sliced to tatters, and her head flopped loosely to the side. Even at the distance at which the photograph had been taken, the frayed tendons of her neck evidenced where a knife had cut her throat to the spine. My image of Mona decompressed in an instant from that of a vital woman at war with her place in society to a torn sack of flesh violently ripped from the world. I wanted to retch.

"You were so angry, you nearly cut her damn head off," Stewart said in a quiet but venomous voice, and rattled the photograph in front of my face.

I turned away, stupefied by the simultaneous assault of multiple emotions. Grief, rage, and fear clawed against orderly consciousness. The tumult stunned all thoughts from my mind, and my head began to throb under an intensifying roar. Through the sudden blank roaring like a spear came the memory of her last look at me as she backed away from a kiss. The look went straight through me and I gasped.

"Don't want to admire your own work?" Stewart chided.

The gasp brought air deep into my lungs. I remembered to breathe. Breath restored order. Breath was good. I looked at the photograph again, and rage conquered grief and fear. "I liked this woman. She wasn't a close friend and she wasn't an angel but I liked her and I want you to remove that photograph from my face. If you don't, the interview ends here with a call to my lawyer."

"Relax, have a stick of gum, or maybe I can get you a cup of coffee?" Stewart offered in abrupt conciliation. He lowered the photograph, but positioned it face up on the table. The photograph was his wedge. It had gotten a reaction, and he likely thought its presence would pry the composure from my sense of logic. Discomfited by guilt, I would begin to lose track of my story, panic, and let slip a damaging remark. Then, or so he thought, he would have me. Stewart fished out the jumbo pack of Wrigley's and pointed a stick in my direction.

I shook my head, and waited for him to come to me.

"I talked to the bartender this morning," he said, chomping rapidly to work the new stick into a wad. "Duke. Works at the West Beach Cafe. Doesn't look like a Harvard graduate, but would you believe the guy is worth almost half a million? Tends bar because he likes the work, and invests on the side. Smart guy." Stewart folded his hands behind his head, and leaned back in his chair, as though we were talking about investments, or unusual success stories, or anything but murder. "He says he saw Ms. Demonay flashing the pictures at the bar, then he overheard the two of you arguing about money. At one point you raised your voice and accused Ms. Demonay of extortion. He said it was none of his business, but he thought you were being reamed."

"There were a half dozen other conversations going on around the bar. Maybe we had the best act going that night, but Duke still only caught about a third of what we said at best. Do you want to spin theories or hear the rest of the conversation?"

"I wasn't aware that you were willing to talk about your conversation with Ms. Demonay."

"The man in the photographs is Jack Burns. On my first night as his bodyguard, Mona snapped some candids of Burns and another woman."

Stewart brought his chair sharply up and asked the name of the other woman.

"Dusty something."

"You don't know her last name," Stewart said, and it sounded like an accusation.

"Why should I know her last name? I was just the bodyguard and she didn't give me her business card. She comes from Oklahoma is all I know."

Stewart wrote the name on a pad and, when I couldn't produce an address or number for her, said: "A hooker without a last name or a way to contact her. That's not going to help you."

"Mona also showed me photographs that featured Jack Burns's face," I added.

"That's a convenient defense, but meaningless. These were the only photographs found in her purse."

"Then whoever killed her wanted the incriminating photographs of Jack Burns," I speculated.

"So you say," Stewart replied, not buying it, and asked: "Anything else?"

"Mona was attempting to find a way to blackmail Jack Burns, but he died before she could get the angle on him. She brought the package to me, which included the Polaroids and a copy of a pornographic movie Burns had appeared in twenty years ago. When Burns died she lost her buyer, and she was hoping I knew someone who would be interested.''

Stewart pulled the gum from his mouth and rolled it between his thumb and forefinger, contemplating the wad like a truth talisman. His mustache jutted out and, smacking his lips, he said: ''That is one hell of smooth story, but what the hell, you're one hell of a smooth guy, aren't you? The problem is, I don't believe it. Maybe if you woulda told it to me this afternoon, or when we first sat down, I'd feel different about it.''

''Then why aren't you arresting me for murder, if you think you have a case?''

His smile was smugly confident as he thumbed the spent gum into the ashtray. ''Now there's a bright idea. Thanks for mentioning it, because I never would have thought of it myself.''

''Somebody has to do your thinking for you, considering how little of it you do for yourself,'' I said, angered by his arrogance. ''You find sex photographs in a dead woman's purse, talk to a bartender, and jump to the conclusion that she was trying to blackmail me. You pop up on my doorstep to talk about it and discover I'm getting ready to flee the country. You don't take the time to check out my story and you don't even look very closely at the photographs. The woman's face is clear enough but the shots are so tight that the man could be anybody. But there is another photograph in the woman's purse, and it just happens to be me. You assume that because my photograph is in her purse that I'm the one in the sex shots.

''You don't stop to ask yourself how I could be blackmailed by sex shots that don't feature my face or any other recognizable part of my body. I know you haven't had much time to put it together, but your work is sloppy and I guess you must have relatives on the force because you have the reasoning capability of pig iron and couldn't have made detective on ability alone.''

The color rose in Stewart's face as he listened to my outburst, but he didn't say anything until I had finished and he limited his response to a two-word euphemism for the act of procreation. Then he drove me downtown to the county jail and booked me on a traffic warrant.

20

Loathing Harry Selwurst dominated the emotional lives of perhaps a hundred men and women. Stories about Harry circulated the best parties, particularly those to which he had been pointedly not invited due to some past slight to the host. The storyteller had often never met Harry, and told the anecdote as a joke. In certain circles, these anecdotes became known as Mean Harry jokes. Those who knew Harry well seldom joked about him unless the joke was violently obscene or predicted his painful demise. Harry's closest associates regarded him with spurious contempt. His racquetball partner regularly accused him of cheating, and thought him the most immoral man he had ever met. His four ex-wives foamed invective and lunged for high-blood-pressure medication at the drop of his name. His mistress admitted she was in it for the money. His current wife would have left him long ago, had he not tricked her into signing a prenuptial agreement which entitles her to nothing when she divorces him, which she certainly will do, because having nothing without Harry is eminently preferable to having everything with Harry.

Harry Selwurst's unlikability was not the result of a single characteristic or flaw. He was a complex matrix of unenlightened self-interests, annoying habits, and loathsome character traits, untempered by charm. Harry cultivated his detestableness with a misanthropy as devastating as a neutron bomb. Like the neutron bomb, he respected property without reservation, and hated people equally and without prejudice. Harry had his shortcomings, but he was a lawyer, and whoever said you want your lawyer to be a nice guy?

The peculiar aspect of his posting my bail was that Harry Selwurst was not my lawyer. I hadn't called him. I hadn't called anybody. Two hours after Stewart closed the door to the holding cell behind me at L.A. County Jail, a guard opened it again, led me to a grim-faced officer who shoved an envelope containing my personal effects beneath a wire cage and released me into a long fluorescent corridor, at the end of which waited Harry's cheerfully vicious face.

"How does it feel to be a free man?" he beamed, as though to a long-suffering victim of the criminal justice system.

"You're not my lawyer," I said.

"I am now," he announced, then leaned forward in lawyerly confidence and centered his lips an inch from my ear, whispering: "You dumb dickhead, what do you care if I'm your lawyer or not? I filed the papers and posted your bail, so keep your mouth shut and let's get out of here before they change the charge to murder one."

Harry grasped my elbow and smiled grandly for the audience of panderers, prostitutes, thieves, and other diverse manner of felons. His voice boomed in measured theatricality as he whisked me through the central lobby. "It's an outrage. You work your butt off for the system and try to get away from it all, take a little vacation, but does the system let you do it? Hell no! There are murderers on the street, hoodlums who would cut you and watch you die as easy as asking you the time of day, and the system arrests you for not paying a traffic ticket. It's an outrage, and if there is any justice under God's heaven, we'll sue for false arrest!"

The performance ceased when Harry clipped through the double doors at the building entrance, and he deflated like an actor at the sound of "Cut." He released my elbow and slowed his stride, following the front walkway to the parking lot. Three paces and a deep breath outside the building, his voice turned conspiratorial and he said: "You're in a hell of a lot of trouble, but as of tonight they don't have anything except the traffic warrant. Detective Stewart wanted to hold you without charge but the judge wouldn't buy it. Your bail was two hundred and fifty dollars, forfeited upon release, which I paid, so the traffic warrant is now cleared. You owe me two hundred and fifty for the bail, and the rest is negotiable.''

''What do you mean, negotiable?''

''We'll talk about it in the car,'' he said, pointing out a black Cadillac Seville bearing the license plate ISUE4U.

I had ten dollars in my wallet, not counting the two thousand dollars in cash and traveler's checks in Angel's purse, now winging toward Paris. I was east of downtown Los Angeles, thirty miles and a forty-dollar cab fare from my front door. Harry was owed for getting me out, and I'd owe him again for taking me home. It wasn't wise to be in Harry Selwurst's debt.

''How did Angel get your number?'' I asked, pulling up at the passenger door.

His key hit the lock and popped open both doors. I slid into the Seville. The engine started with a prompt purr, and Harry backed out of the slot. I waited until he had turned out of the lot and onto the surface streets before I repeated the question.

''Angel who?'' he queried.

''Cantini,'' I answered, and when he blanked on that, I clarified: ''The woman who called you.''

''She didn't call me.''

''Then what are you doing here?''

''Getting you out of jail, you dumb dickhead,'' he repeated. Harry drove fast and devious, slicing across two wrong lanes at Hill to make a right onto Sunset. The maneuver cut off a truck. The trucker hit us with a blast of his horn, and Harry was quick to respond with a jab of his middle finger. I reached for my seat belt. A red light stopped him at Grand, and I took advantage of the temporary lull.

''Call me an ungrateful bastard, but I want to know how you knew I was in jail, and why you thought it worth the effort to drive down personally to bail me out.''

''I knew you were in jail because I have incredible psychic powers,'' he said without emphasis. His eyes remained fixed on the traffic light. ''Like I knew you worked a couple of days for Jack

Burns before the dumb fuck killed himself. Like I know we are going to find a way to do beautiful business together.''

"How did you know I worked for Jack Burns?"

"Like I said, I'm psychic."

"I'm not, so why don't you just answer the question?"

The light blinked green and Harry gunned the Caddy onto the freeway on-ramp. He weaved into the fast lane and set the cruise control to seventy. Then he turned a smile on me. He didn't look mean. His blond hair was moussed back in an executive cut. His skin was pale, and his eyes a kindly blue. His sensitive, full mouth framed a voice well trained in the dramatic arts of the courtroom, capable of the faint, emotional tremor in moments of sorrow, and the thunderclap when aroused in righteous anger. He was in his late thirties, and his face had the well-fed look of a man who has made it in life and doesn't want any more than to hold on to what he has. Jurors never guessed he made his living carving the livers out of everyone who crossed his path.

"To answer your question, and I always try to answer every question asked of me truthfully, which is why I'm not the most well-liked man in town, I could care less whether you live or die on a personal level." He turned his smile up a notch and chuckled. "But your work is interesting, and you've got a friend. Your friend has money, and he has other friends with money, and friends with money are friends with power."

"First you're psychic. Now I have powerful but unknown friends. We could do this conversation in thirty seconds if you quit the mystery act and told me who sent you."

Harry didn't want to do the conversation in thirty seconds. He leaned forward and plugged in a cassette tape. Mick Jagger's voice strutted and swaggered through the Caddy compartment. Harry beamed, cherubic with his pink lips and blond curls, and said: "Life is much more interesting when there is a sense of mystery."

I tired of the game and guessed: "Frank Worthy, right?"

"If you know the answer, why ask the question?"

"I wanted to let you give something for free for once in your life."

"You may be a charity case, Marston, but you're not tax-deductible," Harry pronounced. He turned up the volume, his head bobbing as Jagger crooned that you can't always get what you want. "Is Frank still pretending he's from Texas?"

"Yes," I snapped, then wondered why Harry had needed to ask that question, and what it implied about Frank Worthy.

"Frank Worthy is such a forthright name. A name that inspires confidence. It's so good it almost makes one think that maybe it's too good."

It was riddle time again. "What are you talking about?" I demanded, annoyed.

"I would never consider mentioning that Frank Worthy might not be above changing his name to fit the circumstances."

"If Frank Worthy isn't his real name, what is?"

Harry just smiled at the question, demonstrating that although he knew the answer, he would not give it cheaply. His counter revealed a game I had not known we were playing: "How's your investigation into Jack Burns going?"

"That's confidential," I replied, figuring that if he worked for Worthy, it would be of little use to deny the investigation.

"I admire your sense of ethics. Just remember that those with ethics are the ones living at the bottom of the hill, staring straight up the ass of those at the top."

"I don't have any complaints."

"And you also don't know what I know about Jack Burns and Frank Worthy," he suggested, heavy on the innuendo.

This was the point in his scenario when I was supposed to ask all trembly with anticipation what he knew. I thought at that time that Paris would provide the answer to Jack Burns's mythical millions, so instead I said: "If you want to cut a separate deal, I'm not interested."

"We can do some beautiful business, you and I," he repeated.

"The only business we can do is the business of saying good-bye."

Harry was not easily denied or insulted. Without bitterness or irony he speculated: "You think I'm an asshole, don't you?"

"Yes."

"You know why I'm an asshole?"

"Natural talent?"

"No. Because I'm the best. I'm so good, I can be the biggest asshole in the world, and still win all my cases, because nobody is even close to as good as me."

Harry Selwurst popped the Caddy out of cruise control and whipped across four lanes of traffic to catch the Lincoln off-ramp. The final chord crashed down on Mick Jagger, and the tape snickered into rewind. At the top of the ramp, waiting for the light to change, Harry slid his arm over the back of the passenger seat and, with a twinkling smile of masculine complicity, asked: "So, did you fuck her?"

I didn't answer. He mistook my silence for embarrassment. His hand dropped to my shoulder and gave it a friendly squeeze. The light changed, and he followed the line of traffic turning right onto Lincoln.

"The guy who killed Miss Demonay made a deposit in her back door before he cut her throat. I don't have to explain what I mean by that, do I? They'll be able to type his blood from the semen. If you fucked her, I need to know what entrance you used, and your blood type. Even if you did, they still won't be able to prove anything, because she was a whore, right? Could have been anybody."

So it wasn't the most rational act. I didn't like getting arrested and I didn't like going to jail, and I didn't like Harry Selwurst. I didn't owe Mona Demonay anything, but I had liked her. The brutal manner of her death disturbed me. I leaned over the Caddy's center console, wrapped my palm around the column shift, and threw the transmission into reverse. The gears screamed with the stripping of metal, and the wheels locked. The Caddy swerved across two lanes of oncoming traffic and jumped the curb on the opposite side.

Harry stopped breathing. His hands welded to the steering wheel, and his jaw clenched tight enough to crack teeth.

"Thanks for the ride. I'll walk from here," I said, and stepped out of the Caddy.

I didn't hear his scream until I had covered half a block. The Caddy door opened, and the scream began as an inarticulate curse.

He was threatening to sue as I rounded the corner, but by then his voice was small and insignificant, and soon I could not hear him at all.

A jogger had found what remained of Mona Demonay in an alley behind a grocery store at Lincoln and Colorado streets in Santa Monica. Her body hadn't disturbed him at first. In the heavy blue predawn light the body blended into shadow. Drunks, derelicts, and the deranged sprawl ragged and dirty-faced in every alley close to the beach. A body near a dumpster is no more remarkable here than a heap of blankets, an old newspaper, a sack of rotting matter aimed at the trash bin and missed. The mute forms are ugly, but not unusual, and not dangerous, so his eye had passed over her body, and he might not have noticed had it not been for the dog. It was a small mutt, and it had chased him on previous mornings, nipping at his heels until he reached for a stone to frighten it away. The dog crouched near the head of the body, lapping at something dark and glistening on the asphalt. The jogger pulled up a dozen yards short of the dog, and noticed that the body wasn't in street derelict rags, and wasn't curled in the typical attitude of sleep. The body was positioned face up, arms twisted behind the back, legs awkwardly spread. The clothing was torn away in black tatters, exposing young and feminine flesh. The jogger faltered, knowing then that he had stumbled across something that would lend him the power of the storyteller whenever the subject of death arose, but would exact the price of nightmare.

The jogger had an impulse to resume his pace, shifting his head to the side in denial of what he had seen, but curiosity proved stronger, and he crept closer. The dog growled. The dark and glistening pool was blood, and the jogger had disturbed the dog's feast. It was a primeval signal, carrion feasting upon human flesh, and it unleashed adrenaline. The jogger bellowed like a beast, and lunged at the dog. The dog dodged aside, and trotted out of range.

It sat on the asphalt, tongue lolled out, waiting. The jogger looked down at the body, the slash of flesh at the throat, the young face, and fought against his own vomit. He knew that when he left the body to call the police, the dog would return to its claim. He flung a stone, but the stone skipped a foot wide, and the dog merely retreated another few yards to wait. The enraged jogger bellowed again, and flew a five-minute-mile at the dog's tail before the dog finally gave up and ran without being pursued. Then the jogger stopped at a phone booth, and made the call.

I stood in the alley, straining to see in the darkness, and tried to make the few bare facts seem real by context. I didn't expect to find something the police had missed. The yellow plastic police line, rolled and stuffed in the dumpster, testified to their presence. There were no chalk marks or blood. The bagboys had washed the asphalt clean with a hose. I wasn't hoping to find anything except a little bit of understanding that I could take home with me. Her body had been dumped six blocks from my apartment. I walked them.

A black-and-white and two unmarked squad cars were parked at the curb across from my apartment building. My second-floor apartment door was open, and a uniformed cop stood in the frame, shadowed by the light and casting a long shadow down the stairs. I climbed toward the shadow, the jerk and twitch of muscle weighted by fatigue and despair. The shadow slipped up the steps as the cop bent back inside the door frame and said something to the room. Detective Stewart strolled out onto the walkway, pulled a wad of gum from his mouth, and stuck it under the railing.

"How was Paris?" he cracked, and handed me the search warrant.

I didn't bother to read it. A short bald man carried a plastic trash bag out my front door, nodded to Stewart, and brushed past me on the stairs. I wanted to sit down, and asked if I had the right to enter my own apartment.

"Hang loose for a few minutes, and we'll be outta here," Stewart advised.

I sat on the top step and allowed my head to fall forward onto crossed arms. A gum wrapper floated to the step beside me, and I read the Wrigley's sugarless label before a gust of wind blew it into the yard below.

"If we get any kind of match on blood or fiber, it's not going to look good for you," Stewart speculated, with a portentous touch.

I shrugged. I couldn't tell him anything that I hadn't already said.

Another plainclothesman walked from my apartment, lugging a black case. He didn't give Stewart any kind of a look other than one of wanting to get home. Stewart bowed at the waist with a facetious sweep of his arm toward my apartment door and announced, "It's all yours," then clipped past my shoulder and followed the black case down the stairs.

What's left of it, I thought.

My apartment smelled of cigarettes and strange bodies. The contents of drawers and cabinets had been emptied into a heap in the center of the living room floor. A patch was missing from the rug. White fingerprint dust clung to every slick surface. I knelt to the floor and gathered the detritus of my life. A small square had been snipped from each of my shirts, trousers, and coats. They would compare the fibers from the rug and my clothing with fibers mingled among Mona's clothing and embedded in her flesh. They would not be able to find a match. My story would stand, and I would not be arrested. My life would not be changed.

I stood and surveyed all of the things that I owned, the paper, metal, glass, and cloth which represented thirty-five years of a not particularly notable life. Each object associated with a memory of some place or time, and all now violated. I no longer owned them. They were witnesses of my guilt or innocence, giving evidence in the court of the police laboratory. I did not own anything except myself, and one day, I wouldn't own that.

I found a hotel room and called it a night.

21

I didn't know what to expect when I flew into Paris for the first time. I had vague impressions of Paris as an ancient city of romance and mystery. I had forgotten that airports and freeways had not been invented in the sixteenth century. The outskirts of Paris at rush hour looked like East Los Angeles on a bad day: a congestion of concrete, cars, and bad twentieth-century architecture. That I had traveled one-third of the world's circumference to land behind the belching tailpipe of a Mercedes truck did not put me in good humor. Collapsed in the backseat of a Peugeot taxi next to Angel, I railed: "So this is Paris? Whoever called Paris the City of Love must have had a thing for traffic jams."

Angel told me to shut up and asked for an account of my arrest.

The narrative distracted me from the traffic, and as I finished it the taxi had pulled off the freeway and into the eighteenth district of Paris, which did not look like East Los Angeles at all. A different quality of time loomed from the ancient buildings, as though the present encompassed several centuries within a single moment. To a native of the minimall, automobile, and neon culture of Los Angeles, where history is best represented by the wrecking ball, the vibrant blending of present and past evoked a sense of wonder. Later, as we traversed the city, I would come to regard the plan of Paris as a living archaeological dig; a cross section of time radiating from an ancient core at the Ile de la Cité to the modern outskirts.

Angel had orchestrated a meeting with our Paris contact, Henri Grall, at a working-class café in Montmarte. The café was nearly empty, and the sidewalk tables had been pulled in for the evening. I had noticed the weird emanations of blinking blue lights in the overhead nineteenth-century apartment windows as I stepped out of the cab, and guessed that most of the neighborhood was engaged in what modern people find more fascinating than sitting in cafés: watching television. The few remnants of the old guard, to whom coffee, cigarettes, and conversation were still primary to life, eyed us warily as we entered. There are more tourists than Parisians in Paris at some times of the year, and our presence in the café was an encroachment. We were quickly ignored.

The proprietress was glad enough to have us sit at one of the several empty tables. She didn't smile, and neither extended us welcome nor discouragement, but served us mineral water when we ordered it, and did not pretend to misunderstand Angel's accent.

Henri Grall strolled into the café at half past six. The proprietress set out a bottle of red wine and a glass as he approached the bar. He said something to her. She half smiled, adding two extra glasses. Henri centered the bottle on our table, and we stood to greet him.

Henri had a pug's face and the elegant carriage of an aristocrat. His nose swelled with broken cartilage at the bridge and twisted west. A spidery-thin web of scars traced the corner of his mouth down to a block chin. He smiled as we stood, revealing brown-stained teeth alternating with the bright white of new bridgework. The smile was friendly but didn't quite reach the eyes, which were guarded by the surface tension of a man who would talk freely without taking you into his confidence. Angel extended her hand first. Henri took it in his gently, as though handling fragile china, and said something in French. Angel smiled, obviously flattered. He released her hand, and shook mine.

"It is a pity that you look more like Robert Taylor, and less like Kojak, now that I have met your beautiful partner," he sighed, affecting great remorse, which was then split with a grin. Henri

FALSE PROFIT • 155

clanked the empty wineglasses onto the table and topped them with red wine. We drank first to the friendship between the French and the Americans, rife with the quarrels and strange appreciations of most good friendships, and then to the camaraderie of our profession.

"What has Angel told you about our problem?" I asked, once the progression of toasts had emptied our first glasses and begun the second.

Henri shook a cigarette out of a pack of Gitanes. He wedged the smoke in the corner of his mouth and let it dangle, considering me from behind the surface of his eyes. Angel looked at the cigarette as though it was about to leap from his lips and bite her throat. Henri lit the Gitane and said seriously: "If it doesn't bother you for me to tell you this, don't be so American. We have a bottle of wine in front of us, and if we start talking work right away, the job will be done and the wine will not, no?"

The advice was not easy for a slave of the Protestant work ethic to accept, but I thought what the hell and slipped a cigarette from his pack. I lit it and asked Henri a few questions about his past. The smoke bit into my lungs with a harsh pleasure. It had been a year since I had last smoked a cigarette, and Angel regarded me with shock until she too thought what the hell and lit one for herself.

Questioning people is one of the things I do best, and Henri was happy to talk about himself. His father had figured prominently in the post–World War II black-market trade. Henri had initially followed his father's footsteps, beginning as a teenage burglar, then anticipated the 1960s boom in drugs like any good entrepreneur, and advanced his career as a smuggler. When his friend and partner had been murdered by rivals, Henri had methodically tracked down the killers. With the realization that revenge killing was a philosophical hair plucked from the same head as murder, Henri had opted to set up the killers instead with a one-hundred-fifty-thousand-franc cache of heroin and a well-timed call to the police. He had enjoyed the thrill of hunting them down, and as he had had the singular luck of having never been arrested, enrolled in the police academy at age twenty-five. That didn't last, and by thirty he had found the middle ground between crime and law enforcement as a private detective.

Henri's story captivated me, and when the second bottle of wine appeared on our table, I had forgotten about work. I floated in a jet-lagged and tipsy euphoria. Henri uncorked the bottle, poured another round, and lit his third Gitane.

"If this woman, this Kathy Maddox woman, has been to Paris before, it is not as easy to find her as it was the last one, Francis Gamine," Henri mused through a haze of smoke. "She could be almost anywhere. If it is her first time, then it is easier, because she stays at places tourists usually stay."

I shrugged. I shrugged because I had jet lag abetted by three glasses of wine, and great chasms stretched where there should have been thoughts. I remembered why I always worked first and drank second, but after that it was blank. I signaled the proprietress and asked for coffee. In Spanish. She looked at me, startled, then hid the half smile the French reserve for complete idiots. I then recalled why Kathy Maddox should suddenly be important.

"You are not a student of language," Henri observed, grinning.

"I'm afraid not. I majored in head-breaking and small weapons fire in college. Didn't have much time for languages," I said.

"Me too," Henri agreed, and we had an understanding.

"We have to assume that Kathy Maddox has been to Paris before, or is with someone who knows the city," Angel said.

"Or otherwise why would she have come to Paris at all?" I speculated, completing Angel's thought.

"Then it will be very hard, but it gives us a little hope, that she is a devotee of Sappho."

Henri raised his eyebrows, either avoiding the curling smoke from his Gitane or seeking agreement. I looked at Angel, who returned the same look to me.

"Sappho?" I asked.

He shrugged his shoulders, and gestured broadly with his hands, expounding: "Sappho was one of the greatest poets of ancient Greece, but it is not her poetry that is remembered today. She was from the island of Lesbos, also remembered for the wrong reasons. A great poet, yes, and also a great lover of other women."

The proprietress set a demitasse of black liquid on the table. I wafted the cup under my nose and sipped. It was strong and a little gritty, and the wires in my brain began to snap with current.

"So Ms. Maddox will be easier to find because she is a devotee of Sappho, or in English, a dyke," I clarified.

Angel leaned across the table and stared earnestly. "You don't have to use that word. Henri was making the point that sexual tastes are unimportant. Sappho was a great poet."

"Which Kathy Maddox is not, so we don't have to look in the poets' cafés, just the gay bars, right?"

"Stop being so flip," Angel warned, and the look in her eyes seared me.

I stopped. I knew I had crossed that shifting line between humor and hate, when the joke can no longer excuse the attitude. That I was afflicted with the boys' locker-room stereotype of lesbianism troubled me. I had unconsciously assimilated what would have been repugnant had I bothered to think.

"Did you bring the photograph?" Henri asked.

Angel retracted the burn of her eyes from my flesh and dug into her purse for a white envelope. She opened the flap, flipped the envelope, and several copies of the original photograph of Kathy Maddox spilled onto the table. Henri twisted his head to the side, contemplating the multiple images of the same face scattered amid the wineglasses, before selecting one and lifting it for closer inspection.

"Her face is plain, but there is still something striking about her visage, yes?" he observed. "I know the hotel clerks here, and it seems natural that I show this photograph to them. I start with the tourist hotels, and maybe I might have a little luck. The gay bars, I don't know, but I would be as the expression goes: *un poisson hors de l'eau.*"

"Translation?" I asked, turning to Angel.

"A fish out of water," Angel explained, adding: "I know of one fish at this table who could do with a bit of fresh air."

Henri didn't know what she meant by that, but I did, and to avoid the explanation, asked for a briefing on the gay bars where Kathy Maddox would most likely be found.

"There are two major clubs in Paris: the Monocle, and, appropriately enough, Sappho's. There are other what you call 'hangouts,' but I would try first the big clubs. I do not think it is very dangerous, but they are not in a very good area, and you should be careful," Henri cautioned.

"I can handle myself," Angel said, and turned to me, still angry from my previous remark. "It's this homophobia of yours that worries me. I think maybe you ought to come to the clubs with me and see for yourself."

Right or wrong, apologies are difficult. I just shrugged and said: "I'll tag along, if you'll have me."

Henri laughed, and I asked what amused him.

Henri Grall emptied the bottle of wine into his glass, and lifted it to his lips. "A personal question, if it is okay," he requested.

I was glad for the diversion. I nodded.

"You two are in love, no?"

I looked at Angel. She smiled. So did I.

" 'Love the limb-loosener, the bittersweet torment,' " Henri quoted, and quaffed the last of the wine. "It's from Sappho. She was famous in her time for poems of love. Not lesbian poetry. Poems of love. It does not matter who you are, or who you love. Love is, after all, love."

22

The Monocle was smoke and sweating women, flashing lights and loud music. Angel pressed through the crowd, working her way to the bar. I tethered to her like a safety line, smiling and nodding my innocuous best at every face pressed against me in the crush. The bar was standing room only. I resisted my chauvinist tendencies and let Angel order the beer, turning my back to the bar to admire the crowd, which struck me as no different from the mix at any nightclub, except of course for the absence of men. Women elegant in evening gowns mingled with jeans-clad students, conservatives in skirts and plain white blouses, and avant-garde types in ever-fashionable black, who sported raspberry-, grape-, or rainbow-colored hair. A jackboot-and-leather contingent roamed through the crowd in numbers no greater than that of any dance club in a major metropolis. I could discern no set pattern to the pairings. Women danced with lookalike partners, and opposites in dress and attitude. Some danced as couples, others in amorphous, interchanging groups. It all seemed strange yet ordinary, like the unexpected juxtaposition of familiar objects—a pear, say, with a pair of scissors—which causes the eye to reconsider each.

That I did not exist within this world was troubling. No one noticed me. I had expected hostility. The women had not come to be angry with men. They were at the Monocle to parade their sexuality, dance it, celebrate it, and possibly, if the circumstances worked out, get laid. I was outside the circle of that shared sexual celebration, and as dancers in a circle face inward, aware of nothing but the dance and the unity of the circle, I was invisible. Gazes passed through my face as though through air.

Angel handed the photograph of Kathy Maddox to a stout bartender with ash-blond hair piled on top of her head. The bartender examined the photograph by penlight next to the cash register, as Angel shouted across the bar a story about looking for an American friend. The bartender sent it back with a shrug. The woman next to Angel asked for the photograph, glanced at it, then used the interchange as an opportunity to engage her in more intimate conversation. Angel smiled politely, slipped the photograph from the woman's fingers, and moved to the next woman at the bar. She worked quickly and easily, showing the photograph, deflecting passes, laughing, and moving on.

I watched a woman in white balloon pants and shoulder-padded blouse on the edge of the dance floor. Her skin was Mediterranean olive, and her black hair lustrous. She smoked a cigarette on a long silver holder with one hand, and in the other dangled a leash. At the end of the leash sat an obedient poodle, white like her outfit. Women streamed to her. Each was met with a sad smile, a shrug, and a shake of the head. I wondered if she owned a different poodle for each colored outfit, or maybe just dyed the one to match.

Two women squeezed through the crowd lining the dance floor, arms around each other, and heads pressed together. They wore jeans, cowboy boots, and UCLA sweatshirts. Angel approached them with the photograph. They nodded in unison and both began to talk. Angel pressed her ear close to their lips, listened, then spoke into the ear of the taller one. They conversed, shifting to hear over the din of the music and crowd, then the three of them hugged, giggling. I didn't think I'd ever understand the principles of girl talk.

"How are you doing?" Angel asked, pressing her lips to my ear.

"Fine," I answered.

"You don't feel uncomfortable?"

"I love being totally unnecessary."

"You're not unnecessary, darling," she replied, and I felt a little better until she tagged it with "You're just superfluous." Then she said that the two sweatshirted women had just shared a beer with Kathy Maddox at Sappho's.

The Sappho's crowd had a rougher edge. Workshirts, leather bomber jackets, bright metal chains, jackboots, and similar badges of the dated macho ethic dominated by attitude if not number. Flamboyant exotics darted in bright costume through the smoky press of bodies, trailing plumes of color. Faces were red-swollen with drink. The sound system over the dance floor had been turned to the brink of pain, and the dancers moved with libidinous abandon. In the claustrophobic crush at the edge of the dance floor, I sensed a dangerous combustion of excitement and panic.

Angel shouldered through the crowd and spotted Kathy Maddox sitting alone at a corner table, obscured by the pressing crowd of dancers, drinkers, and sex-change artists. A half dozen tables crowded with leather-and-chain biker clones, pale faces aspiring to brutishness, separated Kathy from the dance floor. Angel dragged me to the bar. We talked for a moment about the approach, settled on one, and ordered beers.

The peak hours of frenzy were approaching, when the promise of sex and the consumption of alcohol mingle in a wild bacchanalia on the dance floor. We drifted toward Kathy's table, watching the dancers and pretending conversation. Angel turned smartly on her heels, and scanned the biker crowd. Her eyes fixed on Kathy in hesitant recognition, until Kathy became aware of being watched. Angel glanced away. Kathy looked up, curious. Her face hung round as a moon in the darkened corner, her native paleness flushing with color as the club's revolving lights flashed on the flat surface of her skin. The large-boned blockishness of her body, cloaked in black leather, loomed heavily beneath the face, dwarfing her tight-lipped mouth and receding chin. Eyeglasses inscribed perfect twin circles in silver and glass over her pug nose, and behind the glasses her eyes seemed small and myopic. She compensated for the tough hand nature had dealt her with a tough look. Her blond hair was cut short and spiked in the front, and fanned to the shoulders in back. The black leather jacket, blue jeans, and jackboots were studded with silver buckles, and wrapped in silver chains.

Kathy studied Angel, thinking perhaps that Angel was interested, and wondering what to do about it. Finally unsure of herself, she turned back to her beer. The tough look didn't quite work. Behind the eyeglasses, her eyes did not have the dead certainty and blank brutality of the tough. It was too obvious that she cared about things, and could be hurt.

Angel drifted a step closer to the table, glanced to the side, as though distracted, then stared openly at Kathy, waiting for her to notice. When she did, and looked up, Angel kept her eyes steady, and put a question into them. Kathy cocked her head to the side, uncertain and wary. Angel navigated through the chairs and tables, peering intently into Kathy's face. I followed with a shambling, loose-limbed gait, shoulders slumped and expression bored in the attitude of a jaded and slightly drunken older brother.

"Excuse me, but is your name Kathy?" Angel shouted over the din.

Kathy nodded, pleased that this attractive woman seemed to know her.

"I can't believe it!" Angel squealed, and sat confidently in the chair next to her. "I met you at Partners, in Los Angeles."

Kathy scrutinized Angel's face, then blushed in the confusion and embarrassment of not recognizing her in return.

"You were Martha's friend, right?" Angel cried, girlish and chatty as I had never before seen her. "It was a couple of years ago. We just met for a second."

Kathy smiled and, unwrapping her hand from the beer, offered it to Angel. "I'm sorry, but I must have had a lot to drink that night, because I don't remember your name, and you are definitely worth remembering."

"I'm Angel."

Angel turned in her chair and motioned me to sit. I squeezed past a couple of leather jackets, and extended my hand across the table.

"This is my brother, Paul."

Kathy briskly shook my hand.

"So you two know each other?" I asked.

Kathy nodded. The hook was set.

"Small world," I said, and pretended disinterest by focusing my eyes on the dance floor.

Angel began to work at stretching the connection. "I ran into Martha just last week. Whatever happened to you two?"

"I met someone else," Kathy said, and shrugged.

Angel held her eyes and smiled. "I know the feeling. It seems to happen all the time, doesn't it?"

Kathy blushed, flattered, and asked: "How long are you in Paris?"

"Two weeks, maybe more. And you?"

"I just moved here, actually."

"How wonderful. But it's so expensive now, what with the dollar. How can you afford it?"

"I came into an inheritance," Kathy explained with a wry smile.

"I wish I'd come into an inheritance. I'd love to move to Paris," Angel said, and rested her hand casually on Kathy's arm. "Have you found an apartment yet?"

"Not yet. I'm staying at a hotel on the West Bank."

"That's incredible. So are we," Angel lied. "The Hotel de Suez, on Boulevard St. Michele."

"I'm just around the corner, at the Albe."

"Are you with your friend?" Angel asked, and by now the question was not a pump for information, but part of a seduction.

"She's in Paris, but at a different hotel, near the Eiffel Tower."

"So where is she? She hasn't abandoned you, has she? Paris is so romantic a place that I'd think it dangerous to leave you alone," Angel confided, and the invitation seemed so genuine that jealousy began to jangle my nerves.

"We're supposed to meet tonight. It's complicated. Her brother is here, and she wants to spend time with him. So we're in different hotels, and, I don't know, it's a little frustrating."

"Don't tell me she is still in the closet," Angel admonished.

"It's a little more complicated than that," Kathy admitted. "I don't know how I get into situations like this. She's a wonderful person, but it's like she's got all these sides to her. She's like one of those Chinese puzzles, you know, the boxes, where there is a box inside one box inside another box, each getting smaller and smaller, until you get to the last box, and you open it up, and discover that it wasn't the last box at all. There is another one. And it just goes on.''

"It sounds like you don't think you can trust her," Angel observed.

"I know I can't trust her, but I've got no choice. We're sorta in business together."

"I'm in the fashion industry myself. Sports apparel. Sweats, leotards, that sort of thing. What kind of business are you in?"

"That's pretty complicated, too. I'm not really sure what kind of business it is, but we're in it."

She brought the beer to her lips, and looked out into the crowd. Her face brightened. I followed the direction of her glance, and spotted a woman parting the wall of bodies at the edge of the dance floor. She was dressed to turn heads, like a thirties film star in a tight black dress, white polka-dot scarf, black sunglasses, and a black turban wrapped around her blond hair. Her pace slowed when she noticed that Kathy was not alone. The sunglasses worked against her. She dropped her head to peer over the top of the frames and, scanning me, glanced quickly to Kathy and shook her head.

I jerked my chair back and leapt forward as she bolted into the crowd, figuring a woman in heels would be an easy catch, but Kathy lunged across the table and grabbed a fistful of my jacket, yanking me off balance. Kathy screamed something in French. I dragged her over the table, and when her body fell to the floor, the weight took me down with her. She clutched at my jacket with her other hand, screaming the same phrase in French, and managed to lock onto the sleeve. I stripped out of the jacket, but my feet slipped in a slick of beer as I tried to stand, and she wrapped an arm around my throat, wrestling me down again. It took a moment to twist away, but by then she was not alone.

A boot caught me under the chin. The concussion flipped me onto my back. A snarling woman in torn blue jeans raised a jackboot. I rolled, the boot glancing off my shoulder as it smashed down.

A beer bottle splintered glass across my face. I rolled again, into a thicket of kicking boots. My arm lashed out to deflect a blow to my groin. I caught a steel-toed boot and twisted with it, bringing someone down. A heel clipped the back of my head, and I released the boot, trying to cover up. My body shook and writhed under concussive boot blows to my ribs and back. I curled my knees into my chest, dimly aware that if I stayed on the ground, I would be dismembered.

The blows diminished, then stopped. I glanced through my protective covering of arms to a body skittering over mine, arms flailing as though in flight. Angel loomed overhead. She twisted around an onrusher and kicked high, sprawling the woman over a table. Her feet planted and kicked again, and her hard-edged hands swept clear a circle in the crowd. A husky woman with black-spiked hair came at her with a chair. She sidestepped it, and threw a short, crushing hook. A figure in a brown aviator jacket darted in as the chair wobbled from Spiked Hair's hands. Angel flowed with the impact, grasping the jacket, and with a quick corkscrew wrench of her back hurled forward. Aviator Jacket soared over Angel's shoulder and thumped with a yelp of pain onto a distant table, scattering bottles and glasses onto the floor.

Spiked Hair broke a beer bottle over the edge of her chair. Blood streamed from the corner of her mouth, and her eyes gleamed with the stupid rage of the bar fighter. She tossed the chair aside, and thrust the jagged bottle-end at Angel. Angel feinted left and spun right, snatching the wrist behind the bottle. Spiked Hair stumbled forward. Angel grabbed the hair at the back of her adversary's head and snapped her knee sharply up, cracking it across Spiked Hair's face as she forced it down. Spiked Hair dropped to the floor and didn't move.

I staggered to my feet and pressed against Angel back to back. Shocked and angry faces circled us. None of them belonged to Kathy

Maddox. Angel crouched, her hands at a deadly angle of readiness. No one dared breach the circle. Angel shuffled forward, and the circle broke. She relaxed, her supple body confident in its power, and strode victorious through the tunnel forming at her approach.

23

I dogged Angel's heels through the ancient twisting streets of Montmartre toward the Métro. Angel ran fluidly, her strides long and agile as we flew past the late night revelers. Women in short leather miniskirts strutted amid the shadows, and men crouched in doorways, faces briefly illumined by cupped cigarettes as they offered sex, or drugs, or both. Angel darted into a darkened side street. The side street was narrow as an alley, and canopied by eighteenth-century stone apartments. The pale blue flickering of a television cast weird shadows from a second-floor window. The street curled into another street, and Montmartre began to spiral labyrinthine as my feet pounded the pavement. Oxygen burned my lungs deeper with each breath. The nightscape blurred, and faces caricatured to dark masks on vision's periphery. The alley burst into a sudden noise of lights and traffic at Place Pigalle, where seven avenues merged into a lopsided circle. The stairs descending to the Métro yawned ahead, marked by a sign bearing a blue field circled in red. Angel took the steps two at a time and pulled open the massive glass storm doors guarding the entrance. I squeezed through without breaking stride, and skidded to a stop before a splay of arrows pointing to a half dozen different boarding platforms. Angel braked against the wall, glanced at the signboard, and sprinted left. I followed, and we ran shoulder to shoulder down the corridor, dodging clusters of pedestrians and their packages. She waved a yellow ticket as we neared the turnstiles. I snatched it from her hand on the run, and slid into the turnstile. The turnstile clicked and groaned, scanning the magnetic stripe on the back of the ticket. It released, and I bolted through, a step behind Angel.

A crowd gathered beyond the turnstile. The train idled just past the boarding platform. I straightened out of the sprint and pulled up. The juxtaposition of the train and the waiting crowd seemed awry. The train had overshot the platform. Faces pressed against the windows of the rear compartment, gazing out in horror and curiosity. The crowd, which should have been moving toward the train, clustered well behind the last compartment. The crowd was silent and stationary. The faces in the crowd were bent down toward the tracks. A woman stumbled away. She covered her face with her hands, and cried out. Angel wove through the center of the crowd. I heard her swear. I wedged in beside her, my feet tipping at the edge of the platform, and looked down.

Kathy Maddox lay on the tracks below. Her battered head was twisted at an impossible angle from her body. Her face stared up at the crowd, the left eye obliterated by the pulp of blood and skull, the right eye a blank horror. The body wrenched in the reverse direction, the front tip of one shoulder dug into the track. Her back was a hemorrhage of blood and bone. One hand was severed nearly through, and clenched like a discarded glove along the rail.

Angel leaped down to the track, and knelt near the head, probing the carotid artery for an improbable pulse. I dropped and crouched at her side. Angel looked at me, and I knew without seeing the hopelessness of her eyes that Kathy Maddox was very dead. Cosmetics, pens, paper, and a hairbrush were strewn along the track, spilled from a black leather purse a couple of yards from Kathy Maddox's body. I eyed the purse like a vulture. I needed a diversion, and whispered: "You feel a pulse. Call for a doctor."

"It's useless," Angel said.

"Become hysterical. Just do it," I ordered.

Angel nodded, and moved her fingers further up Kathy's neck. She gasped, and began screaming in French for an ambulance. I wandered down the track, and bent to pick up a brush. I looked at it, as a man approaching shock might, when the sight of a common object grounds him to reality. I did not want it to seem as though I was conscious of what I was doing. I crouched on the track, and collected a pen, notebooks, lipstick, and cosmetic case, and carried the objects to the black purse. I opened the purse, and carefully lowered them inside. Nobody objected. My hand palmed a hotel key as I lifted the bag. A second, smaller key was affixed to the ring next to the hotel tag and key. I slipped the keys into my pocket and lowered the purse next to dead Kathy Maddox.

I felt for a pulse at the neck, just as Angel had done, but shook my head. "It's no use. She's dead," I said.

I circled Angel's shoulders with my arm, and gently stood her up. Angel was shaken enough for her shock to seem authentic. The death was brutal. Two gendarmes jumped onto the track, their uniforms slick blue-black and heads capped. The one who approached us was tall and thin and pigeon-faced. He flapped the backs of his hands at us, and we stepped away. I shook my head when he began speaking French.

"I'm sorry, but we're American," I said, having learned that this one phrase was synonymous to saying that you did not speak any language except English.

The gendarme nodded, and looked at Angel, who stared vacantly at the ground. While his partner knelt to examine the body, the gendarme struggled with his English through a series of questions. He seemed to believe me when I stated that we did not know the woman's identity, and had jumped down to the tracks to administer first aid, which we had quickly determined to be futile. When the gendarme asked how the woman had fallen, I shrugged my shoulders and replied that I had not seen the accident. A man shouted from the crowd, and his voice was joined by an elegant young woman in a red coat. The gendarme turned sharply, and though my French is minimal, I sensed his surprise at what they had shouted. He held up a hand, commanding silence while he glanced at our passports. My stomach turned jittery at the thought that someone had witnessed me palming the key. The gendarme noted our names in a black book, returned our passports, and dismissed us with an abbreviated bow. Angel and I scaled the platform, and as we slowly moved through the crowd parting at our approach, I glanced back at the gendarme. He was huddled with the shouting man and the woman in the red coat, scribbling furiously in his black book.

A white ambulance flashing blue lights screeched to the curb at the head of the Métro steps as Angel and I ascended to the street. I stepped off the curb, turning my back to Angel, and scanned Place Pigalle for a cab as the paramedics hurried a stretcher out of the back of the ambulance and carted it down the steps. I wanted to get to the Hotel Albe quickly, and impatiently called for Angel's advice. Hearing no response, I glanced over my shoulder and saw her striding at the edge of Place Pigalle toward Boulevard de Clichy. I caught up to her at the corner, thinking that she merely sought to improve our chances at catching a taxi. Keeping pace, I asked: "What did those people shout to the cop in the Métro?"

When Angel didn't answer or slow her stride, I caught her elbow and pulled. She whipped her elbow from my grasp, and turned toward the window of the closed café, laying her cheek against the cool glass. In the reflection, her expression walked a tightrope between anger and grief.

"What is it?" I asked softly.

"They were shouting that it wasn't an accident. That the woman was pushed into the train as it approached the platform," Angel responded, then sat on the sidewalk and wept.

It confused me. That Kathy Maddox had been pushed was strong argument for a quick search of her hotel room, and I wanted to tell Angel to stop crying and get moving. She had seen death before. I did not think it appropriate that she should be so quickly dislodged by grief over a woman she barely knew. The best part of any partnership is trust, and it was that, I suppose, that stilled my impatience. I sat on the curb, allowing her privacy, and waited. The weeping abated, and Angel called my name, asking me to sit beside her.

I crouched on the sidewalk. Angel wiped her nose with a sleeve, sniffled, and pressed the palm of her hands against her eyes. Her face was red and swollen from weeping. The hands dropped and folded across her lap. She stared at the space between us, and confessed: "There is something that I haven't told you. I wanted to tell you earlier, but I guess I just didn't."

I waited, and in the silence her voice picked up again, gathering courage as she said: "About five years ago, I had an affair with a woman."

The words slowly tumbled through my consciousness, touching upon disbelief, jealousy, then striking rage. Rage at myself. I remembered my idiot remarks about dykes, the adolescent attempt at cuteness that proved my callowness. In my brittle and ignorant malevolence toward an experience about which I knew nothing, I had caused pain. I tried saying "I'm sorry," but the attempt seemed stupid and futile, so instead I asked: "Do you feel bad about it?"

Angel nodded, immediately contradicting herself with: "No, not really. It just happened. I had a few bad experiences, which convinced me for a while that all men were jerks, and she was there to pick me up and hold me and help me feel whole inside myself again. She liked women and wasn't afraid to admit it. I didn't want to be with a man. I was tired of getting hurt. So I gave it a try. It worked for a while, and when I felt strong enough to decide that I really did like men, we ended it. She is still my friend and there is absolutely nothing sexual about it."

My first impulse was to tell her that it didn't matter to me with whom she had slept or why, but my first impulse was wrong. It did matter to both her and me. The experience had shaped her in part, and a quick unconsidered acceptance of it would not help me understand her any better. I wanted to talk about the experience with her, and I wanted to tell her that I was sorry for being a jerk, and, to tell the truth, I wanted to find a cab, take it to the Hotel Albe, and search Kathy Maddox's hotel room. The conflict short-circuited my brain so I just held her, which seemed to be what she wanted most. Then Angel pushed away, her face startled with a sudden distracting thought, and asked: "The woman at the club, the one coming through the crowd to meet Kathy. Who was she?"

I had not considered the distance of the woman from our table, and had assumed Angel had seen her as clearly as I had. Angel is nearsighted, and, from a vanity both athletic and cosmetic, refuses to wear glasses or contacts.

"The woman was Nina Gamine," I replied.

24

The taxi dropped us beneath the green awning of the Hotel Albe a few minutes before midnight. I slipped the hotel key from my coat pocket and glanced at the room number while Angel paid the driver. The second key dangling from the ring was small and silver, and marked by a four-digit number printed in yellow. I wondered what the key unlocked, and why it had been slipped next to the hotel key. Angel offered the palm of her hand, and I slapped the keys down. I opened the door for her, and she strode into the lobby, prepared to launch into a story about fetching an overnight case for Kathy if challenged. The story proved unnecessary. The concierge slumped on his arms over the counter, asleep.

The turn-of-the-century lift was a metal cage creaking down the six floors of the hotel. We didn't want to wait, and jogged three floors up the staircase. The lift passed us on its way down. I glanced inside the cage, glimpsing a thin young man with blond hair. I didn't see his face. When the lift hit bottom, he stepped from the cage with a floral-print suitcase. I thought it a little late to check out, but it didn't strike me as wrong until a little later, after we checked the room.

"So what are we looking for?" Angel asked, shutting and latching the door.

"A couple of million dollars would be nice. Failing that, a lead to Nina Gamine," I answered, searching the bathroom. A toothbrush and a tube of Colgate rested on the sink. A spent towel bunched on the floor. In the shower, nothing.

"What kind of a coincidence is it that Nina Gamine knows Kathy Maddox?" Angel asked, the closet door scraping as she opened it in the entryway.

I flicked off the bathroom light and stepped around the bed, feeling under the mattress. Nothing. Angel patted down the pockets of a jacket hanging in the closet. I surveyed the room. There wasn't much to search.

"The odds of it being a coincidence are as great as both Nina Gamine and Jack Burns stumbling separately into our office, which is to say that it is no coincidence at all, although I can't pretend to understand the mechanics of it."

"Maybe we can track Nina through her brother's old address," Angel suggested, then remarked: "It's odd, but there isn't a suitcase."

Brilliance comes to the gifted in a sudden flash. With me, the sudden flash is the realization of my stupidity. I swept the vertical blinds aside and looked to the street below. The man with the suitcase I had casually witnessed in the lift stood across the street from the hotel, looking up at the room window. The lit façade of the hotel reflected onto his pale features. At that distance, and with the light behind me, I don't think he could see my face, but the fact that I was there, in that room, startled him. The attitude of his head, the pale and fragile-boned face lifted across his shoulder, gazing up as though to heaven, was the mirror image of the photograph Nina Gamine had presented in my office two weeks before. He stumbled back against the curb, lurched away from the hotel, and hurriedly lugged the suitcase down the sidewalk.

"That was Francis Gamine," I blurted, and sprang for the door.

I took the stairs two at a time, nearly separating my shoulder at the turns as I gripped the stairposts and wheeled into the next set. Angel galloped at my heels. I took the last four steps in a leap, hitting the landing with a loud thump. The concierge woke and yelled as we flew past the desk. I shouldered through the lobby door and broke into the street.

"How far is the nearest Métro station?" I shouted, and sprinted in the direction I had seen Francis Gamine lugging the suitcase. I imagined it filled with fifty thousand twenty-dollar bills.

"St. Michel is around the corner," Angel called, a half dozen yards behind.

I was good in sprints, but with any kind of distance my heart threatened to blow through my chest. Angel caught me at Boulevard St. Michel, and we took the stone steps down to the Métro in cadence. I struggled to keep up through the corridor leading to the platform. My lungs whimpered and wheezed like a sick animal. I glanced at my partner. Angel had yet to break into a sweat. I said a silent prayer to Nautilus, the New Age God of fitness, and promised to begin training when I returned to Los Angeles if the pain in my chest didn't kill me first.

"It's past midnight. This is the last Métro," Angel called over her shoulder, and hurdled the turnstile in a fluid leap.

I stutter-stepped on the approach, and didn't get enough height. The turnstile caught under my lead foot, and I pitched forward, stupidly trying to brace my fall with an outstretched hand rather than tucking and taking it on my shoulder. The hand gave away, and I belly flopped, cracking my chin on the concrete floor. My brain spun inside its skull cage, and when it righted, I saw Angel leap onto the last Métro as it pulled away.

I couldn't suck enough air into my lungs, and paused on hands and knees, waiting for my heart to thrash clear out of my chest and bound like a red rabbit onto the platform. I stood. My body creaked. I'd pounded the fluid from my joints, and could feel size-seven bruises from the boot blows to my ribs and legs. I was ready to call it a night. I looked up, absently brushing my coat. Francis Gamine charged up the stairs on the opposite platform.

It took me a moment to put it together. I guessed that he had seen Angel board the train and jumped to the other side. I dropped to the tracks and scaled the opposite platform. Boots clicking unevenly under the strain of a heavy load echoed in the corridor ahead. I followed the sound to the entrance and picked up my pace, not wanting to lose him on the street. He slowly climbed the stairs to

Boulevard St. Michel, jerking the suitcase up the steps with both hands. From behind, he looked thin and weak. He wore jeans, a sweatshirt, pointed black boots, and a suede jacket. He didn't look like a junkie, except maybe by his weight. He looked like a good kid. At the top of the stairs he hesitated, and I couldn't tell what he was doing. From my angle at the base of the stairs I could only see his head turning back and forth as though searching for something. A cab, I supposed. He moved right, toward Ile de la Cité, and I slid up the stairs. He walked with a stutter and lunge of the big suitcase with each step. His head was active, spinning as he heaved the suitcase forward, and I sensed that he was looking for me as well as for a cab. He crossed the Seine at Pont St. Michel, and I hung well back of him on the other side of the bridge. When I noticed a taxi cruising Boulevard St. Michel, its vacancy sign lit, I stepped off the curb and hailed it.

The taxi driver was a plump and gray-haired woman in slacks and a blue jacket. A brown and white cocker spaniel rode shotgun, his tongue lolling out in friendly greeting.

"Do you speak English?" I asked before getting in.

She shrugged and shook her head, in that peculiar way the French have of saying maybe yes, maybe no, maybe a little bit. I looked over the roof, and spotted Francis Gamine at the opposite end of Pont St. Michel, across from the Palais du Justice, hoisting the suitcase into the backseat of a waiting taxicab. I handed the driver a hundred-franc note and said: "Follow that car."

She leveled me with droll eyes and replied: "You are kidding, no?"

I told her that I was very serious.

"You are a gangster perhaps? Monsieur Capone from Chicago?"

I assured her that I was Monsieur Percy from Los Angeles, thinking it wise to bend the truth a bit regarding my name. Her glance was skeptical. The cocker spaniel pulled in its tongue, inched back on the seat, and regarded me with suspicion. But the driver tracked the cab across the bridge, and, when it moved, slid smoothly into the light late-night traffic.

"So, Monsieur Capone from Chicago, you must tell me why we follow that car."

Nothing could sound crazier than the truth. So I told it. "Because the man in the car is carrying the suitcase of a murdered woman. I don't know what is in the suitcase, but I think it might be money."

"Or maybe just dirty laundry, no?" the driver cracked, watching my reaction in the rearview.

"That's possible," I admitted.

"So this man, did he kill her?"

"I don't think so, but maybe."

The amusement fled from her expression as she regarded me. The cocker spaniel whined, and she reached over to give him a reassuring pat. She said: "This is very serious, this business."

Paris by night flew past the windshield, Renaissance buildings hulking in the darkness, their facades swept with the headlights of passing cars, or dimly illuminated by twentieth-century neon.

The driver followed the taxi like a pro, maintaining a couple of car lengths between herself and the target. The Eiffel Tower, lit like a beacon, ascended over the elevated Métro tracks along Boulevard Suffren. I gawked. Francis Gamine's taxi pulled up at a gray stone edifice, lit by a dim white sign announcing the Hotel Europe. My cabbie continued down Boulevard De Grenelle, and turned left at the next street. She whispered something to the dog, who squared his haunches on the seat and braced a paw against the dashboard. She then whipped the wheel around, and the cab swung in a hundred-degree arc, parking at a corner with a view of the hotel entrance.

Francis Gamine paid his driver, and struggled with the case, lugging it out the door and onto the sidewalk. He peered both directions down the street, but he was new at being hunted, and didn't know what to look for. He didn't give the parked cab a second glance. The front door to the lobby was locked. Francis straddled the case and rang the buzzer.

I folded another hundred-franc note and held it up, saying: "I need a favor."

"Of course. His room number, no?" she answered, turning in her seat.

"The number to both sides and directly above his room," I added.

The driver understood, and after I dropped the note into her proffered hand, she stepped out of the taxi. I took the moment alone to think about the money. It didn't matter that I didn't know how much was in the suitcase. It might not have contained any money. Just dirty laundry. The fantasy of a million dollars attracted and held me. The cocker spaniel watched me with interested eyes, so I told him that a million dollar bills placed end to end would stretch almost a hundred miles. It wouldn't buy everything, but it would buy enough.

The dog drooped his jaw over the back of the seat and sighed, maybe thinking about all the dog biscuits a million dollars would buy, or just missing his owner. I closed my eyes for a moment, and was doing a hundred twenty-five along the Pacific Coast Highway in my new Ferrari Testarossa when the driver slid behind the wheel and gave me the room numbers. I thanked her with another hundred-franc note. I could afford to be generous. I was almost a millionaire.

The concierge had treads under his eyes and was not happy at being disturbed again by the buzzer. His bed was a cot next to a stack of books behind the front desk. He scratched his head and tried to understand my French while I tried to decipher his English. I told him that it was late and that my luggage had been lost at Orly Airport, that I had stayed at the hotel on a previous visit and wanted the same room. It was booked, he said. I said I wanted the next room over. Booked also. I tried the one directly over Francis Gamine's room, and it was free. He gave me the key, and pointed to the stairs.

The room was on the fourth floor, and faced a side street. The furnishings were shabby, and the paint job antique once-white. I moved across the balding carpet and opened the window. The room did not have a balcony. The window was recessed into the facade of the building. A row of bars stretched across the bottom of the windowsill. I stuck my head out the window. A narrow concrete ledge wound around the building, meeting a window at each room. I looked down. The ledge to the next floor appeared to be a ten-foot drop. I unbuckled my belt and strapped it around one of the vertical bars at the base of the window. A six-foot body and a two-foot arm, plus a three-foot belt, would get me there with a foot to spare. I stepped out onto the ledge, and lowered myself over the side, holding on to the window bar to let myself down easily. I dangled six inches short. I took a deep breath, and dropped cleanly onto the ledge, hugging the wall for support. A flock of pigeons ascended from the ledge below with a clamor of flapping wings. I ducked, wingtips brushing my back, and my balance shifted dangerously over the ledge. My arms flailed at the air as I hovered between safety and a hard fall. The wall smelled sweet when balance returned, and I pressed my face to the coolness of it, breathless.

Vertigo loosened its grip, enabling my legs to move without trembling. I crouched next to the wall by the window. The vertical blinds were cracked open. I peered through the cracks. Francis Gamine paced by the window. Nina Gamine sat on the edge of the bed, legs crossed, shoulders crimped inward, her nails in her mouth. The turban hat was upended on the pillow, looking like an empty flower vase, and her blond hair fell straight and hard to her shoulders. Francis paced to the corner of the room and shouted something with the word "death" in it. Nina shook her head, and went back to her nails.

I pressed the inner corner of the window. The window was locked. It was like watching a movie without sound. The visuals informed me of the basic relationships and little else. Francis Gamine lit a cigarette. Nina wafted her hand across her face. Francis shrugged and walked to the window. I pancaked against the wall. The window squealed and opened six inches.

"Is that better?" Francis asked, his voice riding clearly through the gap in the window.

"I wish you wouldn't smoke," Nina complained, taking her nails from her mouth.

"Well, I wish you wouldn't do a lot of things," Francis retorted, thin and frail shoulders slumped as he considered the tip of his cigarette. His body hopped with nervous energy, the weight shifting from foot to foot. His hands clenched and fisted the cigarette to his mouth, and his eyes flitted around the hotel room like a bird in an electrified cage. I wondered if the rumors were true about an addiction to heroin, but his sweatshirt was bunched over his arms, concealing track marks, if there were any, and his nerves could have come from the presence of his sister.

"What do you want me not to do?" Nina asked, her voice pained but patient, as though speaking to a child.

Francis shook his head and smoked angrily, plunging the cigarette between his lips and ripping it out again.

"Tell me, Francis, and if I can stop or change, I'll do it."

He coughed and, covering his mouth, muttered: "You can start telling me things, for one. You send me halfway across Paris for a suitcase. You tell me to be careful, that someone might try to follow me. Well, somebody follows me. What for? I don't know. You won't tell me."

Francis jerked the suitcase onto the bed, and demanded: "What's in here?"

"Open it and find out," Nina suggested, and her voice conveyed a challenge both tactical and sexual.

"I can't. You don't have the key."

A butter knife lay among wineglasses, an ashtray, a bottle, and the scattered crumbs of a loaf of bread on the writing desk along the far wall. Nina stood, straightened the silk sides of her dress, and leaned to grab the knife. She thrust it toward Francis, confident yet excited by the surprise that would be waiting for him inside the suitcase. Francis butted his smoke and jammed the knife under the suitcase latch. He worked it back and forth, pried the tip up, and the latch gave. He tried the same technique with the other latch, and the suitcase snapped open. He reached into the case and lifted a woman's blouse and a pair of blue jeans.

"So? Third-rate clothes," he said with a contemptuous glance at the garments.

"Dig a little deeper," Nina suggested.

His hands disappeared into the suitcase. He stepped back, his mouth drooping, and stared at his sister. It was a strange smile that she returned to him, an aroused confusion of money and sex. Francis bent over the case again, tossing pants, underwear, and socks aside. Both hands emerged with neat green rectangular bundles. I couldn't read the denominations, but I bet they weren't singles. I thought about smashing through the window and snatching the case. I could be out the door before they were over the shock.

"This is a lot of money." His voice was awed as he clasped the bundles against his chest with one hand and clutched another handful. Francis paused, looking at the money in his hands and what remained in the suitcase, until fear mingled with greed and he stepped back, a green bundle slipping from his chest onto the bed, and asked: "Where did you get this?"

"I stole it from a thief. No. From a couple of thieves," she admitted, proud.

"The two who followed me?"

She shook her head, and the reminder that he had been followed troubled her. Nina slipped a couple of bundles from the suitcase, and held one against her cheek, briefly reassuring herself in the feel of the crisp, cool bills against her skin.

"Then who were they?" he pressed.

"Private detectives. From Los Angeles."

He dumped the green bundles back into the case and slammed the lid, shouting: "This is trouble. What the hell are you doing?"

"It's for us," she answered, quiet and confident. Nina slid smoothly toward her brother, still holding the bundle of cash, and sought to wrap her arms around him in a moneyed embrace. Francis stumbled back, and sought refuge from his discomfort in the pack of cigarettes lying on the bed. She circled him. He looked aside, and stuffed a cigarette into the corner of his mouth. When he lit the match, Nina blew it out and plucked the cigarette from his lips. She grabbed his chin in the palm of her hand and pulled his face toward her. He shook the hand off, but didn't back away. Her hand returned, and gently caressed his cheek. He closed his eyes, the fight draining from him with each sweep of her fingertips along his skin. Her voice was a soft and compelling seduction as she murmured: "We can't live together in the States. You knew that. That was why you ran away. We couldn't live here, not without money. Now we have the money. Lots of money.''

Her hands cupped his jaw, and gently lowered his lips to hers. A sweet pain clenched his eyes and deepened as the kiss lingered. When they finished it, they pushed back and regarded each other, his face lost with the knowledge of what was to come but still wanting it, and hers confident of her desire. Nina shivered, and her eyes swept the window. I sat back quickly on my heels. Her heels clicked to the sill. I gripped the rail with my left hand, and clenched my right, ready to chop down on the face that appeared. It didn't. The window squeaked shut, and the latch clicked in place.

Still clutching the bundles of cash in one hand, Nina met her brother between the bed and the window, and they embraced in a violent tumble onto the bed. Hands clutched at arms, legs, hair, and clothes.

Nina ripped her brother's shirt open, and claimed his neck with her mouth. His hand centered on his sister's sex, and her hips shifted with a fierce desire. The paper bands binding the cash bundles split apart, and twenty-dollar bills scattered over the pillows and bedspread like a shifting green stain beneath their twisting bodies.

I watched, embarrassed yet fascinated, thinking that I should turn away to allow them their privacy, yet unable to tear my eyes from the tumble of bodies. Then I remembered Mona, and the previous time I had witnessed, with the same loathed excitement, sex through a glass, and turned my back to the window.

I stared across the narrow cobbled street at a gray-haired woman in a nightdress staring back at me. She flung open the window to her apartment, and yammered French in a shrill voice. I set my forefinger against my lips. She responded by raising her voice an octave.

''Une affaire de amour,'' I rasped.

She was surprised I'd spoken, and stopped railing.

''Pardon?'' she called, cupping her ear.

''Une affaire de amour,'' I repeated.

''Une affaire d'amour, ou une affaire de coeur,'' she corrected.

''Merci.''

"Pas du tout." She nodded, and shut her window.

I sat back on my heels, and looked at the moon rising over the rooftops of Paris. It took me a moment to conjure from memory the face I had seen in childhood, when, gazing up into the starry Montana sky, I had imagined it as a yawning old man in a sleeping cap. That image comforted me. When I took my first woman into the woods at night, the moon approved with a smile and sly wink. The woman and I made love, and after it was done, we held each other and looked up at the sky. He had seemed kind, then, beaming down on the loss of innocence, and love seemed a natural and wondrous thing.

Tonight, his mouth opened in roaring laughter. A jaded roué, the moon. *La luna.* The patron saint of lovers and lunatics, the celestial prankster who compels a moose to fall in love with a cow, and a brother to make love to his sister. The night voyeur supreme, who suspends the internal gravity of the human heart, tumbling reason and emotion until the relationship between the two tangles and snaps. Straight and gay and every permutation between looked up at the moon in the city of love, and thought the face of the moon kind, or sly, or seductive. The moon roared with laughter.

The splintering of wood snapped my communion with the moon. I pulled myself to the window and looked through the vertical blinds. Another crash jerked Nina and Francis from their naked embrace. A man stumbled through the shattered door, and thrust a pistol toward the lovers. It was an Austrian gun, a Glock, half plastic, which can be disassembled to look like nothing to airport security. A thick black mustache brushed over the lip of the man who held it. Bruises fanned out under his eyes like purple wings. His face was swollen, and I thought that he had taken a hell of a beating. He was thick around the middle, about forty, and looked like he had lived too well to be deadly, but the pistol in his hand was unmistakable. It backed the lovers against the bedstead.

Nina knew the man. She slipped from the bed and walked to him. Her hands, which had protectively shielded her small breasts, floated palms up in a suppliant opening of the arms for peace. He stopped her with the upraised Glock. Their mouths moved in an exchange of words that I didn't hear. He held the gun loosely in his right hand,

and the fingers of his left drifted over her breasts, as though recommitting the caress to memory. His fingers pulled first one nipple, and then the second, erect. She smiled against terror. He smiled back, a gruesome show of teeth, and shoved her down, jerking the pistol over and blowing her brother's eye through the back of his skull.

I hammered at the wood frame where the window latched, and on the second blow, when Nina's howling grief blew through the glass, the latch gave, and the window swung free. The man did not react quickly. I wanted him to turn and run, and feared that he might raise the gun and shoot me, but he did neither. He stood, the gun at his side, his eyes flitting dispassionate between Nina howling at his feet and my face in the window.

"Drop the gun," I said, and my voice scraped from my throat like a croak.

He shook his head. Nina crawled onto the bed and reached for her brother's ruined face. The man watched her, and when her fingers first brushed the cheek, he lifted the gun and shot her in the back. She pitched into the blood streaming down her brother's chest.

The muzzle swept its black hole toward me, and I was stuck. The first shot showered glass onto the street outside. I took the air elevator and rode the three stories down the fast way. The roof of a Citroën rushed up from below. My legs glanced across the roof and my body followed with a deadening thump. I rolled without knowing I was rolling, and the second fall was only a cessation of movement and brought no pain. The senses began to fail, and the flow of information to my brain slowed to a ballet of distortions. Sounds became nothing more than waves, objects dull shapes, and my body a loose construct of wires and rubber.

Dull explosions sounded above me. I awkwardly pulled on the wires that controlled my head, twisting the wires back to give my eyes a look at what was over my shoulder. A cutout figure leaned out the balcony. Brief flashes of light flowered from his hand, and I thought that he was trying to give me something beautiful. The cobblestone near my head burst into shrapnel. I rolled away from the point of impact, and sheltered under the Citroën.

The world returned in a rush, and most of it was pain. The pain was everywhere simultaneously, but with concentrated effort I fought it down to a white-hot ankle. I curled into a ball and looked at it. I didn't see any bone. I figured the ligaments were gone, and that if I didn't move quickly, I'd be gone as well. I scrambled out from under the car. The ankle wouldn't take any weight. I balanced on one foot, and hopped away from the hotel, stumbling once when I jerked my head around in the panic of being caught from behind by a slug. Windows over my head flung open, and shouts punctured the night. I hopped and crawled to the next boulevard, wiped the tears from my eyes, and hailed a taxi.

25

I climbed the last two of the four flights of stairs to Henri Grall's Montmartre apartment on my butt. I struggled to my feet and hobbled to his door and knocked until my head filled with a spinning rush of air, forcing me to my butt again. When he answered, I had about given up and was using the back of my head as a battering ram, determined either to wake him or to knock myself insensate in the process. Henri pulled the door open to the chain barrier, and glanced down. He was dressed in briefs and a muscle T-shirt, and his black hair jutted in determined tufts above a puffed face. We didn't know each other that well, and, sprawled in the hallway by his door, I could have been drunk. Behind the sleep-bruised eyes he was not amused at having been disturbed. I tried a wave and a weak smile. He nodded and asked what I wanted. I pointed to my ankle, and said that a doctor and a bit of advice on how to handle local police problems would make me feel a hell of a lot better. The chain clacked against the doorframe as he released it and swung the door open. He helped me to my feet, and I borrowed his shoulder to an armchair by the door. I lowered myself gently into the chair, gripping my pantleg and pulling my ankle onto the footstool. Henri knelt and cradled the ankle in his palms, gently testing the range of motion in the joint. I tried to be manly, but I think I groaned once or twice. He removed the shoe and sock, and whistled. The ankle was badly bruised.

"With an injury like this, you should go to hospital, no?" he remarked, feeling down from the tibia to the tarsal bones.

"I don't think that is a very good idea," I said, and told him why.

He listened to the narrative, patiently probing for the shift in bone that signifies a break, interspersing questions about pain in my ankle with requests for clarifications in my story. His surprise at the three murders, if he felt any, did not play down to his face, which remained impassive behind his web of scars. When I finished, he lowered the ankle gently onto the footstool and offered to make a few phone calls. I asked that his first call be to Angel, and he agreed, padding slowly down the hall to a back bedroom.

I settled back into the armchair, and cast my eyes around Henri's apartment. It was simple and dark, a one-bedroom flat with an exposed kitchen, and a window fronting a quiet street. The furnishings were spare and worn and likely hadn't been much more attractive when new. The armchair was a rough brown tweed worn through to white stuffing at the elbows. It was part of a sitting group that included a blue vinyl sofa left over from the sixties, and a yellowing Plexiglas coffee table. The stereo and television set were propped on a wooden board extended between two crates. The effect was anonymous and depressing, with a dingy fatalism curiously redeemed by the solid wall of 1940s film noir posters plastered above the sofa and stretching into the kitchen. *Phantom Lady, Out of the Past, They Live by Night*: the evocative titles towered in bold print above the heroically doomed faces of men and women confronting a morally shifting and ambiguous world. The posters explained the furnishings. Anything worth owning can be taken, so it is best not to own anything.

The bedroom door opened and Henri emerged buttoning his jeans. He had located a doctor willing to make a late-night house call, a man with a thriving practice among the denizens of the Paris netherworld who sometimes required medical care but not police attention. I thanked him. He opened a pint-size refrigerator and plopped a bag of ice on the counter. The bedroom door down the hall opened again, and a thin adolescent, his skin a dusky Arab brown and his black hair curly, padded naked into the bathroom. Henri wrapped the ice in a towel and knelt at my ankle. His hands were careful, and with a quick warning glance he cautioned me against speaking about what I had just seen. I didn't read the look clearly, and between the pain, the shock, and the lack of sleep I opened my mouth when I shouldn't have and blurted: "I thought . . . "

"You thought what?" Henri challenged.

"I thought I should mind my own business," I said.

Henri wrapped the iced towel around my ankle and secured it with twine. His eyes fixed on the towel and the shape of the ice surrounding the ankle, and he remarked: "You should know more than most that appearance and reality are parallel lines meeting only at infinity, and then perhaps not at all. If I explain, you will not be any wiser, because I might be confused about what is real and what is only appearance. Some night I might be one thing, but on another, who knows?"

He lit a Gitane, and let it burn untouched on the counter while he put a kettle to boil and measured coffee grounds into a filter. A soft rapping drew him to the door and he opened it to a small man in a long gray trench coat bunched by a belt at the waist. The man was small and precise, his face thin and angular and ebony black. His body moved from point to point with a swift elegance, each motion precisely perceived and executed. When he removed his coat, his fingers uncinched the belt and loosed the buttons in a quick series of confident twists, and his feet seemed to sense the optimum number of steps, equally spaced, that would bring him to the couch and back again. He introduced himself to me as Slim.

Slim manipulated the ankle joint, and determined that ligament damage was likely. He proposed a temporary cast, and suggested that I get an X ray as soon as possible. Slim pulled a needle from his bag, unwrapped the sterilizing plastic, and filled it from a vial. It was just a local anesthetic, he said, and would not impair my reasoning capacity. I replied that that was good, because my reasoning capacity was marginal and any further impairment would drop me out of the primate range. Slim searched for his spot, and poised the needle above the skin. Four sharp raps sounded at the door, and he jumped, startled. Angel with her usual impeccable timing. I told Slim that company was expected, and he relaxed, sliding the needle smoothly under the skin while my attention was occupied with Angel's entrance.

Angel nodded briefly to me, and watched the chamber behind the needle slowly empty into my ankle. "This is what happens when you don't stay in shape," she pronounced, with a merciless concern for my well-being. "Your muscles lose their elasticity with fatigue, and when you push, something pops."

"If Mr. Olympia had fallen as fast and far as I did, he'd have left a hole the size of a bomb crater," I replied, and recounted the events that concluded with the injury. As I talked, Slim soaked two rolls of plaster bandages in warm water and, splinting the ankle, wrapped the bandages around the splints. The teakettle whistled, and Henri poured a round of coffee. The commotion of voices, door action, and whistling attracted the Arab boy, who, dressed in jeans and a muscle shirt like Henri, stumbled groggily into the room, slumped against the wall, and hung an unlit Gitane out of a disconsolate mouth. He appeared between sixteen and nineteen years old. His face had an innocent brutality to it, with full sensual lips and a wide nose, and heavy-lidded eyes.

"This guy with the bruises under his eyes, you think he was an American?" Angel asked when I had finished.

"Nina knew him, and he didn't seem to be hired muscle, so yes," I answered.

"Don't forget the plastic gun," Henri added, standing in the kitchen over a steaming cup of coffee. "Those guns, they look like nothing to security at the airport. He could have come from America with it hidden in his underwear, no?"

The Arab boy laughed in the corner. Slim glanced over his shoulder when he heard the laugh, and the Arab boy sent him an abbreviated salute: one finger tipping against the corner of his right eyebrow. Slim said something to the Arab boy, knowing him, and the boy shrugged, expressionless, then broke into a wide grin.

"So who is he?" Angel asked.

I admitted that I had no idea.

"How much money they steal?" pitched in the Arab boy, lighting his Gitane and tossing the match into an empty Coke bottle.

"We don't know," I admitted.

"And none of your business," Henri added.

The Arab boy shrugged, feigning disinterest while he blew a smoke ring from the perfect circle of his mouth.

"We don't know how much money is involved, or where it is. We don't know who shoved Kathy Maddox onto the Métro tracks, and we don't know who the guy is who shot Nina Gamine and her brother," I admitted.

"You know what I think?" Henri offered, gazing shrewdly from behind the rim of his coffee cup.

"No," Angel and I chimed.

"I think you don't know much of anything."

I thanked him for the observation. Slim trimmed the edge of the cast with a pair of scissors, allowed himself a small smile of satisfaction, and said:

"This is a very interesting story, which I will naturally forget the moment I leave this room. But from this killer's description, you should consider that his bruises were caused by a broken nose. Disruption in the cartilage here will often cause bruises to form under the eyes. The nose could have been broken accidentally, say by falling, or in a fight. It is also possible that he had his nose broken in order to change it."

"You mean plastic surgery?" I guessed.

"That is one possibility," Slim said. Wiping his hands on a towel tossed to him by Henri, Slim advised me on caring for the cast, and presented his bill: 300 francs. He offered to throw in a used pair of crutches, waiting outside in his car, for an extra hundred fifty. I thanked him, and Angel counted 450 francs into his palm. Henri said something to the young Arab, who shrugged his shoulders in a world-weary "Why not?" and accompanied Slim out the door to fetch the crutches.

"I think this is a very bad predicament you are now in," Henri mused, lighting a Gitane and settling heavily onto the couch. "The police have your names from the incident at the Métro, and they will sooner or later trace Kathy Maddox back to Sappho's. They will then learn of the fight, and it will lead them to suspect you. You were also seen outside the window of Nina Gamine's hotel room. It is not good.''

''I'm also morally obligated to report what I saw to the police,'' I said, not looking forward to a delay of days or weeks while the French police sorted through the investigation.

''I will make certain your statement, anonymous of course, is submitted to the police,'' Henri offered. ''If they find this man, and need you to testify, then I must request that you give your word to return and testify.''

I gave him my word.

''You have only a few hours before you must leave Paris. I suggest you use your time wisely.''

Angel and I took Henri's suggestion. I made a complete statement to Henri, who took meticulous notes in a burgundy notebook, and we caught the first morning flight out of Orly Airport to Los Angeles.

26

I took two pain pills over the Atlantic, and awoke from a strange dream on the far side of another continent. In the dream, I methodically wormed on my belly amid a landscape of giant thorns. Impaled on the thorns were fantastical creatures with green sluglike bodies and weeping human heads. Tears glistened with the brilliance of precious stones in their eyes, and sprinkled onto the ground.

I did not wake with a start, but hovered between worlds, trying to hold on to the dream images like fragments from a shattered stained-glass window. I pieced the dream together again in the darkness. Angel slept beside me. There is little to distinguish between the darknesses of different cities, or nations, or continents, and I thought I was in Paris. My eyes adjusted to the Hopper poster on the far wall of Angel's bedroom, and consciousness traversed a continent in a split second. The last vestiges of dream splintered beyond recognition.

I sat up and tried to slip quietly out of bed. My left leg was heavy and resisted movement. I pulled back the covers. The full impact of memory struck me. I did not want to remember, and memory fast-forwarded to where consciousness had last left me, waiting impatiently for the pain pills to take effect. There, memory blacked out, and I wondered how long I had been asleep.

I hobbled into the bathroom. A fresh washcloth hung on the

railing. I soaked it, and rubbed off the accumulated hours of bed sweat. My body was purpled in bruises and streaked red with abrasions. It hurt. I examined the ankle cast, and remembered the deaths before the fall. I shut the bathroom door and switched off the light, hiding the shame of the sickness welling up from my gut. I gripped the sink.

Death images burst from the darkness: jagged bone ends, severed limbs, and bright red arterial blood cascading from ripped and flapping membranes of flesh. The boiled red and bloated face of Jack Burns roiled in a jet stream of green bubbles, dissolving into the ghastly red death smile along Mona Demonay's throat, and the horrified, popping eyes of Kathy Maddox on the tracks of the Métro blinked into the bullet-disintegrated eye of Francis Gamine. Nina Gamine pitched forward with a balloon-burst of blood, and like a film running backward, the blood sucked back into the hole in her skin and she stood in reverse, before pitching forward again, trapped in the perverse loop of memory.

I swept the images back to darkness. I pretended that I was okay. But I wasn't. My stomach was poisoned by blood. Consciousness narrowed to a single focus, and grief came like a terrible vomiting. Thoughts compressed to nothing and my mind blanked. I remembered nothing, and became nothing, convulsing in solitude and sorrow.

When it had finished with me, I ran the hot water, and scrubbed my face. I didn't want to see myself in the mirror, and felt blindly in the darkness for a towel. I scrubbed fiercely. My skin came alive under the roughness of the cloth. I took a breath, and balanced.

Angel was sitting on the edge of the bed when I hobbled into the room. Her eyes told me what she had heard. I glanced over her.

"How long have I been out?"

"About twenty hours. Are you okay?"

"Me? I'm fine," I said, and leaned against the windowsill, looking out over the rooftops at the ocean, a blanket of blue-black threaded with silver highlights from my old friend, the moon. "A little beat-up, is all."

"Are you hungry? I could maybe get something," she offered.

I told her that I was not hungry, and stood at the window trying to wrap a little understanding around the unstable whirl of the last few days. Angel silently slipped her arm around my waist, and I felt the comfortable weight of her head rest against my shoulder.

"What are you thinking about?" she asked.

"I'm thinking that the world is not designed with our happiness primarily in mind," I answered.

"You should have learned that lesson in childhood," she chided, and it brought me out of self-pity.

"I'm a little slow on the uptake at times," I admitted.

Angel guided me onto the bed, and I collapsed against the sheets. She lowered herself on top of me, and I felt shielded by the warmth of her body. Angel stripped off her nightgown and pressed her belly against mine. Her face hovered over me and, awed by her beauty and her strength, I watched the minute incremental changes in her eyes as her features swelled in passion. I sought her hands. Our palms pressed together, and we laced fingers. We moved slowly, luxuriating in each layer of skin on skin, molding from our two passions a single welling of desire. Her mouth folded onto mine. Time and gravity had no consequence for a few precious moments, until the spending of our passions settled me gently into a sad and this time dreamless sleep.

Money smells as strong as blood to the human species of jackal, and I apparently reeked of it. The drive from Angel's apartment to my Wilshire office is about three miles, but in that short distance I spotted two tails: a gray Chevy sedan, and a white Datsun hatchback.

The Mustang is a four-speed, and though I could about manage the clutch, brake, and gas pedal with one foot, there was no question of outrunning anyone. I felt like a wounded buck shadowed by a pack of wolves. I lost sight of the Chevy around the corner from my office, and as I pulled into the parking lot, the Datsun drove by without slowing. I thought maybe I was just paranoid, until I looked out the office window and spotted the Datsun parked on the street, and the Chevy under a tree on the other side of Wilshire.

The office answering machine logged a couple dozen calls. I

rewound the machine and let it run while I started Ms. Coffee and scooped the mail from behind the door. The first message was from Harry Selwurst, threatening to sue. I tossed the mail onto the desk and opened the center drawer. The imitation ruby eyes of the Egyptian lady stared up at me. I lifted her by the hilt, and ran a finger along the narrow blade, thinking about Mona and the moment she had given it to me. The next message was from Ian Waddington, wondering where the hell I was. *Times* reporter Richie Warner called to say he was writing an article about Jack Burns and wanted to talk to me. Between the messages from Harry, Ian, and Richie, there were a dozen dial-tones left by callers electing to leave no message. I figured that Frank Worthy was trying to get in touch, but was hesitant to leave his name. Let him wait. The last caller had not left a name, but her voice and its Oklahoma drawl was easily identifiable. The message was a simple suggestion to meet that night at Pinks, a trendy Westside dance club.

I called Ian Waddington and asked him what he had learned about Jack Burns.

"Nobody seems to know much about where Jack Burns came from. I heard stories that he was a Harvard MBA, but there was no listing of a Jack Burns at student records. Somebody else told me that he had worked for a major investment firm, but that didn't check out, either."

"Then how did he get started? Send away to a match-cover correspondence school on investment counseling?"

Ian barked sharply three times, a grating sound which passed for laughter. "How do half the scam-suckers in this town get started? The entertainment business, naturally. In the late seventies, he produced a couple of flicks."

"Porn?"

"Not quite, but I guess that depends on the ethical standards of your community. The first one was about the adventures of a sexually liberated woman in various exotic lands, and the rest were sequels. My local video merchant described them as hard R films with soft-focus sex."

I asked the titles, and Ian listed them. I felt the small satisfaction of information congealing into a pattern that begins to answer itself, like the remaining blanks in a crossword puzzle clued by the words filled in. "How did Burns make the leap from producer to investment counselor?"

"He used the experience to leverage himself into organizing and selling limited partnerships in film productions. A production company would come to him with a package, and Burns would sell it. Most of the films were losers, but the investors were into it for the glamour and tax write-offs, so it didn't really matter. That gave Burns his contacts in the entertainment business when he moved into more traditional types of investments."

Porn actor to movie producer to investment broker. The arc of Jack Burns's life began to make sense. I still didn't have any idea where he had hidden his money before he died, and asked: "What about hidden assets? Did you have any luck tracing him to partnerships or companies through which he could have sheltered anything?"

"Broke, broke, broke," Ian repeated. "I ran a computer check on corporations and partnerships, and his name was flagged only once. Burns had a hundred grand invested in a real-estate limited partnership called Sea View Estates Development Company."

That clicked. Frank Worthy had said he'd been involved in construction.

"Frank Worthy? Never heard of him," Ian said when I threw the name at him.

"He's a real-estate developer from Texas. What would it cost me for you to make a quick check on his assets?"

"Your left nut."

"Do you want it Federal Express, or will regular mail do?"

He said regular mail would be fine. As I hung up the phone, I heard the front office door open, and a cheery, unmistakable voice rang out: "Hey, dickhead. Welcome home."

Harry Selwurst's blond head peered slowly around the doorframe, as though half expecting a knuckle greeting. When he noticed the cast propped up on my desk, his blue eyes crinkled with malicious bonhomie. "Hey, break a leg."

"No thanks, already have."

"So break another. You deserve it."

"Thanks."

"Does it hurt much?"

"Not much."

"Too bad. No such thing as too much pain for a dickhead like you."

"I get the idea you don't like me, Harry."

"You're wrong about that. It's only because I like you so much that my lawyer hasn't called your lawyer with a lawsuit over that stupid stunt you pulled the other night. As your lawyer, I'd be talking to my lawyer, who happens also to be me, so chances are good we could settle out of court."

I didn't invite him in, but I didn't pull out a gun and shoot him, which was the only invitation he needed. He cleared a space on the edge of the desk and leaned against it, bearing down on me with an inane grin. His suit was a beautiful blue Italian wool blend, with light yellow stripes. Yellow was the power color of the season, and his tie would have shamed a lemon. His face was tan but unwrinkled, likely a gift of plastic surgery, and women might have found it attractive in a boyish sort of way. I found it annoying.

He didn't say anything. He just grinned. He was close enough for the smell of his cologne to turn my stomach. Even with the power tie he looked like the kind of guy you wanted to slap.

"So why the smile, Harry?" I finally asked.

"Because I'm the best lawyer in town. I'm so good, I got you off the hook on that prostie killing."

"Must have taken all your skills, considering the police were pissing into the wind."

"It's true, they didn't have much." Harry slipped a manicured hand into the side coat pocket and flipped open a black leather notebook burnished to a deep shine. "The blood under her nails was Type A, and you're pure O. The hair follicles were close to yours in color, but not a precise match. Clothing threads and the rug sample were both negative. About all they had were those incriminating photographs, and you with no alibi. By the way, I had no idea you were so well hung." He shut the notebook and slapped it absently on his knee. "Still, I've seen convictions with less. I've seen lab reports misfiled, lost, or just plain ignored. A good detective can get a witness to identify just about anybody for anything. When a good cop goes to work, he can convince a priest that Mother Teresa is a hooker."

Harry winked, and waited for my smile. I grimaced. He spun off my desk and glanced out the window, whether to check on the white Datsun or just to enjoy the view, I couldn't tell.

"So I figure you owe me," he said, facing me again.

"I owe you my thanks. Thank you, Harry. Now we're square."

"How was Europe?"

"I've got work, Harry," I said, trying to brush him off.

"You've got work. That's a joke. I checked. The only thing you've got going now is what you're doing with the guy whose name cost me the transmission in my Seville."

"I'm sure you figured out a way to bill Frank Worthy for it," I answered.

"You have the IQ of a dumbwaiter if you think this is about transmission money. A couple thousand isn't going to break me."

"You want an apology? Okay, I'm sorry. I got annoyed. If I knew you were going to bug me about it, I wouldn't have done it, not because I didn't want to do it, and not because I didn't feel great doing it, because I did. I wouldn't have done it because it brought you back to my office, and I've got a cast on my ankle and can't throw you out."

"Apology accepted," Harry said, and slid off the desk. He pulled a sheaf of papers from the breast pocket of his suit. "Time to get down to business. If I'm going to be your lawyer, we have to sign the documents."

"I don't want you as my lawyer."

Harry's face lengthened in a court show of anguish. He regretfully pocketed the papers. "That grieves me. It will grieve you as well. If I'm not your lawyer, then the client privilege is not in effect, and I'll be duty-bound to report what I know to the police."

I fingered the Egyptian lady and idly contemplated performing an impromptu proctologic surgery, making Harry Selwurst an even more perfect asshole. Instead I used the Egyptian lady to scratch an itch inside my cast, and said: "Maybe I'd feel threatened if I knew what I was being threatened with."

Harry nodded and wandered toward the window, pressing his hands together and raising them to his lips. "I read an interesting report in *The New York Times* about two Americans found shot to death in a hotel room in Paris. That is where you were, wasn't it? Paris? One of the deceased was a client of yours." Harry turned from the window and sprang the name on me. "A Miss Gamine."

"That's a pretty wild guess on your part."

"Who the hell do you think referred her to you?"

That answered one question, and raised a few others.

"What about Burns? Did you send him to me as well?"

Harry spread a fatuous smile and shrugged. I took it to mean yes, but couldn't take it far enough to trust it.

"I placed a call to the French police, with the best interests of my client in mind, naturally. A man fitting your description was seen outside the hotel room of the deceased, suspended on the ledge, shortly before shots were heard. The same man was then seen jumping out the window, injuring his leg, before disappearing down an alley." Harry stooped to examine my cast, and flicked his finger against the plaster. "Funny, but you seem to have hurt your ankle."

"So what's the trade?"

"I represent you. You give me ten percent of the grand prize, straight off the top."

"You're taking a big percentage of something I don't know anything about to do nothing but do nothing."

"What price freedom?"

"Maybe you'd better tell me something about this mythical take."

"You know why I hate bullshit? Why I hate it has nothing to do with morals. I don't hesitate to turn the truth into a lie, if I can get away with it. All in the spirit of debate, right? But bullshit is a lie that attempts to pass itself off as the truth by force of will alone. It's not even clever. It's a waste of time. So do us both a favor, and don't waste our time."

"Maybe you'd better tell me something about this mythical take," I repeated.

"Three million dollars," Harry breathed into my face. "I know it exists. You know it exists. Frank knows it exists."

"The police figure Burns was deep in debt when he died."

"They were looking at his investment company. That's not where the cash was coming from."

The surprise must have played as far as my features, because Harry grinned and said: "I'm starting to earn my ten percent, aren't I? Perhaps ten percent isn't enough." Harry again slipped the folded sheaf of papers from his suit, and spread them on my desk. They empowered him as my attorney. "I was Jack Burns's lawyer. Frank Worthy has his reasons for not telling you everything he knows. I won't tell you everything I know, either, but maybe between the two of us you can get enough answers to find what we're all looking for. Without a deal, though, I'm not going to tell you anything."

"Ten percent is too steep. Make it four."

"Something else I can do for you is to help you keep your percentage. Frank Worthy will take it away from you if he can. I know enough about Mr. Worthy to keep him off both our backs."

"Four percent," I repeated.

"Cheap bastard," he muttered, but handed me a gold Cross pen, and I signed the papers.

"Nina Gamine was fronting a real-estate development company in Venice Beach," Harry began. He folded the papers carefully back into his breast pocket, and plucked the pen from my hand. "The plan was to sell limited partnerships in a condominium development called Sea View Estates. Another company made a fortune with the same idea across the border in Santa Monica. Through Burns, Sea View Estates sold about three million in partnerships to forty separate investors. I filed bankruptcy papers on the company late last week."

"Why Nina Gamine? Why did Burns need a front?"

"He didn't want to be legally liable for Sea View Estates when it went down the toilet, would be my guess. I sincerely doubt they had any intention of following through with the construction."

I hoisted my cast from the desk and pulled a sheet of paper from the drawer. On the top of the sheet I doodled a large box, inside which I wrote "Sea View Estates." I connected the Sea View box with a smaller box below it, representing the limited partnerships.

"They sell limited partnerships in the company, then split the take," I speculated. "Nina Gamine leaves the country. Burns claims that he's been swindled along with everybody else. His reputation suffers a bit, but he's not legally responsible."

Harry leaned over the desk, fingers arched into an inverted V to support his weight. "The investment money was split into business accounts at twelve local banks. There were three signatories on the accounts: Gamine, Burns, and a company called Sweetwater Investment Corporation."

"What do you know about Sweetwater?" I asked, writing the three names next to the Sea View box on my sheet of paper.

"I've talked so much I'm losing my voice, and I've heard so little from you that I think I'm going deaf. Give."

I gave. I told him about the strange love triangle of Kathy Maddox, Nina Gamine, and her brother. I described the man who broke into the room, and the shooting. He listened patiently, and sharply questioned the gaps in my narrative when I dissembled. He was good enough to get more out of me than I had wanted to give. The suitcase piqued his interest. He wanted to know how large it was, and how much it weighed. I didn't catch on when he first asked about it, and when I did, I covered by giving the suitcase Herculean dimensions. I couldn't make it large enough to fit three million dollars, however, and he knew it.

"Now it's your turn. What do you know about Sweetwater?" I asked.

"Absolutely nothing," he grinned.

"Three million dollars missing and you don't know? That strains belief."

"This is a contingency case for me. Why put in the work when I can get you to do it for me?"

Naturally, I didn't believe him, and said: "You're a devious son of a bitch."

He took it as a compliment, saying thanks with a courtly bow of his head. "Sweetwater appears in the partnership agreement, but the papers didn't list an address. Legally, Sea View Estates was a joke. None of the papers was correctly filled out or filed."

"What kind of money had Sweetwater invested?"

"A hundred grand. You're thinking that this guy who did the killing is connected to Sweetwater."

I nodded, and asked: "Did Nina Gamine have a clear draw on the money?"

"The money was drawn out of the accounts over a period of three days. Twelve checks were written, payable to another company called United Ventures."

"Here we go again. What do you know about United Ventures?"

"What am I supposed to do, hand you the fucking thing on a platter? Withdrawals in excess of five grand needed two signatures, so the checks all had signatures and countersignatures," Harry continued.

"Who signed, Gamine and Sweetwater?"

Harry wagged his head. "Gamine and Burns."

"Doesn't make sense. If his signature is on the withdrawals, then Burns can't very well complain that he has been swindled."

"He could claim that his signature was forged."

"Okay, so that was how it was supposed to look. Nina Gamine forges a series of checks, draining the accounts of Sea View Estates, and disappears. Burns is supposed to collect a share, probably with Sweetwater. But that wasn't how Nina Gamine planned it. When it comes time to make the split, she arranges Burns's death, and runs with all three million."

"Sweetwater is burned and tracks her down," Harry interrupted. "He pumps a couple of rounds into her and her brother, and runs with the money. Now, dickhead, the three-million-dollar question is who is Sweetwater, and where is he hiding?"

When Selwurst cleared the door, I called the Federal Reserve Bank. The receptionist routed me to a guy named Victor who worked the vault. When I asked him how much three million in twenties weighed, he said: "Hell if I know. That's a weird kinda question."

"I got a bet going with a buddy," I said. "Think you could figure it out?"

He thought it over, said "Sure," and yelled to somebody else in the vault: "Hey, I forget, what does a bundle weigh?"

Victor turned his voice back to the phone. "Two point four pounds a bundle. You got twenty grand in a bundle. So how would you figure it out, yeah, you'd divide 'em first. So twenty grand goes into three million a hundred and fifty times. Then you multiply 'em. A hundred and fifty times two point four pounds is about three hundred and sixty pounds."

I thanked him and went to work on my calculator. The red suitcase Francis Gamine carried out of Kathy Maddox's Paris hotel room would have weighed seventy pounds maximum. Clothes were in the case, so I figured the case contained maybe sixty pounds in cash, or approximately five hundred thousand dollars. Two and a half million short of three million.

27

The Hall of Records is a dull gray government building downtown where Los Angelenos cluster in labyrinthine lines, waiting for the machinery of society to validate the births, deaths and other seminal events of their existences with a number and a county seal. Angel had picked me up at the office and given her report during the ride downtown. The small key that had been hung with Kathy Maddox's hotel key had been identified by a locksmith as the type commonly used by storage facilities. We speculated that Kathy Maddox had stored her belongings before flying to Paris, and it was a good bet that her belongings included three hundred pounds in twenty-dollar bills. With about a hundred self-storage facilities in the Greater Los Angeles area, the problem was one of legwork.

I had my own problems with legwork, learning how to hobble on crutches through the crowds at the Hall of Records. Angel and I were routed through business registry to a short and rotund black woman bustling between blinking phones, microfiche files, and a two-foot stack of unstamped forms. Huge round eyeglasses spanned the width of her face and extended down her cheeks, giving her the appearance of a big black owl. Angel asked for the file listing the fictitious business-name statement of Sea View Estates. The clerk plucked one-handed a square blue plastic sheet from a file box and pointed to the microfiche machines along the wall, her opposite hand clacking in an uninterrupted form-stamping rhythm.

Angel pressed the plastic sheet into the slot and raced the cursor through a list of businesses beginning with *S* registered in the county. She overshot her target and backed into Sea View Estates Developments.

The business was registered as a limited partnership. The names on the document were Mike E. Mouse, Don L. Duck, and Cindy Rella.

"We've got a problem," Angel said to the clerk.

"We've all got problems," the clerk rejoined mercilessly, "and I've probably got more than most."

The phone buzzed. She picked up the receiver, told the line to hold please, and dropped the phone down again.

"What are your problems?" I asked.

Her eyes were bright when she laughed, surprised by the question. "You got all day I could tell you. One of my problems is I don't got all day so I couldn't tell you even if you did. So to save us all some time maybe you had just better tell me your problem."

"We have some wrong names registering this company," Angel said.

The clerk leaned her elbows on the counter and took a deep breath, as though it were her first full stop all day. Her head swiveled down the counter in both directions, checking the lines, the phones, and likely the supervisor. She decided she had time to talk.

"What do you mean by wrong?" the clerk asked.

"We know the owners of this company, but the people who registered the company are not the owners."

"You mean they put fictitious names on the fictitious business-name statement," the clerk clarified, and when our heads bobbed in unison, explained: "That sometimes happens. We don't check any of the names people submit."

"You don't ask for identification?"

"Someone could register as the Sweet Lord Jesus and we wouldn't know the difference. Sounds crazy, but true."

"Then why register at all?"

"It's required by law, first of all. But shoot, we all know that just because something is required doesn't mean much, otherwise we wouldn't have prisons and a long line of folks waiting to get in and out of 'em. It's the banks that enforce this thing. They like to have something on paper before they cash the checks. Banks won't open a business account unless they got county papers."

"So if somebody already has established banking ties, they don't necessarily need county documents to open an account under a fictitious business name," I speculated.

"I wouldn't know. I'm not a banker. But I can tell you that if somebody doesn't have a good relationship with a bank, they sure as heck are gonna need to show they've registered with us."

We submitted a list of businesses and names we wanted to check, and the clerk pulled a small stack of plastic microfiche sheets. We went to work. Registered businesses were filed by business name, and cross-registered by name of owner. The paper on Jack Burns was straight. He was listed as the sole proprietor of his investment firm. Nina Gamine didn't show in the files. Sweetwater Investment Corporation, named by Harry Selwurst as co-owner of Sea View Estates, was owned by another company, Magnolia Enterprises. Magnolia Enterprises listed itself as a California corporation, but had not registered as a business in Los Angeles. Angel swapped microfiche sheets and located United Ventures, the company on the receiving end of the checks from Sea View Estates. It was registered as a wholly owned subsidiary of Sea View Estates. A blind check of Sea View Estates would result in an endless loop. Cozy.

I sketched a flow chart of the relationship between Sea View Estates and the principal players. Sea View was owned by Burns, Gamine and Sweetwater. Sweetwater was owned by Magnolia. United Ventures was a subsidiary of Sea View. I collected the microfiche sheets and walked them to the clerk, who motioned for us to wait while she clamped the state seal one by one on a sheaf of documents, and gave directions to the Hall of Records to a caller on the telephone.

"We still don't know anything about the third man," Angel said.

"You mean companies Sweetwater and Magnolia. Those names mean anything to you?"

Angel shrugged. The clerk hung up the phone, plucked the microfiche from my hands, and remarked: "They're both cities in Texas."

"Beg pardon?" I said.

"Cities in Texas," the clerk repeated patiently. "Sweetwater and Magnolia. I got kin in Magnolia. It's right outside Dallas."

I blew her a kiss, and said: "If it were up to me, sweetheart, all your problems would be over."

She arched her back and sauced me with a jaundiced eye. "Honey, half my problems come from men who promise to solve my problems."

I camped in the corridor while Angel slogged through the Texas state bureaucracy on the telephone, attempting to pinpoint ownership of Magnolia Corporation. The swelling in my ankle was slowly subsiding, which opened a crease between my skin and the plaster. The pain was lessening, but as the air began to circulate inside the cast, the pain was replaced by an unbearable itching. I worked the blade of the Egyptian lady deep into the crease, and wriggled it about, getting just enough of the itch to fool myself into believing I was making progress.

"This is never going to make sense," Angel complained, retrieving her long-distance calling card. "Magnolia is owned by a Frank Knott."

I whipped the calling card from her hand and plugged it into the phone. I called Ian Waddington's office, held impatiently while he completed another call, and skipped the pleasantries when he jacked into the line. "Forget Frank Worthy. What do you know about Frank Knott?"

"I don't want to forget Frank Worthy. You ask me to check on him, the least you can do is listen. I'm looking at his TRW right now."

I told him to go ahead, thinking at the moment that perhaps my hunch was wrong.

"Frank Worthy sells used computers in Reseda. His net worth is about three grand, and his Visa card shows a string of late payments," Ian said, and barked three times with laughter.

"What about Knott?" I pressed.

"Frank Knott, as I recall, was a major-league player in the Houston real-estate market. The oil bust absolutely murdered him. He has a high rise in downtown Houston with a ninety-percent vacancy rate, and a new housing development in the suburbs which hasn't sold a unit in a year. He recently has been sniffing around Los Angeles for investment capital, which is how I know about him. Nobody wants to touch him. Frank Knott is all-star, hall-of-fame broke."

Fraud is often the last resort of once-successful businessmen who, when facing the oblivion of bankruptcy, resort to maintaining wealth by any means possible. Money is integral to identity, and honesty has less net worth. Frank Knott had been desperate enough to throw into an investment scam with Jack Burns. He had lied to me regarding his name, the nature of his business, and his investment in Sea View Estates. I suspected that if I found the money, he would kill me for it, and I wondered if he hadn't already killed in his chase for the chimera of wealth.

28

Pinks was in. Being in, it didn't advertise. People heard about it by reading the gossip columns, the ones that say such-and-such famous person could be seen with so-and-so other person who is not quite but soon to be famous. Pinks didn't have a sign or a front door. The entrance was in the back alley of a fashionable shopping street, downwind from a dumpster. There wasn't any reason to be in the alley, except to go to Pinks. Being there didn't guarantee admission. Being in meant keeping other people out. The doorman wouldn't let someone in unless he liked his shoes, knew his name, or, at the very least, knew his agent's name. He was a trendy art type who wore sunglasses and a red goatee like a paste-on disguise. He didn't know my name, and he didn't like my cast or the sneaker I wore on my other foot. But he liked Angel's Parisian leather dress, a Chanel number cut nine inches above the knee and adorned by slashing buckled straps, under which she wore a white cotton jersey casually rolled to the shoulders. I smiled and scraped by in her wake, feeling a bit like Charles Laughton's Hunchback shuffling behind Esmeralda.

Angel grabbed my arm and waited for her eyes to adjust to the smoke, darkness, and noise. Pinks offered the latest in postapocalyptic decor. The walls were pitted brick, and the floor chipped concrete. The chairs and tables were bought thirdhand from the local soup kitchen. The charge was ten bucks a head to get in, and it was packed with a young and hip dance crowd.

We wedged past the bar, tended by an albino woman with blood-red lips and eyes like a spider's web, and lucked into a table set against the far wall. The first late-night crush was on, and as I watched the mosaic of bodies pressing in and out of the crowd, my mind sorted the fragments of what I knew and didn't know about Frank Knott, and what I would say to him when we met later that night.

Dusty approached us from behind, and I didn't see her until she settled into the chair at my side, coolly sipping a beer. "Is this your girlfriend?" she asked, nudging her chin toward Angel. When I introduced Angel as my partner, Dusty gave her a longer, more serious look, then stretched out her hand with a "Glad to meetcha."

I would not have recognized Dusty in the crowd, so completely had her appearance changed since I had last seen her, in Burns's Malibu castle. The Rubenesque proportions of her body were jacketed by a denim coat, stiff jeans, and old leather work boots. Her red hair was pulled back in a severe ponytail, and without the definition of makeup, her face was round and freckled. She looked like a country girl who should have been drinking beer and just now learning about sex in the back of a pickup truck on a moonlit dirt road.

"I don't know what y'all know and don't know, so I'll just talk and let me know if I bore ya, okay? First thing y'all should know is I'm scared as a cat to even be here talkin' to you. Sure, gettin' cut is a risk you take, but shit, when you're gettin' five hundred a trick, you're not exactly hangin' out with guttergrease."

Dusty took down half her beer in a long pull, and wiped her mouth with her jacket sleeve. She looked up, her eyes scanning the crowd, then hunched forward, pitching her voice as low as she could. He words were just audible over the din of rock and roll pounding from the dance floor. "If I was to talk to the cops, which I'm not going to do for the simple reason that they'd listen real polite to what I had to say, then tell me to get on my knees, I'd tell them that a lot of Mona's business came to her from a lawyer we called the Worm. Now I'm no

Sherlock Holmes but it seems to me that by asking this guy a few questions you might be able to find out who Mona was supposed to be meeting the night she was killed.''

"His name?" I inquired.

"Didn't I say it?" Dusty asked, startled. "Harry Selwurst."

That figured. Harry was the ultimate parasite. When he wormed into a situation, the more somebody ate, the fatter Harry got. I asked whether Harry had sent Mona to Jack Burns.

"We call it a referral, and yes, he did. She gave me a ring and said that the Worm had scored us another winner," Dusty answered, pronouncing the concluding word "wiener."

"When did you first meet Jack Burns?" I asked, wondering whether Mona had lied to me about that as well as how she had been introduced to Jack Burns.

"The night before you answered the door."

"Had Mona known him before that?"

Dusty paused before answering, shifting in her chair as she scanned the crowd, as though looking for someone who might be looking for her. "She got there a couple of minutes before I did, and she didn't seem to know the guy at all. If somebody is a regular, you get to know his tastes. He was stoned out of his mind, and for the first half hour it was kinda weird, 'cause we didn't really know what he wanted, and he acted like he didn't know where the hell he was."

"What did Harry Selwurst get out of it?" I asked.

"He got his rocks off or a pimp's cut of the take. Sometimes both."

"Did Mona tell you that she was going to meet somebody referred by Harry Selwurst on the night she was killed?"

"Not exactly, but I got my suspicions," Dusty answered, then shrugged in a sudden loss of her convictions. "I dunno. It coulda been some crazy. It's been open season on call girls for a coupla years in this city, and nobody seems to mind much, including the cops. But I keep thinkin' how the girl had been tryin' to work a scam on Jack Burns. Did she tell y'all about that?"

"The night she died."

"But Jack Burns is dead, so who would want to kill her to keep the porno past of a dead man secret? Don't make sense.'' Dusty twisted toward the crowd, again looking for someone. Her head stilled, and her right hand tipped up to the corner of her eyebrow. She propped her elbows on the table and asked: ''Y'all remember that Jack Burns acted in that porno film some years ago? Well, I'd like to introduce you to the star, and she is a star, so treat her like one, okay?''

I glanced up and met the eyes of a dark-haired woman. Her gait was slow and cocky as she strolled to the table. She wore black silk pajamas, Oriental-style, slashed by a red belt. A wry, world-weary smile lifted the corner of her lips, painted invitational red. She was as thin and small-busted as a ballet dancer, and moved with a dancer's confident ease. Her eyes were dark and, set against the pale white of her skin, glowed with a luminous and obdurate burn. Her hips rolled to a stop at the edge of the table. I stood. She extended her hand and said in a low and husky voice that her name was Sash. I took the hand in mine. A sudden jolt of adrenaline rushed through my nerves, and my hand began to unaccountably shake. I withdrew it, and introduced Angel. Touching her hand, and held in the fleeting embrace of her eyes, I had felt enveloped by a sexual energy as elemental and polymorphous as heat. Sash was undeniably a star, though a dark one.

''This little one here lost a friend, and I'm here to help her if I can,'' Sash began, softly kissing the patch of skin between Dusty's temple and eye. The kiss seemed simultaneously maternal and sexual, and I became aware of Sash's age, which would have been about twice Dusty's. As her skin was smooth and supple and nearly flawless, Sash could have passed for twenty-five, but she radiated a confident and controlled inner power beyond the ability of anyone that young. ''Most of the people I know who have died took their own lives, one way or another. There is little you can do then, except feel a little sorry for them, yourself, and the world. But Dusty tells me that Mona Demonay was murdered, and there is something we can do about that. We can take revenge. I'm hoping that what I can tell you, which isn't much, will help you find her killer. And when you find him, you'll let us know so we can cut his balls off.''

"The hell with his balls. I'm going to take my .45 and blow his brains out, the son of a bitch," Dusty threatened.

It was just talk, and a little bit of a tough-girl act to impress Sash. I ignored it and asked: "Did Mona talk to you before she was killed?"

"We spoke briefly on the phone. She asked me about an adult film titled *Television Blues*. Not one of my finer vehicles, but among the first. It took me back, I'll tell you. I was younger then than this one, here." Sash smiled, and caressed Dusty's cheek with a single scarlet nail. "Mona asked me about my co-star, a man she knew as Jack Burns. I didn't recognize the name, but she described what he looked like, and it could have been him."

"Do you remember what his name was back then?" Angel asked.

Sash cast a lingering gaze at Angel, and told her that she was quite lovely. Angel blushed, but her eyes flashed as though the remark both flattered and demeaned her. She repeated the question.

"I'm too vain to admit how long ago that film was shot, although I'm happy to say that my looks have weathered the years better than my memory. I just don't remember. The first name is correct, Jack, but his last name wasn't Burns. I don't even recall his stage name, which I suppose you could look up if you could find the film. But it wouldn't do you any good, because adult film actors are rarely billed under their real name."

That would explain why Ian Waddington was unable to trace Burns back further than fifteen years. He changed his name when he switched professions. I asked Sash what she remembered about Jack.

"Not much. *Television Blues* was only a three-day wonder, but we shot it back to back with another film, so I knew him in total for about a week. Dusty told me that Jack became some kind of a financial heavyweight, which I find a little hard to believe."

"He conned people into believing he was, but his real gift was for fraud. Does that conflict with what you knew about him?"

"Could he have been a con artist? Sure. He was a very good actor. Most adult film stars have big dicks and small brains, but not Jack. He wasn't Einstein, but he was quick enough. Except around drugs.

The man was a monster with the pharmaceuticals. He wasn't an addict, but he did like to binge. Every night after shooting. But everybody in adult films likes their medications, and the only reason I remember it is because one night he miscalculated and was still too stoned to shoot the following day.''

It all fit into the profile of Jack Burns as I had known him, but the information didn't add up to anything more than I already believed I knew. As charming as the company was, I slid my chair back and was about to launch into a polite good-bye when Angel asked:

''What happened to Jack after the film was shot? Did you ever see him again?''

''I suppose he dropped out of the adult film industry shortly after *Television Blues,* because I never ran across him again, although I seem to vaguely remember something about stage acting,'' Sash answered. Her dark eyes blanked, and then brightened as an image dropped into place. ''I forgot about the looping. We shot most of the action sequences MOS, or without sound, and two weeks later met at a sound studio to record the moans and groans. It's been too long for me to remember clearly, but I think Jack said he was going to move to New York and try stage acting.''

It was another detail that fit within the duplicitous pattern of Jack Burns's life, and I made a casual note of it. I asked Sash to give me a call should she remember the name Jack Burns used when she had known him, and thanked her for trying to help. When Angel and I left Pinks, Dusty and Sash were holding hands across the table, talking about prospects for work in the adult film business. A long and hard stare later, the pattern of Jack Burns's life would shift like a deeply embedded holograph suddenly illuminated by a simple change in perspective.

29

I waited for the limousine at the corner of Santa Monica and Robertson. An adolescent of about sixteen sauntered past, all muscles in a white tank top and tight blue jeans. Aware that a man on crutches at night seems an easy target, I idly wondered how I would handle it if he tried to jump me. He noticed the attention and turned to ask for a cigarette. I told him I didn't smoke. Then he gave me the look, said he didn't much care what he sucked on, and named a price. My first instinct was to hit him with my crutch, but I got a look at his eyes, and that stopped me. He didn't look hungry, or hopeful, or greedy, or excited. He didn't look much of anything. His eyes were holes to nowhere. I told him I wasn't interested. He shrugged, plugged his hands in his hip pockets, and ambled away.

The limo slid up to the red zone and parked. I reached for the passenger door. It was locked. I knocked on the window. The chauffeur circled the front of the car. He was a large black man in a navy blue turtleneck. The turtleneck was an extra large and stretched taut over an upper body contoured like an inverted mountain. His hair was cropped close to his head, and his face was round and massive but bore an amiable smile. I thought he just wanted to open the door for me, but he touched my elbow with a light but firm hand and said: "If you'll please raise your arms for a moment."

"I can't raise my arms," I replied.

"I'm sorry, sir, but I can't let you in the car until I check you."

"If I raise my arms, I lose my crutches. If I lose my crutches, I fall down," I explained.

He stepped back and considered the problem. "How about if you just hold your arms out?" he suggested.

He seemed like a nice guy who wanted to do his job. I let him do it. When he had finished, he rapped gently on the window. The door unlocked with a dull click. Frank of the mutable last name glared at me from the far side of the limo, palming a pale blue Stetson. I set the crutches lengthwise along the floor. Frank offered his hand. I took it. He squeezed too hard and held too long for the shake to remain a gesture of friendship. His grip was good, but the grip of his eyes was stronger, and I couldn't have cracked that with a sledgehammer.

"I was a little disappointed you didn't come to talk to me when you first got back into town," he said, smiling.

Frank put another five foot-pounds of pressure into his grip, to certify that I was getting the point, then dropped the hand. The limousine rolled into traffic.

"The funny thing about sending someone out to look for your money is you don't exactly know what he's gonna do with it once he finds it," Frank mused in cracker-barrel style. "You gotta trust the man to go against his baser instincts. People will do almost anything for money. Hell, not almost anything. Anything. And that's what I worry about. Why take twelve percent if you can get away with it all?"

"No reason, except trust," I said.

"I got a problem with that. Jesus trusted Judas. Caesar trusted Brutus. Neither of them lived as long as I have. The problem with trust is you can't trust it. You can only trust people to do the right thing if they fear you. A man has to know that if he betrays the trust, you'll hunt him down and take it out of his hide. The kind of money we're dealing with here, the man has to know that he won't live to spend it if he tries to cut a different deal."

"I get the distinct feeling you're trying to tell me that you don't trust me."

Frank broke into an easy grin, and his eyes twinkled blue as the turquoise stones in his belt, bolo tie, and rings. "We're just sittin' on the front porch, talkin'. I trust you. Just as long as you understand our agreement, we'll get along fine."

I no longer understood our agreement, but I had spent the man's money, so I told him how I had spent it. He listened with a sharp interest, tilting his head ten degrees forward to get closer to my words, although the limo drove quietly and he had no trouble hearing me. He seemed to recognize Nina Gamine's name, but he asked me to repeat what she looked like. I thought he was trying to throw me off.

"So we have half a mil in a suitcase taken by somebody we don't know, and a hell of a lot more money than that floating around unaccounted for," Frank repeated when I had finished. "So far, I've put ten grand into this, and I've got nothing on account but a lame detective."

Frank thought about it long enough to decide he wanted to fix himself a drink and think about it some more. He clinked ice in a tumbler and trickled an ounce and a half of bourbon over the ice. He settled back into the seat and queried: "This guy with the bruises and mustache, you wouldn't be making him up, having stashed the cash someplace safe, would you?"

I said I wouldn't.

"Then who the hell is he?" he drawled.

"I was thinking you knew him," I said, and waited.

"Doesn't ring a bell. Why should I know him?"

I let the question hang, then took a good shot at him.

"I was thinking he works for you, Mr. Knott."

Frank Knott uttered a short and sharp grunt. A sheepish smile curled his lip and he said: "I guess the rumors weren't true. You do know your ass from a hole in the ground. But I don't know what the hell you mean by this guy working for me."

"I'm talking about Sea View Estates," I said. "A limited partnership headed by Jack Burns, Nina Gamine, and a company called Sweetwater Investment Corporation. Sweetwater is owned by another company, Magnolia Enterprises. You are the sole owner of Magnolia, and control Sweetwater."

"If that's what the papers say, it must be true. But if you'll pardon my French, what's the big fucking deal?"

"Sea View Estates was a scam from the beginning, and your investment with Jack Burns wasn't more than one hundred grand. That's the deal," I said.

"Bullshit," he drawled, and he didn't say it the short way. He stretched the "bull" and cut the "shit" fast and hard.

"Burns had the Southern California money contacts. You knew real estate, and how to structure a deal that would look unbeatable on paper. Burns needed money fast to prop up his Ponzi scheme. You didn't get out of Texas fast enough when oil prices collapsed. Loans are being called and your credit line has been cut."

"Bullshit," he repeated, turning the word short and hard. Like the Eskimos, who have over a dozen intonations for snow, a good Texan can say "bullshit" a dozen different ways and mean something different by each one.

"After your debts are subtracted from your assets, I doubt if your net worth is much more than mine, which is zero," I pressed. Knott grimaced. He looked down at the drink in his hands, listening. "Had you been able to wait for your money, Sea View would probably have been a winner, but you both needed cash fast. Nina Gamine was brought in to take the fall. You would either find a way to dump her permanently, or give her a cut of the take and ship her overseas. It was supposed to look like embezzlement, with both you and Burns victims of Nina Gamine."

"Now you've stepped from bullshit into some serious horseshit," Knott pronounced, his voice grim.

"But Nina Gamine got greedy, or maybe she thought you weren't going to let her live to spend her share. It doesn't matter because she's dead now, and nobody cares. You hired me to track the money, and somebody else to track me. I found Nina Gamine and the money, part of it at least, and your man was there to collect. But he blew it, because he thought the suitcase contained more than it did. You've recovered a fifth of the three million, and want to find the rest."

Knott nodded, his thin-man face widening in chagrin. He took an inch off the level of his bourbon, and said: "That's one hell of a story. If it were true, by your accounting, I'd be five hundred grand richer than when I started."

"I cross-checked with some people in the investment community. Burns brought the investors to you, or maybe I should say marks, and you helped with the close."

Knott spread his mouth in a rich, burnished laugh, and said: "A hell of a story. I wish it were true."

"If you have a different story to tell, tell it," I suggested.

"I thought the project was legitimate. Jack Burns approached me about a year ago with the idea. I was new in town, and hadn't connected to the local money that I needed to work my own deals. So I threw in with him. His reputation seemed okay, and he had good money contacts. Burns's problem was that he didn't know shit about real estate. I do. So we set up a partnership. The deal looked good, because it was good. We had a line on beachfront property, and hired an architect to draw up the plans. Burns and I both kicked in some seed money, and the investors flowed in."

"What about Nina Gamine?"

"I thought she was a major investor."

"Right."

"You think I brought home a gusher when I'm telling you I hit squat. Burns described her as key to the deal. She promised to invest a certain sum, and to bring in some of her friends, who were supposed to be old Pasadena money. He introduced me to her over dinner at some fancy restaurant over in Pasadena. She was an old dowager in a wheelchair. Mean as hell. Wouldn't trust the preacher with the Sunday collection. She insisted on being a signatory to the bank accounts. I thought it a good idea at the time, thought it might help keep Burns honest."

"Did the woman have a cane?"

Knott grinned, either from chagrin or admiration, or possibly both, and said: "Hell, yes. She just about clobbered me with it once when I didn't get out of her way fast enough. But you described Nina Gamine as being considerably younger and more attractive."

"I did. You met Jack Burns's mother, not Nina Gamine."

Knott's eyes drifted out the window with the dazed glitter of a man who just realizes he's been had. His shoulders seemed to gain five pounds, and he sighed: "Well, shit."

"You were right about trust," I remarked, bringing him back.

"What about it?"

"You can't trust it."

"Sure as hell can't," he agreed, then straightened his shoulders, and the cogs began to turn. "We still have our deal. I'll live up to my end of it, and I expect you to follow through with yours."

"I don't think so. If I find the money, and that's a big if, considering I have no idea where it is, it will be divided among the Sea View investors, prorated according to their investment. You've hired me and I appreciate the work, so I'll subtract the amount of your investment in Sea View, plus my expenses, before I turn the money in. That should gross you about one hundred and twenty grand."

Knott reached a big bony hand to the console on the other side of the wet bar, and pressed a silver button. "Raymond, the site, please," he announced, and I noticed the small microphone next to the button. "I'm disappointed. I thought we had a deal, and what I'm hearing now is that we don't have a deal." He glanced at the blue Stetson on the seat, and traced his finger along the rim.

"You lied to me about who you were and how much you had lost to Burns, so now we have a different deal."

"I don't want a different deal. I want the deal we agreed to."

"Can't have it."

Knott slipped his hand from under the Stetson and pointed a toylike .32 automatic at my chest. A man points a gun at me, I look at it. It wasn't a dangerous gun, as guns go. It fit easily in the palm of his hand, and the barrel was short. A short barrel sacrifices accuracy for size. It couldn't have hit an aircraft carrier at a distance greater than thirty yards. At three feet, it was enough gun to pin my guts to the seat. I looked at Knott. He didn't seem any more serious than his gun. He could have been holding a drink by the expression of bemusement on his face.

"Come on. What are you going to do, shoot me?" I asked in

disbelief—thinking that, if he did, such a small gun might not kill me. Not immediately, at least.

"A lame detective is about as useless as a three-legged thoroughbred. If you don't tell me what you've done with the money, I'll have to put you down."

I didn't appreciate the metaphor, and said: "You heard my story. I don't have any better idea where the money is than when we started."

"I don't think I can trust you. I'm sure that you're honest, in your own way, but greed does funny things to a man. It can make a man compromise himself faster than a two-dollar whore. It makes the honest cheat, and a coward bold. Three million dollars is a lot of greed."

"Eight percent is all the greed I can handle. If I took a bigger bite, I'd choke on it."

The limousine slowed, turned, and the road changed. I glanced out the window at a huge pit, flanked at the top by Cyclone fencing. The limousine braked slowly down a steep dirt incline into the belly of the pit. I didn't like it.

"I remember you were offered twelve percent, and my memory is not poor," Knott corrected.

I played the only card I had left.

"I had to deal for information and a little protection. I made the deal with a guy who knew something about Sea View Estates. Four percent seemed a little high, but he told me he knew enough about you to keep you off my back, should you suddenly get greedy. It seems to me you're getting greedy. You know the guy. Your lawyer, Harry Selwurst."

The limo scraped dirt at the base of the incline, and rolled to a smooth stop in the night shadow of a bound stack of steel reinforcement bar. I looked at Knott. He smiled, and shook his head. His voice pitied me.

"Son, your leg ain't the only thing about you that's lame. Harry Selwurst is a conniving son of a bitch, and he's the last man on earth I'd hire as my lawyer."

The door opened behind me, and a hand gently gripped my shoulder. Raymond's head bobbed politely when I turned, and he helped me through the frame as Knott stepped out of the car and circled the black trunk. Raymond handed me my crutches, and asked Knott if there was anything else he could do. Knott told him to wait in the car. Raymond wished me a pleasant evening, more out of habit than cruel irony, and returned to the driver's seat.

The construction pit covered about an acre of ground, and was lined in massive vertical slabs of concrete towering thirty feet to street level. Steel supports jutted out of the walls at six-foot intervals, and dipped into the pit like giant oars. Huge columns sprang incomplete from the dirt into the dark sky, ending in jagged concrete edges and splayed steel bars. The ground was littered with the detritus of construction, aluminum cans and paper wrappers. I pressed the tip of a crutch against a soft-drink can, and heard the metal give with a sharp crack.

Frank Knott saluted me with the automatic and, pitching his voice into the night, said: "This is going to be a high rise in six months. Fifty-five stories of steel and glass. A man couldn't ask for a better tombstone."

"You were in on the con at the beginning, weren't you?" I asked, my heart thumping at the thought that Knott had chosen a good spot to disappear me.

"What difference does it make?" he shrugged.

"You tried to keep your real name secret because you planned to kill me if I found the money."

Knott sighted the little automatic on my chest and swung it a couple of degrees to the side. The gun kicked three times, the small-caliber fire amplified by the pit into the sound of a cannon, and my right crutch splintered from under me. I hobbled and balanced over my left crutch.

"I want you to tell me where you've hidden the money, and if you don't, I'll kill you," Knott threatened, beading the automatic on my chest again.

I told him he was full of shit, the adrenaline coursing fear through me like a fast-running river, and the automatic kicked again, skittering my left crutch from under me. I tossed away the dead end and balanced on one foot. Knott palmed the automatic and snapped it into firing position.

A horn blast shattered the tableau. Knott's head jerked toward a tan pickup truck careening down the ramp. Angel clicked her headlights into bright, and swamped the pit with light as her wheels fishtailed at the base of the ramp. The door to the limousine cracked open, and Raymond hulked out of the driver's seat, shouldering an over-and-under semiautomatic shotgun. Angel saw the gun and hit the brakes about twenty yards from the back of the limo, skidding to a dust-whirling stop.

What we had was a problem of escalation.

I waited for the dust to settle, and said: "Come on, Frank. Everybody knows I've been working for you, and everybody knows you tried sandbagging me into thinking you lost three million. You're just angry because I found out about it, and that's no reason to shoot me."

Frank Knott tipped his head back and let loose a howl, out of which emerged the words: "I need that money!" Then he lowered the gun.

I motioned Angel to pull forward and said: "I'm real sorry that you're broke, but I don't have it, and if I do find anything, I'll let you know."

Raymond pivoted smoothly with the shotgun as Angel's pickup crept forward, waiting for a signal from Knott, who held his automatic loosely at his side. I muscled up the back of the truck, and flipped into the bed. Angel cranked the wheel and gunned it up the ramp. The dirt smoothed into pavement. The cool night air rushed over me. I laughed, my mind racing heady with excitement. The stars glimmered overhead, and I drank them in. My heart slowed its wild adrenaline charge, and I wondered why I should feel peace at the end of fear.

30

Harry Selwurst had a suite of offices in a bank building on Ventura Boulevard in Encino. The receptionist was barricaded behind a counter, teller window, and locked door as protection from irate clients, which I supposed to be many. She inquired whether I had an appointment, and when I handed her my card, read my name aloud and asked if she had pronounced it correctly. I said that she had, and she instructed me to wait in the lobby until she could let Mr. Selwurst know I was waiting. I sat in a black leather armchair, next to a man in his mid-thirties with a brush cut and wire-rim spectacles. The man regarded me with a look of curious skepticism, as though he were about to ask me a question, and then not believe my answer. His eyes were an intense brown, and though I turned my back and scanned a magazine, it is difficult to ignore someone whose complete attention is focused on the very flick of your eyes across the page. I looked at him, and that was all the excuse he needed to introduce himself.

"This is an incredible coincidence. I'm Richie Warner of the *Times*. I've been trying to reach you for days," he said. His voice carried the harsh and nasal accent of a native New Yorker.

"I've been out of town," I replied.

He repressed a smile with a quick flick of his lips, having heard that line before, and said: "I'm doing a story on Jack Burns, and

Sheriff Kohl suggested I talk to you. You were the one who found his body, right?''

"No comment," I replied.

"It's a simple yes or no answer. No comment required. Kohl mentioned that you were hired by Mr. Burns to act as his bodyguard. Is that correct?''

"No comment," I repeated.

"These are facts easily corroborated by other people," Richie said reproachfully.

"Nothing personal. If I answer one question, all it will do is encourage you to ask me another. You'll move from facts corroborated by others to stuff only I know, which I don't want to tell you."

"Do you mind telling me why you don't want to talk about Mr. Burns?" he asked, in a tone of patronizing politeness that suggested he was a reasonable man and I was not.

"What I do is confidential between myself and my client."

"Who in this case is, I might point out, dead," Richie interrupted.

"That doesn't matter. If my name appears in the papers, my other clients get nervous. Nobody likes to have their private business conducted by a celebrity."

Richie jumped me with his response. It wasn't the first time he'd had this conversation, and he was confident that his argument would coerce me into talking. "All the more reason you should talk to me. I'm allowed some discretion in what I write, so I don't have to attribute any quotes directly to you. You already feature prominently in the story, but in what context and how often your name appears in print hasn't yet been decided."

"Meaning that if I don't talk, you'll do a hatchet job on me."

"Not at all. I'm just saying that you have some control in how your name appears in the story if you decide to talk to me."

The secretary announced to Richie that Mr. Selwurst was ready to see him. Richie tapped me on the arm, advised me to think about it, and said he hoped that he would see me later. I wondered if there was a back exit from Harry's office. A phone rested on a tinted smoked-glass end table between my chair and a black leather sofa. I cradled the receiver against my shoulder and called the office. Angel picked up after a couple of rings, and I asked her how the search was going. She complained that the work was boring. She had called the dozen storage facilities closest to Kathy Maddox's apartment without any luck in matching the key. I suggested she expand her search to the area surrounding Los Angeles International Airport, and after exchanging a couple of sappy yet essential lovers' sentimentalities, we hung up.

I occupied the remaining minutes working the tip of the Egyptian lady down to my ankle, until Richie Warner swept down the hall, scribbling furiously in a small flip-top notebook. The receptionist called my name, and Richie gave me a look of rife with significance when I passed him at the gate leading to the corridor. He said that he would meet me in the lobby, and I just nodded. The receptionist led me down the corridor to a corner office, knocked on the door, and opened it. Harry stood behind his desk, beaming fatuously, and called me his good friend while motioning me to a chair.

"You're not Frank Knott's lawyer," I said, declining the seat.

"I never said I was," Harry replied, still beaming.

"The hell you didn't."

"I precisely recall having said you had an important friend. You jumped to the conclusion that I was referring to some mysterious character named Frank Worthy, whom you now name as Mr. Knott. You may remember that I never mentioned either Mr. Knott or Mr. Worthy."

"Then why the hell did you bail me out, and who the hell is this important friend?"

"I guess it won't do any harm to tell you," Harry said. He grinned and spread his arms wide in fellowship. "I'm your important friend, dickhead."

The thought of any kind of friendship with Harry Selwurst sobered me. I had suspected that he was using me, but not the depth of his duplicity, and I charged: "You knew Knott had hired me."

Harry shrugged and said: "Word gets around."

"And you thought that if you could get me to believe you were working for Knott, I'd accept you as my lawyer, and you'd be able to find a way to put the bite on me if I found what happened to Jack Burns's cash.''

"That is a bit uncharitable. I didn't think you'd get anywhere on your own. It's only fair that I be rewarded for services performed.''

"Bastard," I sputtered.

"You're only angry because I'm smarter than you are.'' Harry grinned.

"You didn't even bother to tell me that Frank Knott was lying to me about his name.''

"I gave you a few hints and you chose to ignore them. Had I told you that your client was a crook, you wouldn't have believed me. Now why don't you relax a bit, sit down, and rest your leg,'' he coaxed, motioning to the chair.

I didn't move. Harry nodded, accustomed to irate clients, and sat calmly behind his desk. He folded his hands before him, smiling pleasantly, and asked:

"Who told you that I did not represent Mr. Knott?''

"Mr. Knott, just before he tried to make me the cornerstone of a new high rise.''

"You mean he tried to kill you?'' Harry exclaimed, shocked.

"Right after I told him I had a deal with you. I suppose I also jumped to the conclusion that you could protect me from him.''

Harry did not seem happy that I had mentioned his name to Knott. He brushed invisible dust from the surface of his desk, frowned, and said: "I'll see what I can do.''

"Meaning you can't do anything.''

"What do you care anymore? The man tried to kill you. When you find the money, we cut him out of the deal. Split it fifty-fifty. I don't want to share my money with a guy who just tried to kill my partner.''

"Fifty-fifty? Partners?'' I stammered, astonished by his audacity.

Harry riveted me with sincere blue eyes, and pitched: "I'm connected to some heavy hitters. You know the type. These guys can drive a kneecap three hundred yards with a one-iron. I'll send them around to Knott, and I guarantee he'll be pissing in his boots by the time these guys are done. No way Knott will bother us.''

"These heavy hitters, what do they look like?" I inquired.

"I don't know. They look like thugs." Harry shrugged.

"One of them wouldn't be about five foot ten, one eighty, with a bushy mustache, would he?"

"Why should you care what they look like?" Harry quarreled.

"Knott didn't seem to know who the Paris shooter was. He denied hiring him. Somebody hired him. Maybe it was you."

Harry was stunned into a moment of silence. Only a moment. His voice swelled to operatic dimensions as he thundered: "That is an absurd and slanderous accusation."

"And that isn't an answer."

"I didn't hire him."

"That didn't sound very convincing from a man who lies for a living."

"You would believe a man who just tried to kill you, over your own lawyer?" Harry cried, incredulous.

"Yes," I said.

Harry stared at me, jaw gaping. I leaned forward on my crutches and returned his stare. He read my eyes, and regained control of his jaw. Cunning slipped a smile over his lips. He got it.

"You're pulling my chain, aren't you?"

"And you're pulling mine. Four percent is what we agreed to, and four percent is what you'll get."

"I assume Knott is out of the picture. That leaves you with ninety-plus percent, assuming you find the money. Greedy. Very greedy."

"Knott's share is going back to the investors."

Harry chuckled, and waited for the punch line. There wasn't one. He clucked his tongue in disappointment, and said: "We're not talking about little old ladies who have lost their pension, here. This is not rob from the rich and give to the poor."

"I won't tell the fraud squad about your cut."

"Wise up! These are millionaires! Do you think a couple hundred K is going to make any difference to their lifestyles?"

"Unless they ask me. If the police ask me what happened to the rest of the money, I'll tell them that I had to cut a deal. I won't volunteer your name. Unless they ask me.''

"Go ahead. I'll just deny it.''

"And with a little luck, the investors will take you to court. Maybe they won't win, but you know as well as anybody how quickly legal costs mount up.''

"I think maybe I'll send some guys around to your apartment. Nineteenth Street in Santa Monica, apartment D, right?'' Harry threatened.

"You just talked yourself out of the four percent.'' I planted my crutches and whirled toward the door.

"Hey, dickhead. Just kidding, right?'' Harry called, anxious.

"Sure. Just kidding,'' I said, and crutched to Harry's desk. I flipped one of the crutches and held the base in a two-hand grip, like a bat. "It's baseball season again, Harry. You like baseball?''

Harry watched me, wary but annoyed, and asked: "Why should I care about baseball?''

"Because it's a great game of reflexes,'' I said, and swung the crutch at his head.

Harry squealed and ducked. The crutch whiffed six inches over the top of his blond curls. He pulled his face off his desktop blotter and shouted: "What the hell are you doing?''

"Strike one. Tell me about Mona Demonay,'' I suggested, and cocked the crutch against my shoulder.

"What about her?''

I swung again. Harry flopped out of his chair and hugged the carpet, shouting: "Are you crazy?''

"Strike two. Don't get so excited, Harry. We're just playing games with each other, aren't we?''

I propped the crutch under my shoulder. Harry peered up from the carpet. I gave him my used-car-salesman smile, the one with the five-mile, five-minute guarantee.

"Yeah, we're just playing games,'' Harry sighed, relieved. He pulled himself up by the edge of the desk and straightened his tie.

"You were pimping for Mona,'' I asserted.

"That's a slight exaggeration. I referred her services now and then," he answered with a glib smile.

"Who was she meeting on the night she was killed?"

"I haven't the faintest."

I flipped the crutch into a two-handed grip again. "I've got two strikes on me, and I can't afford a third. Your head is coming at me like a curveball hanging so fat I can count the stitches."

Harry yelped and dove under his desk before I swung, wailing: "It's the truth, dammit. I hadn't turned her on to anybody since Jack Burns."

I hobbled around the edge and pushed his chair out of the way. Harry had wedged himself against the farthest corner under his desk, and the top of his blond head quivered like the exposed tail of a rabbit.

"When did Burns first ask you to send him a hooker?"

"The day before he hired you. He messengered me a note requesting a two-girl special. He gave me a call requesting the same thing last year."

"Did you send Mona to him last year?"

"No, I was running someone else. Why the hell does it matter?"

I could have said that it mattered because she had been brutally murdered by someone who didn't want stories about Jack Burns's past to go public, and that someone had also likely murdered three people in Paris. I could have explained that I had a notion of justice that extended to hookers and lesbians and incestuous lovers, and though each had been guilty of greed, none had deserved to die for it. But his secretary burst through the door and asked what I had done to Mr. Selwurst, so I told him that it didn't matter. It didn't matter at all.

Richie Warner wasn't in sight when I crutched through the lobby, and I thought that maybe a little luck was running my way until I reached my car door in the parking lot and heard him call my name from the interior of a silver Volkswagen Jetta parked the next slot over. He pointed to a diner across the street and suggested: "Whaddya say we have a cup of coffee?"

I needed a way to screw a couple of people and it occurred to me that the press was as good a way as any. I nodded and Richie stepped out of the Jetta, leaning over the driver's seat to retrieve a zippered black case. We jaywalked to a delicatessen wallpapered with autographed celebrity photographs. I didn't recognize most of the faces, which meant that I hadn't been watching enough television lately and was falling rapidly behind what passes for cultural literacy in Los Angeles. Richie selected a table with a picture-window view of the traffic on Ventura Boulevard, and asked me how I had discovered the body of Jack Burns.

"I want a guarantee that you will keep my name out of your story," I demanded.

"Just for telling me how you found the body? That's not enough."

"How about I tell you a few stories about how Harry sent a couple of hookers to see Jack Burns on the night before he died?"

"What, you mean Selwurst?" Richie asked, automatically reaching for a pen and pad of paper in his case.

"How about I tell you how one of the hookers started a blackmail scheme that involved Burns and possibly Harry Selwurst, and that she was found last week dumped in an alley with her throat cut?"

Richie shifted sharply in his chair, tossing a few details into his notebook. His eyes did a backward burn as he thought through the implications of what I had just said, then lit with the expression of curious skepticism I had seen earlier in the lobby. If he printed without attribution what I told him about Harry Selwurst, and later discovered that I was blowing smoke, the *Times* would be legally liable for slander.

"You're wondering whether your contacts in the police department have been holding out on you. I don't think they have. I don't think they know as much as I do. They've got other things to do, and I've been living Jack Burns for the past two weeks. I can also tell you about an ex-millionaire from Texas named Frank Knott who built a fraudulent real-estate scheme only to see it collapse with the death of his partner: Jack Burns."

"I think I can do the story without using your name," Richie said, the potential angles to the story juicing his imagination.

"I can tell you about finding Jack Burns's body now, but the rest is going to have to wait a couple of days."

"Impossible. The story has to go to print the day after tomorrow."

"This is not hard news. Jack Burns has been dead for two weeks. You're working on a profile story. Put it off, or run it in two parts."

"Production has already assigned the space. I can't put it off," Richie objected.

"Then we have a serious problem, because I can't compromise what I know."

Richie tapped a nervous rhythm onto the tabletop with the tip of his pen, thinking. "If I agree, you're not going to jerk me around on this, are you?"

I said that I would stick to my word. Richie pocketed his pen, and pushed back from the table. "I have to call my editor to clear it. Give me five minutes."

The phones were in a back corridor, next to the rest rooms. Richie wedged his black zippered case into the corner on his side of the table, and, walking past the deli counter, disappeared into the corridor.

It wasn't ethical but every now and then I blindfold ethics in the face of opportunity: I reached across the table to grab Richie's zippered case. I slipped a manila folder from the case and flipped over the front cover. The folder contained notes on Richie's investigation, and a rough draft of his article. I hurriedly checked his notes, glancing every couple of seconds toward the back corridor. The last item in the folder was from the *Times* photo bureau. It was a photograph of a group of men standing in a semicircle around an actor whom I recognized as having once won an Academy Award. The photograph was dated 1986, and one of the men had been circled in red grease pencil. A handwritten scrawl in the margins noted that the item was the only photograph of Jack Burns on file.

I slid the folder back into the case, returned it to the corner, and joined Richie at the bank of phones in the back corridor. Richie was arguing about deadlines with somebody on the other end of his line.

I placed a quick call to Angel. The machine picked up, and I left a message, hoping that she would get it in time.

"We got a deal," Richie announced, hanging up his phone.

I tapped him on the shoulder on my way by and said: "Great. I have to run," crutching quickly through the delicatessen.

"Wait! You gotta tell me about finding the body," Richie said, chasing me onto the sidewalk.

"I'll call you," I answered, and took off across Ventura Boulevard.

"We just get started and already you're jerking me around!" Richie shouted angrily.

I didn't have time to argue with him. Also, he was right.

31

"What do you want?" Valerie Burnside squawked through the intercom when I rang her buzzer.

"It's Paul Marston," I announced.

"I can see that, you idiot. What do you want?" she repeated.

I bent and looked into a peephole positioned wheelchair-high on the door, and said: "I want to talk to you."

"What do you want to talk about?" she demanded.

"Jack."

"We already talked about him."

"I just met with the agent in charge of Jack's insurance policy," I lied.

"Hold on," she commanded, and I waited for the door to open.

I waited several minutes. The hot Valley sun slanted along the porch, and cut a stripe up my leg. The flesh beneath my cast began to pop with sweat, and a drop rolled in an excruciating trickle down to my ankle. I bent to scratch it with the tip of the Egyptian lady, and sighed with a small contentment when the itch subsided. I thought that Valerie Burnside had wheeled away to fetch her nurse, but when the door finally inched open, she was alone, and looked up at me with fierce suspicion.

"What new information?" she demanded, barricading the door with her wheelchair.

I didn't say anything. I looked down and waited. Her gray hair had been recently styled in sharp curls that circled her head like a wreath of scythes. A blue afghan draped over her lap. Her right hand clutched the cane like a club, and her eyes sliced from the cane to my face, as though measuring the distance in contemplation of clobbering me.

"Well, come in, I guess," she relented, sheathing the cane in the holster at the side of her chair.

With deft movements of her strong hands, Valerie backed the chair and turned it. Her voice was a shrill complaint as she wheeled down the hall. "You should have called. I don't like people to drop in unannounced. Just because I'm stuck in this wheelchair doesn't mean that I don't have things to do. Things more important than jawing with people for whom I have little regard." She wheeled to her spot, a noticeable gap in the wagon encirclement of sofa and end chairs around a marble coffee table, and drew her cane. She pointed the rubber tip toward the sofa, and nodded.

"It's more comfortable if I stand," I said.

"Suit yourself. Looks like we're about on equal terms now," she noticed, pointing to my cast. "Don't bother to tell me how you broke it."

"Pulled a ligament, is all," I said.

"I said don't bother," she interrupted. "There is nothing more boring than hearing someone else talk about their infirmities. I have enough of my own, and the last thing I want to hear is yours."

I planted my crutches and swung a few lengths toward the dining room. Two chairs stood at the far end of the dining room table. I looked for photographs along the walls. There were none.

"Where are you going?" Valerie demanded.

"I was hoping I'd see your nurse here," I said, turning back. "What was her name?"

"Mary. I fired her."

"How do you manage?"

"None of your business," she answered, and centered the harlequin glasses on her nose. "And speaking of business, on to yours. What's this about the insurance policy?"

I clumsily twisted around, and, setting the crutches along the back of the sofa, sat on the arm.

"Sit like a white man," she carped.

I ignored her and asked: "Has there been anyone from the insurance company out to see you?"

"Yes. They sent someone out last week. Like yourself, half bright and not entirely trustworthy. He didn't lead me to believe there would be any problems with the claim."

"Do you expect them to tell you about their investigation?"

"Investigation?" she echoed.

"Of course not. You won't hear anything about it until they can prove the problem with the claim."

"You're speaking a lot of nonsense. What problem with the claim?" she fussed, temper growing.

I shrugged, as though the problem was out of my control, and let it drop: "With the identification of the body."

She scrutinized her nails, dug into the handle of the cane, and turned a penetrating gaze inward. "That doesn't mean anything to me," she snapped, shrewdly understanding that too great a contemplation was an admission of guilt. "I identified the body. There is no question in my mind that it was the body of my son."

"The coroner's report goes into graphic detail, not only about the cause of death, but in describing the physical condition of the body," I began.

She lightly tapped her cane on the floor, and commanded: "Get to the point. What is the problem?"

"The coroner reported that Jack was prematurely bald. Other reports indicate that he had a full head of hair."

She watched me carefully, trying to read between the lines of my face. The thick lenses of her glasses magnified her sharp predator's stare.

"That's ridiculous," she snorted. "Jack had male pattern baldness, just like his father, and just like my father. He had it on both sides of the family."

"I know. He wore a wig, and not a very good wig. I helped

identify the body, as you remember. Perhaps if you had a photograph of Jack. A photograph of you and Jack together. That might help prove it.''

Her distrust burned upon me with an unwavering glare. "Wait here," she commanded, and wheeled from the room.

I had no intention of waiting for her return, but skulking about was limited by my cast. It is no easy matter to move crutches silently along a hardwood floor. I hobbled as quietly as I could through an archway into the dining room, and from there poked my head into the kitchen. The house was clean, and well ordered. Nothing seemed out of place, which was extraordinary in a household that had just lost its nurse and housekeeper.

I returned to the living room in time to prop myself against the end of the couch and appear relaxed when the rubber wheels of Valerie Burnside's wheelchair snickered into the room. She thrust out a photograph with a grudging defiance. While I studied it, she lay her cane across the armrests of her chair, and drummed her nails along the polished oak.

The photograph had been taken in natural light. Valerie Burnside perched stiffly in her wheelchair, squinting against a sun that washed her skin a pale gold. The man kneeling next to the wheelchair circled her resistant shoulders with his arm. Even with the overexposed film effacing the details of his skin, the wig was obvious. The man was Jack Burns, as I had known him. The photograph had a glossy texture and an unblemished surface. It had been taken recently, and infrequently handled.

"Ever meet a Texan named Frank Knott?" I inquired, handling the photograph.

Her response was a curt and prompt "No."

"He was your son's business partner in a real estate venture called Sea View Estates."

"Jack didn't tell me much of anything about his business affairs," she explained.

"Frank Knott claims otherwise. Said he had lunch with you and Jack. Jack pawned you off as a wealthy investor from Pasadena named Nina Gamine, which, coincidentally, is the name of a young girl who was murdered in Paris last week."

"Sounds like a lot of rubbish to me," she replied coolly. "Maybe this Mr. Knott is behind my son's financial problems. I think he skinned my son of his last dime, and now wants to divert suspicion by blaming Jack."

I nodded, as though accepting the explanation, and flipped the photograph face-up, asking: "When was this taken?"

"A couple of years ago," she answered.

"It's too recent," I concluded, and slipped the photograph into my breast pocket.

"You asked for a photograph. I gave you one."

"Do you have an older photograph, taken maybe five, ten, twenty years ago?"

"I'm not the sentimental type. I don't keep photographs."

"This isn't a photograph of your son, is it, Mrs. Burnside?" I asked, softly.

"Of course it is."

"You can't count on the insurance money. All the insurance company has to do is refuse to pay under suspicion of fraud. Which they certainly will do when your son's clients report that the man in this photograph is not Jack Burns."

"A mother knows her own son," she said, tight-lipped.

"Then your only alternative will be to sue them. In court they will question the identification of your son's body. I identified it, but in court, I'll testify that I was the victim of an elaborate hoax, and identified the wrong man. You will be the only person willing to testify that your son was the man cremated under the name of Jack Burns. Maybe because you're an old woman in a wheelchair, the court will have pity on you, and you'll win. But it will take years, and the lawyer fees will take most of the award."

"My son is dead. I saw the body. You requested a photograph, and I've given you one. Apparently, it's not enough. I lied when I told you I didn't have other photographs. I have them, all right. But they are stored away in boxes in the garage. I can't get to them, because of this." She gestured the cane toward her crippled legs. "But if you want to see them, we'll go take a look."

Valerie Burnside glared at me, and my certainty dimmed.

"Let's go," I said.

She holstered her cane and thrust her hands forward on the wheels. The chair sped across the hardwood floor into a narrow hallway. She negotiated the hall corners with routine expertise, slowing the wheel nearest the corner with the handbrake, and propelling the second wheel with a quick flick of her hand. I gimped behind, not nearly as expert, nor as fast. She sped through the kitchen and into the pantry. At the pantry door she stopped, leaned forward, and backed the chair as she swung the door open. A ramp led down to the garage. She clipped the light and, braking to slow her descent, rolled into the garage.

I spotted the tips of my crutches on the edge of the ramp and looked over a gray Chevy sedan parked along the far wall. Boxes were neatly stacked midway to the open-beamed ceiling behind the Chevy, and followed the wall to the ramp.

Valerie Burnside pivoted her chair and immediately drew her cane.

"Come on," she commanded, and pointed her cane at the wall next to the door.

I couldn't see at what she was pointing. I shifted to get a view of the garage on the other side of the door. It was clear. I leaned carefully forward, until my head broke the plane of the door. Valerie Burnside tipped her cane to a spot seven feet from the floor. The wall was bricked by boxes of uniform size and shape, all clearly labeled with a black broad-tipped marker. I crutched down the ramp, and glanced behind the Chevy. The door to the side yard was closed.

"It's up there. The box marked 'Family Documents,'" she said, thrusting her cane.

I propped the crutches against the hood of the Chevy and limped to the boxes. I took a last look over my shoulder, and reached up to the box, inching it out of its slot. The door to the side yard behind me opened and a voice commanded: "You can just keep your hands where they are."

I started to turn my head.

"And don't move," the voice added.

I splayed my hands flat against the box, and my chin dropped to my chest. Leather soles scraped on concrete behind me.

"Hello, Jack. How was Rio de Janeiro?" I asked.

32

Valerie Burnside eyed me like prey brought down on the wing. Something round and hard tipped against my spine at the twelfth vertebrae. A hand smoothed down my left side. The hand disappeared behind my back; the soft flap of a gun changing palms, and another hand searched my right.

"How did you know I was in Rio?" Burns asked, and the leather soles scraped again, backing away.

"The bruises under your eyes suggest a nose job. Rio is the best city south of the border for plastic surgery."

"The problem with you is that you're not smart enough to be really good, but just smart enough to get killed," Burns said.

"What are you going to do now?" Valerie Burnside asked, wheeling her chair forward.

"That's my worry."

"This is my house. That makes it my worry."

"It also makes you accessory to whatever happens," I suggested, and carefully turned to the new face of Jack Burns. I compared it to the face in the photograph from Richie Warner's folder. The nose had been shortened and thinned, the bags under the eyes excised, and the skin pulled taut and pinned at the back of his neck. His new face was round, and the effect of the surgery seemed to flatten it of salient features, leaving only a bushy mustache growing from a remarkably porcine countenance.

Burns waved the Glock at me, the same half-plastic gun I had seen him use in Paris, and said: "I don't need your opinion, thanks. If you give it again, I'll shoot you."

"If that gun goes off, you'll have a couple of plainclothes cops at your door in thirty seconds."

"Police? We can't have the police," Valerie shrilled.

"I told you not to worry about it," Jack Burns repeated. "I checked. I know every car on the block."

"They aren't in a car," I improvised.

"Come on. This is a suburban neighborhood," he said scornfully. "Where are they? Up a tree? Hiding in the azalea bushes across the street?"

"I can't have you kill him. Not here," Valerie warned.

"Trust me, Mom."

"Trust you? Why should I trust you? You've been a fuck-up since you were born," she jeered.

I thought that he would lose his temper. He didn't. He smiled with the seeming pleasure of the familiar, and said: "On the floor."

I dropped to my knees.

"Not on your knees," he reproached, waving the gun. "On your stomach, with your hands behind your head."

The side of my face pressed against cold concrete. I cradled the back of my neck in my hands and watched through the crook of my elbow Burns sidestep the wheelchair and kneel at his mother's side. He gripped her arm just below the elbow and squeezed, his voice patient and kind as he said: "Snap, crackle, pop. Just like the breakfast cereal." He increased the pressure until his mother cried sharply in pain. "Do you want me to break your arm, Mom?"

"You wouldn't dare," she challenged.

Burns laughed, then twisted her arm, drawing another cry of pain. I had the perverse impression that she enjoyed it.

"Whose little boy am I?" he asked, his voice a singsong.

"You're my little boy," she parroted.

Burns's face engorged with blood, and he shouted: "Given my genetic background, you still don't think I'll break your arm?"

"Let go," Valerie commanded, and Burns promptly released her. They stared at each other with an understanding beyond my comprehension, two twisted souls in violent harmony. Valerie nodded sharply, breaking it off, and Jack rose, gripping the back handles of her wheelchair.

"When you kill him, you have to arrange it so he doesn't leave much of a mess," she instructed as he wheeled her up the ramp, and the thought of my existence being reduced to a stain was not a great comfort.

Burns descended from the ramp and lifted a folding chair from a nook in the wall and spread the legs to the sides of my head.

"I see you had something in common with Nina Gamine," I said, face on the floor.

Jack Burns slipped a cigarette out of his blue blazer, and lit it one-handed with a silver Zippo. "What's that?" he inquired, clicking the Zippo shut.

"A warm and wonderful family life."

"We had many things in common, primary among them greed," he sighed in a whirl of smoke. "Greed, and a tendency to betray those whom we considered our business partners."

"Then she betrayed you," I guessed. "She was supposed to meet you after you had your face changed in Rio. She took the money and joined her brother instead."

His black loafers shifted on the concrete. I thought for a moment about my chances should I grab the foot and try to topple him. Suicidal, I concluded.

"We were going to disappear," Burns mused. "I would be legally dead, and with a three-million-dollar bankroll, we could live anywhere in the world. She was supposed to have met me in Rio, but when she didn't show up, I knew I had been betrayed. She had control of the money, you see. Very stupid of me." He laughed. His laugh was a rich texture of chagrin, admiration, and anger. He brought it down to a smile, and cut the smile with a drag on his cigarette. "I knew about her brother. I thought it gave me a hold on her, because I understood it. Not that I've experienced anything like it, of course. I knew the danger. The terrible temptation. But she was a complex woman with a simple desire. More complex than I, yet simpler." He laughed again. "I didn't know that she had hired you to find her brother. Had I known, I might have realized the setup. I didn't even know about Kathy Maddox. She fooled us all, even her brother. I doubt he knew what the hell was going on when I shot him."

"How many have you killed so far, four, five people?" I asked.

He dropped the cigarette butt next to my head. The acrid smoke stung my nostrils. He crushed it with his loafer. "I haven't killed anybody," he claimed cryptically.

"Right."

"Has Jack Burns killed anybody? Jack Burns is dead. How could a dead man kill anybody?"

"The guy hired to play your corpse for the benefit of the coroner, the guy who once did a porn film and was probably an out-of-work actor, that guy is dead, not Jack Burns," I corrected.

"No great loss. He was so busy screwing around with the whores that he almost blew the scheme. He was a nobody before he became Jack Burns. He took over Jack Burns, and then Jack Burns killed himself."

"If Jack Burns killed himself, who killed the actor?" I challenged, trying to shake his solipsistic riddle.

"Greed, of course. Do you understand what I'm saying?" he asked, nudging my ribs with a black loafer.

"Not at all," I admitted.

He nudged me again with his loafer, and said: "Get up."

I pushed myself off the floor.

"Not all the way up," he commanded, making a small circle with the barrel of the gun. "Keep your hands behind your head, but sit. Try to get a little more comfortable."

"If you want me to be comfortable, put away the gun," I suggested.

He grinned, appreciating the mock attempt at cunning. I slid the cast forward and leaned my back against the Chevy. He smiled down on me, his eyes surprisingly kind.

"It is a question of identity," he explained. "Without an identity, there can be no responsibility, no one on whom to affix the blame or praise for an act of charity"—he gave an ironical smile and completed the sentence—"or an act of crime."

I laughed, and that stopped him.

"You find it funny?" he asked.

"Having an argument on ethics with a mass murderer? Yes, I find it absurd," I remarked. His mouth tightened like a wire when I said "mass murderer." Mortality lit a fast fuse in my brain. I realized it might be healthier to play it straight, and added: "But fascinating. Please, go on."

He nodded, and tipped his eyes into the air, recapturing his thoughts. "It all has to do with self-image, and self-hate. Some people turn to religion to rid themselves of this hate, others to psychoanalysis, and a few to crime. Most criminals, of course, have a poor self-image."

"You don't seem greatly troubled by it," I observed.

Burns shrugged away the objection and stared blankly for a moment, as though listening to voices in his head. "Oh, I know I have talents. I'm smarter than most people, and I have a type of cleverness that allows me to make my way in the world. I know perfectly well why I have been an artist all my life. A confidence artist, that is. I like humiliating people, revealing them for the fools that they are. We're all a pack of greedy fools, aren't we?" Burns laughed and nudged me twice with his foot, until my head bobbed in agreement. "You see, I really was quite self-aware before I decided to do away with myself. Freud's folly was in believing self-awareness leads to positive change."

"You've gone through analysis, then," I said.

He grinned, his eyes dark points of arrogant self-loathing, and confided: "I'm an expert at it. Psychiatrists are easy prey for a good con. I studied psychiatry off and on, you see. I knew what the shrinks wanted to hear, all the claptrap about my mother, you know, and I made them fight for it, before giving what they wanted in a big show of emotion. Oh, I was great in having breakthroughs. I was a very satisfying patient, and I won't pretend that I learned nothing. I learned much. I learned how much I despised myself, and it prepared me for the ultimate sacrifice, the sacrifice of self.''

"You mean arranging your own death," I concluded.

"Yes!" he cried, animated by the pleasure of my understanding. "I was in an unbearable dilemma. I hated myself, and I hated others. I am too intellectual to believe in the possibility of redemption. The only solution was to destroy myself. To arrange my own death. I formulated the plan, and the plan included building a new self with someone I loved." The glow on his face subsided when he thought of Nina Gamine. "It didn't work out, but I don't suppose myself unhappy, because I have no self. I am not happy or sad. I am free."

"Enlightenment through greed," I scoffed.

"It's a form of superconsciousness," he agreed, "to live totally without conscience. You have to surrender your ego to a greater force to be truly liberated.''

"But you haven't given your life to a greater force," I objected. "You've just given yourself the freedom to act without conscience."

"What is the nature of the greater force? Certainly it is not one thing, but many things. To a true capitalist, the greater force is money. The love and desire for money have driven me throughout my life. Money is my greater force. The sweet metallic ring of coin has been my personal mantra." He laughed, pleased with his poetic combination of words. Then his eyes glazed, as though fixed on some eternal distant point visible only to the chosen, and he spoke in a voice bled of humanity. "But I have grown. I am no longer interested in just money. I'm drawn to the spiritual side of it, to the metaphysics of greed. My self no longer exists, save as the manifestation and instrument of the greater force of greed. I have died, and now I am risen. I am the prophet of greed. I have given my life for it, and like all holy men, am somewhat mad.''

When he called himself a holy man, and mad, his eyes fixed upon me with the fervor of the religiously devout, and I was convinced that he was, if not holy, wholly mad. Then it was gone, quick as a shade drawn down a window.

"This has been a very enjoyable conversation, and I'm pleased that you have an open mind and a questing spirit," he said, drawing a second filter-tip from his breast pocket. He flicked the Zippo into flame, and drew in a heavy dose of smoke. "I have not had an opportunity to talk to anyone like this since my transformation. But we must press on to the business of the money."

"I don't have it, and I don't know where it is. Simple as that," I said.

"But you do, after all, hold the key to the money." Burns laughed nervously. He inhaled smoke deeply into his lungs, held it, and exhaled. His face emerged from the cloud of smoke with a cunning expression, his prophet-of-greed persona neatly shed to reveal the smooth operator at his core. He held up his hand to prevent my response. "I'll tell you what I mean by that. When Nina didn't show up in Rio, I took a risk and used my new passport and identity to fly back to the States. I had to discover what had gone wrong. I also had some unfinished business to take care of regarding an extortionist."

"Mona Demonay?" I guessed.

"Yes. A pity. So good-looking, so greedy, so few brains." Regret filmed his eyes, but I couldn't tell whether he mourned her looks, her greed, or anything at all. "I didn't think I'd have to do anything about her, you know, until I saw her talking to you."

Oh Christ, I thought, I don't want to be responsible for this. "You were watching my apartment?" I asked.

"Of course. I figured you'd go for the money when you heard it was missing. Everyone always does go for the money, don't they? I watched you, and Knott, although it took me a few days to discover that you were working together. Or are you working for Selwurst? I'm not really clear on that."

"I'm not working for anybody right now," I said.

"I understand the impulse. Business partners are to be betrayed. You're not suggesting that you want to cut a deal with me, are you?"

"I don't like your track record."

Burns cracked a smile. "Good observation. I followed you to Paris, you know. I sat about ten rows back from you on the flight over. When I saw Kathy Maddox, Ms. Butch in her leather jacket and leather pants, scrambling out of that dyke nightclub, then it all came together. I'm sorry to say that I lost my temper. I followed her to the Métro, and without thinking, gave her a shove. It was stupid of me, I know. I should have cornered her somewhere, and gotten it out of her, before I killed. But, as I said, I was not rational."

"Gotten what out of her?" I asked.

"The key, of course. I was in the crowd when you were down there on the track, pretending to be a concerned citizen. Your partner gave a good performance. Everybody was looking at her, and of course, at the body. Nobody was watching you, except me. I saw you palm the hotel key, then followed you to Nina. Again, I confess that I lost my head a bit. She told me about a key, about Kathy's hotel key. You have the key, and I want it."

"We turned it in at the desk," I lied.

"If you're going to lie, at least do it intelligently," he sighed. "You didn't turn it in. You didn't have time. I was watching you, remember."

"What is so important about a hotel key?"

"That is something you definitely don't need to know," he advised.

"Then we're at an impasse."

"I'm holding a gun on you, and we're at an impasse?" he exclaimed, incredulously.

"I don't think you'll shoot me, unless I give you no other choice. Not because you're such a nice guy, but because you need me. I'm not going to give that key in exchange for a bullet in the head."

"I could tie you up and beat it out of you," Burns offered, more in the manner of suggestion than threat.

"I don't think you're good enough. That's not meant as a challenge. It takes a special skill to get someone to talk, if they know they'll be killed once they do. You have to be a master at manipulating pain. Too much, and you put the guy out. Too little, and the thing drags on for days. You have enough raw talent, but not enough experience."

He grinned, and crushed the smoke with his heel. "That's the best backhanded compliment that has ever been paid me. So, we're at an impasse. What do you suggest we do about it?"

"We have no choice but to cut a deal," I said.

The idea pleased him. Burns knew how to cut deals like a magician knows how to cut cards. "You're the one with the product. Name your terms."

"I want two things out of this. I want to stay alive, and I want money. Around a guy like you, those two items might be mutually exclusive, so I have to be careful. I want enough money to make it worth my while, enough so that you know that I'll want to keep my mouth shut to hold on to it. But not so much that you'll think it's worth killing me."

"That sounds like about fifty thousand to me," he offered.

"You must think me as cheap as you are greedy. Two hundred thousand," I countered.

"That is out of the question. You're bargaining for money that isn't yours."

"Right. You stole the money fair and square, right?"

"Okay. Eighty thousand."

I agreed. He backed to the trunk of the Chevy, and digging into his pocket for the key, opened it. The gun did not stray from its brutal fix on my chest as he reached into the trunk, and lifted the floral-print suitcase from Paris. The air in the garage was still. I was sweating heavily, and drops trickled along my skin inside the cast. It itched. The impulse to bend and work the Egyptian lady to the spot was resisted the moment before I moved. A sudden and violent scheme sparked my thoughts.

Burns set the case on the floor and told me to open it. I flipped the latches, and spread the case to a top layer of men's clothing. I folded back the clothing. Twenty bundles of twenty-dollar bills, each bundle five inches high, lined the sides of the case.

"Each bundle contains twenty thousand," he said.

I set four bundles on the floor. Burns tossed me a paper bag and I stuffed it. The package weighed about ten pounds. I shut the case and slid it toward the trunk of the car. He lifted the case into the trunk and shut the lid.

"Okay, now the key," he demanded.

"We'll have to take a little drive to get to it. We'll use my car," I said.

"I don't think so," Burns objected, and pointed the tip of the gun toward the Chevy. "You drive."

I collected the sack and hobbled behind the wheel. He hit the garage-door opener, and climbed into the passenger seat. I cranked the engine, and backed out the driveway, looking for Angel's pickup. The only car I recognized was a white Datsun parked midway down the street, and I wondered if it was the same one that had followed me the other day. I pulled the Chevy out onto the street, backed it to the Mustang, and cut the engine.

"What the hell are you doing?" Burns demanded.

"I told you we had to take a little drive, and so we have. The key is in the car."

The calculations of betrayal teemed behind the gaze he leveled on me. His gun hand tensed when I reached for the door.

"You can't shoot me. Not here. It would make too much of a mess, and I haven't told you where in the car I've hidden it."

He grinned and, draping a section of newspaper over his gun hand, said: "Why would I want to shoot you? We have a deal, don't we?"

I set my cast on the street and grabbed the bag of cash with my right hand to cover the movement of my left, which unsheathed the Egyptian lady from the space between the cast and my leg. I crossed hands, concealing the lady in the curled lip of the bag, and limped around the Chevy. Burns slipped out the passenger door, keeping pace with me on the other side of the Chevy. He tipped the barrel of his pistol into my spine when I reached the trunk of the Mustang. I fumbled for my keys.

"I'm going to open the trunk, and reach inside the tire compartment for the key, so don't get nervous," I advised.

The tip of the key struck the lock wide, and bounced off. I tried again, groping for the lock like a drunk.

"You're the one who's nervous," he observed.

His animal awareness alerted him to the danger. The barrel of the gun bore deeper into my spine. I keyed the lock on my third attempt, and opened the trunk.

"Don't move," Burns warned, before I could reach inside.

"Shit," I muttered.

Burns laughed knowingly, and chided: "Hiding a little something in here other than the key? A gun, perhaps?"

Burns pulled me away from the trunk by the collar of my shirt and shoved. I staggered back, gripping the lady in my right hand behind the bag.

"You tell me where the key is, and I'll get it," he ordered.

I directed him to look in the spare-tire compartment under the mat. The gun drooped a bit from its bead on my chest as he dipped sideways into the trunk. I planted my broken leg and hoped enough spring remained to dodge the muzzle of the gun. Without turning his head from me, he felt for the mat with his free hand and stripped it back.

I timed his eyes. They switched from me to the trunk and back to me again.

"Where?" he repeated.

"There's a blue tool kit. It's in there."

His eyes swept to the trunk. I lunged, aiming for the gap between his twelfth rib and pelvis bone. Burns jerked the gun and fired. The round percussed against the side of my face, and I stumbled into him fatally high. The lady struck for his heart, plunging through the space between two ribs with preternatural aim, and the force of my fall carried her deep into him. Burns twisted and fell back against the bumper. The gun clattered to the pavement. He clung to the inner rim of the trunk, mouth gaped open, eyes shocked wide. I pulled the blade. The lady had fallen short of his heart, but had ripped through his right lung, and he gasped for breath. I wrapped my arm around his waist, and cradled his head. His arm slumped free of the trunk. I lowered him gently to the pavement.

I kicked the Glock aside, and glanced up to the figure of a man running toward us from the open door of the white Datsun. I shouted for an ambulance. Burns shuddered under my hands. The muscles in his neck violently corded as he tried to suck air into his lungs. Then he wheezed and blood trickled from the corner of his mouth. Burns tore at his throat, writhing on the ground. I straddled his stomach to pin him and pulled his hands away. His face distended to an angry red swelling, and his eyes rolled in bulging panic. Blood spurted from his nose and he wheezed again, trying to sit up. I pushed him back down, uncertain how to save his life.

The man from the Datsun stood over me, watching. I shouted at him again, calling for an ambulance. He didn't move. I looked up. He was young, between twenty and twenty-five, with a pale acne-scarred face and shoulder-length sandy brown hair. I assumed the blood had shocked the wits from him, and screamed at him again. He backed away, spotted the pistol, and picked it up. I assumed wrong.

Burns hacked, choking, and sprayed my arms with blood. His face had swelled to bursting, as though someone had drawn a cord around his neck and jerked it taut. His skin color was radically shifting from red to blue. I pressed my ear to his chest, listening to a soft hiss of air deep inside. A liquid gurgling poured from his throat. Burns was drowning in his own blood. I grabbed his shirt, and flipped him onto his side, hoping to clear an airway.

Barely conscious, Burns clawed at the asphalt with his free hand, trying to reach the paper sack and my eighty grand. The young longhair crouched on his heels over the sack, and his eyes lit when he opened it.

"Thanks, dude," he said.

There was nothing I could do about it. He bunched the sack under his arm and trotted away. I heard the Datsun's engine catch, and it blew past in a stream of squealing tires and exhaust.

I turned Burns's body so the head sloped down toward the curb, trying to keep his lungs from filling with blood. His mouth drained a steady stream of red to the gutter. I had my hand on Burns's wrist, and felt his pulse slowly dwindle to nothing as he turned blue as glacial ice. I hated the man and what he had done, and had I stopped to consider the pain and terror Mona Demonay had felt before her death, or the value of the five lives lost to his greed, I might have just waited for the inevitable cessation of blood flow and cardiac arrest. I had acted in self-defense, and done what was reasonable to try to keep him alive. But not everything possible.

I knelt at Jack Burns's head. Consciousness had fled, and his eyes had closed. It was going to be messy, and I regretted having to do it, but did not question the imperative to save a life, any life, when possible. I pinched his nostrils and, keeping him on his side, tilted his head back. Drawing a deep breath, I sealed his mouth with mine, and forced air into his lungs. Blood spurted into my mouth as I forced the air in, and I spat it to the curb. I worked him for five minutes, forcing air into his lungs and spitting out blood, until an ambulance arrived and two paramedics replaced me with a tracheal tube and oxygen tank.

33

I was hosing the blood from my face when Angel squealed to a stop across from the ambulance. I could tell from the worried set of her face that she was wondering how much of the blood was mine as she vaulted from the truck and dashed across the street. I dropped the hose and wiped my hands on the grass, telling her that I was fine, and that the man lying in the street was Jack Burns. She asked me more questions than I could handle, and I waved them off, hobbling to the Mustang. The police had yet to arrive, and I didn't want to be there when they did. I asked her about the key, and Angel said that she had matched it to a storage facility near the airport in Marina Del Rey. I told her that I'd meet her there after a change of clothing at my apartment, and drove off. Two squad cars flew past on Ventura Boulevard at twice the posted limit, freezing traffic with a blast of lights and sirens. I didn't stop for them, and they didn't stop for me. Stewart would throw me in jail for leaving the scene, but I didn't care. I was temporarily a free man.

Angel was leaning against her pickup in the parking lot of a three-structure storage complex off the Marina Freeway when I parked the Mustang. I slipped a new pair of crutches out of the backseat, having dropped by a medical supply store to replace the previous set after a quick shower and change of clothing at my apartment. The new crutches were aluminum, and the late-afternoon sun glanced from the metal surface in a blinding glare as I swung toward the front building.

"I got to Valerie Burnside's as soon as I could," Angel said, staring at the ground as she met me.

"It was my fault. I should have waited for you rather than going in alone," I replied, trying to make her feel better.

"Yes, you should have waited," Angel agreed, and I thought that would be the end of it until she bit her lip and admitted: "I stepped out of the office for a minute, and didn't check the damn answering machine when I got back. I'm sorry."

"Don't worry about it. I'm just glad you didn't pull the same stunt I did. You could have come out here alone to pick up the money."

"You really think it's here?" she asked, slowing her pace to my crippled step and swing.

"I can't figure where else it could be."

"Two point five million is a lot of money. Are you afraid I might double-cross you?"

"Not at all."

"Why not?"

"Money can't buy you love."

"No, but it can buy you a lot of like," Angel suggested, laughing.

I liked to hear her laugh, and realized that we hadn't laughed together since I had been arrested for Mona Demonay's murder. Our obsession with the chase had strengthened our partnership, but I had lost the heady euphoria of loving her, and missed it. A temporary optimism swept through me. I sensed that death had done with us, and for a moment felt almost happy.

Angel led me to the middle building, and we followed a sequenced set of numbers down a long gray hall of doors. The lights in the hall were fluorescents on a timer system. Black switches were built into the walls at thirty-foot intervals. Angel hit a switch and the hall ahead of us flickered into light. When she pressed the next switch, the hall behind was pitched into darkness. The hall of doors seemed endless, and the flickering lights and stale air were the atmosphere of a dream. Many nights I had dreamed of hallways filled with doors, particularly

when I was young and faced with life's panoply of choices. I
expected the doors to open, and strange creatures to flit across the
hall quick and unbelievable as ghosts, disappearing again behind
rapidly shutting doors. The image struck me as absurd, and I
chuckled.

"What is it?" Angel asked, startled.

"I was remembering a dream," I said.

"Paul?"

"What?"

"When this is over, I think we should take a vacation."

"Right."

Angel halted at the door matching the number on the key, and
turned it in the lock. She felt for the light, and the room fluttered
fluorescent. I kicked the rubber stopper, and propped the door open.

The room was a square gray space with cinderblock walls and
twelve-foot ceilings. It was depressing as hell. Boxes and sticks of
furniture were stacked against the walls. The furniture had the shabby
veneer of thrift-shop purchases.

I nosed through the belongings, disappointed when I did not
immediately see a pair of floral-print suitcases like the one Kathy
Maddox had carried to Paris. We checked the obvious first, searching
through the stacked boxes, then moved to the drawers when we
didn't find the money. Angel suggested that maybe we had gotten
careless and missed one of the boxes, so we methodically searched
each again. Our last hope was the furniture. Angel poked around the
couch, feeling the cushions, and crawling underneath to check the
springs. I prodded a mattress and box spring propped against the
wall. They weren't stuffed with twenty-dollar bills. Angel thumped
a chest of drawers, and gauged the sound for a false compartment.
After we had gone through everything twice, I slumped into an
armchair and admitted that the money was not in the room. Angel
moved around the back of the chair and gently massaged my neck. I
kissed her arm absently, thinking, and she asked: "If we do find the
money, what are we going to do with it?"

"Return it to the investors," I answered.

"Do you think the investors will give us a reward?"

"The rich don't get where they are by giving away money. I think we'll get a round of thanks, and a steak dinner for our troubles. Down the line, some fat cat might get into a tight spot and remember our name. That's about it."

"Then why are we trying so hard?"

"Because I like steak dinners," I said, and struggled to my feet.

It was a flip answer, and Angel smiled at it, but her question was working something deeper inside me. I had been distracted by the thrill of finding the money, and greed had inured me to the awareness of other things. I was standing in the midst of the sole remaining possessions of a woman brutally murdered. I had ferreted through the accumulations of her life as though her death had no significance. The top drawer of a bedroom chest yawned open. I leaned my crutches against the chest and felt through the drawer. It was filled with costume jewelry: brass, plastic, and ceramic adornments of no financial or aesthetic value. I wondered where she had bought each one, and when she had worn them. I eased the drawer shut, and opened the next. Angel sensed what I was doing and opened a box, slowly sifting through its contents. Jeans and t-shirts, the type with jokes or political slogans emblazoned across the front, filled the next drawer. As I fingered through each item, the image of Kathy Maddox formed clear enough in my head that I could replay and examine the details of her face, the way she moved her hands when she talked, the timbre and cadence of her voice.

I moved to the writing desk. The bottom drawer contained an ordered file of receipts, warranties, and old bills. A receipt lay across the top of the file, as though it had been stuffed into the drawer at the last moment. I unfolded the sheet of paper. The macabre contents gave me pause.

"Kathy's ex-lover, Martha. What did she say about the dogs?" I asked.

Angel looked up from her contemplation of a high school yearbook, confused by the question and why I had suddenly asked it. "That Kathy and her new lover, Nina that is, had shown up at Kathy's apartment with two Great Danes. That would have been about two days before Kathy took off for Paris."

"And the dogs had been in good health?"

"Of course," Angel replied.

Angel carefully set the high-school yearbook back into the box and stood to read over my shoulder. The bottom-line cost on the receipt was $1,586, paid to Dog Heaven Cemetery and Crematorium, Inc. The charges were incurred for the caskets, burial, and grave markers for two Great Danes named Jack and Frank.

34

It was past midnight when Angel turned the pickup truck into the parking lot at Dog Heaven, and cut the lights. The lot was empty and dark. Angel circled the truck and lifted a pick and shovel from the back bed. She cradled the tools under one arm and spotlit the pavement with a beam from her flashlight, testing it one last time before clicking it off and crossing the lot in darkness.

The pet cemetery was in the crook of two freeways in the industrial South Bay section of Los Angeles. The freeways were elevated, passing just beyond the far corners of the cemetery, the long slabs of curving concrete perched gracefully on stilts marching into the distance. Night traffic was sporadic, and the distant roar of semi trucks sang a lullaby to the eternal sleep of the dead.

Earlier in the evening I had driven the Mustang to a video rental store on Main Street in Santa Monica and parked on the street, crutching through the store to a back exit and Angel's waiting pickup truck. We had then aimlessly cruised for two hours, waiting for night to deepen and watching carefully for tailing headlights. I had decided not to carry a gun. Angel can't shoot worth a damn, and as my mobility was limited by the cast, I was too easy a target if somebody decided they wanted to shoot back at me.

The grounds at Dog Heaven were screened from the surrounding warehouses and industrial buildings by a perimeter of tall conifers gradually browning in the Southern California heat and smog. The front office was lit by a solitary low-wattage bulb hung over the doorway. A half moon hung high in the city-bright night. I followed Angel up a broken stone pathway that led past the front office to the gravesites beyond. The pathway circled a sculpture on a stone pedestal in front of the office. The sculpture was a plaster-cast triad of a dog, a chimpanzee, and a cat. The sculptor had not been talented, and the animals stood as sadly deformed guardians over the cemetery. I stopped and examined the chimpanzee. I thought of William Holden and the scene in *Sunset Boulevard* when he is led through a dilapidated mansion to meet a reclusive movie star who believes he has come to take her dead monkey for burial. Surrounded by candlelight, the chimp wore a three-piece suit and was laid out in a casket. That spooked me. Angel hissed and I jumped.

"The dead are dead, Paul," she admonished in a low whisper, and motioned me to get moving.

If the dead are dead, I wondered why the ancient obsession with ghosts, spirits, and hauntings. I imagined the ghosts of little dachshunds, poodles, and Scottish terriers flitting around the cemetery on short pale legs, chasing phantom cats and each other, rolling in the grass, happily pissing on trees, and, a little ashamed of my own irreverence, I chuckled.

"What are you thinking about now?" Angel whispered.

I didn't think Angel would appreciate the cartoon absurdity of the image, so I just said "Nothing," and followed her around a six-foot hedge to the gravesites. The grave markers were set flush with the ground. A hundred ground-level red lights flickered luminously through the cemetery, spilling an eerie red glow along the grass. The half moon cast blue shadows high up the trees and in the dark recesses of the grounds. I approached one of the lights and bent over my crutches to examine the candle flame set in red glass. It appeared to be a memorial light, perched over a grave that bore the florid inscription THE LOVED ONE, and gave the birth and death dates of a dog named Southern.

Angel diligently canvassed the rows of gravesites, pinning the beam of her flashlight on each granite marker as she passed. I crutched slowly through a separate section of the cemetery. When I came upon the first picture, printed onto a sheet of aluminum for long life, I stopped to contemplate. The inscription read simply MY BEST FRIEND and hung below the photograph of a shaggy mutt with a happy canine smile and flopping tongue. The dog was named Max, and seemed to have more hair than wits, but there was something about Max's attitude toward the photographer that stirred a sense of pathos. I propelled myself forward, trying to concentrate on finding the graves of the Great Danes. As I scanned the grave markers, I encountered more photographs. Each dog gazed at the photographer with a similar animal trust and dependence, and I became increasingly depressed. The inscriptions were all heartfelt and unabashedly emotional, more so than in cemeteries for human beings. The love for these creatures had been unconditional, and I felt as though I were moving though a cemetery for children.

Angel called my name in a hoarse whisper, and I wheeled around on my crutches, spotting her in a far corner of the cemetery. She beamed the flashlight onto the ground at her feet, then clicked it off.

I swung rapidly along the pathway until I reached her. She handed me the flashlight and lifted the pick. I shone the light onto a large granite marker bearing the name JACK, which listed the current year as the internment date. Above the name was chiseled the inscription IN GOD WE TRUST. Fitting. I slid the beam one marker over and found Frank, resting under a similar inscription.

"I don't like doing this," Angel admitted, hesitating over Jack's grave. "Maybe we should call the police."

"They wouldn't believe us," I said. Indeed, Sheriff Kohl hadn't. I had called him from a pay phone after finding the receipt, and told him about Jack Burns. When I mentioned that I thought the money was buried in a pet cemetery, he had just laughed, thinking it a joke, and hung up.

Angel crossed herself, a lapsed Catholic but Catholic nonetheless, and swung the pick. It bit into the grass with a sharp swish. She worked the tip under the grave marker, and pried it free. The ground beneath the marker was loosely packed. Angel dropped the pick and dug the blade of the shovel deeply into the grave, spading the dirt to the side. She dug rapidly, nervous with feelings of desecration, and the spaded dirt quickly mounded to the side of the grave. About two feet down her shovel thunked something hard. She knelt, and swept aside the dirt to reveal a gray metal surface. It took another five minutes of concentrated digging to clear the dirt from the top and sides. The casket measured four feet in length by two in width. Angel squatted, grasping the handle at one end, and hoisted the casket up to the grass.

We stood over the dull gray thing, dreading the inevitable lifting of the lid and the shock of decay. Angel took another step back and, taking the flashlight from me, said: "Bad leg or not, you do it."

It was fair, but I still regretted it. I knelt next to the casket. Angel fixed the light on the lid. It was secured by two metal catches. I flipped the catches free, took a deep breath, and raised the lid. The flashlight illuminated a stuffed green trash bag. Cautiously, I allowed a little air to filter through my nose. Most of the gases of decay were still trapped in the bag. I reached into my coat pocket for a jackknife and slit the length of the bag, feeling a slight puff against my hands as the gases escaped. I ripped the plastic back, revealing the carcass of the Great Dane. Angel swore behind me. The dog had been dead about two weeks, and its body was still intact. Decay had ravaged the animal's eyes, which had melted from its sockets, and its tongue rolled black from the side of its jaw. I buried my mouth in the sleeve of my coat, and took a breath. The stench was bad enough to choke me for a moment. I instructed Angel to fix the beam back on the animal, as she had turned away in revulsion when I had first ripped open the bag. She guided the light to the animal's soft underbelly, and I counted the neat march of stitches stretching from its legs to its chest. That was all the evidence I needed. I wondered whether or not the owner of the cemetery knew what had been buried here, but imagined that Kathy and Nina had brought the dogs already wrapped in plastic bags. The head of the Great Dane had not been tampered with. The owner had likely taken one look at the head, not found anything amiss, and stuffed the dog, bag and all into the casket.

Angel called to me the moment before I heard it. I glanced to her as I pushed myself up, and caught the fear in her eyes. I twisted toward the sound. A hulking square shape sped onto the cemetery grounds, and above the sudden roar of its engine I heard the smashing of glass as it crushed the memorial lights in its path. It was a blue Chevy van. I had seen it before, and the memory coalesced with my uncertain future into a surge of terror. I would have run if my leg had let me. Angel quickly knelt and shouldered the pick. I pushed her aside and told her to run. She cursed me, so I cursed her in return and pushed her again, shouting that if they caught us both, they would kill us both. She sprinted with the pick toward the perimeter of trees.

I faced the van, and my eyes were seared by light when the headlights snapped into high beam. I stumbled awkwardly back. The van engine sputtered into silence, but the headlights remained on high beam, pinning me buglike against the night. The driver door jutted out with a creak, and a figure jumped onto the grass. Blinded by the headlamps, I didn't recognize him. He leaned over the side door and ratcheted it back. Three men stepped out of the belly of the van. One of the men was my clone. His leg cast gleamed in the headlamps as he hobbled forward on crutches. The four men fanned out, their shadows towering through the cemetery as they sauntered past the front headlamps. They were backlit, their faces black-masked by shadow. I figured I could take the guy on crutches, but I didn't know about the other three. The tall one with the cowboy hat was easy: Frank Knott. The figure on the left broke away to circle me to the side, and by his long hair I identified him as the driver of the white Datsun.

"Hey, dickhead. You seem to be in grave trouble," a voice called, and I didn't have to see the face to recognize Harry Selwurst.

The longhair covered my left, palming the Glock he had taken from Jack Burns earlier that afternoon. The guy on crutches was Gilbert Stern, whom I had last seen in the lot behind the Fifties Cafe. He wore jeans, a windbreaker, and a .357 Magnum. I nodded toward his cast and asked: "Something wrong with your leg?"

"The same thing that's gonna be wrong with your neck," he grunted, sighting me against the big gun.

"I see you've met my clients, Roscoe Krantz and Gilbert Stern," Harry announced in jolly spirits. He bowed to the longhair, boasting:

"Roscoe here gunned down a rival cocaine dealer, and Gil there likes to hurt people for a living. I got them both off on technicalities."

"They've been working for you all along," I said, less a question than a revelation.

Harry just grinned.

"Where did the girl go?" Frank Knott interrupted.

"She didn't tell me," I replied, trying to appear fearless but the fight-or-flight response juicing my nerves like a hot wire.

"If you're hoping she'll help you, don't. We slashed her tires, and Frank's man Raymond is waiting in the limo, just in case," Harry advised, and told Roscoe to turn off the van lights.

Roscoe backed toward the van, keeping the gun on a level plane with the ground, and killed the lights. I blinked away bright spots in front of my eyes, waiting as the irises made their minute, incremental adjustments and I could see again in the flickering red cemetery glow. Frank Knott brushed past me, more in a hurry than the others, and peered into the casket, muttering: "Well, I'll be damned. It's just a dog."

Harry pulled a flashlight from his pocket and shone it down onto the carcass, inquiring: "What the hell are you doing here, Marston?"

"I don't know. What are you doing here?"

"Following you, stupid."

"Since when have you and Knott been partners?"

"How long has it been, Frank? About twelve hours?" Harry asked.

Frank nodded absently, not interested, and asked: "What's with the dog?"

"I thought I'd find the money buried in the casket. I was wrong."

Frank grabbed Harry's flashlight and knelt before the casket. He fixed the beam on the dog's carcass and, after a quick examination, noticed the stitches. "Damn, those gals were clever. Gimme a knife."

Harry caught the excitement in his voice, and held his hand out toward Roscoe, who slapped the palm with a stiletto. Gilbert watched the knife, and said in a softly malevolent voice:

"When this is done, maybe we're gonna bury you in that dog's grave."

Harry clicked the stiletto blade with a sharp snap, and bent over the casket. Frank pointed a bony finger at the animal's belly, and Harry laughed high and giddy with anticipation. He plunged the knife deep into the belly, and jerked it with a sharp gutting cut. The stench was getting to me, but didn't seem to bother them. Frank couldn't wait. He dug his hands into the carcass and violently ripped its sides open. Harry dropped the knife onto the grass. His hands gripped the animal's skin, and tore away large chunks of decaying flesh.

I imagined how it had been two weeks ago, when Kathy and Nina had brought the two Great Danes into the apartment. Kathy had drugged the animals, and together Kathy and Nina had lifted them into the bathtub to slit their sleeping throats. They had gutted the dogs, lined the cavity of bone and hide with plastic, and stuffed it with bundles of twenty-dollar bills. A quick stitch job with needle and thread, and the job was done. Whatever pity I had felt for Kathy and Nina shifted to the Great Danes.

Piercing laughter screamed from Harry's throat as he dug his arm up to the elbow into the carcass and withdrew a shaking fistful of twenty-dollar bills. Frank Knott stripped away a rotting hunk of fur, and hooted exultantly. He buried his hands deep into the bundles, and began to laugh, low and hard. The two of them doubled over the carcass, bumping shoulders as they howled and roared in laughter, pulling the money and bits of flesh and fur against their chests.

A high-pitched beep tone sounded from the van. Harry and Frank were too gleeful to hear it, but Roscoe stepped quickly back and said: "The transmitter."

Gilbert shrugged and answered: "That car ain't gonna move with its tires slit. Maybe the thing is on the fritz."

The homing device began to beep in a regular rhythm. Harry noticed the sound, and his laughter abruptly ceased. He nudged Frank and stood, clutching bundles of cash against his chest, listening.

"What is it?" he asked.

"I know we slit the tires on the sucker, but the pickup is definitely moving," Roscoe said, and turned toward the parking lot.

Knott's black limousine slowly turned into the cemetery from the same groundskeeper's back road that the van had taken. The headlamps and parking lights were doused as the low black shape rolled in a funereal pace over the graves, scattering floral tributes and shattering memorial lights beneath its tires. The beeping of the homing device increased in rate as the limo approached. In the flickering red glow, I thought I discerned the gleam of broken glass on the driver's side.

"Whatever the hell is going on, Raymond is here to tell us," Frank said, standing uncertainly.

"Maybe the girl got away," Harry whispered, and Frank opened his mouth to answer when the limo's headlamps stabbed the high beam into our eyes.

Roscoe shifted nervously, trying to shield his eyes and sight his pistol against the glare. The homing device increased to a steady beep, and Roscoe muttered to himself: "The bug is in the limo."

The driver's-side door swung open as the limo braked to a sudden stop. Roscoe shifted his gun toward the movement, noticing too late the broken glass and what it signified. Gilbert braced on his crutches, drawing down on the door. Angel slipped out the passenger side. Shielded by the long hood of the limo, she froze us all with the business end of a shotgun and a threat:

"I've got a shotgun and your driver is dead. Who wants to be next?"

Against the glare of the headlights, it was difficult to see Angel clearly. Roscoe and Gilbert were caught aiming in the wrong direction. One of them would not make it to the end of the long swing of their sights toward the voice on the other side of the car.

"The shotgun is a semiautomatic," I shouted. "If you think you can see enough around that light to shoot, you had better be good, because you'll only have one try before you're blown to hell."

It was tough talk, and mostly bullshit. Angel isn't very good with a gun because her nearsightedness reduces distant objects to blurs, and I raised my voice because I wanted to make certain she knew which of the five figures was me should anybody start to shoot. It was convincing enough. Gilbert and Roscoe had no place to go. It had to be a semiautomatic because she was in Raymond's car and Raymond's gun was a semiautomatic shotgun. Neither wanted to chance going up against it. They didn't move, and they didn't lower their guns.

"Look, maybe this isn't such a good idea," Harry called, his greed quickly diminishing in confrontation with mortality. "It's only money, right?"

"You're right it's only money," Knott bellowed, and kicked the casket at his feet. "And I'd gladly kill every son of a bitch here to keep it. So don't think I'm gonna let you just waltz out of here with this carcass."

"You can keep the money," I said, and crutched the long way around the exposed grave, keeping clear of the line of Angel's shotgun and the four men.

"Wait a minute, dammit! If he goes, he brings the police in," Knott objected, wanting to block my path but not daring to move and make himself a target.

"We just deny everything," Harry argued, his voice fluttering with tension. "The money disappeared with Nina Gamine, and she carried the secret of its location to her grave in Paris. That's the truth and there is no way Marston can prove otherwise if we shelter the money properly."

I thought I could trust Roscoe and Gilbert to do the smart thing and let me go. I wasn't taking the money, and they lived close enough to the edge of society's void to drop into obscurity with whatever amount Harry had promised them. I swung around the grave toward the limousine.

"That's not good enough!" Knott shouted, dangerously near the sudden movement that would pitch us all into blood and death.

I stopped and looked at him. His face had gone apoplectic, the skin stretched taut and red as though his angry skull was about to split out of his face. His eyes were glazing over in preparation for a desperate act, and I realized with chilling horror that Frank Knott preferred death to bankruptcy.

"You're damn right it's not enough," I countered, to defuse the slow tick of destruction that had worked into his brain. "I worked my butt off and what do I have to show for it? You double-cross me, Harry double-crosses me, and I can't even make the rent on my office this month. You're damn right I'll go to the police, because so far I haven't heard anybody suggest a better deal."

Knott stared at me for a long while before the glaze went out of his eyes. He nodded and attempted a good-ole-boy smile which cracked up somewhere between the intent and his mouth. "Well hell, why didn't you say so?" he cried. Greed understands greed. Knott bent over the casket and plunged his hands into the carcass, plucking out bundles of cash and stacking them against his arm.

I hobbled to the limousine, relieved to have the driver's door between me and the line of fire. I tossed my crutches into the rear compartment. Knott followed me to the door. I sat behind the wheel, and he tossed five bundles amounting to a hundred grand onto my lap.

"If you do go to the police, I will invest my money into a contract that will cost you your life. Is that clear?" he warned.

I knew he meant it, but that was tomorrow's worry, so I just said: "Clear as rain, Frank." I shut the door to a shower of glass from the shattered driver's-side window, and eased the transmission into reverse. Angel stood on the doorframe, bracing the shotgun on the top of the roof, as I backed toward the groundskeeper's road. I swung the back end of the limousine around at the exit. Angel lifted the homing bug from the dash, having placed it there as a diversionary tactic after spotting it magnetized to the undercarriage of the pickup. She tossed the bug onto the road, and jumped into the passenger seat.

We cruised out onto the deserted streets, heading for the freeway entrance. I picked up the shotgun with my free hand. The safety was locked on, and the firing chamber was empty. Angel was brave, but not particularly gun-smart. I decided not to tell her about it. The distant pop of a single shot sounded in the night, and I wondered what it meant. Harry and Frank would be in a hurry to get out of the cemetery, and would not realize until later that night that only half the money had been stuffed in the dog. Maybe they would think I had double-crossed them, and maybe they would be smart enough to drive back to the cemetery to look for the second Great Dane.

"What did you do with the driver?" I asked, the wind whipping fragments of the window onto my lap.

"He's in the trunk, and don't worry, I didn't really kill him. But he is going to have to see a doctor," Angel admitted.

I thanked her, and she accepted the thanks with a perfunctory "Just doing my job." I looked at the bundles, which had spilled onto the seat between us, and said: "This is a lot of money. What do you think we should do with it?"

"The police should believe our story now, don't you think?" she answered, and I loved her for it.

The South Bay police took one look at the money and sent a squad car to Dog Heaven. The responding officers initially reported that everything looked in order, and only after Angel and I tried to place a call to Sheriff Kohl did the precinct commander agree to instruct the officers to check under the grave marker of a Great Dane named Jack. They found Frank Knott buried under the marker, curled in the fetal position. He had been shot through the head at point-blank range by a Glock 9-millimeter pistol, which had been tossed into the grave with him. Detective Stewart of Homicide was called in with a team of forensics experts. The Glock was later traced to Jack Burns, with copies of the ballistics report forwarded to the Paris Préfecture de Police.

Harry Selwurst denied everything, but when threatened with a murder charge, admitted that he had been at the cemetery, trying to reclaim several million dollars that had been stolen from his clients, Jack Burns and Frank Knott. Harry claimed that he had left the money under Frank Knott's care once it had been dug up by two workmen he had hired on the street, whose names he could not recall. The police theorize that the two workmen killed Frank Knott and took off with the million-plus in twenty-dollar bills. The district attorney is still considering charges against Harry Selwurst, but as neither Roscoe Krantz nor Gilbert Stern has yet to been found, the case rests solely on my testimony.

The $1.25 million buried in the carcass of the second Great Dane was confiscated by the police, subjected to a violent legal dispute between the creditors of Jack Burns and Frank Knott, and still awaits distribution to the investors of Sea View Estates.

The District Attorney's Office declined to charge Jack Burns with the murder of the out-of-work actor who had been boiled to death in Burns's hot tub, but thought it had enough physical evidence to try him for the murder of Mona Demonay. The trial drew headlines for six months, with the prosecutor's case resting primarily on motive, opportunity, and fiber evidence. Jack Burns produced a star turn on the witness stand, and the jury returned a verdict of not guilty. He was immediately rearrested on an international warrant, and extradited to France, where he was tried for the murders of Nina and Francis Gamine. The French prosecuting attorney had a ballistics match between the Glock and the bullets that had killed the Gamines, and an eyewitness to the murders—me. Jack Burns's act wasn't nearly as compelling in translation. A French jury convicted him of both murders, and he was sentenced to life in prison.

Richie Warner of the *Times* was not able to substantiate much of what I told him regarding Harry Selwurst, although he did write several excellent pieces on Jack Burns, which he managed to leverage into a lucrative deal for book and movie rights.

Angel and I drove out to Palm Springs for a couple of days when the first round of questioning was over, and rented a condominium with a private pool and sundeck. We talked about the problems of our relationship, and made love, swam and sunned and drank champagne, and rediscovered most of the joys as well. We couldn't afford the trip, but took it anyway and charged it all on plastic. That's the American way.

FOR THE BEST IN PAPERBACKS, LOOK FOR THE

In every corner of the world, on every subject under the sun, Penguin represents quality and variety—the very best in publishing today.

For complete information about books available from Penguin—including Pelicans, Puffins, Peregrines, and Penguin Classics—and how to order them, write to us at the appropriate address below. Please note that for copyright reasons the selection of books varies from country to country.

In the United Kingdom: For a complete list of books available from Penguin in the U.K., please write to *Dept E.P., Penguin Books Ltd, Harmondsworth, Middlesex, UB7 0DA.*

In the United States: For a complete list of books available from Penguin in the U.S., please write to *Dept BA, Penguin,* Box 120, Bergenfield, New Jersey 07621-0120.

In Canada: For a complete list of books available from Penguin in Canada, please write to *Penguin Books Ltd, 2801 John Street, Markham, Ontario L3R 1B4.*

In Australia: For a complete list of books available from Penguin in Australia, please write to the *Marketing Department, Penguin Books Ltd, P.O. Box 257, Ringwood, Victoria 3134.*

In New Zealand: For a complete list of books available from Penguin in New Zealand, please write to the *Marketing Department, Penguin Books (NZ) Ltd, Private Bag, Takapuna, Auckland 9.*

In India: For a complete list of books available from Penguin, please write to *Penguin Overseas Ltd, 706 Eros Apartments, 56 Nehru Place, New Delhi, 110019.*

In Holland: For a complete list of books available from Penguin in Holland, please write to *Penguin Books Nederland B.V., Postbus 195, NL-1380AD Weesp, Netherlands.*

In Germany: For a complete list of books available from Penguin, please write to *Penguin Books Ltd, Friedrichstrasse 10-12, D-6000 Frankfurt Main 1, Federal Republic of Germany.*

In Spain: For a complete list of books available from Penguin in Spain, please write to *Longman, Penguin España, Calle San Nicolas 15, E-28013 Madrid, Spain.*

In Japan: For a complete list of books available from Penguin in Japan, please write to *Longman Penguin Japan Co Ltd, Yamaguchi Building, 2-12-9 Kanda Jimbocho, Chiyoda-Ku, Tokyo 101, Japan.*

FOR THE BEST IN MYSTERY, LOOK FOR THE

FOR THE BEST IN MYSTERY, LOOK FOR THE

☐ MURDOCK FOR HIRE
Robert Ray

When he is hired to find a dead man's missing antique coin collection, private detective Matt Murdock discovers an international crime ring that is much more than a nickle-and-dime operation.
     *256 pages   ISBN: 0-14-010679-0   **$3.95***

☐ BRIARPATCH
Ross Thomas

This Edgar Award-winning thriller is the story of Benjamin Dill, who returns to the Sunbelt city of his youth to attend his sister's funeral—and find her killer.
     *384 pages   ISBN: 0-14-010581-6   **$3.95***

☐ DEATH'S SAVAGE PASSION
Orania Papazoglou

Suspense is killing Romance, and the Romance Writers of America are outraged. When a fresh, enthusiastic creator of the loathed hybrid, Romantic Suspense, arrives on the scene, someone shows her just how murderous competition can be.
     *180 pages   ISBN: 0-14-009967-0   **$3.50***

☐ GOLD BY GEMINI
Jonathan Gash

Lovejoy, the antiques dealer whom the *Chicago Sun-Times* calls "one of the most likable rogues in mystery history," searches for Roman gold coins and greedy bird-killers on the Isle of Man.
     *224 pages   ISBN: 0-451-82185-8   **$3.95***

☐ REILLY: ACE OF SPIES
Robin Bruce Lockhart

This is the incredible true story of superspy Sidney Reilly, said to be the inspiration for James Bond. Robin Bruce Lockhart's book tells the thrilling story of the British Secret Service agent's shadowy Russian past and near-legendary exploits in espionage and in love.
     *192 pages   ISBN: 0-14-006895-3   **$4.95***

☐ STRANGERS ON A TRAIN
Patricia Highsmith

Almost against his will, Guy Haines is trapped in a nightmare of shared guilt when he agrees to kill the father of the man who will kill Guy's wife. The basis for the unforgettable Hitchcock thriller.
     *256 pages   ISBN: 0-14-003796-9   **$4.95***

☐ THE THIN WOMAN
Dorothy Cannell

An interior designer who is also a passionate eater, her rented companion who writes trashy novels, and a rich dead uncle with a conditional will are the principals in this delicious thriller.   *242 pages   ISBN: 0-14-007947-5   **$3.95***

FOR THE BEST IN MYSTERY, LOOK FOR THE